Advance praise for

QUEER CORNERS

"*QUEER CORNERS* IS A RIVETING NOVEL WITH
AN UNFORGETTABLE CAST OF CHARACTERS. THE TONE
IS OFTEN SATIRICAL BUT THE UNDERLYING MESSAGE
IS SERIOUS AND HEARTFELT. MR. OLSON HAS WRITTEN
A PAGE-TURNER THAT APPEALS TO THE BAWDY
AND THE SOUL."

— QUENTIN CRISP, AUTHOR OF *THE NAKED CIVIL SERVANT*

"AS AN ADMIRER OF DONALD OLSON'S PREVIOUS
THE CONFESSIONS OF AUBREY BEARDSLEY, I WAS AT
FIRST ASTONISHED TO READ A NOVEL SO DIFFERENT
FROM IT. BUT I WAS SOON WON OVER BY THE VIGOUR OF
THE WRITING, THE SPARKLE OF THE WIT, AND THE FORCE
AND SHARPNESS OF THE ATTACK ON RELIGIOUS BIGOTRY."

— FRANCIS KING, AUTHOR OF *ACT OF DARKNESS*, *THE WOMAN
WHO WAS GOD*, *DEAD LETTERS*
AND FICTION REVIEWER FOR *THE SPECTATOR*.

"GAY OR STRAIGHT, READERS OF ALL PERSUASIONS
WILL ENJOY THIS ROMP THROUGH THE IDIOSYNCRASIES
OF HUMAN NATURE. SARDONIC BUT EMBRACING,
OLSON'S WIT SKEWERS EVERYONE—AND LEAVES US
WAITING FOR MORE. RECOMMENDED FOR THOSE OF US
WHO LIKE TO LAUGH—AT LEAST IN PART—
AT OURSELVES."

— ROBIN KARR-MORSE, AUTHOR OF *GHOSTS FROM THE NURSERY*

Novels by Donald Olson

The Secrets of Mabel Eastlake

Paradise Gardens

A Movie

The Confessions of Aubrey Beardsley

QUEER CORNERS

BY

DONALD OLSON

BRIDGECITY BOOKS

Published by:

BridgeCity Books
1717 SW Park, Suite 616
Portland, OR 97201
Tel: 503-220-4171
Fax: 503-220-4081

Distribution of book:
Independent Publishers Group
814 N. Franklin St.
Chicago, IL 60610
Tel: 800-888-4741

Publisher's Cataloging Data:
Olson, Donald S.
Queer Corners
1, Fiction. I. Title.

ISBN 0-9623683-6-9

Cover Design & Layout by Jeffrey Smith
Cover Art by Michael Cacy
Author photo by Peter Sanders

Made in the United States of America

DEDICATION

For

Gary and Rachael

Francien and Isaac

And for the real heroes and heroines of this story:
the men and women who fought in Oregon

MORALITY IS SIMPLY THE ATTITUDE WE ADOPT
TOWARDS PEOPLE WE PERSONALLY DISLIKE.

OSCAR WILDE

PART ONE

CHAPTER 1

"WHAT'S GOING TO HAPPEN TO THE HOUSE?" SUSAN BARK WHISPERED to Jay Zucker.

Standing side by side at the back of Whitney's Funeral Home, they surveyed the room to see who was already there. Everyone, as it turned out. Susan and Jay were the last to arrive at Delmont Percy's early-morning "power funeral." Thin, doleful strands of organ music floated through the chokingly sweet-scented air.

"I think it's going on the market," Jay whispered out of the side of his mouth. His deep, intimate vocal style had been perfected over years of noisy restaurant work.

"How much, do you suppose?" Susan asked in hushed tones.

Naturally she was curious. All of Delmont's neighbors were curious. Delmont's was the choicest house in Queer Corners. It had a certain historical cachet—as well as half-an-acre of gardens and a fabulous view of Portland, Mt. Hood, and the Cascade Range—that was certain to increase its market value. The house was a solidly built Queen Anne and in that, perhaps, was not so different from its deceased owner.

Several years earlier, at Delmont's urging, Susan Bark had used a tiny portion of her enormous divorce settlement to snap up a perfectly darling replica of a half-timbered Elizabethan cottage one street up from him. She'd renamed it Bilitis Cottage and now lived there with her American lover, Carolyn Corbett. Susan had always been grateful to Delmont for putting her onto the house and chagrined that Delmont's gardens always managed to look more English than her own.

"What do you think?" she asked in her tweedy English accent. "Two fifty? You know what's happening to real estate on the hill."

Jay didn't answer. Looking up at the coffin, he could just make out Delmont's long thin nose and see his hands folded on his chest. It was only now, when he was about to approach his neighbor for the last time, that the full impact of Delmont's death hit him.

Jay lived next door to Delmont, and across the street from Susan and Carolyn, in a classic Sixties Modern house. Delmont had been more than just a neighbor to Jay. He had a sardonic verve and worldly, well-traveled sophistication that Jay, a refugee from New York, appreciated in Portland's duller moments. "I can't believe he's gone."

"I'll miss those heavenly daiquiris," Susan said. "And all the fun we use to—" Her voice caught in her throat. Gone forever the cocktails, candlelight, lively gossip and witty badinage of Delmont's seasonal parties. She raised to her nose the scentless autumn bouquet she'd brought as a tribute and gave a forlorn sniff. "Should we go up now?"

Jay nodded. Susan put her hand on his arm, something she'd never done before, and together they slowly walked up the aisle. Those who didn't know them thought they made a lovely couple.

Delmont, touched up in death, his cheeks padded, lay before them in a zippy cobalt-blue casket.

Susan cocked her head and tenderly appraised the deceased. "He looks quite peaceful, doesn't he?"

"Yes," Jay whispered.

"Of course he would *never* have worn that much mascara and blusher in public," Susan observed. "And I wonder who picked out this vulgar casket?"

"I think Terry did." Jay looked over his shoulder.

"I might have known." Susan shot a reproving glance in the direction of Terrence Bennett Terwilliger III—Terry the Turd as they all secretly called him—sitting in the front row, his face half-hidden behind large Gucci sunglasses. The room was uncomfortably warm, but Terry was swaddled in his winter mink. Trying to ward off the chill of death, Susan thought. Delmont's oldest and cheapest friend lived in the Mock Tudor mansion on the other side of Delmont's Queen Anne. He had been a resident of Queer Corners longer than any of the rest of them.

Terry sidled over to them in a half-crouch. "They put him in the wrong casket," he whispered.

"The wrong casket?" Susan blurted out.

"This *isn't* the one I ordered."

"I should jolly well hope not," Susan said, lowering her voice again. "It looks like something more suited for Liberace. I'm surprised they didn't put Delmont's name in rhinestones on the side."

"It's too late to do anything about it," Terry said, quickly slipping back to his front-row center seat beside Leonora Halsey, his companion at all prominent social events. Leonora, of the banking Halseys, smiled and twiddled her fingers in Susan and Jay's direction.

"Honestly," Susan sniffed, turning back to the coffin. "Delmont always had such impeccably good taste. It would break his heart if he knew he'd be spending eternity in this thing." She slipped on her glasses to better appraise the gold scarab ring glinting on Delmont's pinkie. "That's the priceless ring he got in Egypt for practically nothing," she murmured. Such a pity it would be lost forever. She'd admired the ring so often during Delmont's final weeks that she was certain he'd leave it to her in his will.

Jay, hiding a bewildering rush of grief and anxiety under the perfectly composed demeanor of a maitre d', stared down at Delmont. Packaged for death. Once Delmont had been just as young and perhaps just as handsome as Jay was now. In the prime of his life. Then bingo, suddenly it was all over. The table reservation was cancelled. Congestive heart failure. They'd all watched him fade before their eyes.

Susan, who preferred the bracing scents of her kennel to the cloying perfumes of a mortuary, felt the worm of a headache creeping through her temples. "Cheerio, you charming old bugger," she said to Delmont. "I'll miss you." She tucked her bouquet into the casket, eyed the scarab ring one last time, and turned away, searching for Carolyn.

Jay stood looking into the coffin for a moment longer. He could not imagine Queer

Corners without Delmont. Delmont was really the first single person to colonize the neighborhood and make it a desirable place for the unmarried to live. Delmont had moved in forty years earlier, just after the war, when Harry Truman was president and, as Delmont liked to recall, "there were still plenty of horny sailors hanging around in the bars." Delmont's antiques business had flourished, he said, "because I was the only person in Portland who knew how to pronounce Louis Quatorze." Delmont's home was a showplace. A collection of minor Impressionists hung on his walls and the built-in vitrines were stuffed with Fabergé eggs he claimed to have laid himself. He had a shrewd business sense that Jay envied. "Everything is luck and timing," Delmont used to say.

Jay hesitated, then tentatively put his hand out to touch Delmont's. The ice-cold non-thereness of Delmont's flesh shocked him and he quickly drew his hand away. He could not bring himself to say goodbye. All he could think of to say, silently sending the words to his old friend now on the far side of eternity, was *thank you*.

▼ ▼ ▼

As Susan and Jay went to take the seats Carolyn was saving for them, Jay, the consummate host, nodded and smiled at those mourners who were patrons of Chez Jay, his restaurant. Some of them were even important enough to merit a flirtatious wink. Jay doled out his winks very carefully. Today it was more of a reflex than a come-on. He desperately needed to remind himself that he was alive.

"Doesn't Delmont look nice?" Carolyn sighed as Jay and Susan took their seats beside her. "So peaceful. So real. Like any moment he might sit up and offer us all a daiquiri."

"Don't be morbid," Susan reprimanded her.

Peter Love, sitting directly behind Jay, Susan and Carolyn, leaned forward to ask, "How much for Delmont's house, do you think?"

Everyone in Queer Corners took an active interest in real estate, discussing property values on "the hill" as though the figures were vital sports statistics. But it was really rather too much, Susan thought, that Peter Love should be interested in property values. It was Peter's arrival in Queer Corners, after all, that had excited the last round of market speculations among the more established residents. The neighborhood had been abuzz for weeks when it learned, just three years ago, that a black interior designer from Washington, D.C. was moving into the 1920s Mediterranean across the street from Delmont. The older residents were shocked at the price—$220,000—which set a new record, yet secretly pleased since it meant that the value of their own homes had probably doubled, even if Peter was black.

Delmont's Queen Anne was in mint condition and twice as large as Peter's Mediterranean. It had a "reputation." It was also on the unobstructed view side of the hill. Susan hazarded a new guess. "Two seventy-five?"

"I think three hundred—minimum," Jay murmured to Susan and Peter. "Sissy Parker's handling it."

"Well, that's a relief anyway," Susan said. Sissy Parker, padded like a linebacker, was sitting on the other side of the room. A lesbian realtor who'd been a member of the

Million Dollar Club for ages, Sissy knew Queer Corners very well. She'd sold Peter his Mediterranean. There was every reason to assume that Sissy would bring in a new resident who'd fit in with the sexual demographics of the neighborhood.

"Do we have to talk about real estate now?" It was the disapproving voice of John-Don Webster, Peter's white, Portland-born lover. Athletic, sweet-faced John-Don was a little too radical for Susan's tastes. But, as Delmont liked to point out, John-Don had the benefit of good looks and excellent legs, which he showed off in his running shorts.

"Why not?" Peter said. "Anyway, it's not the price so much as who'll be moving in. Did Delmont leave a will?"

Really! Susan, to signal her disapproval of the question, slid forward in her seat, keeping her ears peeled for any further information Jay might reveal. "Those gladioli are *vile*," she whispered in a friendly aside to Ito Kudomono, in front of her, nodding towards the sprays of hideously colored flowers that flanked the coffin. "Delmont hated hybridized gladioli. What idiot was responsible?"

Ito, grieving the loss of his old friend, merely gave a sad smile and a shrug. Ah, the memories. It was Delmont who'd first hired Ito, just out of school, to landscape the grounds of the Queen Anne house on Skyview Boulevard. It was Delmont who saw to it that the reworked gardens were written up locally in *The Oregonian* and nationally in *Garden World*. It was Delmont who'd recommended Ito as a landscaper of genius to all the other old Portland families. Ultimately it was Delmont who'd been responsible for Ito's prosperity and his eventual move to Queer Corners, where he lived in a forbiddingly modernist steel-and-glass cube set atop enormous pylons. That's why Ito, who lived in a world of horticultural symbols, had anonymously sent the huge sprays of gladioli that reared up on either side of his friend's coffin. It was Ito's way of remembering Delmont as he'd first seen him, in his gardens on Skyview Boulevard, surrounded by gladioli.

"Yes, there was a will," Carolyn Corbett whispered to Jay and Peter.

"How do you know?" Susan asked, annoyed that Carolyn was whispering confidences behind her back.

"Because Delmont told Wellfleet and Wellfleet told me. Didn't you, Wellfleet?" Wellfleet Stipple, the gimpy choir director who had a small adobe-style bungalow next to Carolyn and Susan, had been waiting for his opportunity to join the group's discussion. He leaned over and said, "Just before he died Delmont told me about his will."

"Right, he told you he was leaving everything to—" Carolyn saw that Jay, Peter, and Susan were breathlessly waiting for details. So, apparently, was Terry Terwilliger, who was leaning so far back in his chair that they could see the intricate construction of his hair implants. But just then the service began and, as if on cue, her soft blue eyes began to water and Carolyn turned her attention from the here to the hereafter.

▾ ▾ ▾

It wasn't until afterwards, when Delmont's neighbors were gathered in a post-internment knot at Sunset Memorial Cemetery, that the details of his will were made known. According to Wellfleet, Delmont had left everything to his sole surviving relative, a niece in Florida.

"Her?" Susan was aghast. "Everything?"

"Almost." Wellfleet had been given Delmont's cherished Boesendorfer grand, but this wasn't the time or the place to mention it.

"She's practically illiterate," Susan sputtered. "She lives in a *trailer*."

"Not for much longer," Wellfleet predicted.

The horrible thought suddenly occurred to all of them—what if the trashy niece who lived in a Florida trailer park moved into Delmont's lovely home and became their neighbor?

"You don't mean to say—" Susan, unable to finish the question, brusquely tugged the sleeve of Sissy Parker's suit, drawing the passing realtor into the Queer Corners enclave. "Sissy, what's happening to Delmont's house? We heard the niece got everything."

Sissy nodded. "Yup, that's right. I called her yesterday to see if she wanted me to sell."

"And?" Susan asked for all of them.

"Yup, she does. I got an exclusive. Open house on Sunday."

"Open house?" Terrence Terwilliger III, patting the carefully woven strands of his dyed black hair, snorted his disapproval. He'd shaken off Leonora and come over to sniff out information from his neighbors. His eyes were red and swollen, not from crying but because something had gone wrong during his most recent facelift. Despite his mink coat he looked cold and oddly pale under his new Palm Springs tan. "Usually things in the neighborhood are taken care of privately."

By which he meant that houses in Queer Corners were generally earmarked for friends or friends of friends and sold quickly, under the table as it were, before anyone else knew they were listed. More of a controlled market that way. It was always Delmont, with his vast social network, who put others onto the houses. Delmont was the one with the widest circle of rich gay friends.

"If any of you know of anyone—" Sissy's question trailed off into the clear, hot air of Indian summer.

"What's the asking price?" Terry wanted to know.

"Well—the way things are moving on the hill—it's a hot market right now—lots of Californians moving up after the earthquake—that teeny ranch down on Maywood Drive just went for close to three—of course they'd just put in a new hot tub and—"

"Sissy, how much?" Susan interrupted.

It was impossible to ignore that imperious English accent, and God knows, over the years Sissy had tried. "Four-eighty-five," she blurted.

"Four hundred and eight-five thousand *dollars*?" John-Don Webster slowly enunciated the price in a shocked tone. "You mean someone would pay almost half a million dollars? For a house in our neighborhood?" John-Don was an underpaid high-school teacher with socialist tendencies. He stared at Peter Love, his partner, with disbelief.

Peter, however, was delighted and couldn't repress a smile. He looked at his fellow householders and could see the same dollar signs glowing in their eyes.

"Well," Sissy shrugged with capitalistic nonchalance, "that's what the market is like right now."

"But who will buy it?" Wellfleet wanted to know. "At that price—"

"Open house—anyone can buy it," Ito said.

"That's just the point," Terry said irritably. "The wrong sort."

"Heterosexuals—with children," Susan shuddered.

"Jesus," Peter muttered, his smile wilting.

"Sissy, don't you have any gay people interested?" Jay asked.

"A nice gay couple," Carolyn suggested.

"That house is made for a homosexual," Peter insisted. "Straight people would never appreciate it."

"Never understand it," Wellfleet added with a soulful nod. "All the loving care Delmont put into it."

"Museum quality," Terry murmured.

"Goodbye Debussy," Wellfleet said. "Hello hip-hop."

"Delmont's superb gardens!" Susan cried. "Heresy to see them ruined!" And never again would she be able to wander through those bursting flower beds, free as Adam before the Fall, snipping off all the roses and columbine and sunflowers and delphiniums that her trug could carry.

"Well, I'm working on it," Sissy said, "but the price automatically puts most single buyers out of the ballgame." She smiled her meaningless realtor's smile and backed away before they could pin too many false hopes on her.

"I don't think we can count on Sissy," Susan said grimly.

"Delmont had a lot of straight friends, but I know he wouldn't want one living in his house," Jay said.

"Would you?" Terry asked rhetorically.

"Maybe some children would be nice," Carolyn murmured, pressing her soft, wide hip against Susan and tenderly picking dog hairs from Susan's corduroy jacket.

"Shrieking all day and leaving their plastic toys on the sidewalk?" Susan winced at the thought. "No thank you. Toys 'R Not for Us."

"Amen," Peter added.

"Straight people aren't so bad." Carolyn's remark was met with a flurry of groans.

"They're fine," Susan snapped, "*in their place*."

"That's why suburbs were invented," Terry said.

"God, can't you just see it?" Jay exclaimed. "Campers in the driveway. Huge boats parked on the street. Mobile homes. Riding lawn mowers."

"If straights moved in it just wouldn't be Queer Corners anymore," Peter said. "It would be—"

"Straight Corners." John-Don let out a doleful laugh.

"It wouldn't be ours," Jay said. "It would lose its special identity."

"I hate the way they think they can just move in wherever they like," Susan grumbled. "Simply barge in and take over."

"Let's face facts," Peter said, "the last thing we want is an influx of noisy heterosexuals. They destroy property values and make life miserable for everyone around them."

"They're moving in all over the hill," complained Terry.

"We've got to keep Delmont's house in the family," Jay insisted.

"How?" asked John-Don. "It's easy to stand here and talk about it, but I don't know anybody who can pay half a million bucks for a house. Do any of you?"

"I think we've all got some phone calls to make," Susan said. "Pronto."

CHAPTER 2

"AGAIN," WELLFLEET SAID IMPATIENTLY. "TRY TO STAY ON PITCH THIS time." He tapped middle C on the piano while sternly peering up at Tina Pedersen over the tops of his reading glasses. His bad leg ached terribly and it wasn't even raining.

Tina, a five-foot-eight, 250-pound college freshman from Yakima, Washington, cleared her throat and nervously twitched her behind like a chicken about to drop an egg.

"Well?" He tapped the key again, then again, and once more.

"I don't think I can," Tina whispered.

"Why not?"

Tina bit her lips and avoided his dark, piercing eyes. Eyes the color of bitter chocolate. "It's—you're—"

"I'm what?" Wellfleet always liked the dark little surge of energy he got from brow-beating his private voice students. "Too demanding?"

Tina licked her dry lips. "Sort of," she murmured.

"Tina, why are you here?" Wellfleet asked.

"To sing, I guess."

"You guess?"

"To sing," she corrected herself.

"Wrong," Wellfleet said with a sour smile. "You're here to *learn* how to sing. You do want to sing, don't you?"

"I guess so. If it's what the Lord wants me to do."

His response was a mistake, and he knew it the moment the sharp words flew from his mouth. "What the hell does the Lord have to do with it? The Lord doesn't care if you're a singer or not."

She was speechless in the face of his heresy. He'd frightened her. If she wasn't a passive instrument of the Lord, what was she? Tears sprang to her eyes and with a defeated air she clumsily turned to gather her things.

"Where do you think you're going? Your lesson isn't over yet."

"I can't," Tina whispered, her throat clenched tight as a fist. "It's too hard. You're so critical."

"Do you think singing is easy?"

"When I'm in church choir it's easy."

"That's because in a choir you're invisible," Wellfleet said. "It's easier to hide when you're in a crowd. You don't have to assert your own identity. And a voice is a kind of identity, Tina. Part of it, anyway. It's you. And it's a promising voice, but you have to train it if you want to take it anywhere."

The truth was, it was potentially a magnificent voice. Somewhere in her egoless depths even Tina knew that. But Wellfleet firmly believed that praise weakened the iron-clad resolve and discipline an artist needed to develop in order to survive.

"Maybe the Lord doesn't want me to be a soloist."

"Oh the Lord, the Lord," he grumbled impatiently. "Stop worrying about what the Lord wants and ask yourself what you want."

"I want what the Lord wants," she sniffled.

Wellfleet, who taught in a private Baptist college, came up against this assertion in one form or another every day. Over the years it had turned him into a closet atheist. It was becoming more and more difficult for him to listen with any sympathy or understanding to students and colleagues who invested their every fart with religious significance.

"The Lord isn't going to teach you how to sing," he said. "I am. Maybe he gave you the voice, but he isn't going to teach you breath control and pitch and enunciation and make you run the scales. That's what I'm here to do."

"You don't believe in God, do you, Mr. Stipple?"

The stubborn, assertive tone in Tina's voice made him nervous. Hitlerjugend, here we come. "What makes you say that?"

"The things you say—and Mimi Strang said so, too."

Mimi Strang, a former student, who'd stopped coming for private voice lessons because she needed more time to run the Christian Students' Association. That's what she'd said, but of course Mimi was a liar, as they were all liars, avoiding the truth whenever it was upsetting or inconvenient. The real reason Mimi Strang had stopped coming was because she and Wellfleet had developed a mutual aversion to one another. They were antagonists, and they knew it. Mimi gabbling on and on about the Lord, as if she were possessed, until Wellfleet had finally had enough and forbad her to mention the Lord's name in his house. "In my house, I'm the lord," he'd said.

"My private beliefs have nothing to do with teaching you how to sing," he said carefully to Tina. "Now are you going to finish the lesson or not?"

"No," Tina said. "I really have to go. I'm helping Mimi organize the reception for Ron Labonne next week."

"Who?"

"Ron Labonne." The very name sent a shiver of adoration through the overweight girl. "The head of the American Christian Alliance. The Christian Students' Association invited him to speak. We have to raise a lot of money to pay for him, so I told Mimi I'd help her bake cookies and stuff."

Wellfleet slammed the lid down on the piano keys. "So it's more important that you go bake your stupid cookies for Ron Labonne than finish your lesson with me."

"I promised." Trying not to cry again. Trying to get out as fast as she could.

Wellfleet watched as, turning her wide back to him, she nervously stuffed sheet music into her backpack. The enormous rump, the colossal thighs that rubbed together as she walked, the soft bib of fat under her chin, the wide shelf of her massive breasts—trapped inside that frightened, ungainly eighteen-year-old mountain of flesh was a voice of pure gold. And somehow Wellfleet knew that he would never be able to mine it.

"Is it okay if I ask some of the choir members if they want to sing when he comes?" Tina asked on her way out.

"When who comes?"

"Ron Labonne. Mimi thought it would be nice if we did a couple of hymns. She said she'd play the piano."

"It's your voice, Tina. Do with it whatever you want."

When she was gone, Wellfleet went to the kitchen and popped a couple of Tylenols. His leg hummed with pain. He limped out to the deck and looked down at the street below. Tina, with her heavy, elephantine gait, was lumbering past Delmont's house on her way down the hill. And there was Sissy Parker, pounding a For Sale sign into the front lawn.

Dead. Gone. Kaput. Mai più. A life over and done with. A huge empty silence where once there had been friendship, understanding, camaraderie, music. Wellfleet couldn't bear to think about it. His first instinct when Tina left had been to call Delmont. To unload. To defuse. To turn it all around and make it funny, or at least tolerable. That's what he and Delmont always did when they were confronted by the unbelieveable stupidity of the world. Delmont, so delightfully wicked, so adept at lancing sacred cows.

Word had already gotten out, of course, that Delmont's house was for sale. Rich women with blonde pageboys and cellular phones slowed down and inched past in their Mercedes, cruising the place. The very sight of them enraged Wellfleet. "We don't want you!" he'd silently shriek. But he was powerless, of course, to stop them from their chronic shopping.

He was feeling his own economic inferiority, that was part of the problem. "Call your friends," Susan had said. "We need to get one of our kind in here *fast*." But who could Wellfleet call? He had no friends outside of Queer Corners. He'd alienated, or tried to alienate, everyone at the college—and they were, after all, the very last people he wanted as neighbors. Not that any of them could afford it.

Wellfleet was the poor boy on the block. On Delmont's advice, he'd purchased his little Spanish-style adobe back in the Seventies, when the market was flat. The house was cheap because it needed major repairs. It still needed them. But Wellfleet had enough trouble scraping up his monthly mortgage payments.

"You don't get rich teaching music," he periodically grumbled to Carolyn Corbett, his neighbor and closest friend now that Delmont was gone.

So the dry rot crept like a melanoma through the plaster walls, the floors sank and shifted, the cracks in the lower foundation walls widened, and the termites feasted with the carpenter ants on the joists.

Of course even in its presently dilapitated condition he could sell and make a bundle. And then go where? The little rotting adobe was the closest he'd ever come to having a real home. He loved it as a monk loves his damp cell. Overshadowed by an 80-foot Douglas fir, hidden by massive rhododendrons, covered with so much English ivy that half the windows wouldn't open, let alone admit light, the house encapsulated Wellfleet's personality. He felt a close kinship with its small, dark, out-of-kilter rooms.

Sissy Parker was now pounding "Open House on Sunday" signs up and down Skyview Boulevard. Tomorrow the open-market fate of Delmont's house would begin.

It was so frustrating, so unfair. Delmont had helped everyone in Queer Corners find their homes. Now, when Delmont's own beloved house was on the block, it was up to them to find an appropriate buyer. What could Wellfleet do? Nothing.

Someone would buy the house, but who? Only Californians, lawyers, doctors, and double-income high-tech yuppie couples would have enough money to pay the astronomical price.

Wellfleet watched as a huge, bright red American car—a car so undisputably vulgar that Delmont would have called it a "pimpmobile"—slowly cruised by.

He fought back a sudden stifling premonition that Queer Corners was about to be heterosexually integrated.

CHAPTER 3

"LIFT THE TAIL AND CHECK HER VULVA," SUSAN CALLED FROM HER STUDY.

Carolyn, in the living room, winced. "Do I have to?" The bulging eyes and permanently dour expression of Lady Caroline, their Ruby English toy spaniel, didn't make such intimacies easy.

Lady Caroline had always reminded Carolyn of Bette Davis in *All About Eve*, and now that the dog was in heat the resemblance was positively uncanny. It was like asking Margo Channing to lift her skirts so you could examine her twat.

Carolyn kneeled on the floor and coaxed Lady Caroline to her. But when she tried to lift Lady Caroline's tail, the dog snapped and, to Carolyn's relief, skittered away. "She doesn't want me to," Carolyn called.

Susan, who was busy researching the bloodlines of Lady Caroline's stud-in-waiting, signalled her impatience with a loud, aggrieved sigh. Lady Caroline was to be bred the moment her oestrus cycle was in full swing. It was a matter of practically split-second timing.

Susan had already collected two grand in downpayments on the unborn pups. A litter with impeccable lineage could bring in as much as five thousand dollars. And there was Carolyn, dithering and embarrassed and unable to lift the dog's tail!

"Must I do *everything*?" Susan complained.

The impatience, the implicit criticism in her lover's voice, acted on Carolyn like a sharp tug on a leash. She slowly crept over to where Lady Caroline was hiding and pulled her out from under the table. "There, there," Carolyn murmured, pacifying the nervous, pop-eyed spaniel. "Mummy just wants to make sure that her little darling is ready for Lord Nelson."

To lessen the shock to Lady Caroline, they'd decided to have the deflowering take place in the comfort and safety of their home. The moment Lady Caroline was ready, Susan was to call Lord Nelson's owner, who demanded pick of the litter and four hundred in cash as a stud fee.

"Well?" Susan called from her study.

While rubbing the spaniel's stomach, Carolyn tried to pull Lady Caroline's tail away from her privates. The bitch kept her tail clamped down like a chastity belt. Another struggle. Whimpers. Carolyn tightened her maternal grip around the squirming dog. "Come on now, mummy just wants to see—"

Finally she managed to pry the tail up and get a good look. There was shy Lady Caroline's vulva, exposed like a hot, swollen, recently opened orchid. Slightly dripping. Distended. Purplish. A Georgia O'Keefe painting, a Judy Chicago plate. Carolyn's heart throbbed with sympathy. The salty currents of her own fertile feminine energy swirled through her veins. She remembered all too clearly what it was like to be biologically ready to conceive—the sense of power, the sense of powerlessness. The receptive mistress awaiting the impregnating master . . .

"Well?" Susan appeared in the doorway of her study.

"I think she's ready," Carolyn said.

Susan slipped on her reading glasses and came over to verify the diagnosis, unceremoniously pulling up the dog's tail and prodding its swollen organ with her finger. "Right," she said. "I've checked and double-checked the bloodlines. No inbreeding that I can see."

Carolyn had been shocked to learn of the unscrupulous breeding practices in the animal world. Susan had told her everything, of course. And Carolyn, after four years with Susan, had seen with her own eyes more than enough evidence to break a simple dog lover's heart. The mother/son, father/daughter, brother/sister cross-matings that produced genetic abnormalities of all kinds. Hip dysplasia, anemia, hemophilia, bone disease, heart disease, heads too big for the body, vaginas too small to allow normal birth to take place, immune system problems, congenital hernias, progressive blindness, neurotic personality disorders——the catalogue of inbred heterocanine horrors was endless.

"What about the owner?" Carolyn asked. "What do we know about him?" She wanted everything to be perfect for Lady Caroline, of course, and imbued the impending penetration with a romanticism entirely unsuited to its brutish goal. For Carolyn, it was a kind of wedding ceremony. She and Susan were giving away the bride, as it were.

"The owner's reliable," Susan said. "He raised Lord Nelson himself, without a handler—"

"Just like a gay father," Carolyn said approvingly.

"—and he's *very* selective about who Lord Nelson mounts. Doesn't go in for frozen sperm at all. Lord Nelson won Best in the Breed and Best in the Show before retiring, so he's top-dollar breeding stock."

"Well, us wants our little girl to have the vewwy best, doesn't us?" Carolyn viewed the dog, which she and Susan had purchased together, through a haze of anthropomorphic sentimentality. Lady Caroline had been named for Carolyn, after all, even though Carolyn had really wanted another sleek, sloppy Labrador, not the little goggle-eyed toy spaniel Susan's discerning breeder's eye had picked out. Carolyn tried to love Lady Caroline as she would an ugly, finicky, demanding stepdaughter.

Susan's view of the dog world—like her view of the world in general—was far more practical and far less emotional. She loved dogs as a master might love his slaves or a tyrant his subjects: so long as they obeyed and produced income. Yet, curiously enough, she had a true affinity for canines, and they and their owners responded instinctually, even gratefully, to her commanding English superiority. The obedience school she ran from Windy Hills Kennel was the most popular in the state. It was there, as a matter of fact, that Susan had first met Carolyn.

Carolyn had made the mistake of taking in a stray mutt, which proceeded to chew up all of her Mission oak furniture and destroy the interior of her car. She'd tried everything to get the dog to behave, and in desperation signed up for obedience classes at Windy Hills. The first day of Walking with a Leash class the ill-mannered mutt bolted from the training group and disappeared.

Susan, struck by Carolyn's flaming red hair, gentle blue eyes, and high, strawberry-and-cream coloring, comforted and eventually sold her a black Lab. The Lab was hit by a car, and Carolyn blamed herself.

That led to intensive therapy—Windy Hills offered individual counseling and group workshops in Pet Loss and Pet Grieving. Susan pumped the psychologist she'd hired to lead these sessions for information on Carolyn Corbett.

"Carolyn feels that she's being punished for something," the psychologist told Susan. "Beneath it all there's an abandonment issue that has nothing to do with pets."

One thing led to another, there was a brief courtship, and then four years ago Carolyn left southeast Portland's comfortable lesbian ghetto and moved into Bilitis Cottage, Susan's rose-covered neo-Elizabethan manor on "the hill." She had become completely infatuated—as had many before her—with the tall, tweedy dog breeder whose brushed-back hair, English accent, and dismissive, aristocratic manner reminded her of Vita Sackville-West. Secretly, even though she had large breasts and no writing talent, Carolyn thought of herself as Virginia Woolf.

"There's that hideous red car again," Susan said, peering out one of the casement windows. "Parked in front of Delmont's. The second time today."

Lady Caroline squirmed free of Carolyn's arms and sullenly pattered off to lick her trickling vulva. Carolyn joined Susan at the window. The sight of the red car sent an unexpected shiver of agitation down her spine. "My Goddess—it has fins!" she exclaimed.

What was it—a '59 Caddy? It looked sharkish, dangerous, reminded her of the Sixties, of Southern California where she'd grown up, of cruising and dragging down Main with her friends, an illicit bottle of beer tucked between her thighs and a joint hidden from view. A series of vignettes from her past life—all of them wildly embarrassing and totally unknown to Susan—whizzed down the highways of Carolyn's memory. She squirmed inwardly as each presented itself for her mortified emotional inspection. The clumsy, impatient hands she had allowed to touch her, the hungry, desperate need to feel loved: it was like remembering an illness.

"Cold?" Susan asked, turning away from the window, her dark hazel eyes sharp and impatient.

"No—well, a little—maybe. Are you?"

"I'm not the one who's shivering." Susan turned back to the window. "If you'd just take to wearing a sweater when the weather turns damp you'd acclimate your body properly."

"I know."

"You're always knitting the damn things, why don't you wear one yourself?"

"I'm fine," Carolyn murmured.

Susan's tone was slightly repentant. "Well, if it is chilly in here, you'd better turn up the heat. Lady Caroline should be kept as comfortable as possible."

Carolyn, hypnotized by the red Caddy, didn't move. Twenty years earlier she would have seen the car as totally cool, a huge necking palace with aphrodisiacal amenities such as electric windows and push-button radio. But now, in the light of the downsized, streamlined, environmentally conscious Nineties, it looked somehow corrupt. "Who's inside?" she asked, squinting out at the car.

"Can't tell—tinted glass." Susan frowned and let out an annoyed sigh. She had an entire repertoire of sighs. "It can't be a lesbian, that's for certain."

"Why not?"

"Have you ever seen a lesbian driving a car like that?"

No, Carolyn hadn't. The rich lesbians she knew—mostly Susan's friends—drove immaculate Mercedes convertibles, BMWs and Jeep Cherokees with air fresheners fastened to the ashtrays. The middle-class but upwardly mobile lesbians from her old neighborhood drove sporty Toyotas and Volvo station wagons plastered with bumper stickers commanding people to Love Mother Earth and Honor Diversity. The poor ones—not that she and Susan really knew any poor lesbians except for Cassandra Taylor—drove battered old junkers and beat-up pick-up trucks with beaded seats and dice hanging from the rear-view mirrors.

To drive a car like the one parked in front of Delmont's—to take it *seriously* as your automotive mode of transport—you had to have a sense of humor or be an old car buff like the long-vanished seducer she'd never told Susan about.

"Do you think they're looking?" Carolyn asked nervously. "The open house isn't until tomorrow."

"They're either looking or casing the place," Susan said. "Maybe they're casing the whole neighborhood."

"Here?" Carolyn shrilled. "Us?"

It was Carolyn's one great fear that she'd awaken one night and be confronted by a man wearing a ski mask and clutching a butcher knife. She'd woven this fear into a great tapestry of many scenes: being bound and gagged, being raped, watching as the dangerous intruder ransacked the house and harmed Susan: once her mind got started, it wouldn't stop. "Should we call the police?"

"You can," Susan said. She ran her hands through her hair and stretched. "I have an appointment in the Heights."

"Now? What for? It's almost six o'clock."

"Oh, that silly bitch wants to talk to me about her show dog."

"What silly bitch?" Carolyn asked with a twitter of apprehension.

"You know—Flavia Billingsley—the one who thinks her Corgi may be anorexic."

"Why can't she see you during normal kennel hours?"

Susan smiled. "Because she's rich, darling." She kissed Carolyn on the tip of her nose and went to get her corduroy jacket. "And she's paying me for a private consulation."

"What about Lady Caroline?" *What about our daughter*, Carolyn wanted to cry. She followed Susan out to her dashing new Land Rover. "You said she's ready."

"I'll call Lord Nelson's owner and have him delivered tomorrow morning. You'll have to be here."

"But we're so busy at the library—we're switching over to a new computer system—I can't take any time off."

Susan's face registered displeasure. She fastened her seat belt with a grim deliberateness that made Carolyn's stomach curdle. "Darling, why are you being so difficult?"

"I'm not—"

"Yes, you are."

"It's just—oh all right, I'll go in at noon."

"That's a love. Cheerio." Susan backed down Santavista Terrace, pausing for a moment alongside the red Cadillac parked in front of Delmont's house, and then roared off down Skyview Boulevard.

If only Delmont were still alive, Carolyn thought dejectedly. She could simply walk down and knock on his door and he'd invite her in for a daiquiri. He would make her laugh. "You know very well Susan's bark is worse than her overbite," he'd said once, when Susan had blown up about something and stormed out of the house.

It wasn't the same with Wellfleet, who'd become her closest friend in Queer Corners after Delmont's death. Wellfleet exuded a bitter air of gloom and exasperation that sucked Carolyn in like a poisoned garden. Misery loves company.

It was nearly dark. The Indian Summer had been a short-lived mirage. Winter was closing in. Sodden sycamore leaves, their edges crisp with frost, lay stuck to the asphalt like fat importuning hands. A high, sharp wind blew and the giant Douglas firs on the ridge above whispered and nodded. Carolyn shivered. She hated the wet grey gloom of an Oregon winter, viewed its impending arrival as she would a dreaded relative.

She loved Santavista Terrace during the daylight hours but was afraid of it at night, especially when she was alone. It wasn't like her cozy old neighborhood in southeast, where the land was flat and the houses so close you could watch *Jeopardy* through your neighbor's window.

The neighborhood where she lived now—she still refused to call it Queer Corners—had too many dark places. Wild pockets. When the sun was shining you saw beautiful houses and gardens; when night came on the hills reclaimed something of their uncultivated past. Just a month ago a cat owned by some people higher up on Santavista had been killed by a hungry bobcat straying down from Forest Park.

The red Cadillac hadn't moved and Carolyn had a sudden fear that she was being watched. She was about to turn and head back into the house when one of the car doors opened and a black shape leapt out of the vehicle and streaked like a shadow around the side of Delmont's house. They were letting their dog out to root around and poop in Delmont's garden! She was disgusted but didn't have the nerve to go down and confront whoever was in the car.

She heard nails clicking on the pavement behind her and whirled around with a sharp sense of foreboding. She'd left the front door open. There was Lady Caroline, outside, sniffing the night air. Air filled with invisible scents, glandular secretions that a human couldn't smell, powerful feral odors that could inflame Lady Caroline's already heightened hormones and drive her into an uncontrollable frenzy.

"Caroline," Carolyn murmured, keeping her voice calm, "go back into the house." She took a step towards the spaniel, hoping to force her to turn around. "Caroline, go back. Don't be naughty. Good dog."

But Lady Caroline, in heat, wasn't a good or a bad dog. She was just a dog, and she cocked her head as though she couldn't believe, now that she was outside and free, that her mistress wanted her back in the house. Before Carolyn could reach her, Lady Caroline barked, bolted down Santavista Terrace, and disappeared.

CHAPTER 4

JAY ZUCKER WAS IN HIS HOT TUB, SIPPING A PRIZE-WINNING OREGON
Pinot Gris with Chipper Johnson, when he thought he heard strange noises next door.
Trying to look interested as Chipper prattled on about his improbable acting career, Jay
cocked his head and listened more carefully. It sounded as though something or someone was slowly moving through the underbrush.

Maybe it was just a scavaging raccoon. They periodically tipped over Jay's garbage
bins, and one night not so long ago he'd awakened with a scream to see one of the
bandit-faced mammals staring at him through the bedroom window. Jay, in a seductive
mood, didn't want anything to put a crimp in his efficient style. He had to be back at
the restaurant in an hour.

The hot tub, a navy-blue six-seater surrounded by Italian terra-cotta tiles and
hidden from view by a slatted cedar screen, occupied a corner of Jay's back deck. The
deck, a good twenty feet off the ground, was built on stilts over Jay's steep, sloping,
bramble-infested half acre. He was a minimalist when it came to yard work.

Hearing the sound again, Jay turned and nervously peered through the screen down
into Delmont's dark, deserted garden. Once a source of such lovingly cultivated pride,
the garden, untended since Delmont's death, was already reverting back to a state of
primal, weed-choked wildness.

"Like everyone says if you're like totally serious about like being an actor, then,
like, well, you know, you're supposed to like go to New York," Chipper was saying.
"Do you like, you know, think I should like do that?"

Jay couldn't see anything. Relieved, he turned his attention back to Chipper,
secretly shifting his position so that a jet of fizzing, chlorinated water would hit him at
just the right angle. Ahh, one moment of pure physical bliss, a sparkling effervescence
as sweet to his stressed-out, hemorrhoid-swollen, forty-five-year-old asshole as Veuve
Cliquot was to his tongue. "I don't think anyone should go to New York," he said,
trying to get a glimpse of Chipper's big Scandinavian cock through the bubbling water.

"You don't?" Chipper's perspiring face, red from the hot water and the wine Jay
had been pouring, was as simple and honest as a big slab of rare beef. His white-gold
hair had been cut short in that butch, crew-cut, neo-Nazi look favored by the young. A
ring, cheap silver already tarnished by the chlorine, pierced his right nipple.

Jay, a refugee from New York, never ceased to be amazed, amused and aroused by
the blond Nordic giants of the Northwest. He loved their flat twanging voices and
husky corn-fed bodies. Unlike New York, where men wearing cowboy boots walked
like they were in pinching high-heels, the guys in Portland strode around in their big

comfortable clodhoppers as if they were John Wayne. They seemed to know so little of the world. And for ten years Jay had had extraordinary luck with them. A miracle! A plump, guilt-ridden, freshly divorced Jew when he came to Portland, Jay had turned himself into a city-wide heartthrob.

"New York's a pit," Jay said. "A cesspool."

"It is?" Chipper sounded interested. He was from a small town in southern Oregon. His old man beat the shit out of him, he said, when he stopped going to the Fundamentalist Foursquare Church. He'd left his father's cattle ranch and worked as a white-water rafter on the Rogue River before packing up his aspirations and migrating north to the city. That was after he met Ginger Rogers, a swollen-faced Republican who'd left Hollywood to settle in an agreeably homophobic neck of the woods just north of the California border. Ginger, Chipper claimed, told him that he had "possibilities"—though what they were, she didn't say.

"There are lots of small theatres here in Portland," Jay said, working the bait. "In fact, I sit on the board of one of them."

"On the board? What's that mean?"

"It's the governing body," Jay explained.

"Cool. Which theeder?"

"The Mousehole."

"Never heard of it."

There was no reason why he would. The Mousehole was as experimental as you could get without being run out of town. But it gave Jay an opportunity to exercise his wit with Portland's smartest oddballs.

As owner and maitre d' of Chez Jay, he had to meet, greet and seat more than his share of conservative, buttoned-down businesspeople. He had to smile and be eternally affable to the dwindling lunch crowd and then the dwindling dinner crowd and then the nearly non-existent after-dinner crowd. Sometimes he got tremendously bored with them, and grew sick of catering to their fat-assed comfort and pleasure. The gym helped. So did The Mousehole. And sex, of course.

"Maybe you should think about television," he said, scooting an inch closer to Chipper. He spread out his arms so Chipper could see his well-defined biceps and triceps. His chest, unlike Chipper's, was covered with a mat of thick black hair, the gray plucked out with a tweezers every morning.

"Fer shure," Chipper exclaimed. "Like get my own series, you mean, and have a laugh track and all that neat stuff." He sobered. "But then I'd like have to like go to L.A., wouldn't I?"

The howl, coming from almost directly below the deck, froze them in the hot water.

"Jesus," Jay gasped, "it's a wolf!"

"Nah, that ain't no wolf," Chipper said, relaxing again. "I used to hear wolves all the time around the ranch. That's probably like just some *rilly big* mean old dog."

A sudden volley of powerful barks confirmed Chipper's hypothesis. Jay, fighting back a wave of instinctual panic, couldn't move. He hated large dogs, loathed large dogs, grew weak in the knees and began to sweat when he saw large dogs. When Jay was a small boy, his grandfather had told him terrifying stories of the vicious mastiffs that accompanied the Christians during their periodic pogroms of the shtetls in Eastern Europe. Then his father had told him terrifying stories of the throat-ripping German Shepherds that the Nazis used as attack dogs in their extermination campaigns.

His heart began to hammer as sounds of growling and snapping plant stems rose from the darkness. Whatever it was, it was destructive. "Why isn't it on a leash?" he said, his voice a gulp. People on the hill never let their dogs run unattended.

Now there was another sound—whining—then a yelp. Pattering feet. A rustle of leaves. Another sharp yelp. Chipper rose from the water, his body steaming in the cool night air, and leaned across Jay to look out through the cedar slats. "It ain't one dog, it's two." He began to laugh.

"Are they fighting?" Jay asked.

"Hell no, they ain't fightin'. They sure are fuckin', though."

▼ ▼ ▼

"See ya round."

Jay, in his thick white terrycloth robe, smiled, nodded, and opened the front door. He wondered if Chipper would kiss him. A peck on the cheek maybe.

Nothing. Flat as day-old Pellegrino. Unemotional. A little embarrassed, or bored maybe. Eager to get away.

Jay watched as Chipper, in big black boots and leather jacket, clomped out to a pickup truck and out of his life.

The moment he closed the door, a mood of grim foreboding sheared through his thoughts. Okay, so for once in his life he couldn't perform. So what?

So what? Jay Zucker could always perform! As daring as a trapeze artist, as agile as a Russian gymnast, as experienced as Casanova himself, Jay prided himself on never letting anyone down sexually. And there he was, Mr. Seduction, with eager super-Aryan Chipper—as limp as a noodle! It was a devastating first. There he was, frantically trying to connect, but his usual sexual energy seemed to be floating somewhere just outside his body, ungovernable, out of reach.

Impotent. The word nailed itself into his thoughts, cracking the plaster of his self-esteem. He headed for the Valium, hoping to head off pharmaceutically the spurt of malevolent taunts echoing in his head. Impotent. Middle-aged queer. Graying *fegalah*. Almost bankrupt. Empty. Alone, alone, alone.

Another glass of Pinot Gris would help the Valium.

If only Delmont were still alive. His deceased neighbor had gradually become like a father to Jay—a gay father who could dispense the clear-headed advice (and occasional bank loans) of an older generation.

"Have you ever been impotent, Gay Dad?"

"Of course, Gay Son. It happens to everyone. Don't panic."

"Don't panic," Jay said out loud, pushing up the rheostat and flooding his marbled bathroom with the harshest, most humiliating light it could produce. He dropped his robe and stared at himself in the full-length mirror. Flexed his muscles. Took a deep breath to expand his hairy pecs. The panic roosted in his body like a queasy hint of some strange flu.

He examined himself front and rear, looking for clues. Scabby growths, discolorations, lesions. Nothing.

He'd had panic attacks before, but they'd always been business related. The hammering heart, the insomnia, the desire to crawl into bed and pull the covers up over his head—he'd talked to Delmont about all of the symptoms. This was something deeper. Maybe it had to do with Delmont, with the grief that Jay, Mr. Smile-For-The-Customers, had never had time to express. Or was afraid to express.

And, of course, as usual, customers were in the back of his mind. Like an actor, he had to prepare for his nightly role as the charming solicitous host of Chez Jay. Thanks to the traveling road show of *Jesus Christ Superstar*, playing just down the street from Chez Jay at the Civic Auditorium, the restaurant was fully booked. That wasn't happening much lately—another cause of nerve-jangling concern. Cassandra would do the early seating until Jay arrived at seven to handle the heavy dinner crowd.

Delmont had told him that he should never let a panic attack keep him from going about his normal routine. The best thing to do was to keep going. Nip it in the bud. Show it who was boss. "It's a test of inner strength, dear," Delmont said.

Jay, taking deep breaths to keep his hands from shaking as he knotted his tie, looked down from his bedroom window into Delmont's garden. Dark, dark, dark. The little accent lights no longer clicked on automatically at dusk to illuminate beds of roses and ferny crevices in the rock garden. Were the two dogs gone? Jay pushed open the window and gulped in a draught of sweet cold air.

That's when he saw a figure—not a dog but a human—slowly following the shadowy pathways that wound through Delmont's garden.

Softly calling someone's—an accomplice's?—name.

They were going to break into Delmont's house, which was still filled with his valuables, and make off with the goods.

A clear, cold shot of adrenalin pumped through the haze of Valium and wine. Robbing his dead friend's house! If he didn't stop them, he'd be the next victim. He hadn't left crime-infested New York to be robbed in Portland, Oregon.

He pulled a small unlicensed gun from his bedside drawer and, quiet as a thief, slipped out his front door.

▼ ▼ ▼

Jay knew the garden, even in the dark, like the back of his hand. Delmont, nocturnal as an owl, believed in old-fashioned nightcaps, the kind with ice, not the kind you wore on your head. Jay would sometimes stop over at two in the morning and they'd walk down into the quiet garden, their drinks tinkling like alcoholic wind chimes. There they'd talk. Jay would unwind from another frantic Chez Jay day.

Delmont's garden had been created from the steeply sloping hillside behind his house. It was an old garden, tangled with neglect when he moved in. Ito Kudomono had trimmed back the drooping conifers, torn out the suffocating ivy, shored up the retaining walls at each level, added a new rock garden, replanted the flowerbeds, and sprinkled rhododendrons, azaleas, and flowering dogwoods under the Douglas firs.

From the first level there was a panoramic view of the city rising against the backdrop of the Cascades and Mt. Hood. At night the lights of Portland sparkled with cozy allure. As you descended, the view disappeared, the air grew chillier, and the looming giant fir trees spread darkness all around.

Jay, sure-footed as a dancer in his thin Ferragamo loafers, stealthily followed the brick stairs down the side of Delmont's house and peered around the side. He saw the figure almost at once. It was creeping along through the shrubbery, bent almost double, two levels below him. Whispering something at regular intervals. A crack addict? A homeless person? A madman? A thief?

He quickly darted over to the rock-hewn steps on the opposite side of the terrace, his heart whacking him like a fist. "Stop where you are!"

The figure heard him. Gasped. Froze.

"Don't move. I have a gun." His palm sticky against the weapon's handle, Jay kept his eye on the figure as he slowly stepped down to the next level. "Put up your hands. Walk over here. Don't try any funny business or I'll put a bullet through you." Which was a laugh, since he was terrified of guns and this one had no bullets.

The figure, stooped like a foraging primate, slowly rose. Up went the arms. As it moved closer Jay recognized his overweight neighbor, wearing blue jeans and a dark jacket, her hair hidden under a cap.

"Carolyn!"

"Oh, Jay, it's you!" She put a hand to her chest and let out a tense hoot of nervous laughter. "Don't shoot, sweetie!"

He laughed too. "What are you doing out here?"

She couldn't quite catch her breath. "Lady Caroline ran off—I left the door open— she's in heat—I saw her come tearing down here."

"Oh oh," Jay said.

Carolyn winced, preparing herself for the worst.

"There was another dog—"

"Oh no," she groaned.

"I didn't see it, exactly, but I heard it."

"It was from that car—"

"What car?"

"That disgusting red Cadillac parked in front of Delmont's," Carolyn said indignantly. "They let their dog out to do it's business. Lady Caroline ran off. I freaked. I ran inside to change my clothes so I could search for her. The car was gone by the time I got down here."

They both turned in the direction of a holly tree that grew on the far boundary of Delmont's garden. The holly was whimpering.

"Lady Caroline?" Carolyn ran to the tree, got down on her knees, and lifted the lowest branches. "Where are you?"

"Is she there?" Jay asked, suddenly fearful that the mysterious dog—the *rilly huge mean old dog* from the red Cadillac—would leap out and lunge for his throat.

"Ouch!" Carolyn was having a hard time with the prickly holly leaves. Jay went over to help her, gingerly lifting the heavy branches so she could crawl underneath.

"There there," she soothed.

As she inched deeper under the tree, all Jay could see was the flat-footed soles of her Birkenstocks and her rump straining the seams of old Gloria Vanderbilt jeans. "It's all right. Mummy's here. Come on. Don't be afraid." A sharp painful yelp.

Jay stood back as Carolyn withdrew the small, filthy toy spaniel from its hiding place under the holly tree. Cradling the dog in her arms like a precious child, she went to sit down on a step. "What did he do to you?" she whimpered, stroking the shivering animal, picking leaves and burrs from its coat. She pried back Lady Caroline's tail. "Oh my dear Goddess."

"What?"

"I think she's been raped." She looked imploringly at Jay. "Don't tell Susan. Please!"

▼ ▼ ▼

The hum of the restaurant was money to Jay's ears. Nearly every table was filled with people he'd never seen before, people who looked unaccustomed to dressing up for a night out but felt obligated to do so. Fat men with sagging bellies wearing pale-blue or rust-colored polyester leisure suits with white patent-leather shoes. Skinny old farts with weathered faces, Stetsons and string ties. Women with teased, dyed hair, wearing colorful but strangely unflattering outfits. Where had they come from?

"American Christian Alliance," Cassandra whispered to Jay, giving him a quick, conspiratorial look. She smiled graciously at a waiting couple, both of them wearing fringed buckskin jackets, and said, "Your table's ready now. Follow me, s'il vous plait."

"You got french fries here?" the man asked.

Cassandra didn't miss a beat. "Of course we have french fries, sir. This is a French restaurant. You'll find them on the menu under pommes frites."

She was back a minute later. "Help," she whimpered. "I think I'd rather be in hell."

"That bad?"

"It's some sort of fundamentalist Christian convention. They got a special discount on tickets to Jesus Christ Superstar. They all want Diet Pepsi and ketchup with their steaks. And they've never heard of tips."

"Sorry I'm late. I had to help Carolyn Corbett find her dog."

"I thought she had a pussy," Cassandra said.

Jay laughed, half in love with the tiny blonde whose eyes always held, for him, a sly, mischievous glow. If he'd been straight, Cassandra was the sort of woman he'd go for. "No, a dog. I nearly shot her."

"The dog or Carolyn?"

"Carolyn."

"New tie?" Cassandra asked, fondling the silk.

"On sale at Nordstrom's Rack."

"I won't tell."

"You look hot." Cassandra, braless, was wearing a black floor-length sheath, luminous liver-colored lipstick, and, in honor of *Jesus Christ Superstar*, eight-inch platform heels. The men were staring, the women looked sourly indignant.

"When you told me we actually had a full house I dolled up. I thought maybe some rich glamorous dyke would give me a pinch and invite me to her chateau in the Loire

Valley. Then this crew showed up." She turned her sharp little face to survey the diners. "Don't tell anyone you're Jewish or they'll attack you with their steak knives."

"Yeah, I know. We killed Christ."

"Okay, I'm out of here. Am I waitressing for brunch tomorrow or seating?"

"Seating. I'm taking the day off."

"Good," she said. "You need to do that once in awhile."

She'd just turned to leave when the door opened and a new couple walked in.

The man entered first, not bothering to hold the door for the woman trailing behind. He had a wide, pitted face, almost elliptical, which he tried to lengthen with a long, drooping moustache. A face that reminded Jay of a catfish, or some hearty, primitive bottom feeder. Thinning hair the color of cordovan shoe polish and artfully scraped up from the temples. Eyes that looked like blue sucked candy from a distance, but hard as microchips when he got closer. Wearing a dark suit that almost fit before he'd put on those extra pounds. Carrying a cellular phone, a no-no because Chez Jay was an officially designated cellular-free zone.

Once she was in the door and saw the crowd, the woman, like some strange hothouse flower, suddenly blossomed into life. She had a blonde Sixties flip with bangs that hid her forehead. Her age-scratched face, hidden behind putty-colored makeup and pink lipstick, grew animated. "Look, hon, it's like a full house on Sunday!"

Batting eyelashes as long as rakes, she clicked past her escort on gold high-heeled slippers and headed towards the reservations podium. Jay and Cassandra were suddenly drowning in a sea of perfume.

"We don't have a reservation," she cried, "but I hope you can find us a little table somewhere!"

Her voice, throbbing with loud, inexplicable emotion, carried into the crowded room. Heads turned. Someone said, "Look, it's Cornette Terwilliger!"

"Ron Labonne's with her!"

A moment later the diners were applauding. One after another, still chewing their food, they popped up from their chairs and gave the couple a standing ovation.

The woman threw open her arms to embrace the crowd. "We're all here for Jesus!" she cried. "Did you all thank Jesus for your food? Jesus is the chef of life!"

"Give us a prayer, Cornette!" someone shouted.

The clapping grew louder. The woman cast an adoring glance at her escort and held out a hand with nails so long they looked like varnished garden spades. She beckoned him to her side. The man, tilting his head back and jutting out a non-existent chin, joined her.

They stood like a Prom King and Queen as the crowd chanted: "Ron and Cornette! Ron and Cornette!"

Cornette, giggling, baring her teeth, clutched Ron's arm like an excited schoolgirl. Then she shushed the crowd. "Have any of you ever known Ron to be shy?" No, they roared. "Well, maybe you're wondering why he's acting so shy right now."

"Why you so shy, Ron?" someone yelled.

It was Ron's cue. He disengaged himself from Cornette. She stepped a little to one side, staring up at him with trance-like devotion.

"Friends," he said, "you know that God created man and woman to love and cherish one another. It's the holiest joy on earth, to come home from a hard day's work and find your little woman waiting for you, with a smile on her face and a few soothing words and dinner on the table. Isn't that so?"

Silence. The seated couples didn't look at one another but kept their eyes riveted on Ron Labonne as he stepped into their midst.

"You know my story. I'm not proud of it. How my first wife run off and left me with a son to raise myself. How I prayed that she'd come back. 'I'll forgive her, God, if she'll just come back and help me raise our precious son in a Christian home.' That's what I prayed for. I prayed that Jesus would light her heart, and show her the way back to me. But she was lost to drugs and drink."

"I'd be, too," Cassandra murmured to Jay.

Tears dripped from Cornette's eyelashes like fat raindrops. Her eyes were squeezed shut and she was nodding.

Jay and Cassandra looked at one another, amused and horrified at the same time.

"Everyone said, 'Ron, she's no good. Don't waste your life waiting for her. Don't sacrifice your son. He needs a mother.' They meant well. But as a Christian, I felt it was my duty to do everything in my power to patch up my marriage. Marriage is a sacred institution to me. So I waited and prayed and then one day I heard the voice of Jesus. And He told me what to do. I moved to southern Oregon and started the American Christian Alliance—the ACA—on a shoestring, in my garage, because I could see from my own experience the way this country was turning. How special interest groups were doing everything in their power to overturn the values that have made this country of ours the greatest on earth. How government was caving in to their unChristian demands."

Cornette surveyed the murmuring crowd through half-open eyes and cleared her throat as if she were about to speak.

"Friends, the time finally came when Jesus said to me, 'Ron, stop agonizing over the past and start thinking about the future. You're a lonely man in need of a helpmate. Your son's at a crucial age now—he's almost a man—and he needs an example. He needs to see how a Christian guy can find happiness with a Christian gal.' And then a miracle occurred. This lovely lady, known to millions through her television ministry, came to an ACA fundraiser. I took one look at her and I knew she was going to be my wife."

An excited gasp ran through the restaurant. Cornette opened her eyes wide, beaming and shedding tears of joy.

"So I asked her to marry me. And another miracle occurred. She said yes!"

Everyone laughed. "When you tying the knot?" someone asked.

Cornette flashed a diamond ring. "We already did!"

Ron held up his hands to quiet the deafening applause. "She's giving up her ministry in Dallas—"

"Not giving it up, hon," Cornette quickly added, "just moving it up *here*—"

"—and moving here to Portland—"

"With my daughter!" Cornette slipped in.

"—so we can do the Lord's work together, hand in hand—one big Christian family."

"We wanted you to be the first to know!" Cornette cried. "And we're going to be sitting there with you tonight at Jesus Christ Superstar—with growling stomachs if we don't get something to eat real fast. God bless!"

They didn't bow, but acknowledged the clapping by joining and triumphantly raising their hands. Then, the show over, Cornette waved and the two of them turned to Jay and Cassandra. Following her husband's line of vision, Cornette's eyes immediately fastened on Cassandra's freestanding breasts.

"Hey guy," Ron said to Jay, "you got valet service here?"

"No, we don't," Jay said.

"Then do me a favor and run my car over to a garage. I'm in a tow-away zone." He tossed a ring of keys to the stupefied Jay. "It's the red Cadillac parked right out front. There's a dog inside, but he won't hurt you."

"His name's Pharaoh," Cornette said.

"I'm afraid I can't do that." Jay tossed the keys back.

Ron's cellular phone warbled.

"This is a cellular-free zone," Cassandra said.

Both Labonnes ignored her. "This is Ron Labonne. Yeah, yeah. They did? Well, the Lord's obviously giving us the green light and telling us to step on it." There was a smile playing on his lips as he clicked off.

"Who was it, hon?" Cornette asked.

"The realtor. They accepted our offer on the house."

CHAPTER 5

CASSANDRA TAYLOR KNEW A BARGAIN WHEN SHE FOUND ONE. SHE HAD a lucky sixth sense about these things—the right time, the right place, the right price. She wasn't rich, but she looked as though she might be. In fact, she hardly had a dime to her name. So when she saw the carriage house Terry Terwilliger was offering in exchange for low rent and minimal housekeeping duties in his own Mock Tudor, she accepted on the spot. That was almost a year ago.

The carriage house was the find of the century. Terry parked his huge green Mercedes below. There were two rooms above: a small dark one, where Cassandra slept, and a large open one, which she used as her studio and living space. At some point in the distant past, one of Terry's serial live-in boys had convinced the old cheapskate to knock out the far wall of the large room and put in a small balcony with glass doors. There was also a skylight.

Cassandra loved this light-flooded eyrie more than any home she'd ever had. And, being an army brat, she'd had many. They were never called "home," though; it was always "the base."

Perched high above the city, she could see the soft contours of the Cascade foothills and the sharp, dramatic profile of Mt. Hood. The flattened cone of Mt. St. Helens, visible to the northwest, looked benign enough but everyone knew the volcanic power cooking below its surface. The shifting, shimmering colors of the mountains—magenta, purple, crimson, forest green, polar white—inspired Cassandra. Sometimes, when a bank of wet coastal clouds moved in, she wouldn't see the mountains for days. Then, one morning, she'd look out and there they'd be, calmly silhouetted against a clear blue-gold sky. Her spirit would expand. She'd feel a secret, powerful connection to this small western city nestled in a valley between the Cascades and the Coast Range.

Cassandra was sharp and observant. During her year in Queer Corners she'd found out quite a bit about this exclusive little corner of Portland and the people who inhabited it. Delmont Percy, Terry's oldest pal, was the sparkling doyen of the neighborhood. Everyone revered Delmont—even Terry, who kept most of his adoration for himself. Cassandra hadn't known Delmont except by sight. Before he got sick he sometimes came over to Terry's for cocktails, and she'd hear the two of them cackling and laughing. Last Christmas Jay had taken her to a party at Delmont's. The house was awesome. When Delmont saw her eagerly studying his collection of minor Impressionists, he came over and told her a little bit about the history of each one. A real gentleman. When she told him about her own work, Delmont made a vague promise to come over and "have a look." She'd been elated. But the visit never materialized. Delmont became frail. She knew what was going on—Jay was so concerned—and didn't have the heart to press the old, dying collector to make good on his promise.

The Queer Corners colonized by Delmont Percy was a gorgeous place. Cassandra was thrilled by her luck in living there. The area—called Queen's Heights but locally referred to as "the hill"—had once been covered with ancient stands of Douglas fir. Most of these towering giants had been hacked down before the turn of the century, but enough remained to give the streets a foresty Northwest feel. The roads, cut in sharp switchbacks up the side of the hill, were hellish in snowy or icy weather, which increased their appeal. Beautiful walls of stacked basalt, covered with English ivy, helped shore up the hill and prevented the houses from sliding away. Forest Park buffered one side of the hill from further development, but garish, ungainly homes—contemptuously referred to as McMansions—were springing up like gigantic fungi all around Queer Corners, threatening its peaceful, perfect, tasteful way of life.

Living in this wealthy enclave Cassandra felt safe and secure for the first time in her penniless life. Special. Everyone liked her, although they wished she wouldn't park her beat-up pink VW bug on the street. She was "cute," smart, and, as an artist, had a certain *je ne sais quoi* that made up for her lack of money. She'd sold one painting to Carolyn Corbett and another to Jay Zucker. Terry was a hold-out, but he was a Republican, like her parents, so that was to be expected.

▼ ▼ ▼

Early Sunday morning, before her brunch gig at Chez Jay, Cassandra made her usual visit to Terry's house. One of her "duties" was to make Terry a good cholesterol-laden Sunday breakfast. He was sitting in the kitchen bay, the Sunday *New York Times* spread out on the table, when she arrived.

"The last time I went to Rio I got robbed," he grumbled, evidently in response to a story he was reading in the Travel section.

"How was Palm Springs?" Cassandra asked. Terry and his mysterious jaunts to Palms Springs. He'd gone back again after Delmont's funeral and had returned late last night. The clanking vibrations from the antiquated electric garage door had awakened her.

"There wasn't any Floris soap in the upstairs shower," Terry complained.

"You're out of Floris."

"Why didn't you tell me? Now it'll take two weeks to order some from London."

"You can order it from New York," Cassandra said.

"They don't have the scent I like. I'll have a cappuccino—foamy, you know the way I like it."

Yes, she thought, flicking on the espresso machine, she knew the way he liked it. She also knew that somebody else was in the house. Upstairs. She'd heard another voice last night, the sound of braying male laughter. There was a plate in the sink, and crystal tumblers that gave off a faint, sour smell of whiskey. And Terry looked nervous. A bony knee protruding from his paisley dressing gown jiggled up and down.

Who could it be? Who would come home with a sixty-something man with dyed black hair, a defective facelift, and lots of money?

"Scrambled eggs," Terry said, rifling through the Living Arts section. "And some microwaved sausage—five minutes. Warm me a croissant, too."

"Yes, sir," Cassandra said, her ironic military tone lost on Terry.

Something unspoken hung in the air. She could feel it as she gathered the breakfast ingredients, adding her own share. Disagreeable as it was, eating with Terry was one way to keep food bills down.

"You know our agreement about the carriage house," Terry said as he pretended to browse through the New York theatre listings.

A sudden foreboding roiled her stomach. "What agreement?"

"You know—that it was sort of temporary—that I might find someone else who'd be more permanent."

"I'm happy to think of it as permanent," she said carefully.

"Well, you would, wouldn't you? It's such a good deal for you. But I told you to think of it as temporary, just in case I found someone more—" He waved his hand, as if she knew.

"More what? More male?"

Terry glanced at her, annoyed. If there was one thing he hated in a female it was sexual frankness. "Someone who could do more than you do. The yard work and fix-it jobs around the house."

"You never asked me to do any yard work, Terry."

"Well, you're too busy anyway, aren't you? You hardly have time to run a vacuum over the carpets once a week. Working for Jay Zucker, and doing whatever else you do."

"I paint, Terry. I'm an artist."

"Yes, well, maybe I need someone who's not so busy doing other things."

Cassandra was furious. By "other things" he meant "having a life." Enjoying herself, at his expense. That was the implication. Because everything, in the end, came back to Terrence Terwilliger III and his monstrously self-absorbed ego. Cassandra had never become quite human to him because he wouldn't let her. She was a woman, after all.

Well, she wasn't going to curtsy and skulk away like a dismissed maid. She hated fighting. She'd grown up in a military household where fighting formed the very reason for existence. But the carriage house was worth fighting for. She had to bide her time, though. Had to do it carefully, without licking Terry the Turd's ass.

Terry rose with a sigh and plodded over to the window that overlooked a section of Delmont's back garden. With his skinny neck, sharp nose and flapping wattles he reminded Cassandra of an old turkeycock. A mouth pursed tight as a sphincter made him look as though he were sucking on gobbled pennies. "Delmont's house goes on the market today," he said.

"No it doesn't." She sharply cracked the eggs.

"What do you mean?"

"It sold yesterday."

"Why didn't you tell me?" Terry looked back outside, alarmed. "Well, who? What do you know?"

"Someone with your last name," she said, making him sweat.

"Terwilliger?"

"Cornette Terwilliger. Ever heard of her?"

He gasped. "Heard of her! She's my cousin!"

"Well, she's also your new neighbor. She and her new husband, Ron Labonne." Both disgusting, she might have added, but kept the thought to herself. Terry had an excruciatingly high opinion of his family, even the ones he hated.

Terry, as if suddenly possessed, began an agitated dance around the kitchen. "What are you saying? That's ridiculous! It's not true! I haven't seen the bitch for years. It can't be the same Cornette Terwilliger."

"A television evangelist or something?"

"She used family money to buy a cable television spot," Terry sputtered. "Claimed to be born again. Fancied herself another Aimee Semple McPherson. Married some weirdo who stole everything and ran off. Oh God, this can't be true. I have to call Leonora."

Leonora Halsey was Terry's official "girlfriend." His "beard." She was a divorceé as rich as Terry and equally dim—so dim she still hadn't figured out that her beau of twenty years was as queer as a three-dollar bill. Leonora was part of the same "Old Money" crowd Terry hung around with. She always treated Cassandra with suspicious contempt, as if the young woman were a rival for Terry's non-existent affections.

Terry, fumbling for his glasses, was dialling Leonora when a dark-haired young man wearing a pair of bikini underpants appeared in the kitchen doorway. Flustered, his mouth hanging open, Terry hung up the phone. "Billy—what are you doing out of bed?"

The young man, idly scratching his crotch with one hand and strumming on a nipple with the other, eyed Cassandra. "That your cook?"

The mocking tone of his voice set Cassandra's teeth on edge. A face like a ferret— sharp, cunning, and stupid, all at once. She'd seen a lot of those faces on the army bases. Cassandra surprised him, surprised herself, by going over to shake his hand. "Hi, I'm Cassandra."

"Hi, I'm Cassandra," he mimicked. He looked over at Terry, who dutifully cackled in appreciation.

Frightened and instantly wary, Cassandra went back to the stove. There was nothing in his handshake. An empty gesture. Worse, she recognized immediately the emotional dislocation of his personality. Billy was not someone you could trust. Only a person like Terry, completely out of synch with his own psyche and lonely to the point of desperation would give this two-bit hustler the time of day.

"This is Billy Bird," Terry said, "my friend from Palm Springs."

"Hey!" Billy said sharply. "I'm not your friend!"

Terry looked crestfallen. "What do you mean?"

"I'm not your *friend*," Billy repeated. Menace in his step, he playfully stalked Terry through the kitchen. Terry backed away with a nervous cluck, hiding behind Cassandra.

He gasped as Billy suddenly grabbed him around the neck, like a wrestler, and pulled his head down.

"I'm not your friend, I'm your buddy! Your big buddy!" Billy said, pretending to pummel Terry's face. "Right?"

"Oh yes, ha ha, of course, right," Terry said, pulling away, his face red, his artfully woven hair standing up in stiff tufts, his robe torn open to reveal a torso that looked like a plucked chicken breast. He quickly turned around to rearrange himself.

"Say it then," Billy demanded. "Tell Hi, I'm Cassandra your cook that I'm your big buddy from Palm Springs and I want some of them scrambled eggs and a Bloody Mary."

"I'll make you a Bloody Mary," Terry said.

"I'll make you a Bloody Mary, what?" Billy bellowed.

Terry turned around with a fawning grin. "I'll make you a Bloody Mary, Big Buddy."

▼ ▼ ▼

"Oh, that tired old queen," Peter Love said when Cassandra told him the story fifteen minutes later. He threw down the Real Estate section of the Sunday paper in disgust. "Terry the Turd deserves whatever he gets, honey."

"Yes, but what about the carriage house?" Cassandra cried. She could see it from the windows of Peter and John-Don's living room. Her beautiful little sanctuary had suddenly been taken hostage by a hostile force. She'd run over here in an absolute dither, had literally fled the Mock Tudor. It was Jay's house she'd instinctually headed for because it was Jay she was in love with. The truth came to her in a sharp pang of tormented longing. Like a pinball, she'd zinged off in the opposite direction. She couldn't foist her problems off on Jay. He had enough of his own.

She felt awful, disturbing their intimate Sunday morning ritual, but didn't know where else she could go. Peter, wearing a pair of soft cotton sweat pants (and no underwear, she noticed) and a fleecy Donna Karan sweater, was lounging on his Italian leather sofa. Newspapers and magazines were strewn around him. Soft jazzy music was playing.

"How do you know this scumbag wants the carriage house?" Peter asked.

"Peter, he wants everything. I can just see it. He's going to move in and take over. And Terry is such a sucker!"

"Especially when he takes out his dentures," Peter said.

"Okay, go ahead and laugh, camp it up, but it's my home that's at stake." What did any of them, cushioned in their wealth, really know about *home*?

"I'm not camping, honey," Peter said. "This is how I really am. And if you're a smart little dyke you'll play it cool."

"How? I don't trust him."

"Lock your doors," Peter said.

"I never lock my doors," Cassandra said. "I don't want to live that way. That's just it."

John-Don, wearing a rumpled running suit, appeared with coffee for them and mineral water for himself. "That's just what?"

"Her doors," Peter said. "She never locks them."

Cassandra shivered and stared down into her coffee. "Just having him there changes everything. Suddenly it's all out of whack. I feel completely paranoid. He's so creepy. And Terry's so out of touch, do you know what I mean?"

Peter and John-Don exchanged looks. Yes, they knew what she meant.

But they were a couple, Cassandra thought, glancing at a Hockney print of a swimming pool and wondering if one of her paintings would ever hang on the smooth plaster walls. They had one another. Their perspective was different from hers. They had a big beautiful home that no one could take away from them. Entering it, she could feel a stability, an emotional repose that she was afraid she'd never find for herself.

"Everything's changing," she said. "Ever since Delmont died. And that horrible couple that's buying his house—"

It was like throwing a pitcher of cold water on them. What horrible couple? So Cassandra told them about the scene in the restaurant.

"Fundamentalist Christians?" Peter gasped, sitting bolt upright. "In Queer Corners?" He let out a peal of horror-stricken laughter. "Tell me it ain't so!"

"It doesn't seem very likely." Sipping his mineral water, John-Don looked out the window, across Skyview Boulevard, towards Delmont's house. "How do you know it's Delmont's house they're buying?" he asked Cassandra.

"Because they drive a red Cadillac."

Peter snorted. "Honey, are you sure they're not drug dealers?"

"No," Cassandra breathlessly explained, "because Jay ran into Carolyn Corbett last night before he came to the restaurant, and Carolyn said she saw this huge red Cadillac parked in front of Delmont's house, with a big dog in it, and then this horrible couple came in the restaurant and it was like a revival meeting, and the man was head of something called the ACA, and he asked Jay to park his car. I couldn't believe it, the arrogance, he treated Jay like a valet! Anyway, that's when we found out that they drove a big red Cadillac, so it has to be the same people who were parked in front that Carolyn saw, right?"

"I don't think it would hold up in a court of law," John-Don said.

"Well, then his cellular phone rang and he said, this ACA freak said to his wife, 'They accepted our offer on the house.'"

"But you never actually heard him give the address, or say what house," John-Don said patiently.

Cassandra admitted that she hadn't. It was speculation. "But how many people drive red Cadillacs and park in front of Delmont's and have a big dog?" she asked.

▾ ▾ ▾

Sissy Parker was in her beige module at Sarah Sue Seagull Realty when Terry Terwilliger called. He was fuming. "Sissy, I demand an explanation!"

"For what?" she said, eyeing her uneaten chocolate-chip muffin, too tense to sit back and relax in her new ergometric chair.

"You should have told me!"

"Told you what?" She nervously flipped the page in her Women in Art daily calendar and eyed two pale, naked, 18th-century French ladies coyly tweaking one another's nipples.

"Told me that you were selling Delmont's house to Cornette Terwilliger." When Sissy didn't respond, Terry added: "She's my cousin, you know."

"No," Sissy said, "I didn't know." And even if I had, she thought defensively, why would I have to tell you? It was true that Terry had been a client in years gone by. He'd bought a dilapidated late-19th-century apartment house on her recommendation, kicked out the welfare winos who lived there, and converted it to luxury condos which she, in turn, had sold for a tidy profit. So what?

"How much did it sell for?" Terry wanted to know.

"Four eighty," she said, smiling at the thought. In fact, her largest sale ever, and she'd hustled her butt off to make it happen. Met the prospective buyers at weird hours, in the middle of the night, smiling blankly at their rudeness, going deaf at convenient moments. "Think of what it'll do for property values on the hill."

"It's all *down*hill if that bitch moves in," Terry shrilled. "She's from the Texas Terwilligers, the bad side of the family. *Trash*. And here I was, down in Palm Springs, trying to interest my friends in the place."

Another line warbled. "Just a minute, Terry, I've got another call." She put him on hold and picked up Jay Zucker.

"Sissy, what in the hell is going on?" he demanded, his voice deep and edgy.

Jay the dreamboat Adonis. A gay man so handsome that even a dyed-in-the-wool dyke like Sissy occasionally fantasized about him. "Jay, sweetie," she said. The chair, which responded to the tiniest shifts in body weight, tipped backwards with a malevolent jerk and she fell into it with a grunt.

"Did you really sell them the house?" Jay asked.

There was no beating around the bush with Jay: he was too savvy. "Word certainly spreads fast," she said. As fast, for instance, as news of Jay's financial problems with Chez Jay.

"Sissy, do you know who these people are?"

"I didn't run an FBI check on them, if that's what you mean." It was better to know as little as possible, really, about prospective buyers. Personality was superfluous in the open market. You were banned from even thinking about it. Sissy was an equal opportunity realtor, she liked to say. Sex, race, age, religion, physical handicaps, sexual orientation—none of that mattered, so long as you had enough money for the downpayment.

"They're Christian fundamentalists!" Jay shouted.

"Jay, if someone makes me an offer and the seller accepts it, I can't not sell them the property, now can I?"

"Did you tell them this is a gay neighborhood?"

"Of course not!" she huffed. "That's none of their business." She saw Terry's light blink off and realized she'd forgotten all about him.

"But if you were selling to a gay person you'd tell them it was a gay neighborhood, wouldn't you?"

"If that's what they were looking for." She couldn't resist any longer and nervously began to pick chocolate-chips from her muffin.

"Didn't they ask who their neighbors would be?"

"No, they didn't. And if they had asked, I certainly wouldn't have told them you were gay. That would be an invasion of your privacy. I could be sued for saying that."

"I seem to recall that before you sold Peter Love his house you called to let us all know that he was black."

"No," she snapped, "I called to say that he was a wonderful gay guy who happened to be Afro-American."

"Well why didn't you at least let us know these cretins were looking at the place?"

"Why?" she said. "What could you have done about it? Nothing. I told you the house was on the market before it was even listed. I gave you all a chance to find a gay buyer."

"Sissy, these people came into the restaurant last night. They're awful."

"Did you give them a table?" she asked.

"Of course. I can't refuse service to people I don't like."

"Well, there you are," she said triumphantly. Now her other line was warbling again—Terry, no doubt, calling back. "Jay, I'm sorry, but I've got to go."

She hung up, took one gulp of her double cappuccino, and flipped to the other line.

"Sissy? Susan Bark here."

It wasn't her arrhythmia that made Sissy's heart skip a beat. It was that authoritative English voice and all the painful memories it conjured up. At one time Sissy had been infatuated with Susan. They'd even gone out once. Sissy had hoped. And then Susan had met Carolyn Corbett. That led to those stupid drunken weeping phone calls in the middle of the night. It all happened before Sissy had joined AA, of course. "Hello," she said, dropping her voice and trying to sound sexily nonchalant.

"Look here, I'm out at Windy Hills but before I left I got a call from Cassandra Taylor who was working at Chez Jay last night and met some dreadful couple—the woman's evidently Terry Terwilliger's cousin—and she said, Cassandra said, they're going to buy Delmont's house."

"Yes?"

"It isn't true, of course. You didn't sell Delmont's house to a straight couple. With two *children*, I understand. Not when I'd just got Flavia Billingsley interested."

I'll bet you got her interested, Sissy thought. She carefully tipped herself forward as the door opened and Ron and Cornette Labonne entered the realty office. "Yes, it's true," she said, returning Cornette's wave and mouthing "Be right with you."

The Labonnes evidently misunderstood her for they headed straight for Sissy's module.

"Tell me," Susan said, her voice cold, "do these people drive a red Cadillac?"

"Er, yes, I believe so," Sissy said, quickly wrapping up her muffin and stuffing it in her desk drawer. She slammed her listings book atop the two naked ladies. "I have to go now," she said, hanging up on Susan.

"Good morning, Sissy!" Cornette cried. "Well, here we are, ready to take possession!"

"Won't you have a seat?"

Cornette, nervously fluffing hair as stiff and pale as cotton candy, was too excited to perch. "'Yea, the sparrow hath found her a house,'" she warbled, squeezing her new husband's arm, "'and the swallow a nest where she may lay her young, even thy altars, O Lord of hosts, my King and my God.'"

"You are certain that you want this house," Sissy said.

"What's the matter," Ron said, instantly suspicious. "Our money's good, isn't it? You do take cash, don't you?"

"It's not that," Sissy said. "I just want my customers to be happy. There are other houses, you know. Other neighborhoods we didn't have time to look at."

"Sissy's just trying to be helpful, hon." Cornette turned to the realtor, blinking rapidly, as if it were a struggle to keep her eyes open under the weight of her eyelashes. "It's *this* house we want. This one. Isn't it, hon?"

"If you say so," said Ron Labonne.

CHAPTER 8

CAROLYN DIDN'T LIE, SHE SIMPLY OMITTED THE TRUTH WHENEVER IT WAS inconvenient, humiliating, or reflected badly on herself. She'd been doing this for so long that it was an automatic reflex.

Of course, she had a lot to hide—a whole secret life that Susan and their friends knew nothing about and that Carolyn had no intention of revealing, ever ever ever. She called it her "California craziness" and kept the tormenting details of it padlocked in her heart.

Because what would Susan do if she suddenly found out that her timid, browbeaten lover had once been enslaved in a violent paramilitary cult called the Bruderschaft? That she'd taken up with a cultist and had a child by him? That she'd abandoned her infant son and run for her life?

To Carolyn, these were all acts of cowardice, unforgiveable but necessary for self-preservation. Susan would no doubt find them lurid, disgusting, and a reflection of Carolyn's overall untrustworthiness and emotional instability.

She had spent most of her adult life as a fugitive, hiding behind so many assumed identities that her own had somehow gotten lost in the shuffle. The real Carolyn Corbett lay buried deep within her, but Carolyn was afraid of her. It was that Carolyn, after all, who had lead her down the path to hell.

Keeping all of this from Susan was its own form of self-inflicted torture. Wishing that something hadn't happened didn't make it unhappen. Repression of facts gave them more power, not less, because the truth of hidden experience—however painful—remained stubbornly alive. Truth would not go away, no matter how assiduously Carolyn avoided it. But for cowards—and Carolyn regarded herself as a coward—omission was better than admission and repression was better than confession.

For years Carolyn had pretended, without revealing any traceable details, that before she met Susan she'd lived a retiring, quasi-aristocratic life near San Diego, sheltered from the worst of life's financial storms by a sizeable trust fund. She was never quite certain of her sexuality, she said, and too shy to find out. When her parents died, she said, she came up to rainy Portland, where she'd been born, and had been drawn, quite inadvertently, into the east-side's ongoing lesbian luau.

Carolyn's concocted persona—rich, naive, virginal—appealed to Susan, who preferred wifely malleability to husbandly strength in a lover. That lordly lady, Susan Bark, had dumped her old-fashioned American husband (once her citizenship was assured) because *he* wanted to wear the pants in the family. The gall!

Susan's forthright, unemotional English upbringing, so useful in training dogs, had otherwise left her remarkably unsuspicious and ill-equipped to deal with the secret, stormy undercurrents of human nature, including her own. The surface sufficed for Susan. She sniffed out weaknesses and turned them to her own advantage, of course, but she didn't really give a damn where the smell came from. She'd never investigated Carolyn's past because she liked Carolyn, with her soft, acquiescent, petlike talent for taking orders, just as she was.

Of course Carolyn hadn't told Susan about Lady Caroline's escape and subsequent rape in Delmont's garden. Susan would hold her accountable. And it was true: when it came to dogs, Carolyn had the equivalent of a gardener's black thumb. She guiltily assumed it was a form of punishment for abandoning her child. A gleefully malicious reminder from the gods that she would *never escape the consequences of that one unforgiveable act.* She'd run away from her son, her own flesh and blood, so now everything she tried to love would be taken away from her or somehow ruined.

Carolyn, like all closet fatalists, believed that she got what she deserved.

Raised to be an all-American Barbie doll, a married, upper-class Junior Leaguer who'd sit on charity boards and sip white wine at poolside country-club parties, Carolyn had broken free of her social packaging. But it was hardly liberating on the other side of the cellophane. Now she lived her life as though trapped in a gloomy Greek myth, sensing imminent catastrophe all around her and nervously waiting for the ultimate punchline of her fate to be revealed.

So it was with a classic feeling of dread that she'd run back home with the ravaged Lady Caroline cradled in her arms. She saw terror in Lady Caroline's bulging, indifferent eyes and a mysterious pain in the dog's passive expression. "My darling, my darling," she whimpered, frantically envisioning a violent, unstoppable militia of mongrel sperm cells marching down Lady Caroline's pedigreed allée to claim the dainty eggs-in-waiting.

Lady Caroline squealed and tried to wriggle free as Carolyn, holding her with a grip of iron, grimly inserted the nozzle of a douche bag. There were no spermicides on hand or she would have napalmed the raiders taking possession of the dog's fertile cuntryside. Locking the bathroom door so her now-dribbling ward could not escape, Carolyn ran a warm bubble bath and plunged Lady Caroline down into its rose-scented foam, sobbing as she scrubbed. It was as much an ordeal for herself as for the dog.

Susan was due back any moment, so Carolyn quickly rubbed down Lady Caroline with their best Laura Ashley floral-print towels and then fluffed and brushed her under the blowdryer. Luckily, Susan had other things on her mind when she finally returned from Flavia Billingsley's, and didn't even notice when Lady Caroline disappeared under a piece of furniture and spent the rest of the evening noisily licking her enflamed vulva.

The next day they found out that the people in the red Cadillac had bought Delmont's house. Susan, who'd almost talked Flavia Billingsley into buying it, was devastated.

"We're being invaded," she grimly announced to Carolyn after hearing the news from Cassandra. Her stiff upper lip quivered with frustrated outrage.

"Who? Who?" Carolyn wanted to know.

"Heterosexuals—with children." Susan bristled at the thought. "Well, ducks, there goes the neighborhood." From now on, Sissy Parker, realtor non grata, was to be mercilessly snubbed at every opportunity.

Neither Susan nor Carolyn had ever heard of Ron Labonne or Cornette Terwilliger but since Cassandra had described them as "religious fanatics" they expected the worst. Carolyn felt positively hostile. The new owners were, after all, the people whose dog had raped Lady Caroline. *In-laws*, in a nightmarish way, if Lady Caroline bore their cur's litter.

But there was still hope. Dogs weren't stingy with their ova, and so long as Lady Caroline's ripe eggs kept dropping and she remained receptive, she could conceivably conceive a litter that had two fathers. Time was of the essence, however, and Lord Nelson, the chosen stud, was fortuitously due the following day.

He arrived in a black Lincoln town car driven by his owner's son. Carolyn, looking anxiously out the window, saw Lord Nelson, with his long drooping ears and peevish expression, sitting alone on the back seat like a bored, bewigged dignitary touring the provinces. An ersatz coat of arms was painted on the car door.

"Caroline, he's here," she called, keeping her voice gentle. "Come and look, sweetie."

But Lady Caroline stubbornly remained in hiding under the wing-backed leather chair. She hadn't touched the tasty meal Carolyn had prepared for her that morning, perhaps sensing that it was laced with alfalfa leaf to ensure success in pregnancy.

Carolyn stepped outside to greet Lord Nelson's chauffeur and take care of the final pre-copulatory details. The stud eyed her disdainfully through the car window, as if measuring her own suitability for mating. The driver was less haughty, and Carolyn's heart involuntarily went out to him when she saw the scar of a harelip unsuccessfully hidden under his wispy black mustache. The surgically realigned upper lip didn't quite match the lower. One eye was normal, but the other listed off to the side, so she wasn't certain which eye to focus on when she spoke to him.

Queer that Lord Nelson's owner, so obsessed with genetic perfection when it came to breeding dogs, produced such defect-laden offspring himself. The son's Hapsburgian visage and his age, about seventeen, instantly sparked Carolyn's hidden but ever-present sense of guilt. He was the abandoned son she never saw but saw everywhere, marking the changes of his growth and development in the forms and faces of every teenaged boy who passed by her line of vision. She was mother to them all, no matter how thick the acne, how slouched the posture, how tattooed the body, how sullen the face.

But the fiery maternal sorrow that pierced her heart had to be doused in the waters of practicality. Susan had left a long list of disagreeable tasks to be performed before Lord Nelson was allowed to penetrate Lady Caroline. And Carolyn, desperate, was in no position to waffle on any of them. There was no time to be sentimental or modest.

"Did you bring the sperm count?" she asked the driver.

He mumbled something and withdrew a sheaf of papers from the car. "Dad says it's cool."

"Pardon?"

"The sperm count. It's cool."

The figures meant nothing to Carolyn, but Susan insisted on having them as a record. "And, let's see," she checked her list, "a certificate that he's been tested for bloodworms and had a DHLPP booster shot and a serum agglutination test for brucellosis."

"Sure. It's all there."

She leafed through the papers, unable to focus. "Now—um—I'm supposed to check his—uh—his thing."

"His what thing?" the boy asked.

Her cheeks flamed. "His—you know—his thingamajigger—his peepee."

"Oh, sure." He tamped down a smile. "You wanna do that in the house?"

"I suppose so." She certainly didn't want to be seen checking a dog's penis on the street.

The driver hooked Lord Nelson to a leash and followed Carolyn into the living room. Lady Caroline peeked out from beneath the chair and growled. Lord Nelson caught sight of her and flared his nostrils. "Issat the bitch?" the driver asked.

"Yes. We thought we'd have the mating take place here, in the living room, where she's more comfortable." Carolyn stared at the now-quivering Lord Nelson, whose bulging eyes strained to see Lady Caroline. "I'm not exactly sure how to do this but Susan—er, my friend, said we should check to make sure that the penis can extend normally."

Her phantom son laughed. "Don't worry, lady, it extends all right. He's sired litters all over the country and in Japan."

"I'm sure that's true," Carolyn said nervously, "but I have to make sure. Not because I don't believe you but because my friend insisted on it."

"Sure, lotsa people do. I'll hold him up and you can check." Lord Nelson was oddly compliant as the young man lifted him up, exposing his belly, his tufted balls, and the furry bulb of his penis.

Carolyn couldn't bring herself to touch it. "My friend said to check for red pimplelike bumps or growths," she said faintly.

"Okay, he's ready."

"All right—well, let's see—"

"Here." He gently took Carolyn's hand and guided it to Lord Nelson's prepuce. "Now push back—"

Carolyn screamed as the slick, red, bonelike penis shot out and Lord Nelson began thrusting his pelvis back and forth.

"That's called the Whitney Reflex," the young man explained.

Lord Nelson, oblivious to his dignified pedigree, was performing a kind of spastic, obscene hula. He stopped the moment Carolyn removed her hand. Moaned as Lady Caroline leapt up onto the sofa and peeked down at her suitor.

"Look, he's rarin' to go," the young man said. "If you're satisfied I'll let him go."

"Yes, all right." She appealed to the young man. "He is all right, isn't he? No inbreeding or disease or genetic defects."

"He's a champ," the young man said, releasing Lord Nelson. The dog raced over to the sofa and looked imploring up at Lady Caroline, who let out an excited yap but kept her distance.

"How long does it usually take?" Carolyn asked.

"Depends. The bitch usually wants to tease and play for a while before she flags and lets him in." He eyed Carolyn, a spark of mischief in his normal eye. "Just like humans."

Carolyn quickly got to her feet. "Would you like some coffee? Or herb tea? I have Red Zinger or—"

"Sure. Coffee."

But an hour and two cups of Vienna Roast later, Lady Caroline was still teasing and playing. She seemed to love it when Lord Nelson licked and smelled her, but every time she pertly flicked her tail over and Lord Nelson tried to mount, she growled and darted away.

Carolyn, wired by the coffee and trying to make polite conversation throughout this ordeal, finally let out an exasperated moan. "Caroline, for God's sake!" Wasn't championship sperm good enough for her? She hadn't been so finicky with the mongrel from the red Cadillac! Of course that had been the case with Carolyn, too, many years earlier, back in her wild days. Her parents expected her to date and eventually breed with a suitably stable high achiever with executive genes, but she found more excitement with the wild ones, the misfits and outcasts who broke rules and thrived on subversive mayhem.

"I wish she'd just do it," Carolyn said, glancing at her watch.

"Wanna help her?" the boy asked.

Two minutes later Carolyn was kneeling on one side of Lady Caroline, clutching her and stretching her vulva, and the young valet was kneeling on the other side of Lord Nelson, grasping the stud's penis.

"Okay, here we go," the young man said, directing the thrusting penis towards its target. "Ready, aim, fire!" Lady Caroline snapped and squirmed but Carolyn closed her eyes and held firm. A whimper. "Okay!" the young man exclaimed. "They're tied."

The two humans released the dogs. Lord Nelson grasped his mate and humped happily away. Lady Caroline's eyes bulged. Margo Channing, doing it doggie-style. Then, tongue dangling, tail twitching, hind legs trembling, Lord Nelson ejaculated.

There was another fifteen-minute wait while the two canines remained hung in their post-coital position, unable to disengage. Carolyn watched with pained revulsion as Lord Nelson turned around, faced the opposite direction, and began pulling. Lady Caroline, digging her nails into Susan's favorite Chinese rug, pulled in the opposite direction.

"Is he hurting her?"

"Nah, they just have to wait til his dick—er, his penis—like deflates."

Just like humans, Carolyn thought, memories of her past male lovers flickering unpleasantly through her consciousness: once the act is over, they can't wait to get away. Biology, in the end, was simply brutal mechanics.

"How did it go?" Susan asked later that evening.

"Oh—fine," Carolyn said. "It took a while, and we finally had to help her."

"Poor darling, you look exhausted." Susan smiled and brushed a finger along Carolyn's downy cheek. "How about running us a nice hot bath?"

▼ ▼ ▼

Wellfleet, in the back of the auditorium, shifted in his seat to avoid a shaft of sunlight that suddenly shot through one of the high, narrow windows and threatened to blind him. The movement pinched the already throbbing sciatic nerve in his right leg and made him wince. In a strange way he welcomed the pain. It was true, it was honest, it was real. Right now, it was the only reality he could cling to in an unreal situation.

The auditorium—a six million dollar gift from a timber trustee whose son was the architect and whose cedar trees panelled the walls—was stifling. None of the windows could be opened, so the air was as flat and stale as a hermetically sealed cave. Acoustically the Benton Smith Memorial Auditorium was rather marvelous, as Wellfleet knew from having conducted several choral concerts here. Today it was jammed with students, faculty, and administrators listening in rapt silence as Ron Labonne gave a speech billed as "Christian Values in the Classroom—and Beyond."

Flanked by Old Glory and the school flag, dressed in a dark suit, his thick neck bulging above a tight, starched collar, Labonne exhorted the crowd to reject the secular liberalism that was contaminating American education and return to the traditional wisdom of the Bible.

"We see evidence of the decay of Christian values every time we open a newspaper or turn on the television," Labonne thundered. "We see it in the public schools, where innocent children are force-fed a poisonous diet of so-called sex education that brainwashes them into believing every form of deviant lifestyle is okay. But I ask you, who's behind this liberal, left-wing agenda telling children that abortion—sucking one of God's souls out of the womb and tossing it in the garbage can—is an acceptable alternative to rearing a child in a responsible Christian home? Who is the driving force behind this sex-education curriculum doling out condoms like candy and telling children that homosexuality is an acceptable lifestyle? That homosexuals are the same as you and me? That homosexuals should be allowed to marry, to teach, to adopt children, to have special protections under the law?"

Wellfleet, suddenly alert to danger, sat up straight, his heart hammering, and surveyed the crowd, trying to gauge its reaction to Labonne's inflammatory rhetoric. Seated on the stage with the deans and faculty heads, Willard Lansgaard, the white-haired president of the college, pursed his thin lips and nodded meaningfully. Fletcher Davis, the new head of the music department, a failed bassoonist whom God had lead to administrative work after he'd been rejected by every orchestra in the country, flared his nostrils, took a deep sanctimonious breath, and seemed to smile. With the students, who could tell? The poor things had been trained never to question the dubious wisdom of their elders and to accept the most ludicrous interpretations of reality with bland acquiescence.

"I'll tell you who's behind this degradation of traditional values," Labonne went on, his face dripping. He paused, narrowing his piercing blue eyes and moving them like a slow searchlight over the assembled crowd. "You are!"

It had the effect of an electric cattle prod. An agitated wave of terror, of shock, of guilty bewilderment ran through the collective student body.

"Yes, you are! Why? Because it's your taxes, or the taxes paid by your parents, that pays for public education. Your taxes pay for a system ruled by a liberal, leftist, godless group of elite special-interest groups that won't allow a single prayer to be said in the classroom but *will* allow young minds to be debased and seduced into a poisonous social agenda that mocks the traditional values upon which America was built. You are responsible so long as you sit back and do nothing to halt this decline in morality."

He paused, waiting for the crowd to settle. "I started the American Christian Alliance because I know that Christian social activism is the key that will unlock the ignorance of the godless. I know that Christian grass-roots organization is the tool that will force the political leaders of America to sit up and take notice that we will no longer stand by and watch this great country of ours be ground into the filth promoted by special interest groups seeking to undermine the sanctity of the family. The ACA is now one of the fastest-growing Christian political organizations in the country. We're at the point now where we're ready to tackle Satan in his own back yard—the state legislature. And our victory there will lead still others to our cause, because it's God's cause speaking through the people.

"So I say to you young people, now you've gotta become Christian soldiers. Now you've gotta become part of the heavenly militia fighting to regain the hearts and minds of the country at large. You gotta fight and you gotta pray—pray hard—that this great Christian nation of ours will flower with the word of God."

The applause was deafening. The students were on their feet, whistling and clapping. Wellfleet had never heard such applause for his choral concerts. But, then, this was immediate, this was a dare, a taunt, a threat even. It was a trumpeting call to arms, not the remote musical contemplation heard in a 200-year-old oratorio

All smiles on the stage, where everyone was pleased to bask in the enthusiastic glow of a successful speaker, someone who had unleashed the kind of emotional response they themselves were incapable of inspiring. Ron Labonne, who had uncorked this fizzing spiritual champagne, positively glowed as the grinning administrators leapt up to shake his hand.

Mimi Strang moved quickly to capture the crescendo of excitement by leading the Christian Students' Association choir in a soft-rock tune called "His Pain, Your Gain," written by a born-again weightlifter. Tina Pedersen, her voice like liquid honey, was the featured soloist.

Wellfleet, his right leg numb, his head spinning, stiffly rose and lurched out into the foyer as the all-white student congregation launched into a self-conscious version of "He's Got the Whole World in His Hands." A group of beaming girls tittered and fussed over a reception table laden with cans of Diet Coke and huge cookies that looked like frosted cow turds. A banner on the front of the table read: THE CHRISTIAN STUDENTS' ASSOCIATION WELCOMES A CHRISTIAN HERO, RON LABONNE.

"Hi, Mr. Stipple," one of the girls chirped, "wasn't he just like awesome?"

"Awesome," croaked Wellfleet.

"Would you care for a Diet Coke and a fudge-nut granola cookie?"

"No thanks." A double Scotch was what he wanted.

The girls eyed him, whispering among themselves, as he wandered aimlessly around the foyer trying to coax feeling into his stiff leg. The story of his gimpy life. They could engrave it on his tombstone: *Wellfleet Stipple, He wanted to run but could barely walk.* And where could he go? He was expected to stay and mingle with the crowd now beginning to stream into the reception area. Yet the very sight of those smug, smiling, self-beatified faces fueled some rage so deeply buried in his grumpy, pain-addled personality that he wanted to scream obscenities at them.

Of course he couldn't. He could never tell them, any of them, what he really thought, who he really was, why he felt so cornered and cowardly. He was a heretic trying to dodge the Inquisitors, trying to escape the constant threat of exposure and yet aware, in the dim recess where his personal truth lay hidden, that the time would come when he would be unmasked and exposed. The story of his life.

He turned and nearly collided with Mimi Strang and Tina Pedersen as they rushed to take their places in the reception line. For a moment the girls' eyes locked on his, Tina's startled and cowlike, Mimi's narrowed and hostile.

"Oh, hi," Tina whispered, flustered, nervously smoothing the long denim dress that clung to her enormous thighs. She glanced at Mimi, her bird-like companion, whose sharp little face had hardened into cement.

"You sang beautifully, Tina," Wellfleet said.

"Oh!" She melted with the unexpected praise. "Well, I guess it was because I was singing for *him*."

"For him?"

"For Mr. Labonne."

"Oh," Wellfleet said, "I thought you meant for God."

"We always sing for Our Lord," Mimi snapped.

Wellfleet couldn't help himself. "You mean for Mr. Labonne?"

Mimi glared at him. "Come on, Tina," she said, turning away.

"Tina, are you coming for your voice lesson this week?" Wellfleet asked.

Wellfleet heard Mimi whisper, "Tell him no." Tina merely shrugged and let herself be led away, like a docile elephant, towards the crowd excitedly milling around Ron Labonne.

Philistines blindly worshipping the Golden Bull. Why were they always looking for an idol to worship? And why did they always choose the wrong ones, the anti-intellectual demagogues who grew fat and powerful by preying on their fears and ignorance?

"Wailfleet." It was Fletcher Davis, towering over him, wearing a herringbone jacket with dandruff sprinkled into the pattern. "Whut did you think?" he drawled. "Wudn't he somethin' else?"

"Yeah, he was something else all right. The question is, what?"

Fletcher bared his teeth in what was meant to be a grin but looked more like a painful grimace. His large, dark eyes, irresistibly alluring to female students, darted about the foyer looking for someone more important than Wellfleet to talk to. "I found him verrah impressive," he said.

You would, you second-rate ass-licking sycophantic cracker, Wellfleet thought, turning away. Fletcher's corn-pone drawl and smug, unbearably condescending manner drove Wellfleet crazy.

His sour reaction to this son of a Tennessee preacher was fueled by the evangelical politics that had overtaken the college in the last few years. High-paid, bottom-line administrators, more concerned with marketing than classroom performance, were hired to "manage" the departments. Previously, instructors had served as department heads on a rotating basis. The policy had changed just when it was Wellfleet's turn to become chairman of the music department. He didn't want to do it, necessarily, but it brought a nominal increase in salary.

Even more galling was the fact that the instructors had no voice in the decision of who was to run their departments. It was all part of a well-calculated plan that dismantled, piece by piece, the old regulations governing tenure and job security. Wellfleet had tried to foment rebellion amongst the other instructors, suggesting that they organize, make demands, but his efforts—closely watched by Willard Lansgaard, the president, and his hand-picked administrative apostles—ended with a dull thud. There was a glut of teachers, everyone knew that, and in an overcrowded market you had to be content with what you could get. Meek, frightened, unwilling to complain because it was unChristian, unnice, ungrateful, the faculty meekly caved in to the encroachments of Christian capitalism.

So Fletcher Davis, the failed bassoonist whose credentials consisted of a secondary degree in business administration from a third-rate Christian college in Arkansas, and an impeccably Christian background (he'd listed his preacher father as a reference), had been hired to head the music department.

It was undeclared war the moment he arrived.

"I think it's a great idea," Fletcher said, "asking Mr. Labonne to become a trustee. Don't you?"

"I didn't know they'd asked him."

"Oh yeah. All the administrators were informed this morning. Willard's gonna make a general announcement to the rest of the faculty as soon as Mr. Labonne accepts."

"Maybe he won't accept," Wellfleet said.

"Oh he'll accept all right." There was a knowing edge in Fletcher's voice. "Mr. Labonne has verruh strong ideas about the future of this college and Christian education in general. He says we've got to start with a rigorous review of all the faculty. There's some of them that don't quite belong here, you know."

"A witch-hunt, you mean?"

Fletcher laughed. "Lord, Wailfleet, you make it sound downright ugly. It will be a perfectly straightforward procedure. We're going to bring the students into this. They're the ones paying, after all. They've got every right to demand the highest Christian values from those teaching them."

Wellfleet looked up into those dark, slippery eyes. "How old are you, Fletcher?"

"Thirty-six. Why?"

"You're too young to remember the McCarthy era."

"Pardon me, I remember it very clearly. My daddy was head of the Christian Republican Coalition when Eugene McCarthy was runnin' for president. He took me with him to all the meetings. We stopped that dirty Communist in his tracks."

"That's not the McCarthy I meant."

The pained grin, as if Wellfleet smelled bad. "Now that is just like you, Wailfleet, to ask a trick question."

"And it's just like you, Fletcher, not to know a thing about history."

Fletcher's face went blank but brightened again when he saw Willard Lansgaard, standing next to Ron Labonne, wave and motion him over. "Well, I've gotta run, Wailfleet. I see the president wants me to meet our new trustee."

"Yes, you'd better scurry."

"Now you just make sure that those student evaluation forms get back to me in right good time," Fletcher said.

"What student evaluation forms?"

"The ones in your mail box," Fletcher said over his shoulder. "The ones you'll be handin' out to all your students, so they can rate your performance. The ones," he said, "that we'll be usin' to assess new contracts."

Student evaluations? Wellfleet caught a glimpse of Mimi Strang and Tina Pedersen staring with dazed adoration at Ron Labonne. A flicker of dread ran down his scoliatic spine. "Why didn't anyone tell me?" he murmured to himself. But he knew why. It was quite simple. He was the outsider, and outsiders are always the last to know.

And later that evening, when Carolyn Corbett stopped by for a quick chat, Wellfleet realized that even in Queer Corners he was the last to know. Nobody had bothered to inform him that Ron Labonne, the new homophobic trustee at the college, was to be his new neighbor.

CHAPTER 7

OVER THE YEARS, THANKS TO THAT INDEFATIGABLE HOMOSOCIALIZER
Delmont Percy, Queer Corners had acquired its own seasonal traditions. Delmont, the neighborhood's gaytriarch, had presided over a yearly Fabergé Easter-egg hunt, a Rose Festival barbecue in June, a Fourth of July picnic, a Halloween costume ball, a Thanksgiving feast, a December wassail, and a New Year's Eve party. Now that Delmont was dead, the homosocial bonds that knit the neighbors together threatened to unravel and disappear completely unless someone else took over as leader.

In their individual ways, they all sorely missed Delmont the man, but losing their communal gaytriarch was a different kind of loss—with far-reaching implications that no one in Queer Corners really thought about until the second week in November, when the traditional Thanksgiving icons began to infiltrate general consciousness.

All these representations of a holiday that brought friends and family together at the same table to give thanks for what they had reminded the residents of Queer Corners of what they didn't have—Delmont. They realized that, in fact, Delmont had made them into a family of sorts. He'd presided over a table laden with laughter, good food, good wine, and good cheer. Still, no one offered to take his place. After the shock of learning who was going to move into Delmont's imposing Queen Anne, site of so many happy celebrations, they retreated into stupefied isolation.

It was Jay Zucker, finally, who called everyone up and invited them over to his house. Not for turkey—he'd be busy serving that to strangers at the restaurant for much of the evening—but for late drinks. And with a breath of relief, they all accepted.

The night was cold and wet. Brisk high winds keened in the branches of the Douglas firs as the Queer Cornerites left their homes and hurried down to Jay's. Delmont's house, still unoccupied, sat in a dark pool of shadowy memories, its front lawn carpeted with sodden leaves from the horse-chestnut tree in front. The week before, Portland's queen of estate sales, Willa Carruthers, had tagged every item in the house and a flood of strangers had raced through like hungry locusts, stripping the place bare. Now it was empty, like a body without a soul, waiting to be possessed by a new spirit.

Wellfleet, who'd spent the day alone, playing melancholic Chopin études on the Boesendorfer grand Delmont had willed to him, supping on a can of bean with bacon soup, was the first to limp into Jay's foyer.

Cassandra, acting as hostess, instantly sensed Wellfleet's loneliness. A troubling air of low-level depression seemed to hover around him like a miasma. Wellfleet had pulled on a shabby corduroy jacket over an old lint-balled sweater and his face was grim. Cassandra checked her instinct to ask if anything was wrong. She feared his answer.

From the looks of him, it wasn't just one thing that was wrong with Wellfleet's life, it was everything. A real karmic downer. Had he ever been young? Had he ever been in love?

"Oh dear, am I early?" Wellfleet asked.

"Of course not, come in."

Wellfleet, his head down, his thin lanky hair dripping with rain, stepped into the foyer and slowly wiped his funny-looking orthopedic shoes on the mat. He reminded Cassandra of a poor little gnome in a fairy tale, a kind but miserable woodland creature, a Hobbit, harried and haunted by an evil spell.

"Come in, Wellfleet, I'm just trying to light a fire," Jay called from the living room. He felt like an incompetent Boy Scout trying to win a merit badge. "I don't know why these logs won't burn. I paid a fortune for them."

"It's stacked wrong," Wellfleet said, going to help him.

Ito Kudomono, trim and casually elegant in a cream-colored silk shirt and new jeans, peaceful after an evening of meditation in his orchid sanitorium, was the next to arrive. Like Wellfleet, he'd spent the day alone, but unlike Wellfleet, he hadn't groused about his lack of dinner invitations. A vegetarian, he'd turned down three of them.

"Oh, Ito, beautiful," Cassandra said, taking the autumn bouquet of copper-colored mums and fiery-red oak leaves he had brought. "Come on in, Jay will get you a drink when he gets the fire lit. Green tea, isn't it?" She loved the easy, intimate sound of that, as if she and Jay were just another rich, cozy couple entertaining their friends on the hill. Yes, she was so broke she didn't have enough money to buy a tube of paint. Yes, Jay was months behind in his quarterly taxes and facing bankruptcy. All the more reason to lavish fantasy colors on the intimidating canvas of reality.

Ito was followed by Carolyn and Susan. Both of them were stuffed from an enormous turkey dinner prepared by Flavia Billingsley and high from her dessert of Grand Marnier cake and a special brand of marijuana grown in southern Oregon and harvested by lesbians during the full moon. Carolyn, simultaneously giddy, horny, and paranoid from the pot, her red hair tumbling down over her shoulders in a frizzy Pre-Raphaelitish cascade, wore a flowing long-sleeved velvet dress that hid her extra poundage. Susan, her short dark hair gelled into a backswept ducktail, looked severely dapper in a tailored charcoal-grey suit with Hopi-inspired accessories of hammered copper and turquoise. They'd brought a box of Godiva truffles.

"How's Lady Caroline?" Cassandra asked.

"Pregnant, I hope," Susan answered.

Cassandra turned to Carolyn. "I can't wait to see the puppies! Aren't you excited?"

Carolyn nodded, masking her sudden discomfort with a bright lipsticked smile.

Susan squinted down at Cassandra's exposed ankle. "Is that a tattoo?"

"It's called body art," Cassandra said. "I have four of them."

"How extraordinary. Where are the other three?"

"My ankle, my right thigh, my left butt cheek, and my left boob."

"May I see?"

"Susan!" Carolyn giggled nervously.

"Well, I'm curious. Maybe I'd like to get one."

"Oh, you're just stoned," Carolyn clucked tenderly. She'd had far more experience with illicit substances than Susan. She'd gone to places off the map.

Cassandra motioned them into the kitchen, where she unceremoniously hiked up her skirt and lowered her panties.

"Extraordinary," Susan repeated, examining the esoteric images. "A snake on your bum and a rose on your thigh. What's on your tit, my dear?"

"Susan!"

"Why must you always be such an old prude?" Susan chastised her lover. "Carolyn's a sweater-knitter," she whispered to Cassandra. "She worries about everything. Recycling. Loading the washing-up machine properly. Folding the towels a certain way. Well, I love you for your obsessive domesticity, darling," she said, turning back to Carolyn, "but sometimes I do think it's making you old before your time. Look at Cassandra here, she's not afraid to show off her body. She's not afraid to be sexy."

"That's because she is sexy," Carolyn said.

"And you're not?" Cassandra said.

"Carolyn's uncomfortable with her body," Susan explained. "She hides it away. Shelves it, like the good librarian she is. Now do show us your titty tattoo, pet. I can't imagine what you'd have there."

Flattered, suspicious, and teasingly aroused, Cassandra bared her small firm breast for inspection, making sure that Carolyn wasn't left out.

"What on earth is it?" Susan asked, peering.

Cassandra could feel Susan's breath on her nipple. "That's what it is. Earth. Well, Gaia really."

"Gaia?"

"Earth as a living entity," Carolyn said. "A goddess."

"How clever." Susan straightened up. "Do you find them sexy, darling? These tattoos, I mean?"

"Yes," Carolyn said, "I guess so."

"I wonder how they'd look on dogs," Susan mused. "I wonder if I could start a trend."

The door chimed and Cassandra quickly buttoned her blouse.

It was tall, khakied, Bass Weejuned John-Don, his thick blond hair sexily moussed, and Peter, whose pumpkin-colored Italian jacket and dark maroon dress slacks would have clashed unforgiveably on anyone with less sartorial verve. John-Don was freshly invigorated from a rainy late-night run through the hills. Peter was still exhausted and resentful that he'd been roped into helping John-Don and John-Don's parents prepare and serve meals to the homeless in a downtown shelter earlier that afternoon. Institutional settings depressed him. A party boy at heart, he hated the grim, downtrodden realities of life.

"Is Terry the Turd here yet?" Peter whispered, handing Cassandra a bottle of wine. Cassandra said no. "What's the news on your carriage house?"

"He hasn't mentioned it and I haven't mentioned it," Cassandra said. "But that creep Billy—" She couldn't finish because the door chimed again.

Terry Terwilliger and the uninvited Billy Bird, whom everyone had heard of but no one but Cassandra had officially met, were the last to arrive.

Terry was nautical, with crisply pleated white ducks, a navy-blue blazer, and an ascot that bulged from his scrawny neck like a paisley goiter. His tinted, oversized glasses, the kind worn by ageing female movie stars to hide the unacceptable reality of their faces, erased what little character was left in his own. He looked like a stiff-faced mannequin, his woven, aerated hair rising from his head like a pie crust, and he was, of course, empty-handed. "Well," he said, stepping inside, "look who's answering the door."

Billy sidled in behind Terry. His tight black jeans, artfully ripped in the knees and in half-moons under each buttock, were festooned with chains. He wore a black sleeveless leather vest over a white t-shirt, black motorcycle boots, studded black leather wrist-bands, and he literally stank from a mixture of booze and some cloying designer cologne that was oddly out of synch with the butch image he was trying to project. "It's Cassandra the cook," he smirked. "I guess she does doors, too."

"I wish she'd do my windows once in a while," Terry griped.

To keep herself from saying something rude, Cassandra excused herself. On her way to the kitchen she overheard Billy say, "Why do you put up with that bitch any-way? She don't do nothing around *our* house."

"That's going to change," Terry said.

"Yeah? When?"

"We'll talk about it later," Terry said.

"Come on, let's go in so you can show me off to your rich friends."

"Stop!" Carolyn screamed as Billy loped into the living room. "Your boots!"

"What're you, my mother?" But Carolyn's sudden outburst startled him, froze him like an intruder in his tracks. He looked down. Black muddy footprints trailed behind him, across Jay's white carpet, like the pattern in a dance instruction manual. "Oh shit," he said.

Jay, furious but ever the genial host, said, "Why don't you take your shoes off?"

"Do I got to?"

"Well, just look at Jay's beautiful white carpet!" Susan shrilled.

"Take them off," Terry said.

"Fuck," Billy groaned. He leapt back to the Italian tiles in the foyer and pulled off his boots.

When they saw his dirty socks, with bunionated toes sticking out of holes, and got a whiff of his feet, they wished he'd put the boots back on. But it was too late.

"Jay, you should take care of those stains at once, before they set," Carolyn said. "Use a little Lysol and dish detergent."

"I'll do it." Cassandra, who'd come back in to witness the shoe scene, left again. She returned, like Cinderella, with a pail and sponge and began to scrub the carpet as the others silently watched.

Well, here they all were, with one new and highly undesirable addition whom Terry didn't bother to introduce. Now what? The only one missing was Delmont, always the life of the party, always welcoming and joking and putting everyone at their ease, magically blending the group together in the osterizer of his high-spirited affability. His absence had an estranging effect, hardening them into clumsy, separate entities who knew one another but could no longer blur their individual outlines into a generous, collective spirit. Neither Veuve Clicquot nor the fire now roaring in Jay's raised, white-brick hearth could dispel the damp gloom that descended on the Delmontless neighbors.

"I take it you've all heard about Delmont's house," Jay said.

"Too dreadful for words," Susan grumbled, voicing their common sentiment. "Religious fanatics with two children. It couldn't have been any worse if Delmont's niece from the trailer park had moved in."

Ito, with Zenlike composure, suggested that perhaps it would not be so bad. "We don't really know them yet, after all."

"Once you've seen them, Ito, you won't *want* to know them," Jay said.

"What do they actually look like?" Carolyn asked.

Jay thought for a moment. "Like a second-rate club act in a motel dining room." He knew—they all knew—that the new Mrs. Labonne was Terry the Turd's cousin, but that only made it all the more delicious to revile the pair.

"Let's put it this way," said Cassandra, squeezing out her sponge, "they make Jim and Tammy Faye Bakker look glamorous."

"But why here?" Susan demanded. "Why would they choose to live here, in our neighborhood? How could they afford it? Where does their money come from?"

"The faithful," said John-Don.

"The faithful what?" Susan asked.

John-Don, the one political activist among them, had done some research. "The faithful members of the American Christian Alliance."

"What's that?" Carolyn wanted to know.

"Bad news," said Cassandra, scrubbing.

The ACA, John-Don explained, was a right-wing Christian organization Labonne had nurtured in the hot fundamentalist air of southern Oregon. It was basically a political action committee supported by various churches. Anti-abortion. Anti-gun control. Pro-school prayer and the death penalty. In favor of unrestricted logging and unrestricted development. No governmental interference of any kind—except in the bedroom.

"Family values," Cassandra said. "All that hypocritical Pat Robertson bullshit we heard from the Republican convention." On her hands and knees, she looked up to see Billy Bird staring down the front of her silk blouse, an inexplicably hostile look on his face.

"But he's not dangerous, this man, is he?" Susan asked anxiously.

"He's heterosexual, isn't he?" said Peter. "He's a right-wing fundamentalist Christian, isn't he? Honey, the man is dangerous."

"I wouldn't be surprised," John-Don quietly went on, "if the ACA is tied up with some Christian militia group."

Carolyn, demurely sipping her champagne, suddenly choked and began coughing.

"You are saying that our new neighbor is part of a militia?" Ito shifted uncomfortably in his chair. "Carrying guns?" A flood of violent images shattered his peaceful, Zen-induced equanimity.

"I think it's possible. Groups like the ACA are growing all over the country," John-Don said. "They're infiltrating politics big-time. They're like cults, in a way, only now their leaders are more sophisticated. They're all hooked into the Internet and they know how to manipulate people's worst fears."

"I don't think I want to hear this," Carolyn winced. "Not on Thanksgiving. Can we talk about something more pleasant, please?"

But John-Don wouldn't change the subject. "It's a reality, Carolyn, and it won't do you any good to hide your head in the sand. It's what's going on in America right now."

"All right, but doesn't it seem just a tad unlikely that it would go on in our neighborhood?" Carolyn asked. "Just because these people are fundamentalist Christians doesn't mean they're dangerous."

"It sounds like Anita Bryant all over again," Ito said.

"Who's that?" Cassandra wanted to know.

"She was before your time, honey," Peter said. "A fundamentalist beauty queen who sold orange juice but hated fruits. She started this all-American anti-gay hate campaign down in Miami in the Seventies. A truly vicious bitch."

"How much do you actually know about this Labonne?" Jay asked John-Don.

"Personally, not much. I do know that the ACA has ties to the timber and mining industries. They've contributed money to Senator Peckerwood's campaigns."

Susan was horrified. "That drunken lecher?"

"Yeah, the one who said he'd never met a political action committee he didn't like. And in exchange for their money, Peckerwood works on their behalf in the Senate, along with Jesse Helms, Orrin Hatch, and all the other right-wing crackers who get their money." Warming to his captive audience, John-Don strode back and forth in front of the fireplace. "What characterizes all these groups is a shared sense of persecution. They play this up in the most simplistic terms. Us versus them. They're always looking for a group to demonize, to pin the blame on."

"Don't tell me," Peter said. "Blacks. Nigras with their rapist eyes on white women and forcing white men out of their jobs because of Equal Opportunity programs."

"And Jews, no doubt," added Jay. "We control the banking industry, you know."

"And you killed Christ," Susan reminded him.

"Japanese," Ito said, "because of trade restrictions."

"And pro-choice women," nodded Cassandra.

"Yes, you're all right," John-Don nodded. "And gays, of course. Because these people are smart in a pathetic sort of way. They know you can't openly discriminate against blacks or Jews or Asians or even women anymore—"

"Ha ha," said Cassandra.

"—but you *can* still pick on queers. It's always open season on us because we're the only targets left that no one else will stand up for."

"Oh my God, this is too sickening for words," Susan moaned. "Why did Delmont have to die now?"

"Queer bashers moving into Queer Corners," Peter said. "Thank you, Sissy Parker."

"Do you have to use that name?" Carolyn protested.

"What name? Sissy Parker?"

"Queer. It's so ugly."

"Honey, this is Queer Corners," Peter said. "It has been since Delmont moved in forty years ago. We're all queers here, aren't we?"

"Yes," Carolyn sighed, "and I know all about reclaiming the word and turning it around, like blacks do with nigger, but isn't there something else we can call ourselves?"

"What do you suggest?" Peter laughed. "Heterosexually-deficient minority? Hypothalamus-enlarged cross-gender group?"

"I just hate the word queer, that's all," Carolyn said. "I hate gay, too. It's so limiting. We're human beings, we should be defined by our whole spirit, not just our sexuality."

"Honey, it's our sexuality that *gives* us our spirit," Peter said.

"Heterosexuals don't go around calling themselves heterosexuals," Carolyn insisted.

"That's because the entire world has been set up to reflect their image," Cassandra said. "I like queer. It sounds nice and radical."

"The point is," John-Don cut in, "these fundamentalists are hungry for power and they'll stop at nothing to get their way. The means justify the ends. So they pervert religious beliefs and play up conspiracy theories to solicit funds from frightened wonks from the suburbs and small towns. People who believe the world is coming to an end because wealthy perverts are undermining society."

"Oh come on," Terry said impatiently, "aren't you exaggerating a little? I know lots of Christians and I'm certain that none of them feel that way. Episcopalians don't, anyway."

"I'm not exaggerating," John-Don said. "And I didn't say all Christians, I said fundamentalist Christian militia groups, the kind that are springing up all over the country. All over the world."

"So you're talking about a lunatic fringe element," Terry said dismissively.

"It's not a fringe anymore." John-Don's voice was sharp. "Don't you pay any attention to politics, Terry? Didn't you listen to Pat Robertson at the last Republican convention?"

"Terry voted for George Bush," Peter teased. "He's a Bush man."

"Yes, I voted for George Bush," Terry shot back. "I've been a Republican all my life because I'm sick of my tax dollars going to pay for welfare cheats and government bureaucracy."

"I was on welfare once," Cassandra said. "It saved my life." She knew she was treading on thin ice, endangering her lovely little existence in Terry's carriage house, but she couldn't help herself. "Not everyone's as lucky as you, Terry. Not everyone inherits a fortune and gets to spend their life flying down to Palm Springs."

Terry was livid. "What I do with my money is no one's business but my own," he spluttered. "I happen to suffer from Chronic Sun Deficit Syndrome, I *need* to go to Palm Springs for my health."

Everyone but Terry and Billy Bird laughed.

"You've got your disorders out of order," Jay said. "It's called Seasonal Affective Disorder."

Terry was rattled by their unsympathetic response. This kind of baiting would never have happened if Delmont were alive. "All I'm saying is that people can't be as stupid as

John-Don's saying. Live and let live, that's what people want. Do unto others as they would have you do unto them."

For the first time that evening Wellfleet spoke up. "I think John-Don's right," he said. He told them about Labonne's speech at the college. "It's pretty clear who they're targeting."

"Wellfleet, that's awful," Carolyn said, rubbing his bony shoulder.

"Sure, they can start there because it's a private college and doesn't receive state funds," John-Don said. "I wouldn't be surprised if they start harassing the public school board next. Get all the gays out of the high schools."

"There goes *your* job," Peter said. "Thank God they can't do anything about interior designers. Wipe us out and the world turns a boring shade of beige."

"I understand that the woman is your cousin," Ito said to Terry.

"A television evangelist or something," Susan added.

Terry again felt the eyes of the group upon him and nervously patted his hairpiece. "I don't have anything to do with that side of the family," he said defensively.

"Did she know that you'd be her neighbor?" Peter asked.

"I have no idea. I haven't talked to Cornette for years."

The unfriendly interrogation might have ended there if Billy Bird, the uninvited stranger, Terry's new "houseboy," whom everyone was politely ignoring, hadn't piped up with: "Hey, Big Buddy, you told me the bitch visited you here." Having quickly gulped down one glass of Jay's excellent champagne, he now motioned to Cassandra to pour him another. She didn't budge from Jay's side.

There was a certain embarrassed defiance in Terry's pinched expression. "So? She visited me once, about five years ago, asking for money for her new cable television show. I refused."

Billy guffawed from his chair. "He told the bitch to get her fuckin' twat out of his house cause he wasn't givin' no money to no fuckin' Jesus freak. Right, Big Buddy?"

"Really!" Susan groaned, glancing at Jay.

"That isn't what I said," Terry said irritably.

"No, you was probably politer than that. You probably said, '*Please* get your fuckin' twat from my premises, you trashy piece of Jesus meat, because I ain't givin' you a penny!'" Billy sprawled deeper into his chair, roaring with laughter, lifting his smelly feet and clonking them down on Jay's glass-topped coffee table.

"Please remove your feet from my coffee table," Jay said tersely.

Scowling, Billy obeyed. "Scee-use me!" He looked around the room, met the unfriendly eyes of the people he'd thought he was going to impress. This wasn't a group of rich liver-spotted Palm Springs fairies, fawning over his youth, his full head of hair, and his bulging crotch. Maybe if the women weren't here the men wouldn't all be so uptight. "So who do I have to fuck to get a drink around here?" he said, using one of his favorite lines, holding his glass up and addressing Cassandra.

"Why don't you start with yourself?" she said.

Billy, glaring at her, jumped up from his chair. The room was silent except for the alder logs snapping and hissing in the fireplace. Eyes avoided eyes.

"I guess your high and mighty friends don't want me around here, Big Buddy. I guess I'd better go down to the Eagle if I want a drink."

"For heaven's sake, sit down and be quiet," Terry said.

"Hey! What am I, your dog? Fuck you. I'm going down to the Eagle." He tromped flat-footedly to the foyer and angrily pulled on his boots.

Terry trailed after him like a whipped puppy. "Billy, where are you going?"

"I told you where I was going. I ain't staying around no place where I ain't wanted."

"But it's Thanksgiving," Terry whined.

"For you, maybe. I ain't got nothin' to be thankful for. You bring me down here so I can be treated like a piece of shit." He stomped his boots, pulled down his vest, and called out to Jay and his guests, "Hey, man, thanks for nothin'."

"Any time," Jay called back.

"Wait a minute," Terry said, following Billy outside. The wind lifted his woven hair. "How are you going to get down there?"

"In your car, how else? Gimme the keys."

"No, you've been drinking all day."

"Yeah, and I'm going to go down and drink all night, too. Come on, gimme the keys." He smiled his flat, antithetical smile. "What's the matter, don't you trust me?"

"Not when you've had so much to drink."

"I gotta drink, Big Buddy, if I'm gonna hang around with you."

How many times had he heard this before? And each time he heard it, Terry was paralyzed with fear that another love-of-his-life was about to disappear. Why? What was he doing wrong? "I'll come with you," he offered.

"I don't *want* you to come with me," Billy hissed. "Stay here with your tight-assed friends. You can all give one another Geritol enemas. Just gimme the goddamn car keys."

"Promise me you'll drive safely," Terry pleaded. "Promise me you'll come home at a reasonable hour and not go driving all over the city."

"You don't trust me," Billy taunted, "so fuck you." He started up the street.

"Wait. Billy, wait." Terry fished in his pocket and withdrew the car keys. "Here. Be careful, that's all."

Billy snatched the keys. "Go back to your friends. You deserve one another. Go back and let that Cassandra bitch make a fool of you, see if I care."

Terry, his eyes sadly glued to the rump holes in Billy's jeans, watched as the young man stamped up the street, past Delmont's empty house, and into his own Mock Tudor. He couldn't bear to watch Billy drive away, but a moment later the garage door swung open and he heard the powerful roar of his Mercedes being gunned like a cheap American junker. He was always so careful of the car, so respectful of its price, its power, and everything it stood for. Billy chided him for driving like an old lady, but that was precisely why the car kept its value and didn't have a scratch on it. Terry bit his lip as the stately vehicle shot backwards out of its berth, bounced to a stop in the street, and squealed away. For a moment he thought of returning home—but that would mean waiting. Waiting and worrying. So he went back to Jay's.

The door was locked and he had to ring the bell. Jay let him in. Terry had thought that the party would simply stop when he left, and was irked to see everyone chatting as though nothing had happened.

"Is he gone?" Jay asked.

"Yes, thanks to you," Terry said stiffly. He decided he'd punish all of them for their rudeness to Billy. They were, after all, to blame.

Jay, after three glasses of champagne, wasn't in the mood to coddle his rich, stingy neighbor. "What do you mean, thanks to me?"

"You were awfully rude," Terry said.

"Was I? It seems to me that you were pretty rude to bring that stupid little slut down here without even asking me first."

Terry was flabbergasted. "I thought you'd be gracious enough to welcome him."

"I invited you, Terry, because I was trying to keep our Thanksgiving tradition alive. I wouldn't have minded if he'd had any manners, but Jesus—"

"Where did you pick up that piece of trash, anyway?" Peter called from the living room.

"Honestly, Terry." It was sniffy Susan Bark. "He looks like a murderer."

"Frightening," Carolyn chipped in.

Terry couldn't believe his ears. "Delmont would have liked him," he said feebly.

"Delmont would have asked you why he wasn't on a leash," Wellfleet muttered.

Terry looked around the living room. His eyes fastened on Cassandra, standing with Ito by the glass terrace doors. "I suppose you've been telling them all sorts of juicy lies."

Cassandra frowned. "Why would I do that? I'm not a liar, Terry."

"You haven't liked Billy from the first day you saw him."

"Terry, are you blind? He's been baiting *me* since the day he arrived!"

"Why would he do that?"

"Because he hates women." Just like you, she wanted to add, but kept her trap shut for the sake of the carriage house.

There was a palpable air of tension in the room, a sense of unleashed emotions straining to remain polite.

"How I miss Delmont," Ito sighed. And when he said it, they all realized the snappable fragility of their bonds without him. "Whatever happens with our new neighbors, we must stick together. That is what Delmont would have wanted."

"Let's drink a toast to him," John-Don said.

"Out on the terrace," Jay suggested.

They quietly rose and stepped out into the windy night. The rain had stopped. Thick, ragged clouds raced past the moon. The air was bracing and shiveringly sweet. Looking down into Delmont's empty garden they raised their glasses to his memory.

"We must hope for the best," Ito said.

PART TWO

THE MAYFLOWER THAT DOCKED IN QUEER CORNERS A WEEK LATER WAS not a ship but a moving van. Gears grinding, motor roaring, it slowly rumbled up the steep, rain-slicked incline of Skyview Boulevard. With a flatulent hiss of air brakes it came to a temporary halt midway between Delmont's Queen Anne and Jay Zucker's Sixties Modern.

A few branches from the unkempt, thirty-year-old camellia bushes on the boulevard in front of Jay's were snapped off as the truck doesy-doed forward and back in a laboriously destructive parking maneuver. Then a low-hanging limb from Delmont's magnificent chestnut tree was cracked off. Part of the old original curbing, inset with horse-tethering rings that Jay liked to show off to visitors from New York, was crushed by the truck's enormous rear wheels.

With one exception, the natives who had been dreading this fateful moment were away from their homes when the Mayflower arrived.

Susan was at Windy Hills leading a class in Advanced Discipline for Chihauhaus.

Carolyn, sitting at the information desk of the downtown library, was directing bewildered souls to appropriate departments, instructing them on the use of the new computerized card catalogue, and keeping a nervous eye out for the loonies and foul-smelling vagrants who wandered in off the street and plunked themselves down like ordinary citizens.

Wellfleet was handing out student evaluation forms to his third-year choir members, who were to rank his performance as a "Christian instructor" on a scale of one ("Adequate as a teacher but does not incorporate Christian ideals into subject matter") to five ("Excellent as a teacher, incorporates highest Christian ideals into subject matter").

John-Don was trying to interest a bored and restless twelfth-grade class at Hamilton High School in the meaning of the Constitution.

Peter was schmoozing with hip Katrina Parsons, a potential client, over sushi and sake at Obi-Dan.

Jay and Cassandra were at nearly empty Chez Jay, waiting for two angry late lunchers to end their affair and clear out.

Terry was at the Mercedes dealer, trying (unsuccessfully) to get a special deal on a touch-up paint job for those scratches that Billy Bird claimed weren't his fault.

Billy, with the fifty bucks Terry had given him as an early Christmas gift, was roaming from one dark stale-smelling bar to the next, playing violent video games as he kept his eyes open for potential tricks.

Only Ito was at home, sitting at the drafting table in his glass-walled study, sipping green tea as he contemplated a plan of Florence Hill's estate in Dunthorpe. Mrs. Hill, one of Portland's richest octogenarians, had recently returned from a Garden Society tour of England, where she'd fallen in love with herbaceous borders. She knew nothing about gardening, and her late (third) husband, a millionaire manufacturer of wire coathangers, had been even less imaginative than she. The vast grounds of Hillmount, their estate on Military Road, were modelled after a golf course, with long fairways of mown grass. Now, suddenly, at 81, Mrs. Hill had decided to have it all "redone."

Learning through the horticultural grapevine that Ito was the most famous landscape gardener in Portland, the spry old woman had summoned him to Hillmount for a conference. She described as precisely as she could just what it was she wanted. "Like that castle at—oh, I forget where—it was near—oh, never mind—well, it was just the prettiest thing—surrounded by—I can't remember the names, but you know what I mean—big tall things, blue I think, in back, and teeny-weeny little orange things in front, all sort of massed together—and roses, of course—tons of roses—"

As they drove around the grounds of Hillmount on her late husband's golf cart he realized that Mrs. Hill was talking about at least a two hundred thousand dollar project. She wanted "a pretty moat kind of thingamajig" dug around her enormous white neo-colonial house, and "one of those green zig-zaggy doohickies," which was either a maze or an Elizabethan knot garden, Ito wasn't yet sure which. When Ito told her, with a deferential smile, how much it would cost, believing reality would immediately bring the interview to an end, Mrs. Hill merely said: "So? When can you start? I'm not getting any younger, you know."

He said it wasn't quite so easy. It required planning, research, blueprints, soil studies, and a $20,000 retainer fee. She'd written him a check that very day.

It was his largest private commission to date. Nothing of this scope had been done in Portland for decades. It was the Northwest equivalent of Sissinghurst, without the castle.

True, he was tired of creating the lush English-style gardens everyone who read Martha Stewart now hankered for. He'd done his first for Delmont, years before the style caught on with nouveau-riche executive wives and became a fad. He'd created dozens more since then, so many that "cottage gardens" (or "coffee-table-book gardens" as Delmont once called them) had become a kind of Kudomono trademark. But, like any artist, Ito wearied of repetition and longed for new challenges. His clients were rich, but they were also copycats who mostly wanted versions of what they'd already seen elsewhere. Ito made their beds, horticulturally speaking, but had no desire to sleep in them himself.

His own private horticultural tastes were becoming more Zenlike the older he got, and he was trying not to accept every job that was offered to him. It was difficult because Ito was essentially a workaholic with a hungry desire to succeed. His childhood had been one of deprivation and hardship, laboring in his father's fruit orchards east of Seattle before the Kudomono family was interned and the fruit orchards sold at a loss. He'd worked his way through college by doing menial yard work and gardening. That was when he became aware that having a perfectionistic Japanese gardener was considered a status symbol, and resolved to one day be paid appropriately for his services. He moved to Portland but got nowhere until he met Delmont. Slowly, with Delmont's help, he'd established himself amongst the Caucasian elite of Portland as a landscape designer. At first he was cheap, underpricing himself and doing all the work himself. Slowly, as his reputation grew, he raised his fees. And now, with everyone clamoring for "a Kudomono," he was able to charge whatever he felt like. In the greedy Western sense, he'd come to measure his worth by how much he made, just as his clients measured their power by the size of their gardens and the fact that it was "a Kudomono."

But there was a worm in the apple of Ito's success, a reminder of humility, mortality, and the interconnectedness of all things. A strange longing for less, for divestment, for simplicity, for inner peace, for something beyond the fretting turmoil of possession.

In a way, he was trying to disengage himself. Freedom from desire lead to inward peace, as Lao-Tse said. But the sheer size of Mrs. Hill's project, the attention it would create, and the enormous fee involved, still appealed to the capitalistic side of Ito's nature. With what he earned from this one garden he could take time off to travel. And after that he could devote more time to his bonsai, orchids and meditation.

Of course with so much money involved, there had to be a catch.

The catch was Helen, Mrs. Hill's daughter by her second marriage. When she found out what the chatelaine of Hillmount was planning, Helen called Ito and told him that the garden was yet another one of her mother's senile fancies.

"My mother's in the early stages of Alzheimer's," she insisted. "Her brain's shrinking and she isn't in her right mind. So you can just forget whatever she told you, Mr. Kudomono, and send that check back to me." Luckily, Ito had already cashed it.

Mrs. Hill was indignant when Ito called to ask her if he should continue his design plan. "Oh, don't pay any attention to my daughter," she insisted. "She just wants to have me declared me incompetent so she can get her hands on my money."

"I would not like to be caught in the middle of a family dispute," Ito acknowledged.

Mrs. Hill was not to be put off. "Helen always had a nasty streak in her, just like her lout of a father. A couple of years ago she was born again. I said, 'Helen, you were born once already, how can you be born again? With a face like yours, once is enough.' But she joined this church and now she's constantly trying to convert me and gives all her money to these crackpot shysters who tell her the world's coming to an end. 'If the world's coming to end,' I said, 'how come they need so much money?' So who's crazy, Mr. Kudomono?"

"Hm," Ito said noncomittally.

"Right, she is. But while I'm around to spend it, my money is my money, and I'll do with it whatever I damn well please, and I want that new garden."

▼ ▼ ▼

Hearing a crash, Ito looked up from his drafting table. Through the glass wall he saw, on the street far below, a huge yellow truck shearing off a limb as it passed under the horse-chestnut tree in front of Delmont's house. Clumsy careless oafs! Ito revered trees, always had, feeling a close spiritual kinship with their strong, silent presences.

Then, in a synaptic flash, he realized that the moment they had all been dreading had arrived. It was a moving van. The invasion had begun. He spilled green tea all over the drawing of Mrs. Hill's garden as he jumped up to get a better look.

Of all the houses in Queer Corners, Ito's was the most modern and commanded the most panoramic view. The curious thing about the house, considering that its owner was a landscape designer, was that it had no contact with the earth. It was essentially a one-story structure of steel and glass that rested high above the street on sixty-foot pylons. The only access to this free-floating cube was by a daunting exterior stairway that climbed up the side of a carefully landscaped but nearly vertical slope and left visitors dazed and panting.

The vertiginous inaccessability of the house, which discouraged casual drop-ins, suited Ito's nature. Once inside, he was alone and part of the entire landscape—the atmosphere itself. The house was his quiet, rigorously ordered temple. One room was devoted to his orchids, another to his bonsai, and the center atrium, open to the sky, was a Zen garden of raked gravel with precisely set rocks imported at incredible cost from his grandparents' village in Japan. From his front-facing windows he could see, on a clear day, the majestic snow-covered slopes of Mt. Hood, as hauntingly inspirational as Mt. Fuji.

Through his binoculars, Ito focussed on the two men sitting in the cab of the truck. They didn't move until a red Cadillac pulled into Delmont's driveway. A woman with fluorescent white-blonde hair got out and hurried through the rain to take shelter under the gabled front porch. From there she motioned to the drivers. The three of them pointed and gesticulated. With a shrug, the men climbed back into the truck and the motor roared to life. Ito's windows buzzed with the vibrations. The woman backed out of the driveway and parked further up the hill in front of Terry's Mock Tudor. The truck inched forward and turned towards Ito's house. Apparently the Mayflower was going to back into Delmont's driveway.

Ito, watching from above, sensed disaster. The street wasn't wide enough for the truck to turn unless it nosed into his landscaped parking area. And if it did that . . .

He threw up his hands and let out a shrill cry as the enormous cab plowed into one of the slender cypress trees he'd planted at street-level and pinned it back against the concrete retaining wall. With a sharp hiss, the truck slowly crept backwards leaving the tree collapsed against the wall.

A series of meditative mantras rippled meaninglessly through the whirlpool of Ito's fury. Life is change. The clouds cover the sun, but the sun is still behind the clouds. He who smiles rather than rages is always the stronger.

Fuck Lao-Tse, he wanted to murder the drivers who'd killed his tree and destroyed the perfect symmetry of his street-level garden. The drivers hadn't even gotten out to look at their victim. The woman, who'd darted back to the front porch, was equally oblivious.

Propelled by his anger, Ito dashed outside into the rain and clattered down the slippery grated stairs. By this time the truck was jackknifed in the middle of Skyview Boulevard. As Ito was furiously racing down the last flight of steps the rubber sole of his left shoe shot out from the wet metal. With a gasp he twisted to one side, lunging for the handrail. He missed it and fell with a hard crack on his coccyx, banging his jaw on the metal handrail.

He sat, stunned, as pain rushed like a cold tide through his body. His vision blurred. When he looked up, he saw the two drivers in the truck laughing at him.

The pain was excruciating but he hauled himself up with as much dignity as he could muster and limped, bent double, over to his mauled cypress tree. Its trunk had been snapped, severed like a spinal column. Its beautiful, graceful life was over. Men and their destructive machines! Ito, soaked and shivering, turned and hobbled out into the street, towards the cab of the truck.

"You have destroyed my cypress tree!" That was what he meant to scream. But when he opened his mouth to let them have it, his tongue was numb and his battered jaw locked as a searing spasm of unexpected pain shot from his chin to his eyeballs. "You hef dethtwoyed my thypweth twee," he grunted through his clamped mouth.

The driver was smiling as he rolled down his window. "What's that?"

Ito, incoherent with rage, turned and angrily jabbed his finger in the direction of the tree. "Look what you hef done! You incompetent idioth!" His red, burning eyes popped from his head. It was as though a disfiguring, nightmarish mask had been clamped over his face, over speech itself.

The big bland face of the driver stiffened. "Watch who yer callin' incompetent, mister," he warned.

"You should not be dwiving!" Ito shouted through the crack of his mouth. Every word was an effort. "You awe dangewuth!"

With this the door of the cab opened and the glaring driver swung down from his seat. His pendulous white belly spilled out from beneath a too-short t-shirt and his jeans hung so low that when he turned to say something to his partner, Ito could see the crack between his buttocks. Scowling, the driver tugged down the visor of his baseball cap and moved intimidatingly towards five-foot-five Ito, whose aching teeth were now chattering with shock from his fall.

"You got a problem with my driving, Gook-face?"

"How dare you call me thuch a name!" Ito shrilled. "I am going to call your company and have you fired. I am going to thue you."

Perhaps it was the threat of being sued that made the driver turn angrily conciliatory. He lumbered over to have a look at the fallen cypress, his buttocks jiggling above the strap of his belt. "It's just a tree!"

"That twee is iwweplatheable!" Ito squawked.

"Look, you better go talk to the lady," the driver said. "We was gonna park in front by the curb but she tol' us to back into the driveway so none of her furniture'd get wet. Don't blame us, blame her."

With a disgusted grunt and comets streaking through his jolted vision, Ito crept past the driver and towards Delmont's house.

The woman had disappeared. Undeterred, Ito rang the bell. The quiet gong, once so comfortingly familiar to his ears, now sounded hollow and unfriendly. No answer. He rang again, keeping his finger pressed to the button so there'd be no escape for the occupant.

Cornette, who'd run into the house once the shouting began and was trying to block it out by loudly humming a hymn, finally opened the door. She glared suspiciously at Ito, her white-gold hair, soaked by the rain, drooping around her narrow face like a collapsed spider's web She didn't have her eyelashes on and without makeup felt naked and vulnerable. "Stop ringing the bell like that! What do you want? Who are you?"

"I am Ito Kudomono. I live acwoth the thtweet." He pointed and she leaned out to look, following his finger. "The dwiver of your twuck hath dethtwoyed a vewy ware thypweth twee in fwont of my houth."

"It's not my truck," Cornette said, stepping back inside and folding her arms.

Ito tried to calm himself. "Ith that all you hef to thay to me?"

"Well what do you want me to thay—say? I don't own the truck. I wasn't driving the truck. I didn't run into your twee, whatever the heck that is."

"My twee!" he raged, desperately trying to form the simple word with his swollen, lifeless tongue. "My tw-r-ee!"

Cornette, though unnerved by his vocal agony, was not about to accept responsibility for anything. "If you have a problem, talk to the driver about it."

"I have twied talking to the dwiver. He inthulted me."

Her eyes sparked with interest. "What did he say?"

"He called me Gook-face."

"That wasn't very Christian of him." She stood in the dark, empty hallway, silently pondering the situation. "Well, he's probably one of these people who don't know that you can be one God's children no matter what race you belong to. If you believe in Jesus—"

Ito cut her short. "Excuth me, I did not come here to dithcuth Jethuth. I hef had a bad fall and my thypweth twee hath been wuined. The dwiver told me to thpeak with you. You tell me to thpeak to the dwiver. If thith ith your idea of being a good neighbor—" Exhausted, he simply glared at her.

"There's no need to become so hostile." Cornette was stern. "It's just a stupid tree. How much can a silly tree cost? It must be covered by their insurance."

Hopeless! An ordinary day turned into a nightmare. Ito, his lower back stinging with pain, had been stooping forward, unable to stand or talk straight. Now, realizing he'd have to take matters entirely into his own hands, he righted himself. The action triggered a violent physical response. "Aieee!" he gasped, doubling over, his face contorted. He swung out his arms and lurched over to take hold of one of the pillars that supported the porch. He fought back a wave of nausea. It felt as though his testicles were clamped in a vise.

"What's the matter?" Cornette nervously stepped back into the hallway. It didn't occur to her that he might actually be in intense pain. Rather, she wondered if this furious little man wearing khakis, an expensive-looking sweater, and running shoes had been possessed by the Devil and was about to subject her faith to some ugly new trial. A trick. He was an Oriental, after all. He looked deranged. Those tomato-red eyes! And the Devil, which she believed to be everywhere, was always looking for a way in. Maybe into her new home! A thrill of terror ran through her.

"My back, my back," Ito sobbed. His back, the pivot and fulcrum of his life as a gardener, was on fire. A belt of sharp throbbing misery was clenched tight around his hips. Beads of sweat broke out on his forehead. "Hewp me, pwease hewp me," he gasped, clinging with all his might to the pillar of the front porch, afraid to move, his breath short and shallow.

"What can I—?" But her momentary spurt of sympathy quickly gave way to habitual suspicion. "I'm sorry," she said firmly, "but my husband isn't at home. He's on his way up from Medford with our children. There's nothing I can do for you."

Ito slowly turned his head to look at her, and beyond her, into the bare foyer of Delmont's house, where he'd always been welcome. The hideous emptiness of it was magnified by her stiff, unyielding presence. His dark, dilated eyes swam in a pink broth of tears. "Phone—may-I-uth-your-phone?"

"It hasn't been connected yet. My husband has the cellular."

He closed his scalded goggling eyes, afraid he was going to pass out.

"Why don't you try praying," Cornette suggested.

Ito grunted in despair.

She stepped closer. "Open up your heart to the Lord. Tell him you're a sinner in pain. Ask him for strength. He'll listen. He always hears his children when they cry out in need. He cares for you and he shows it through sickness and pain."

"Pleath," Ito moaned, "thtop."

But Cornette was inspired. Fear had left her. She could feel her spiritual tentacles unfurling in the bright, rippling waters of grace, ready to embrace yet another poor misguided soul and pull him in to the bosom of the Lord.

"I'll help you," she said. "Don't be afraid. I'll pray with you. Oh Lord!" she cried over the clanking roar of the Mayflower as it began to back down the driveway, "some-one has come to me in need. He asks for help, for release from pain."

She didn't have time to finish, for when she clapped her hand firmly on Ito's back to exorcise the pain he let out a scream and fell in a heap at her feet.

CHAPTER 9

"HOW THE HELL AM I SUPPOSED TO DECORATE IT?" PETER HELD ITO'S scaly cypress tree upright, at arm's length, as John-Don, on his belly, tightened the screws in the tree stand.

"I'm sure you'll find a way," John-Don grunted from the floor.

"But we always have a noble fir," Peter complained, squinting, appraising, moving the tree an inch to the left.

"So this year we have a noble cypress instead. How does it look? Is it straight?"

"No, dahling, it's perfectly queer," Peter Tallulahed.

John-Don stood and regarded the slender evergreen that rose to the ceiling of their living room. Ito, bed-ridden, told him that of course he could have the tree, but was he aware that the cypress was a symbol of mourning and loss? John-Don hadn't breathed a word of this to Peter, who would have refused point-blank to have it in the house. "I think it's cool," he said.

"Yeah, but what about all my ornaments?" Peter said. "They just won't dangle properly."

"You and your ornaments," John-Don laughed.

For years Peter had been collecting Christmas-tree ornaments. It was a kind of fetish. Adorned with exquisite hand-blown crystal globes from Austria (but made in China), hand-carved Santas from Germany (made in Korea), terra-cotta cherubs from Italy (made in Mexico), sterling-silver snowflakes from Mexico (made in Peru), and tiny glass cherries from Czechoslovakia (made in Romania), his tree was an economics lesson in global market export strategies as they applied to traditional crafts.

"And I've got to consider Delmont's ornaments, too," Peter said."He'd want them to be well-hung."

"Peter's tree" was always admired in Queer Corners. But everyone, including Peter, knew that "Delmont's tree" was more valuable because the ornaments were authentic place-of-origin treasures made before mass-market production techniques took over the world. Those fragile glittering baubles, sitting in a box on the mantlepiece out of harm's way, now belonged to Peter. Willa Carruthers, queen of Portland estate sales, had sold him Delmont's antique collection at a special pre-sale showing not open to the general public. The ornaments were not cheap, and now that Peter had them he felt doubly obligated to have a spectacular tree, one that would do aesthetic justice to Delmont's memory.

"You really miss old Delmont, don't you?" John-Don said.

Peter nodded. "Yeah, I do. I miss his sense of camp."

"You two were always good at that. I always felt kind of left out."

"Honey, you don't understand camp," Peter said affectionately, picking plant debris from John-Don's shaggy blonde hair. "Nobody does anymore. It's a dying art form." He went to the windows and looked out at the dark shape of Delmont's Queen Anne. "But he was more than just camp, you know. Delmont did a lot for me."

When Peter made the Big Move from San Francisco to Portland, Delmont generously stirred him into the city's financial upper crust, giving him a toehold in an otherwise tight (and completely white) market. "We wouldn't be here, you know, in this house, if it weren't for him."

"Yeah, I know."

"Now that I've got his ornaments I have an obligation to make the tree as beautiful as possible. It's not just a tree, you know. It's a statement. A tribute."

"I know, but what could be a better statement than making use of a neighbor's tree knocked down by some idiots in a moving van?" John-Don sighed and scratched his head. "You really hate it, don't you?"

"No, honey, I don't hate it. It's just that I love it when we go out and cut down our own, that's all. I love all that butch lumberjack drag. It's the only time I feel comfortable wearing flannel shirts and hiking boots. Tramping around with a huge ax to find our perfect noble fir. That's my image of Christmas here in the Great Northwest."

"I don't want to do that anymore," John-Don said. "The earth needs every tree it has."

"Honey, we're talking about tree farms. We're not talking about logging old-growth forests and killing spotty owls or whatever they are."

"Spotted, and the motive's the same. Destroying nature for profit."

Peter groaned. He'd heard all this before. John-Don's socialist tendencies had been on the wane since he moved into Queer Corners, but his environmental fervor was growing stronger by the day. "The next thing I know you'll be one of those eco-terrorists, chaining yourself to Christmas trees."

"Maybe." In his more radical moments John-Don did fantasize that he was a Greenpeace hero, going on dangerous eco-missions to wage war with the nature-killers.

"But my clients *expect* me to have a gorgeous tree. When they come over for the Christmas party they want to see something fantastic, something that inspires confidence in my taste. Something that sends out a not-so-subliminal message: Hire Peter Love, Portland's only black interior designer."

Now that Delmont was gone, Peter's party would be the highlight of the holiday season. The guest list extended far beyond Queer Corners. The hundred or so people who looked forward to Delmont's annual wassail bash would be invited. Not only was it Peter's way of keeping Delmont's holiday tradition alive, it was a perfect way to establish contact with all of Delmont's former clients.

"If you were smart you'd get into eco-decorating," John-Don said. "I'm telling you, that's going to be the new trend. Recycled materials, earth-friendly."

"Great, just what all the rich white honkies in the Portland hills want: Christmas tree ornaments made from old tires."

"Look at it this way, it's a Mediterranean tree so, it fits in perfectly with a

Mediterranean house." This was a lie—the tree was Japanese, but Peter didn't have to know that.

Peter's eyes snapped into life. "That's it. You've hit the theme on the head. You're a genius. *Mediterranean.*"

"So stop complaining and start decorating," John-Don said, slapping Peter's butt.

"I can't until you get the ladder and we string the lights."

"Okay, but then I've got to go next door. I promised Ito I'd give him a massage."

"You're giving Ito a massage?" Peter repeated incredulously.

"Yeah."

"Since when are you Mr. Healing Hands? "

"Peter, he can't even walk. He can't move he's in so much pain."

"Is this a full-body massage or what?" Peter hated himself, hated his jealousy, that old unconquerable demon. But he couldn't help himself. "Is he fully clothed?"

John-Don left the room and didn't answer.

"Why don't you ever give me a massage?" Peter called after him. "I could use one, too." The garage door slammed. "Why don't you put those big healing hands on me?"

When John-Don left, Peter dug out his carefully coiled strands of tiny white lights and began unraveling them along the floor. Brenda Lee sang "Jingle Bell Rock" as thick winter rains pelted the windows. Dumb, Peter thought. Dumb, dumb, *dumb*. As if their neighbor Ito could be a threat. But, of course, everyone was a threat when Peter was feeling vulnerable and needy. John-Don didn't understand jealousy. He hated "scenes." John-Don wasn't even aware of all the men who cruised him. But Peter was. He saw those covetous, lingering eyes feasting on John-Don when they were out. He's mine, he wanted to cry. John-Don Webster's mine and you can't have him!

He poured himself just a little bourbon, to calm down. Looked at the jiggling blue and yellow flames in the gas fireplace. Went back to unraveling the Christmas lights. John-Don was something of a Scrooge about the holidays, dismissing all the hoopla as "sickening commercialism." But Christmas was Peter's holiday. He loved it with the fervor of a child.

When Peter was a boy, Christmas was always an extravaganza. The Love family celebrated in a big way. Grandparents, great grandparents, uncles, aunts, cousins, second-cousins, grandchildren, they all converged at the Love's Federal-era townhouse in Georgetown for days of cooking, baking, feasting, singing, church-going, gift-giving, and story-telling.

But so much had happened since then. Over the last few years the holiday had lost much of its old heartfelt warmth and joy. Peter went through the motions, but it was harder and harder to connect with the happy, anticipatory emotions of the season. In a way, Peter now dreaded Christmas. Reminders of dead friends and his estrangement from his family exerted a heavy melancholic tug on his emotions. To counteract the memory bank and to keep his spirits up he threw himself into a desperate flurry of decorating, party-going, and party giving. The people who thought Peter Love was brittle, shallow or annoyingly camp had no idea how hard he worked to keep some semblance of happiness alive and pumping in his heart.

He eyed the telephone. Maybe he should call them. Try yet again to reconnect. A knot of tension tightened in his belly.

His friends were gone, but his family was still alive, still living in D.C., still celebrating Christmas. Without him. Talk about the ghost of Christmas past. Peter Love was it.

▼ ▼ ▼

Peter officially came out the Christmas after he'd left the Rhode Island School of Design. It was the most difficult decision of his life. He was spurred on by his first boyfriend, Nick Colusco, who was active in local D.C. gay politics. "Look," Nick said, "you've got a name but you don't have a life or identity of your own. Your parents are famous in D.C. They're revered, they're icons. But you're just a shadow until you come out and tell them who you really are."

Yes, Peter knew that. Both his parents had been active in the early civil rights campaigns. They'd marched on Selma, stood up to George Wallace's state troopers, seen friends shot and beaten, been called niggers, marched on Washington. They'd marched marched marched with unflagging energy and dedication, through pregnancies and personal calamities, marched through life itself. They'd stood at the side of Martin Luther King singing "We Shall Overcome" and they'd attended the slain leader's funeral.

Their bravery both inspired and frightened Peter, because he didn't know if he had the same kind of courage himself. He was fiercely proud of what they'd done. His father had been given a governmental post under Jimmy Carter. He'd appeared as a spokesman for his race on shows like *Firing Line* and *Meet the Press*.

"Your father understands struggle," Nick said. Yes, but would he understand Peter's struggle?

It was his father's reaction that Peter feared most. By that time there had already been a distinct cooling between them. Mr. Love had expected his son to go into law. When Peter announced that he was going to be an interior designer, his father was speechless with disappointment. Unmanly pursuits made Mr. Love uneasy and embarrassed. If he was so threatened by Peter as an interior designer, what would he do when his son told him he was gay?

Peter never regretted that he'd outed himself. It had changed his life forever, it had robbed him of his family's support, but at least he would never again have to live a lie or conceal who he was.

His Christmas announcement was met with stunned disbelief, denial, anger. His mother wept. His father stormed out of the room. There was no getting through to them on this issue, and eventually he'd stopped trying. Mr. Love took Peter's queerness as a personal insult. No, it was more than that: it was an insult to the entire race. The black community needed every male role model it could get.

His parents still refused to talk about "it." Peter called once or twice a year to remind them that he was still alive. His mother gave him the news about everyone else in the family but never asked about his personal life. There was usually some excuse as to why daddy couldn't come to the phone.

Peter always found it oddly hypocritical that his parents, who'd invested so much energy in destroying ignorant stereotypes, encased their gay son in one. After that bitter

Christmas—his "coming-out Christmas"—he stopped going back to Washington where the old comfort and joy was reserved for others. He exiled himself. Moved to San Francisco. Celebrated Christmas with friends who had been through "the rejection thing" themselves. Turned into a camp disco queen. Took drugs. Danced. Fucked. Tried to find and keep a steady boyfriend who wanted something more than a piece of dark meat. Worked like crazy. Made lots of money. Snorted pounds of coke and danced danced danced. And watched as AIDS sucked away his friends one by one until only he was left, a stunned survivor washed up on the shore of a bleak new land. After twenty funerals he stopped counting.

Dark dark years. Yet every Christmas he valiantly put up a beautiful tree and dutifully laid out a Kwanzaa altar.

Then John-Don Webster came down to San Francisco for a Sierra Club regional conference. One glance at that Nordic, aerobically contoured face, shaggy blonde hair, and shy-stranger-in-the-city air, and Peter knew he was in love. They cruised one another from opposite tables in a cafe on Market Street. They went back to Peter's loft. They talked and laughed over wine. They didn't have sex. John-Don didn't even mention it. But Peter knew what a leper colony San Francisco had become, how fearful of contamination visitors were. The AIDS epidemic hadn't hit Portland as hard as it had San Francisco. But in this terrifying land where terrified men were stalked by The Virus, Peter and John-Don connected. Just when Peter was ready to throw in the towel.

There were just two little problems: John-Don lived 800 miles away and he'd never had a boyfriend. He knew about salvage-logging riders and could quote EPA guidelines from memory, but he didn't know diddly-squat about love. How precious it was when you'd reached a certain age and been through as much as Peter had.

So Peter courted him with letters and long hone calls. He felt it was his last chance to grab the gold ring. He wanted to settle down. He made weekend trips to Portland. John-Don was perpetually eager to see him and titillated by the attention. They had sex. It was lousy, by-the-new-rulebook sex, but Peter was certain that would improve when they actually lived together. That elusive miracle, happiness, burrowed into Peter's heart. And with it, a new perspective. Why stay in San Francisco? Why not make a fresh start? Portland was cute, it was do-able if he could get his foot in the door of the establishment.

On one of his trips to Portland Peter made a point of meeting Delmont Percy, scion of Northwest decorators. "Old decorators never die, my dear," Delmont told him, "they simply change their title to 'interior editor' and move on to a new style." Peter charmed and flattered him, but he was also charmed and flattered by Delmont, and they became friends. It was the first time in Peter's life that he'd known an older gay man.

When Delmont told him about the house across the street from his Queen Anne ("a well-proportioned Mediterranean with Deco overtones, large rooms, stylish detailing, huge windows, a cherrywood front hall and stairway to die for, and badly in need of a gay owners, my dear"), Peter, buoyant with love, immediately wanted to buy it and live there with John-Don. Unforeseen problems. He was richer than John-Don. He was accustomed to luxury. John-Don had never aspired to a house in the hills, but for Peter's status-charged career it was a necessity. John-Don distrusted "status." The problem with the house essentially boiled down to a "class thing."

John-Don seemed to think that living in the house would be an economic betrayal of his staunchly working-class roots. He came from a long line of authentic dyed-in-the-wool Marxists, union leaders, labor agitators, and styleless radicals highly suspicious of anyone with money. And money was everything in Peter's world of covetous, snobby, social-climbers.

When Peter finally sold his San Francisco loft for a tidy profit and said he was buying the Portland house for himself, John-Don took the plunge and moved up in the world. Living on "the hill," in Portland terms, meant he was now upper-middle-class. "It doesn't mean you can't still be a socialist," Peter reassured him. "It just means that you can be a more comfortable socialist."

That was three years ago. And now? They were lovers—or "committed partners," as you were supposed to say in politically correct Portland. And hahaha, John-Don now proudly strolled around inspecting the house and yard like a petit-bourgeoise landowner. And hahaha, Peter could now plumb a sink and install a rheostat while John-Don lounged about self-consciously in their enormous stuccoed living room reading gloomy tomes on the end of everything (nature, literacy, education, common sense, organized religion, liberal ideals, civilization itself).

Peter was in love. John-Don had saved him. Stern, rigorous, prudish, idealistic, slightly square John-Don, the miracle jock, the perfect gay son of perfect socially concerned parents. John-Don was disgustingly healthy, "looked straight" as they said in the personal ads, didn't know how to dance, had never tried drugs. He worried about the environment, worked for liberal causes, and had one credit card which he dutifully paid off in full every month. And—wouldn't you know it?—he continued to be terrible in bed. Fear of AIDS had severely compromised his sexual potential.

There was a peculiar homeness to gay life in Portland. For Peter, who'd become cynical about such things, it took time to adjust to the "niceness" of everything and everyone. John-Don, for instance, was extremely close to his parents. The Websters accepted Peter unconditionally. They treated him as a son. That was "nice" of them, and Peter appreciated it. But he wasn't their son, and he envied John-Don for having what he didn't: a real family.

▼ ▼ ▼

Peter put down the string of Christmas lights and moved towards the telephone. Bit his lower lip. Picked up the phone. Punched in the familiar number. He felt weak in the knees.

His mother answered.

"Hi. It's me."

"Peter? How are you?" Her voice sounded frail, quavery, depleted of its old vigor. Peter was instantly concerned.

"I'm fine, mom. How are you? Were you sleeping?"

No, but she wasn't feeling up to snuff. "It's just one of those things," she sighed.

"One of what things?"

"It happens when you get older," she said evasively.

"How's daddy?"

The news wasn't reassuring. His father had suffered from high blood pressure for years. His last medication had stopped working, so they'd put him on a new one. "It makes him feel queer in the head," she said. "Kind of disoriented sometimes. Where are you calling from?" she asked.

"Portland. Same place I've been for the last three years."

"Oh, you're still there."

"Yes, mom, this is where I live."

She asked what the weather was like.

"It rains a lot," he said, peering out the rain-blurred window. There was movement across the street, in front of Delmont's house.

"How's your business going?" Mrs. Love asked.

"I'm doing very well." Peter moved closer to the window, trying to make out what was happening on the opposite site of Skyview Boulevard.

"I can't remember the name of the firm."

"I'm not with a firm anymore. Not since I left San Francisco. I'm on my own here."

"Is there a black community there?" his mother asked.

"Yeah, but it's small."

"I can't understand why you'd pick a place like that to live," his mother said. "It sounds all white and wet to me."

"Mom, you don't know anything about Portland. You've never even been here."

"Well, I do know a thing or two," she said, a little indignant. "I know that blacks used to be barred from living there, in Oregon." She pronounced it Ore-a-gone; Peter, who'd learned to say Ore-a-gun, didn't bother to correct her. "It wasn't until the \Second World War, when they needed laborers for the shipyards, that blacks went out to Oregon."

"Really? I didn't know that." Peter watched as a man and a teenaged boy began to lug objects from Delmont's garage out to the front lawn. The story of Ito's infuriating encounter with Cornette Labonne had already made the rounds, but no one had seen her or the rest of the Labonnes since. Now everyone in Queer Corners was desperately curious to see what the Labonnes actually looked like.

"The Klan used to be there, in Oregon," his mother said.

"There's still a lot of rednecks, but they're not lynching anyone," Peter said. "Anyway, Portland's very liberal."

"That word has lost its meaning," his mother said in her soft drawl. "Marion Berry is liberal. How's your health, Peter?"

"My health? It's fine. I've lost some weight." As Peter watched, Ron Labonne— who else could it be?—began untangling a thick coil of electrical cord. The task, or maybe the pouring rain, evidently made him impatient, for he thrust the coil towards his soaked, slouching son. The son—sixteen or seventeen?—snapped to attention. He had a stiff, military haircut. Peter couldn't make out if he was cute or not. Probably not, if they were Christian fundamentalists.

"You're not sick are you?" His mother sounded anxious.

"Sick? No, I'm not sick. I've never felt better. People live very healthy lives out here." It took him a moment to realize that weight loss, in her mind, was a sign of illness, probably of AIDS. "John-Don is strictly low-fat. He makes me watch what I eat. No more fried chicken, mom."

She ignored the reference to John-Don. "Sharlene"—his older sister—"came over last night and cooked up some fried chicken for daddy and me. It was almost as good as mine."

"You should lay off the fried chicken, mom. And dad, too, if he's got high blood pressure. You should eat chicken breasts, without the skin, broiled." He still couldn't figure out what was going on across the street. The objects the Labonnes carried appeared to be statues.

"Lionel"—Sharlene's son, Peter's nephew—"reminds me of you. That boy just loves to draw. He makes the prettiest little pictures. He makes all sorts of colorful little things. He says he's going to decorate the Kwanzaa table all by himself this year. We're all so proud of him."

As the figures were set up in front of Delmont's house and the familiar grouping materialized, it became clear to Peter what his new neighbors were doing. He sucked in his breath. Winced. They were setting up a plastic Nativity scene in Queer Corners.

"I always prayed I'd have lots of grandchildren," Mrs. Love went on, "but I guess that's to be denied me. The doctor told Sharlene she can't have any more. And you won't get married, so—"

His sudden anger caught him by surprise. He wheeled around. "What do you mean by that? You make it sound like I should get married just so you'll have grandkids."

"I meant—"

"Yes, ma'am, I know what you meant. But you know what? I'm married already."

"What?" she gasped. "When? Why didn't you tell us?"

"Oh, I've told you. You just never wanted to listen."

"Whatever do you mean?" she laughed, her voice suddenly eager and almost playful. "Peter, you never told us you were married. Who is she?"

"It's not a she. It's John-Don Webster. The man I've been living with for three years." There was an ominous silence on the other end of the line.

"Shame on you," his mother finally said, her faint voice cracking.

Her comment filled with a sudden manic fury. "No," he shouted, "shame on *you*. Aren't you even remotely interested in my life?"

"Not that side of it," she said frostily.

"It *hurts*, goddamnit, that I can't ever talk to you about John-Don. I share my life with him. He makes me happy. I'm in love with him."

"Yes, for as long as those things last," his mother said.

"Listen," Peter said, "I was thinking it was about time you actually met him. I was thinking maybe we could come out for Christmas."

"Come home?" Another long pause. "I don't think that would be easy on daddy."

"Yeah? Put him on the line. Let me ask him myself." This was it. He was doing it. Confronting Big Daddy. Mouth dry, waiting for his mother's response, he turned back to the window. The two Labonnes were still there, struggling to put up their Nativity scene in the pouring rain.

"Daddy can't talk right now," Mrs. Love said. "He can't—he can't stand upset."

Peter glared at the phone. "You're going to keep me away forever, aren't you?" he cried.

"Daddy's worked so hard for others all his life," his mother said, "worked so hard so you'd have the same opportunities as everyone else. He feels you've let him down."

"How? How have I let daddy down? Peter demanded.

"After all his hard work he hoped you'd stand up and take your place in the world."

"And I can't do that as a gay man?"

She let out a scornful little laugh. "Not in Washington. You know how brutal politics can be."

"Yes, ma'am. Especially family politics," he said sharply, wondering why he had subjected himself to their rejection yet again. Why was it always up to him? Fighting for some semblance of composure, he turned his attention back to Delmont's house. A strong gust of wind blew down the blue plastic wading pool the Labonnes had sliced in half and set up behind the Nativity figures. Then Joseph, stiff with prayer, toppled over.

"Daddy wanted you to be a leader," his mother said. "A leader, just like himself. The struggle isn't over yet."

"You call me sometime," Peter said, his voice hollow, "when you want to talk about struggle. I'll tell you about struggle."

"Don't trivialize what I'm saying. Don't confuse it with your personal life. If you choose to live that way, then you have to accept the consequences."

"Merry Christmas," Peter said. He clicked off the phone and tossed it on the sofa. Looked around at his beautiful home, his accomplishment. Sniffed. Wiped his eyes. Turned back to the window.

Outside, despite the moaning winds and pelting rain, the Labonnes were still at it. The wading pool backdrop blew over again, taking the statues with it. Labonne slapped the boy on his arm and pointed. The son shrugged and kept unravelling the electrical cord. Labonne strode over to examine the damage. Bellowed something. The son reluctantly went over. Labonne the Elder pointed. The boy picked up Joseph and repositioned him. Another gust of wind and the lightweight figure went down again. Now Labonne was apparently infuriated.

"What are you looking at?" John-Don asked as he carefully swung the twelve-foot wooden ladder from the kitchen into the foyer.

Peter quickly brushed his eyes and cleared his throat. "The new straights across the street. You're not going to believe this, honey. They're setting up a Nativity scene in front of Delmont's house."

John-Don carefully put the ladder down and joined him. He put a hand on Peter's shoulder. "Are you upset?"

"It's too tacky for words," Peter huffed. "No one in Queer Corners puts up Nativity scenes. It's . . . sacriligious. It just ruins Delmont's house."

"I overheard your phone call," John-Don said. "Some of it anyway."

Peter bowed his head. He didn't realize, until they spurted from his eyes, that he had any tears left to shed on this subject. So unmanly, and in front of John-Don.

"Listen, you can't let it get you down," John-Don said, stroking Peter's heaving back.

"You've got a family. They love you. What have I got?"

"Well, you've got me."

Sweet, magic words. Sweet, magic man. John-Don always came through in the end. Peter pulled John-Don into his arms and squeezed. "You're happy here, aren't you, honey? You love this house, don't you?"

"Me? Yeah."

Peter dove into those clear blue eyes. "You love me, don't you?"

John-Don smiled sheepishly. It was difficult for him to express his emotions. He nodded. "You don't have to ask," he said.

"That's my problem. I do have to ask. I have to be told. Just tell me once in awhile, will you? Make me feel wanted."

"Okay." John-Don eased himself free of the tight embrance. "Hey, come on, let's finish this tree. I can't spend all night on this. Help me with the ladder."

"Okay." But Peter couldn't resist one last glance across the street.

Something had happened. An altercation over the Nativity scene. Labonne père was pushing Labonne fils, jabbing him in the chest. The boy stiffened and lurched backwards. Labonne was shouting. The boy stopped, held his ground, and then threw the coil of electrical cord at his father.

"Oh my God," Peter said excitedly, "a fight, a fight, come and look, they're fighting."

John-Don was trapped in the middle of his delicate maneuvering of the twelve-foot ladder. "I can't. Come and help me with this thing."

"He's hitting him!" Peter cried. "Quick! Get your binoculars!"

"I can't!"

"He's killing him!" Across the street, Ron Labonne was throttling his son. And then the son, protecting himself from the blows, hauled off and took a swing at his father. Labonne quickly got him in a hammerlock and literally dragged him back to the garage.

"Oh Jesus—oh my Lord—John-Don come here! Come and look at this!"

John-Don, rattled by the urgency in Peter's voice, swung around to look. The ladder, balanced precariously on his shoulder, moved with him. And kept on going. John-Don couldn't stop it. He stepped to one side, trying to halt the ladder's momentum. Crunched some of the tiny lights spread out along the floor. Lifted his foot, upsetting his balance, and tottered in the opposite direction as the back of the ladder scythed through the living room.

Peter, hearing a gasp, turned just in time to see the ladder catch the end of Delmont's box of fragile ornaments and sweep it off the mantlepiece.

CHAPTER 10

PORTLAND WAS A SMALL TOWN WITH A BIG MOUTH. YOU HAD TO BE cautious. A mere spark of suspicion caught in the city's gossipy updraft could ignite into rumor and spread as quickly as a forest fire in the dry season. So Jay had never discussed his business problems with anyone but Delmont. Delmont had always been so comforting. Analytical, protective, reassuring, discreet . . . and generous.

Now, with Delmont dead and Chez Jay on the verge of bankruptcy, Jay had to shoulder his financial woes alone. His staff, reduced to a bare skeleton crew, knew something was wrong but Jay couldn't bring himself to tell them how precarious the whole operation actually was. What would happen if someone like Yvor duBouef, his moody alcoholic chef from Brittany, whose sublime rillettes and lavish larding techniques had been praised eight years ago in *The Oregonian*, actually found out how bad things were and walked? Gone forever those superb Chez Jay pommes frites fried the authentic French way, in coconut oil. If Chez Jay folded, a dream, an entire era, an endangered cuisine went down the garbage disposal.

No wonder Jay had such *spilkes*, felt so *vermischt*. For worry he could now outdo his deceased mother, whose anxious voice and endless predictions of imminent disaster had moved in and taken over a corner of his brain. Her voice always reappeared at moments of extreme stress and crisis.

He couldn't go on much longer. Everything he had was pumped back into the black hole of the unprofitable restaurant. Jay was living on credit cards and Valium.

Sleepless nights. Flailing in an endless froth of fret. The thought of undergoing a Chapter 11 bankruptcy proceeding brought on random panic attacks. He'd lose everything, and everyone would know about it. Jay Zucker: has been. What would he do? Maitre d' for another restaurant? Work as a waiter for the same low wages he paid?

Not on your life. Jay Zucker was his own boss.

What then?

Move?

He didn't want to. Where would he go? Couldn't imagine himself back in New York. In Aryan, overweight Portland he was dark and exotic and his muscular chutzpah was duly noted and appreciated. In New York he'd be just another trim horny middle-aged Jew, a little gefilte fish in a big pond. Jay liked it the other way around.

No, Queer Corners had become home. He loved his period Sixties house and his super-sized Nineties hot tub. And he'd grown to like Portland itself: the wide tree-lined streets, the friendliness, the clean wet fragrant air, the WASPy determination to make it work as a city.

Yes, there were plenty of social controls in Portland, lots of eyes in the woodwork, and the pace could be relentlessly slow. But you did get a sense that it was actually growing, getting better as a city.

Which was, in part, why Jay was having such problems with Chez Jay. Over the past few years several downtown blocks had been rehabbed and recommercialized. New restaurants and "food courts" opened. Pedestrian traffic patterns changed. Progress had thrown Chez Jay's once-prime location off-kilter and out-of-center.

And food itself, the whole concept of dining, had undergone a metamorphosis. Everything was "lite" now. A new generation of health-conscious yuppies seemed to live on organic salads and coffee. Every goddamned corner had a cafe, an espresso wagon or a juice bar.

Jay'd had the first espresso machine in Portland and the new generation of caffeine addicts didn't even know he'd been ahead of his time. It was humiliating to have to put a tacky neon "Espresso" sign in his window, next to the one that read "Microbrews," but he had no choice. You had to appeal to the coffeeheads and the beer drinkers, both of whom had developed ridiculously specialized tastes.

Chez Jay couldn't remain the winey, sauce-laden, "romantic dining experience" it had been. It had to change its identity in order to survive. But to what? Delmont wasn't around to give advice. Jay was too proud to confide in any of his other neighbors. The only person he felt comfortable with was Cassandra Taylor. Young as she was, Cassandra was a good ideas person. She had the eye of an artist and saw things from a trendier, harder-edged perspective.

"Okay, I'll play devil's advocate," she said one soggy afternoon, eyeing the label on the expensive Oregon Chardonnay Jay was pouring out for them. He'd gloomily beckoned her over to his favorite deuce. "Maybe you need a whole new look, You know how everyone is into interiors now. Funky doesn't work for upscale."

"Chez Jay's not funky!" he said, shocked that anyone would see it that way. Funky meant old. "It's classic French farmhouse with a charming touch of Paris bistro."

"No, Jay, it's funky. Too old to be trendy and not old enough to be rediscovered." She saw a flicker of hurt in his eyes and quickly added: "I like it, of course, but—well, the carpet's worn, the tables wobble, and the blue-and-white color scheme just doesn't work in this dark space. It's starting to look grungy."

Funky and grungy. He couldn't believe his ears. Heard the death knell tolling. Jay sipped his wine, swallowed his pride and listened.

"You've seen the new restaurants, you know how designed those interiors are," Cassandra said. "Bright, lots of color, not dark old places like this. People want noise and excitement when they're eating. They want to be crammed in a place where it's hard to get a table and they can't hear themselves think."

"I grew up with noise and excitement while I was eating," Jay said. "Teevee blaring, people screaming at one another, phones ringing. I wanted to make Chez Jay a quiet place for people to digest their food and get sloshed in peace."

"I'm with you," Cassandra said diplomatically, "but times have changed. The whole menu should be revamped. How about an advertising campaign that lets everyone know Chez Jay has gone neo-nouvelle? Scrape off those sauces and go for smaller leaner portions. Emphasize fresh quality ingredients. More salads. Drop the farmhouse idea.

It's tired. Say you're bringing Paris to Portland. Go for more sophistication."

"What could be more sophisticated than classic French cooking?" Jay wanted to know.

"Jay, even the French don't eat French anymore."

He knew that. He kept up on the culinary trends. He secretly agreed with everything Cassandra said. But how to make a change, and make it fast, before he went under completely, that was the question.

"Of course there's another idea," Cassandra said, cradling her fingers around the glass, keeping her eyes intently on Jay, "but I doubt you'd be interested."

What did he have to lose by listening? "Talk to me," he said.

"Okay, look, you know how every other major city has a good gay restaurant? I mean *good*, upscale, none of this tacky glittery overdecorated queer-kitsch-crap. Good food, sophisticated atmosphere, and no straights. A romantic place for same-sexxers to bring a date, hold hands, kiss if they want to, and get a really good meal."

"Gays are always welcome at Chez Jay. I always give them the best table. This one, in fact."

"Yes, but it's still more straight than gay. I'm talking about reverse discrimination—a place more gay than straight."

"That's a pretty limited market."

"Is it?" she asked with a flirtatious smile. "You tell me. You're the one who's slept with every gay man in Portland."

Ho ho. Not anymore. Not since his cock went from hard kosher frank to mushy pickle. He hadn't been able to serve up a Famous Jay Hot Dog to anyone since the Chipper Johnson fiasco.

"You could have a special Trick Night," Cassandra said naughtily. "Everyone who's slept with Jay Zucker gets a ten percent discount. That ought to fill the place up."

He laughed, his sagging ego momentarily inflated.

"And cool weird-ohs, even if they were straight, could be thrown in for seasoning. You'd want a few straights around anyway, to titillate the queers, but not so many that the queers would stop feeling it was their place." She was matter-of-fact about it all, quite businesslike.

A gay restaurant. A built-in clientele. His personal cruising establishment. "Hmm."

"Make it good and they'll come back," Cassandra said. "Let go. Pull out the stops. Make it a nightclub, too, like in one of those Thirties movies. Dining as theatre. Cocktails after the show. A light late-night menu. Live music. Turn down the lights to induce romance."

"Keep the standards high, the prices moderate, the food fashionably light, and the bar well-stocked," Jay summarized.

She nodded eagerly.

"Outdo the straights. Show them how high-class queer can be."

"Yes," she said, her eyes glowing. "What do you think?"

Turn Chez Jay into an entirely gay fantasy? Leave the straight world behind? Walk into total queerness? Was he ready for that? It was his straightness, or so he he thought, that turned people on, men and women. If he turned Chez Jay gay he'd lose his best hetero-patrons and have to establish an entirely new clientele. He'd have to work double-hard at projecting his sexy come-back-and-see-me-again image, but that came naturally with success. He was feeling a little tattered now but it was essential to think positively. With a new winning proposition he could reclaim his title as Portland's most desirable gay heartthrob.

"You're amazing," he said.

She smiled and gazed into his dark, sexy, worried eyes.

▼ ▼ ▼

But what would Delmont think? Jay asked himself as he dressed for Peter and John-Don's Christmas party. Would he think it was a sound business proposition?

Delmont's dead, he reminded himself. He doesn't think anything. It's completely up to you.

So why not take the leap? Leave downtown. Leave straightsville. Move over to 23rd Avenue, the new westside hot spot just down the hill. Compete for the cool market. Show them what Jay Zucker was made of.

He pulled on a gray Italian sweater-shirt that accentuated his gym-trained muscles and hid the little roll of fat that had developed around his waist. Love handles—so where was the love? He tended to eat sweets in a crisis. And drink. Both were bad for the waistline. He'd worked so hard to recontour his body, find the form beneath the fat, that it would be nuts to revert back to the *verkokte* 250-pound Jay Zucker of yesterday. The new Chez Jay would *force* him to keep his body in shape.

Jay opened his bedroom window to test the temperature. Did he need a jacket? He stuck his head out and took a deep breath. It had stopped raining and the air was rich, moisture-laden, sweet as champagne. Then, of course, he had to have a look at Delmont's house.

He'd seen the Labonnes only once, that night at the restaurant, but hated them already. Their fucking moving van had crushed his curb. He couldn't tell a tree from a shrub so the destroyed camellia bushes he didn't care so much about. But for the curb, with its old horse-tethering rings, he'd developed a real fondness. And he'd be damned if he'd pay the city for the repair work when it was his neighbor's fault. Ito was in the same boat. The Labonnes refused to pay for his destroyed cypress tree.

Jay had gone over to complain and demand some kind of recompense. He rang the bell but darted away, frightened, when he heard a dog barking on the other side of the door. It sounded like a really big dog.

One other time, as Jay was driving to the restaurant, he passed Ron Labonne in his truck-camper. Jay tried to get Labonne's attention but the man stared stonily straight ahead and made a quick turn into his garage. Jay got the impression that Labonne was guiltily avoiding eye contact.

Bastards. Delmont's beautiful Queen Anne was already succumbing to their trashy standards. Rain-sodden boxes were heaped behind the house. Mud-caked mountain bikes were thrown down in the weedy garden. There was a long chain for the dog, which Jay had never actually seen, and a couple of dirty dog-food dishes outside the back door—an open invitation to scavenging rats and racoons. In front, the garage was often left open, revealing an unsightly accumulation of filing cabinets, house and yard machines, and unidentifiable junk. And, worst of all, the ludicrous Nativity scene was now set up on the front lawn.

There were no garish outdoor Christmas decorations in Queer Corners. No one strung colored lights in the camellia bushes, no one set up sleighs with flashing red-nosed reindeers, and certainly no one *ever* put up a plastic Nativity scene. The most you'd see was a tasteful pine-wreath tied with red ribbons on Carolyn and Susan's oak door.

Otherwise, in Queer Corners, decorating was considered an indoor sport. The richness, joy, and triumphant good taste of the season was discreetly displayed to the street from within. Through the sparkling windows, passersby could see and envy superbly decorated trees, glowing candles, and polished mantlepieces garlanded with pine boughs and holly.

▼ ▼ ▼

Which was just what everyone pulling up in front of the Mediterranean house on the other side of Skyview Boulevard saw.

"Doesn't it look beautiful?" Carolyn gushed. She and Susan had walked down to Peter and John-Don's with Wellfleet, stopping off first to visit Ito.

Yes, Wellfleet thought grumpily as they approached the enormous house: rich and beautiful. Full of rich beautiful people eating rich beautiful food. What am I doing here? He limped along behind Carolyn and Susan as they started up the walk. "It's not as beautiful as Delmont's house used to be, though."

They ignored him. "I love these!" Carolyn cried, stopping to admire the candles flickering in white glass globes on either side of the walk. "Such a lovely effect, isn't it, Susan?"

"Well, it diminishes the impact of that ghastly crèche across the street."

The three of them turned to look.

"Too hideous for words," Susan pronounced.

"Yes, all right, but some people like that sort of thing," Carolyn said.

Susan cast a stern eye on her lover. "How can you be so magnanimous in the face of such monstrously bad taste?"

"In front of Delmont's," Wellfleet added.

Susan shook her head. "Isn't it against the law, Wellfleet, to put religious scenes in public places?"

"That's not a public place," he said. "It's private. They can do any damn thing they want." He sighed. "If you think that's bad, you should see what they're doing at the college."

Susan was aghast when he told them about the "living manger" set up in the student commons. Every day he passed students dressed up as Mary, Joseph, the Three Wise Men, and shepherds, all posed in silent vigil over a doll. They were doing this round-the-clock, from now until Christmas. "You're joking," Susan sputtered. "I've never heard anything so ridiculous."

"And it's not even a Christian celebration," Carolyn said. "Christmas, I mean."

"Yes, Tittikins, we know. It's completely pagan. It used to be a solstice ceremony to honor the Great Mother Fucker."

"Susan!" She couldn't keep the hurt out of her voice. "You're so disrepectful sometimes. I don't make fun of your beliefs."

"That's because I don't have any," Susan said. She turned to Wellfleet. "Did you know that Carolyn's become a goddess-worshipper in her old age? She's been converted. Born again. Haven't you, pet?"

"You make it sound so fundamentalist," Carolyn said.

"You mean you're a witch?" Wellfleet asked.

"No," Carolyn said indignantly.

"She's not a witch," Susan teased. "She's a Wiccan. The Wiccan witch of the Northwest."

Wellfleet was puzzled. "Is that like a vegan?"

Susan let out an amused titter. "Darling, that's too droll. Wiccan is to witchhood what vegan is to vegetarianism."

"You don't know anything about it," Carolyn said testily.

"No, and I don't want to. I'm not going to keep you from flying off to your little Junior League Walpurgisnachts, but don't ever expect me to attend another one of your covens. I don't want to worship *anyone's* mother, Christian, pagan, or biological."

Carolyn was sorry now that she'd brought Susan to the last Great Mother Harvest Festival. But she'd become so infatuated with the Goddess Women that she wanted Susan to share in her newfound sense of spiritual empowerment. It was a disaster. "What in bloody hell are you all worshipping?" Susan impatiently asked during the ceremony. The rattles and bells became silent, the chanting ceased. "A giant vagina?"

No, Susan was not sympathetic. Her hard-edged rationality—that right-brained English upper-crust suspicion of sloppy emotions—didn't allow her to see the value of a group of women seeking to recover sacred feminine mysteries lost through centuries of patriarchal suppression. So Carolyn stopped talking about the Goddess Women. She was used to keeping secrets.

"Here comes Terry the Turd," Wellfleet said, nodding towards a thin dark figure crossing the street.

"Terry?" Susan let out a huff of surprise. "I know for a fact that Peter didn't invite him. Didn't want that wretched boy of his to ruin the party."

But Terry was alone. As they watched, he slipped in something and nearly lost his footing. He cursed and began wiping his shoe on Peter and John-Don's low brick retaining wall. "I wish you wouldn't let that dog of yours out to do its business on the street," he complained.

"What dog are you referring to, Terry?" Susan asked.

"Yours! There's dog doo-doo all over the street, all over my yard, everywhere."

"You must be mistaken, Terry," Susan said. "I never allow Lady Caroline to go outside unless Carolyn's with her and she's on a leash. Do I, Carolyn?"

Carolyn quickly shook her head. "Never."

"And Carolyn always picks up after Lady Caroline. She never leaves home without her pooper-scooper, do you, pet?"

"Well, something's crapping all over the place," Terry grumbled.

"Maybe it's that houseboy of yours," Wellfleet said.

Susan laughed. "Yes, isn't that what those holes in the back of his dirty jeans are for?"

"Very funny, ha ha." Terry irritably dragged his foot along the sidewalk. "These shoes happen to cost a fortune. They're Moroccan snakeskin." He eyed his neighbors suspiciously. "Why haven't you gone in yet?"

"Oh," Susan said, pretending to dig through her small, slim handbag. "we were just looking for our invitations."

"Invitations?" Terry said.

"One can't blame dear sweet Peter for wanting some kind of quality control. So many new invitees this year. He doesn't want just *anyone* barging in." She pulled a small card from her handbag and pretended to read it. "Yes, here it is. 'Please present this card for admittance.' You have yours, don't you, Terry?"

"I'm his neighbor," Terry said. "This is the yearly Christmas party, isn't it? He'll let me in without it."

"I certainly hope so," Susan said.

"We were just up visiting Ito," Wellfleet said. "That cousin of yours must be really crazy."

"Heartless," Susan said. "Utterly heartless."

"Why?" Terry glanced nervously towards Delmont's house. "What did she do?"

"You don't know?" Carolyn gasped.

"I've been in Palm Springs," Terry said. He was aghast and embarrassed when they told him about Ito's encounter with Cornette Labonne.

"I really think you ought to talk to that cousin of yours," Susan said. "Go over there right now and tell her this is unacceptable behavior in our neighborhood. She hasn't offered a word of apology. And that crèche has got to go. Really. It's disrepectful when she's got a Jewish neighbor on one side, an African-American across the street, and a witch just up the hill."

Terry shuddered. "I don't want anything to do with her."

Susan's face brightened as a sleek silver car roared up to the curb in front of the house.

"Oh, look, it's Flavia in her new Jag. I must go say hello."

"I'll go with you," Carolyn said.

"No, darling, you go ahead," Susan said, striding down the walk. "I'll make my entrance with Flavia."

Mortified, Carolyn stood and watched as Susan put out a hand to help slender, beautiful, and perennially chattering Flavia Billingsley from her chariot.

"I'm getting cold," Terry said with a little shiver. "I would have worn my mink, but I didn't want anyone to steal it." He patted his hair and darted up the stairs to ring the doorbell.

"Coming?" Wellfleet asked Carolyn.

"In a minute."

Wellfleet touched her on the arm and left. Carolyn heard the door open behind her. An excited rush of music, babbling voices, and the smell of food filled the air. She heard

Peter warmly welcoming Wellfleet. Heard Terry's whining voice: "My invitation must have been lost in the mail."

Another group of party-goers came laughing up the sidewalk. Then another. Carolyn stiffly moved aside so they could get past her. It was obviously the witching hour, the hour when the yearly Queer Corners party snapped into life.

You're going to have a good time, she commanded herself. You're going to be funny and charming and you're not going to be afraid to talk to anyone, not even that bitch Flavia Billingsley.

She turned away from the two figures locked in rapt conversation on the street. Glanced up at Peter and John-Don's Christmas tree, beautifully silhouetted in the living room window. Someone waved to her from the window. It was Cassandra Taylor. Carolyn, heart fluttering, waved back and joined the party.

▼ ▼ ▼

"It's called what again?" Betty Freeman tucked her platinum-blonde pageboy behind her ears and squinted at the objects laid out on the table.

"Kwanzaa," Peter said.

"Mel!" Betty called over her shoulder. "Come over and look at this!"

Mel Freeman, owner of Freeman Construction, left Cassandra's side and joined his wife and Peter. He was a trim sixtyish, like his wife, with thinning gray hair and a blunt face. The Freemans, who had known Delmont for years, were the richest people at the party.

"It's called Kwanzaa," Betty said.

"What is?"

"Tell him, Peter."

So Peter explained yet again, as he'd been doing all evening, the meaning of the African-American holiday celebrated from December 26 through January 1. "It's based on African harvest celebrations," he said. "They're called 'the first fruits' celebrations."

"Peter celebrates his heritage with all these pretty little doo-dads on this table," Betty said. "Isn't that interesting? Kind of a shrine."

"I suppose you could call it that," Peter said. He hoped they noticed that it was a designer's version of Kwanzaa, the objects chosen with the same meticulous care as his Christmas tree ornaments.

"So what do you believe in?" Mel asked. "What does all this stuff mean?"

"Well, Kwanzaa is really a cultural holiday," Peter explained. "It's not a religious one. It's based on seven principles, called the Nguzo Saba."

"Sort of like a Twelve Steps program," Betty said, eyeing the bowl of rum-drenched eggnog on the sideboard.

"I guess it is, in a way. The Nguzo Saba are regarded as the building blocks of African-American culture." He dutifully enumerated them, trying to figure out if Betty and Mel Freeman were truly interested or just being polite. Through the grapevine he'd heard that they'd recently bought a new house on the coast and were looking around for a suitable designer.

He told them about Umoja, Unity; Kujichagulia, Self-Determination; Ujima,

Collective Work and Responsibility; Ujamaa, Cooperative Economics; Nia, Purpose; Kuumba, Creativity; and Imani, Faith. He did not tell them what had gone through his mind as he ceremoniously laid out his Kwanzaa table that year. How estranged he'd felt from the very community he felt obligated to commemorate. Kwanzaa's first principle, Umoja, was about striving to maintain unity in the African community as a whole and in your birth family. It would have meant a whole lot more if he weren't black and gay.

"Oh, look, a Kwanzaa altar." It was Lorrie Latimer, marketing analyst. "I'm setting one up for my son this year. Maybe you can help me, Peter."

"For your son?" Mel said. He meant, but you're white.

"Yes, Mkeka, he's just turning eight. I was wondering, Peter, if you'd come over and have dinner with Mkeka and me one night. He hardly knows what an African-American looks like. I think it's sooo important to give him black role models."

"Happy to." Peter excused himself and waded back into the crowded living room, snatching a glass of champagne along the way. His experienced nose picked up a faint whiff of pot emanating from the waiter he'd hired from Chez Jay. Peter was instantly wafted back to his old San Francisco party-boy days. How strange it all seemed now. How shocked his guests from the rich, white, well-bred Portland hills would be if he ever told them about the famous "White Christmas Party" where the tree was decorated with cocaine-filled condoms. Even John-Don didn't know about some of Peter's wilder San Francisco escapades.

Thanks to John-Don he had escaped, moved on, reinvented himself, replacing the dead with the living. The party appeared to be a success. People were oohing and aahing over the house, traipsing upstairs and down, inspecting every nook and cranny, just as he'd hoped they would. He had nothing to fear on the design front. Everything was perfect. Delmont would be pleased—except for his shattered Christmas tree ornaments.

"*Gorgeous* tree," Winthrop Faraday hissed in passing. Squat little Winthrop, heir to the Faraday Ford car dealerships, was sipping champagne with Terry Terwilliger. "Where on earth did you find a Japanese cypress?"

"My lover brought it home for me," Peter said proudly.

"I don't know who your lover—"

Terry pointed across the room. "That one."

Winthrop looked from John-Don to Peter and back to John-Don. "That's your lover?" he whispered reverently.

Peter's heart blazed with love. "That's him."

"What do you think of my dishy new playmate, Winny?" Terry asked.

"You mean that dirty little hustler you dragged up from Palm Springs?"

"Billy's not a hustler," Terry huffed. "He's my houseboy."

"Well, your houseboy hit me up for spare change in front of Starbucks the other day," Winthrop said. "What's the matter, Terry? Aren't you paying him minimum wage?"

Bill Tinsdale, of the Tinsdale, Tinsdale, and Tinsdale law firm, plucked Peter's arm and drew him away. "I want your coffee table," he said fervently. "Memphis?"

Peter nodded.

"I want one." Bill slipped a business card into the pocket of Peter's jacket. "Call me next week. We'll talk."

"Peter!" A hand grabbed and whirled him around. It was Flavia Billingsley, thin, manic, and drop-dead gorgeous in a red, low-cut, Christian Lacroix evening gown. She'd just flown down from her inspection tour of the second floor, dragging Susan and Carolyn with her. "Where did you get it?"

"What?"

"You know what! That Betty Page pin-up in your guest bedroom."

"Oh, that. I've had it for ages."

"Sell it to me," Flavia implored, her eyes glittering, stroking the sleeve of Peter's cashmere jacket. "How much do you want? I'll write you a check this minute. Five hundred?"

"Flavia, honey, that's an original Betty Page print. It's not a limited edition, it's a one-of-a-kind."

"If you *ever* come across another one—" Before she could finish, Cassandra Taylor passed her line of vision. In her leather mini-jumpsuit, zippered up the front, Cassandra looked like a punkish version of Peggy Lipton in *The Mod Squad*. Flavia grabbed Susan's arm. "Who's that?"

" Cassandra, our neighbor," Susan said.

"She's an artist," Carolyn said. "I have one of her paintings."

Flavia leaned closer to Susan. "She's darling! Don't you find her extraordinarily attractive?"

"Adorable," Susan said, "but a little bit savage. Beautiful breasts, though."

"How do you know?" Flavia whispered.

"She showed them to me at Thanksgiving."

"To us," Carolyn reminded her.

"Yes, but it was really me she was trying to impress," Susan said.

"Well, you *were* close enough to lick them," Carolyn said.

Susan laughed. "Are we a jealous pet?"

Yes, she was jealous. She knew Susan's past reputation as a Doña Juana. Susan could be a stunningly heartless flirt when she felt like it. Susan hid nothing.

Cassandra wandered back, looking worried. "Have any of you seen Jay?"

▼ ▼ ▼

As he strolled up Skyview to Peter and John-Don's house, Jay slowed his pace to have a look at the Nativity scene. Some kind of primitive lighting effect had been set up behind the blue backdrop. The harsh light silhouetted the figures of Mary and Joseph hunched like praying mantises above a baby Jesus that looked as if it were doing stomach crunches in a messy nest of Astroturf. The figures, insultingly Aryan and historically incorrect, had the eerie blandness of smiling dolls.

Morons, Jay thought. The crèche absolutely ruined the tasteful holiday spirit of Queer Corners. He glanced over at John-Don and Peter's house. Lights on, tree visible, dressed-up figures passing back and forth in front of the windows, suppressed gusts of laughter and music. The street was packed with Mercedes, BMWs, Land Rovers and Cherokees. That's how Christmas in Queer Corners was supposed to be celebrated.

For Jay it was Hanukkah, of course. He didn't go to synagogue, didn't light a menorah, didn't really believe in God anymore, but memories of the old Hebrew rituals were embedded in his consciousness. He'd never connected to the Jewish community in Portland and found it easier to go along with the commercial flow of goyishe Christmasses.

A memory of Delmont's yearly wassail parties shot up through his mind like a bubble. And with it, a sharp dislocating tug of grief and that more recent sensation of aloneness. A lonely New York Jew under a vast Western sky, creating a destiny for himself.

He looked up at Delmont's house. Curtains drawn, no lights on, driveway empty, garage door closed. The plastic tableau with its blue backdrop could just as easily represent aliens from another planet as figures from a Christian myth.

A shadow suddenly rose behind the backdrop, blocking out the light. Jay couldn't make out the shape. What was it? That wild bobcat from Forest Park had been sighted again . . .

He stopped in his tracks as the head of an enormous black dog peered around Joseph's corner of the inverted wading pool.

Oy vey! Was it chained? No, the chain was in back. *Gott im Himmel!* His heart began to pound, an automatic pilot warming up to flight or fight.

The dog saw Jay. Jay watched in terror as it slowly lowered its massive head and fixed him with its black glowering eyes. It's lips rose in an ugly warning grimace. Long sharp incisors glowed in the light. It hated Jews, of that he was absurdly certain.

When Jay took a tiny step backwards the dog began to growl. A hungry menacing rumble vibrated deep in its throat.

What to do? If he moved it might attack. If he stood still it might attack. Don't show any fear. What a *verkokte* joke! His knees were mush, the blood had drained from his head, he was non-kosher dog food if the thing decided to rush him.

Without moving he frantically cast his eyes around for a weapon. Nothing. The only thing he could use was one of the Nativity figures, and they were plastic. Then, as he slowly backed up another step, he felt something hit against the heel of his shoe. A leftover branch from the limb that had been torn from Delmont's tree. But he'd have to move, reach down to get it. And right now that didn't seem like a very good idea.

Where were people when you needed them? They were all at a party, having a great time, and he'd had to do his usual Fashionably Late Entrance. "Someone come out, someone come out," he prayed. But no one came out and the music grew louder.

His worst dog nightmare come true. Grrrrrr. Rrrrrrr. The growl grew deeper as the dog, weirdly illuminated by the blue light, slowly moved out from behind the backdrop.

Huge. Grotesque. Some kind of hellhound cross with German Shepherd in it. Mean. Vicious. Don't faint. Whatever you do, don't pass out. "Nice doggie," he whispered, or tried to: his lips were glued to his dry gums.

The dog wasn't buying any of his sudden sycophancy. It lowered its massive head, swivelled its ears back, and crouched down, positioning itself for attack. Slobbering gasping snarls, like a motor being revved but not quite catching, came out between the growls. The dark targeting eyes were dead to human reason.

Jay could barely breathe. His sweater-shirt was soaked. His body felt stiff, awkward, indecisive. The cozily normal surroundings of Queer Corners suddenly morphed into a sinister landscape of inescapable terror. The almost solid wall of expensive cars and sports utility vehicles parked along the street was impossible to leap over or squeeze through. The weird blue light was like some terrifying detection device, a spotlight that had caught him in the middle of an escape.

Someone come out, please someone come out.

Laughter.

The dog was inching relentlessly closer. Jay stood paralyzed. He thought of his ancestors, thought of all the generations of ordinary hardworking Jews who'd been herded into submission by vicious Aryan dogs.

They both moved at the same time. As Jay lunged down to scoop up the branch the dog lunged for him.

Why couldn't he scream? Because he had to act as fast and decisively as a cornered animal.

He brought the branch down with all his might on the dog's head. He could feel it connect. The dog, caught midbark, choked and reeled to the side. Before Jay could raise his weapon again, the furious animal had raced to his other side. Blood oozed from a cut above its eye. Its mouth was foaming. It snapped at Jay's ankle. Jay squealed and jumped away. The dog's teeth missed his flesh but clamped down on his pants cuff, holding firm as a vice as it tried to shake him, pull him down.

He didn't think. He struck.

The animal gave a dazed yelp and retreated, tearing off a piece of his gray flannel trouser leg. The fabric, hooked on its fangs, hung out of its mouth like a hellish second tongue.

"Mess with me you fucking son of a bitch?" Now he was roaring, now it was his turn. He lifted the club and advanced on the beast. Slammed it down on the right-front paw. A high-pitched yelp. The dog turned tail and hobbled frantically away. "I'm going to kill you, you fucking son-of-a-fucking-bitch!"

But it was all show. He was so pumped up he didn't know what else to say. All he wanted was to get back home and call the police. The dog was whining and staring at him from a few yards away, ready to bolt.

Jay the victorious. Keeping his eye on the dog, he started backwards down the sharply sloping street. Tripped on an uneven piece of sidewalk. Fell backwards.

The dog immediately moved in for an attack. It was still fast, but now favored its battered paw and careened slightly as it raced towards him. Disequilibrium. Concussion maybe.

Jay scrabbled for the branch but couldn't pick it up fast enough. He literally shot into the air, propelled by twin-boosters of adrenalin and testosterone, and landed, on his feet, on the hood of a gray Mercedes. The crazed bleeding dog leapt too, but with its injured paw couldn't get a steady foothold. It slid off, its nails gouging the finish, and tried again.

Jay, scrabbling up to the roof of the car, let out a startled screech as the vehicle's ear-piercing alarm suddenly snapped on. Eeee-ah! Eeee-ah! The sound was deafening.

But it saved him. The dog was terrified and raced off down the street. And Jay, like a flood victim, stood on top of the Mercedes to await rescue.

▼ ▼ ▼

It wasn't jealousy over Susan and Flavia that prompted Carolyn to get conspicuously cozy with Cassandra and invite her to the next Great Mother Meeting. True, she'd ladled down more than a few cups of Peter's heavenly egg-nog by that time. She was finally feeling the joy of a good holiday party in beautiful surroundings. Exquisite food, nostalgic baby-and-gayby-boomer music ("I Saw Mommy Kissing Santa Claus"), an entertaining assortment of rich Hill People, straight and gay, who bought their clothes in New York and travelled regularly in Europe. It all flowed, once she left Susan and Flavia and wandered into the throng.

And Cassandra was certainly receptive when Carolyn, in the midst of all the noisy merrymaking, leaned over and whispered with rum on her breath that she sensed "a great soul" in the young woman.

"Yeah, I've been around the block a few times," Cassandra said, chewing furiously on a wad of gum to keep herself from smoking.

"I mean you have such an aura of independence," Carolyn said. "I admire that. You boogie to your own tune." She brushed crumbs from a buttery, calorie-laden pastry from the lacy front of her long, velvet, Victorian-looking dress.

"I'm looking for a lover just like everyone else," Cassandra informed her.

"Sweetie, why didn't you tell me? I know some *very* nice lesbians."

"It doesn't have to be a dyke necessarily."

"Oh? I thought—"

"Mostly, yes, but I have bisexual undertones."

"Oh." Carolyn nodded meaningfully. "Hmmm." She didn't know where to go with that one.

"When you were sexually active did you sleep with men?" Cassandra asked.

Oh, the sweet delicious ignorance of youth! Carolyn almost laughed. "Yes," she said, "I did. And FYI, I still am."

"FYI?"

"For your information. I still am. Sexually active." She looked around the crowded living room so she could, for Cassandra's benefit, cast a purringly adoring glance at Susan. But her glance turned steely when she saw Susan tit-to-tit in her endless tête-à-tête with Flavia Billingsley wearing that low-cut Christian Lacroix party dress. Oh my, weren't they laughing and having a good time! Carolyn cleared her throat and turned back to Cassandra, pressing her "saddlebag" against Cassandra's lithe leather-clad thigh.

"I'm sorry," Cassandra said. "That was stupid of me. In fact, I was just reading something about how sex gets better as you get older. When you lose that built-in worry of getting pregnant."

Carolyn didn't want to disillusion the poor thing. "Well, my dear, it all depends on how you channel your energy. Sex, you know, is just one part of the tapestry the Goddess weaves for us."

"Yeah, and money's the other part."

"No, sweetie, not necessarily. Love, respect, nurturing—they're all just as important as sex or a financially enhanced partner."

"Not when you're as poor and horny as I am," Cassandra sing-sang under her breath.

"Maybe if you were in touch with your Goddess it would be easier to integrate all the conflicts. The Goddess understands horniness. She understands all sides of a woman's nature because she *is* woman's nature. She's the original Ur-Frau."

"Great name for a perfume," Cassandra said. "What's it mean?"

"It means—" Carolyn sucked in a breath for inspiration. "It means that she is all and everything, your thoughts, your dreams, your body with all its mysteries. And you can boogie with her, sweetie. She'll never turn you down and she'll never stop dancing. That's what I was trying to convey when I wrote my poem about her."

Immediate youthful artistic admiration. "I didn't know you wrote poetry."

"Oh," Carolyn said with a little self-dismissive laugh, "a little. I dabble. For my own pleasure. This one was published in Good Goddess, the national newsletter of the Goddess Women." And closing her eyes she recited in a low quavering voice:

> *"Wild as the sea,*
> *She is you and me.*
> *Tall as the corn,*
> *she is forever born.*
> *Moist as a vagina,*
> *she is the wet Regina . . ."*

She was just getting into it when a shrieking car alarm went off and everyone ran outside to see poor Jay Zucker frantically waving his arms from the top of a Mercedes. What on earth—? Bits of the story were quickly relayed back to the party: Jay had been attacked by a huge dog, *their* dog, the neighbors-with-the-Nativity-scene's dog. Carolyn's head began to spin.

Cassandra ran out to Jay, took charge, led him home. They immediately called the police but the dog had disappeared and the owners were nowhere to be found. Jay couldn't, in fact, say with one-hundred percent certainty that the dog belonged to the Labonnes. He'd never seen it before. Neither had Carolyn. But she knew it was the same dog that had raped Lady Caroline.

▼ ▼ ▼

The event didn't actually ruin the party, but it did change the focus. Peter was livid.

He'd worked so hard and spent so much—two fucking grand—to make everything perfect. It was important, both for his neighbors and for his business, that he maintain the continuity of the holiday-party tradition established by Delmont. Everything was meant to be smooth, luxurious, soothing. His house and by extension Queer Corners itself was on display. There were very high standards to uphold. Anything that so much as hinted at danger or uncivilized, "lower-class" behavior would make the rich hill honkies who were his potential clients bolt.

And now, suddenly, people weren't looking at his house anymore. Instead, everyone wanted to know about the people who had bought Delmont's house. Word spread that white trash had moved into Queer Corners. It turned into a ghastly joke, but one that Peter, and the rest of his neighbors, did not find very funny.

▼ ▼ ▼

At Jay's furious insistence the Animal Complaints Division returned two days later to question the Labonnes, who had by then returned from a Christian retreat. Cornette, who answered the door, got off the hook by saying they didn't even have a dog.

Jay called her a liar. "If you don't have a dog, why are there dirty dog dishes outside your back door?"

"Gracious," Cornette said, "those dishes are for our bunny rabbits. Ron, that's my husband, just hasn't had time to build a rabbit hutch yet."

"What about the chain?" Jay bellowed. To prove his point, he led the inspectors behind the house. The long chain had disappeared.

There was no way to press charges. And since the Labonnes were so rarely seen outside their house, there was no way for anyone in Queer Corners to snub them.

The dog was obviously living on its own, prowling around Queer Corners in the dark dead of winter, gulping down garbage, pooping on lawns, turning even more feral than it already was. Jay told Carolyn he was going to shoot it if he ever saw it again. Carolyn, the dog lover, secretly hoped that he would.

CHAPTER 11

NOW IT WAS JANUARY, IT HADN'T STOPPED RAINING FOR DAYS, LADY Caroline was visibly enceinte, and the Goddess Women were going to meet and celebrate the parturition of a New Year. When the announcement arrived, Carolyn made a xerox, wrote a message on it, and slipped it under the door of Cassandra's carriage house.

"Dear Cassandra, I thought you might find this of interest. If you'd like to attend, please let me know. The Goddess Women would welcome your energy and artistry. Blessed Be! Carolyn Corbett."

It worked. Carolyn was going to pick up Cassandra at Chez Jay at four that afternoon and they were going to drive out to Jeanine Rotter's place on Skyline Drive for the "birthing ceremony." Jeanine, a transplant from Los Angeles, ran Holistic Wellness. In addition to being a channeler and a hypnotherapist, she did cellular repatterning, personal growth coaching, bodywork, crystal energy healing, intuitive readings, and conducted transformative rituals, ceremonies, and celebrations which she called Sacred Theatre. She had invited the Goddess Women to gather on what she called All-Mater Meadow, high atop the ridge that separated Portland from the western suburbs. It was her private property, ringed with century-old conifers, and had a sacred spring running through it. Jeanine had found a curious carved stone there, perhaps an ancient symbol of the sacred Raven Mother herself, which added to the revivalist thrill of the impending event.

Carolyn, fearing more derisive wisecracks about her "pagan pussy pow-wows," told Susan nothing about it. She simply had to accept the fact that Susan was not spiritual, had no desire for personal transformation, and was definitely not interested in Sacred Theatre.

But Carolyn was, and she was in a dither of anticipation. Thank God for the Goddess Women! They were helping Carolyn to reclaim her battered femininity and piece herself back together. They were healers. They fed her spiritual hunger, which grew more ravenous by the day. They helped her to connect to something wondrous and wise outside of her piddly, cowering, suppressed self.

The quest for the Goddess was a quest for communion with the deepest mysteries of womanhood. The Goddess was a tenderly maternal caregiver, connected to the earth and all living things. But she could also be a wild raging bitch. She could give vent to a matriarchal fury that made PMS seem like a pleasant tickle.

The furious side of the Goddess was rarely invoked in Jeanine's covey of Goddess Women. Sometimes Carolyn wished it would be. She identified with that side of the

All-Mater, that churning, hissing, bone-snapping rage. Maybe they all felt it. But the Goddess Women were too accustomed to accommodation, too eager to sooth and placate, ultimately too middle-class to vent their primitive Ur-Angst. They glossed over the Goddess's vengeful, volcanic, devouring, bloodsucking side and concentrated instead on her powerful, fertile benevolence.

It was a secret society, had to be. Sane and healthy as Goddess-worshipping was, husbands, lovers, and families weren't always inclined to be tolerant. Some of the braver members had bumper stickers that read "My Second Car is a Broom" or "Gaia Rights Now," but Carolyn was not one of them. She and most of her sister-acolytes were more interested in giving one another permission to feel their feminine power and connect to the umbilical cord of Life itself.

At the last minute Carolyn decided to bring Lady Caroline along. The poor little thing looked so confused now that she was pregnant. She avoided Susan, who rarely touched her except to palpate with tender relish the six walnut-sized lumps along Lady Carolyn's uterus, each worth five hundred bucks. Instead, she skittered along behind Carolyn, following her everywhere like a needy child, always whining and begging for extra food.

Carolyn was the one who stroked and comforted. She was also a pushover. When Lady Caroline sniffed at the tofu Carolyn offered, pulling back and staring up at her with mortified disdain, she knew her sympathetic mistress—the one with the red hair, not the other one—would crumble up one of those chocolate-covered dog biscuits hidden in a top cupboaard and offer her that instead.

The dog was so listless. The feminine energy of a Goddess Gathering might do her some good. Susan said Lady Caroline needed more exercise, but of course never took her out for a walk herself. Maybe the Goddess Women could do a chant for Lady Caroline's impending whelping. As it was, Carolyn prayed to the Goddess every day that the puppies would be purebred Ruby English and not a cross with the Labonnes' vicious mongrel. How would she explain that to Susan?

Ugh, dark all day for days on end. So dark you had to turn the lights on in the morning. The outdoor sensor lights blinked on at noon. The rain sounded like bacon endlessly sputtering and hissing in a pan. Carolyn couldn't help it, it depressed her. Made her feel like a soporific moth spun into a dense dripping green cocoon. Made her want to hibernate beneath a ton of heavy quilts. Susan, who adhered to the staunch British precept that there was no such thing as bad weather, only inappropriate clothing, kept the thermostat at a bracing 64 degrees. Sometimes it was warmer outside than in Bilitis Cottage. As she soaked her body in a hot organic brew of vervaine and chamomile, Carolyn hoped that a boogie with the Goddess would zap some life into her.

Was it the herbal bath or the idea having a secret rendezvous with Cassandra, of inducting her into the sacred rites? Carolyn was already feeling excited. She was always sniffing around for new converts. She wanted the Portland chapter of the Goddess Women to grow, wanted to help spread the word and the esprit de corps of the Goddess. The Goddess Women were mostly college-educated, professionally established, and rather well off. Cassandra was none of the above. But Carolyn didn't want to be a snob about it. Cassandra had the fierce, fearless imagination of an artist. She had the raw, untrammeled energy of young womanhood. She wasn't afraid to pierce her body or stamp it with tattoos, including one of Gaia. That was Carolyn's first clue that Cassandra might be sympathetic and receptive.

Carolyn finished pleating the tiny bells into her hair, dug out her rattle and beribboned tambourine, went through the lines of the new poem she was going to recite once the Furies had taken possession of her. She slipped into her waterproof poncho and coveted British Wellingtons (made in Taiwan), tenderly picked up Lady Caroline, and headed out to her mustard-yellow Volvo station wagon. When the wind blew, her hair gave off magical little chiming sounds. She felt on the verge of wildness. Receptive to the call of the Goddess.

The sky cleared as she backed down Santavista Terrace to Skyview. The golden beak of the Raven Mother seemed to rip through the thick suet of clouds, sending down a glowing shower of light. For a moment the earth preened and glistened. The evergreens throbbed, each leaf and needle sharply etched in the sparkling crystalline air. To think that this glorious light was always up there, hidden above the black winter stormclouds!

"Thank you, Goddess!" Carolyn shouted.

A minute later it was pouring. The golden light vanished as she turned onto Burnside from Skyview. Rain began to hammer down with sudden heart-pounding intensity. Lady Caroline, curled in her hamper in the back, began to whimper. "It's all right, darling. Don't be afraid." Carolyn turned on her lights and switched the wipers to high. "Mummy's here."

Then it was sleet. Fat slushy gobs smacked against her windshield. Burnside, a traffic corridor cut through a deep tree-lined canyon, was nearly deserted.

On the narrow sidewalk she saw a soaked young man in a denim jacket slogging miserably through the sleet. Mountain bikers occasionally raced along this stretch, but people on foot were rarely seen.

When the sleet became hail, battering like golf balls against Carolyn's windshield, she saw the young man pull his jacket up over his head and dash for cover beneath a thick overhang of ivy.

She never picked up hitchhikers. Never. But he was in danger.

She pulled over beside him and opened the passenger door. "Get in!"

He didn't move. There was a frightened look on his face as he crouched under the ivy, trying to deflect the stinging balls of hail. A cowering young man experiencing the full unabashed power of Mother Nature.

"Get in!" she called again. This time he heard her. Parted the thick curtain of ivy, squinted out at her, ran for the car.

She knew something was weird the moment he jumped in, but couldn't identify what it was. Danger? Fear? Not exactly. There was a prickly sensation at the back of her neck and deep down in her spine, as though an ancient reflex hidden in her body was automatically responding to some kind of powerful sensory stimuli. But what?

He turned once to look at her. The gawky, furtive glance of an acne-stained teenager. Their eyes met, just for a moment. Carolyn's unidentifiable emotion snapped into a higher gear. Her hairbells sent out a shiver of sound as she nervously shook her head. A warm tingling puddle of energy seemed to be spreading down her womb. The feeling was so intense she thought she might be wetting her pants.

"It's pretty wet out there," she said, cautiously starting off, squinting through the frenzied slap of the wiperblades.

"Yeah."

"I thought you might get hurt. This hail—look at it!"

It was frightening and awesome. The street was like the driving range at a demented golf course. Balls of hail popped, clinked, bounced and splattered in a thick whizzing sheet, thundering down on the roof of the Volvo.

"I never pick up hitchhikers," she gabbled, trying to latch onto and give a name to what was going on inside her. "But you looked so wet." *So sad, so dejected, so alone. With that awful military haircut that makes the top of your head look like a glistening red bristle brush. With sad beautiful blue eyes and pale red eyelashes hiding in your gruesome mask of acne.*

Carolyn knew the crippling self-conscious agony of severe acne. In high school, acne had been her sebaceous stigmata. Like her wet passenger, she'd had to maintain some belief in her inherent attractiveness even though the mirror reflected back a pizza-faced monster.

"You shouldn't," he said, forcing her out of her sympathetic revery.

"What's that?"

"Shouldn't. Pick up hitchhikers."

"Oh, I never do," she said, and felt his sudden glance. She kept her eyes straight ahead. He smelled like wet flannel and cigarettes. Her sheepskin car seat was soaked, but it needed a cleaning anyway.

"You picked *me* up," he said, his voice flat.

Trying to make small talk? Or moving onto something else, some horrifyingly violent sexual obsession that twisted *her* into the predator. His big hands, red with cold, were clamped tight on his knees. "It was hailing," she said.

"I don't usually take rides anyway," he said. "They always say it's the hitchhiker you gotta be scared of, but sometimes it's the other way round."

"Have you had some bad experience?" she asked and then bit her tongue. Ninny! Encouraging a total stranger, a male, possibly a maladjusted sex criminal, to reveal the very traumas that motivated him to strangle and eviscerate overweight 42-year-old women!

He didn't answer, just cleared his throat and stretched uncomfortably in his wet clothes.

Carolyn changed her tack. "What's your name?"

"Lester."

She could tell from the way he spat it out that he hated his name. "Well, hi, Lester. Do you live around here?"

"Yeah."

One of those rich privileged Hill Kids who loved to pretend they were poor? She'd recently seen one of her neighbor's daughters downtown, sitting on a sidewalk, begging passersby for change. "Where?" she asked.

"Skyview."

She turned to look at him, her hair chimes sending out a sudden splash of sound, and just as quickly turned back. "Where on Skyview?"

When he told her, she said nothing. Pasted a deflective smile on her face as the boy's identity click click clicked into place. Delmont's address. The Labonne son. The one Peter had seen dragged in a hammerlock to the garage by his father. His mother the heartless creep who wouldn't help Ito. Christian fundamentalists. The Nativity scene. Owners of the dog that had raped Lady Caroline and attacked Jay. Lester Labonne, her teenaged neighbor.

Had he seen her car parked up the street on Santavista? Did he know who she was? Should she tell him?

No, she wouldn't tell him.

But how silly to hold it against him. Especially if he was physically abused. Children in abusive homes were the hostages of their parents. She wanted to dislike and disavow him because of his parents, his blood-line. And intellectually she could, but physically she couldn't. *Couldn't.* Because the sensation in her womb was growing stronger. It felt like a warm sweet puddle rising and overflowing deep within, streaming out of her, joyously released from confinement.

"Get in touch with it, baby," she thought. "Go with the flow. The Goddess is sending a fax through your body." A golden glow of happiness suddenly, inexplicably, surged through her. The feeling was so mysterious, so intense, so expulsive, that she nearly wept.

"Huh?" Lester said.

"Nothing. Just taking a deep breath." Trying to keep from crying.

"I'll get out at the corner," he said as the Volvo reached the crest of the canyon and slowly headed down the slope towards 23rd Avenue.

"Are you sure? I'm going all the way downtown."

"Nah, this is good. Hail stopped."

Carolyn slowed down as the light at 23rd changed to red. Pulled up next to the Uptown Shopping Center. Sara Sue Seagull and her flock of ravenous realtors, Sissy Parker among them, were housed across the street in an ugly new building topped by a giant blue seagull.

Lester searched for the door release. Carolyn wanted to say something to him before he left but couldn't find the words. What words? What did she want to acknowledge? His existence or her own?

"Thanks," the boy muttered.

That was all he said. He quickly got out but then ducked his head back in. Flashed a wan unpractised smile. Their eyes met again. She felt drawn into his essence, into some sad secret pocket of his soul. The light changed. He slammed the door. Carolyn pulled away with the queer feeling that she'd just seen a haunting reflection of herself.

CHAPTER 12

"WELL, CORNETTE, I WAS CERTAINLY SURPRISED WHEN I LEARNED THAT you were going to be my new neighbor." The understatement of the century.

"Yes, Terry, I'll bet you were."

Terry could hardly bear to look at her. Cornette, oblivious to understatement of any kind, was wearing an ill-conceived costume that made her look like a cross between a flamenco dancer, a clown, and a sci-fi queen. More ruffles than his bed-skirt. Polka dots below the waist mirrored above with shiny plastic discs. A wide red leather belt that matched her red high heels, her red fingernails, her red lipstick, and her wide-brimmed red hat. A tight bodice, more ruffles around the scooped neckline, and aeronautical shoulders that flared up like stiff pointed wings. Beneath the shadowy brim of her hat, hidden but industriously working like spiders under an eave, those frightening foot-long eyelashes.

"You're looking real fit," she said.

"So are you. That dress—it's indescribable."

The compliment revved her, got her motor going. She crossed her legs and excitedly leaned forward from the confines of her cousin's chintz-covered chair. "You like it? I call this my power dress."

"Power dress," he repeated numbly. Where had she picked up that awful term? Did she really think of herself as a "player"?

"My viewers absolutely loved it when I wore this dress!" she exclaimed. "So many cards and letters. On-air call-ins. I wasn't sure about it until then. I don't wear the hat on-air of course. It's only for social calls, personal appearances, and funerals."

Terry wondered what she considered this visit, at his invitation, to be. A little bit of each? My God but she'd become loud. She wasn't just speaking up because she knew he was a little hard of hearing. The silent mousy Cornette of his childhood memories now projected a brash confident voice souped-up with the emotional fervor of a preacher. "Can I get you a drink?" he asked.

"Satan's cider, no thank you, sir! But you go ahead, Terry—if you feel the need."

"Me? Heavens no, I hardly touch the stuff," he lied. "I thought we could have tea. Unless it's against your religion or something."

"Why, noooo. A little tea party with my cousin Terry would be simply loverly." When he left the room she called after him: "You always did enjoy playing tea party. I still remember that cute little china tea set you had—the one you'd never let me use."

No answer. Cornette took advantage of her cousin's absence by quickly getting up and snooping around his living room. She'd deliberately not worn noisy jewelry for this very purpose. The room was as tasteful as a magazine, but what would you call the style? Chintz, Oriental rugs, a massive glass-topped coffee table, big gloomy paintings, fragile side tables with curved legs and expensive-looking lamps, all of it presided over by a huge idealized portrait of Terrence Terwilliger III above the fireplace. Not a protective plastic furniture cover in sight. No sign of children. The Lord nowhere to be seen.

Strange little treasures everywhere, sitting on tables, on bookshelves, on the mantlepiece. Terry had always been a collector. He must have inherited them. Some of the objects Cornette vaguely remembered from her awful childhood visits to the awful Portland Terwilligers. "Don't touch anything!" was always her first greeting.

She headed silently towards the built-in mahogany bookcase. No Bible. She scanned the books for incriminating titles, but since she hadn't read anything since high school she didn't exactly know what she was looking for. It wasn't likely that he'd have the two perverted children's books—*Molly Has Two Mummys* and *Two Daddies for Dickie*—whose titles were burned into her consciousness.

Trying to read the titles and induce the contents made her head swim, so Cornette cast her eyes elsewhere along the shelves. She saw a little statue. A little nude statue. Of a boy. *Don't touch anything*, said the frigidly contemptuous voice of her Aunt Irene, Terry's mother. Cornette picked up the statue for a closer look.

"Michaelangelo's David," Terry said from behind her.

She whirled around, dropping the statue. "Oh, gracious Terry, you frightened me! I was just looking—" And as she guiltily crouched down to retrieve the unbroken statue she was that little girl again. Wandering around barefoot, like a scrawny chicken, through the big dark treasure-filled rooms of the Terwilliger's house in Portland Heights. Told not to touch so often that the taboo became an obsession. Her fingers quick to grab and fondle, her sense of trespass heart-poundingly acute. Cornette, from *that* side of the family, daughter of Cameron, the bad sheep of the Terwilliger clan, and Pearline, his manic-depressive wife, caught doing what she had been warned never to do: touch. And all she wanted was to look, to have some little piece of it for herself.

She stared distastefully down at the nude figure in her hand. "What did you say this was?"

Terry took the statue and put it back on the shelf. "I said it's the David by Michaelangelo." Cornette tilted her head back and gave him a blank, expectant, slightly accusatory look. "One of the world's greatest artists."

"Ohhh," she said dubiously. "Well, if that's the sort of thing that people call art nowadays it's a good thing Mr. Helms is getting rid of all those grants for it."

Stupid as ever. Culturally illiterate. No way to connect with her. No desire to. "The original's in Florence," Terry said.

"Florence on the Oregon coast?"

"Florence in Italy. The original's about ten feet high."

"Have you travelled in It'ly?" she asked, regaining her conversational composure. With a practiced shimmy she shook her ruffles back into place and tweaked up her fallen wings.

"Many times."

"You must be putting your trust fund to *educational* uses," Cornette said, smiling as she pretended to look around for the first time. "And into home decorating. Who does all this decorating? You never did get married so I know it's not your wife."

"I do everything myself," he said. Of course when he saw something he really liked he always got Delmont to buy it with his trade discount. That's what friends were for. And then he got Delmont to tell him where to put it. That's what decorators were for. With Delmont gone, he'd have to ask Peter Love to do it all for him, only he had a feeling that Peter wouldn't be quite so accommodating as Delmont.

"Well, you must have a woman's touch, then. Everything's just so pretty," Cornette marveled. "Is that an itty-bitty swimming pool out there on the terrace? You know, I just loved my big pool in Dallas." An above-ground tub of molded fiberglass donated to her during a Praise-a-thon by one of her elderly fans, "Tubby" C. Jackson. She'd thought "Tubby" was one of Lord's chosen, or at least suitable marriage material, until, after the installation of the pool, the old lecher suggested they take their clothes off and climb in so she could baptize him. She'd sent "Tubby" packing but kept his pool as a reminder that the Lord's generosity came in mysterious packages. She never used the pool herself, but Dove, her daughter, did, and got sick with a bacterial infection from the stagnant water. The Lord, speaking again. From then on the pool just sat there, the water evaporating down to a scummy green pond where cottonwoods took root.

"I like to swim," Terry said. "Keeps me fit." Actually, he just liked to sit beside it, drinking martinis and staring into the sparkling chlorinated water of the neighborhood's only pool. His real pleasure came not from using it himself but the satisfying reflection that no one else could.

"But I'll bet you didn't get that tan of yours here in Portland," Cornette said.

"No, Palm Springs."

"Ahhhh," she said, nodding knowingly. "So that's where you've been hiding."

Terry was tanner than usual. His skin, despite slatherings of Guerlaine's alarmingly expensive Issima rejuvenating hydrolastine Super Aqua Serum, looked like beef jerky. She was right: he had been hiding. He'd been avoiding Portland as much as possible since Cornette moved in. To think that his cousin—this particular cousin—was going to be his neighbor! It was mind-boggling. In the hot dehydrating air of Palm Springs he mulled over the situation. It couldn't have been chance that brought Cornette to the neighboring Queen Anne house on Skyview Boulevard. So if it wasn't chance, it was deliberate. A plan, a scheme of some kind.

Scheming, as Terry well knew, was part and parcel of being a Terwilliger.

The great Terwilliger department-store fortune would have been depleted long ago were it not for relentless financial manipulation. Shifting money here, reinvesting it there, dipping into this fund, setting up that one . . . Terry didn't have anything to do with those corporate investment strategies. He wasn't allowed to. He didn't know or particularly care how the Terwilliger money was made, only that he continued to receive the generous monthly checks that made his life so easy. Pay checks for the work of being a Terwilliger.

The disbursement and distribution of the Terwilliger wealth, now in its fourth generation, was a mysterious legal affair hedged about with codicils and subclauses that favored some Terwilligers and humiliated others. Terry's father, Terrence Two as he was called, had inherited the major portion of grandfather Terrence the First's fortune. Terrence Two's younger brother Cameron, Cornette's father, had received a much smaller amount.

This was just as it should be since Cameron, with his history of reckless alcoholic instability, had moved to Texarkana where he squandered what he had and spent what he didn't. Cameron was a sore loser. A loser, period. He'd bitterly contested his father's will and out of sheer spite tied up the entire fortune in endless expensive litigation. He'd made trips to Portland to threaten his ailing mother, who had her own fortune, and bully her into changing her will. But by that time the entire Terwilliger clan had broken up into warring factions. Everyone thought they deserved a piece of the pie.

Grandmother Helen was so sickened by her money-hungry children that she bypassed them entirely, setting up trust funds for her grandchildren, who quickly became as money-hungry as their elders. Terry's trust fund, which he'd been living off and reinvesting since he was twenty-one, came from Grandmother Helen. His father left him no more than a token pittance, just enough to signal his withering contempt for his son. Cornette had received a smaller portion of Grandmother Helen's matriarchal fortune.

For decades stories about Cornette and her ludicrous mishandling of a humble but respectable inheritance circulated among the Portland Terwilligers. Cornette invested in pyramid schemes: cosmetics, mink oil, God knows what. They all folded, of course, but she never grew any wiser. Cornette was like her father: she'd inherited the Terwilligers' propensity to drink, but none of their financial perspicacity. Completely gullible. She married some violent lout who got her to sink money into phony real-estate deals and then headed into the hills, his pockets stuffed with Terwilliger cash. Alone, with her daughter, Cornette found God, was born again, and sank what was left of her Terwilliger money into a cable-television show, *On-Air with Jesus*. Now she was here, next door, and Terry felt unaccountably threatened without knowing why.

"What brings you to Portland?" he asked.

Cornette was staring out at the thick syrup of January clouds. Her view of the city was better, but she rarely looked at it. Too greenly gloomy. She missed the scorching air-conditioned fluorescence of Dallas. "Well, you know I married again," she said.

"Yes, I heard. Whatever happened to your first—"

She cut him off at the pass. "And Ron—that's my husband—thought that Portland was just the perfect place for our new family ministry. It's the new power center, he said."

"Portland?"

"Why yes, Terry. Didn't you know that? This is where it's all happening right now. This is where there's going to be a new awakening. There's everything here. Resources. Easy media access. Ron said the people in Oregon are just ready and waiting for Christ to take over their lives and it has to start here, in Portland, and spread out."

She was going to ask him for money again. Just as she had five years ago. Terry steeled himself for his refusal. He could always feel impending changes in his financial barometic pressure in his bones. "So it's just a coincidence that you ended up next door to me?"

Cornette turned away with a smile. "If you believe in Jesus you don't believe in coincidence, Terry." She sniffed a bouquet of silk flowers. "When you have Jesus in your heart, Jesus leads the way. You haven't found Jesus, have you?"

He sighed. "So Jesus lead you to the house next door to mine?"

"Well, we were looking for a suitable location. Good schools for the kids. Dove, thank you for asking, is fourteen now, and Ron's Lester is seventeen. And then we needed something suitable for our—you know, our social standing."

Terry raised his dyed black eyebrows.

"Ron's already a very powerful force on the political scene here, you know. He's getting Senator Peckerwood to sponsor some important new legislation. We're already raising signatures. And of course people recognize me everywhere I go. So I had no idea where to look, all I knew was that it had to be special. And then I remembered your house. This house. You remember how I visited you here five years ago?"

Terry remained silent.

"My circumstances were so much different then, of course. Oh Lord, I was in need! I thought maybe my family would open their hearts to me."

"You don't mean hearts," Terry said stonily, "you mean pocketbooks."

"The way to the heart is through the pocketbook," she said. "And it wasn't my heart I was talking about. It was the hearts of all those needy souls crying out in the wilderness."

"Cornette, why should you expect me to give money to a right-wing cable-television show in Texas?"

"There you go, putting labels on everything! 'Right wing.' What the ding-dang does that mean? All I do is bring comfort. That's what the Lord asks me to do, Terry. Bring comfort and hope and firm moral guidelines to lost suffering souls from all walks of life. If you think believing in the word of God as it's expressed in Holy Scripture is right-wing, then you're no different from those godless flag-trampling liberals in Washington leading this country right down the gutter. Did you ever see my show?"

"No."

"Well, then, you wouldn't know that On-Air with Jesus just happened to be the most popular cable-access show in Dallas for its time period." She didn't mention that this was two a.m. "I cured a man of his stutter! I got a little pigeon-toed girl to walk straight again! It's right there on video if you don't believe me. I'm the one who started the whole idea of Praise-a-thons, which everyone copies now and I don't ask for a dime in royalties." Tears were starting to run down the gutterspouts of her eyelashes.

"If it was so popular, why did you have to come here for money to keep it going?" he said coolly.

"Oh, it wasn't just the show. I was in need, Terry. You don't know. And when you're in need, you think of family."

"I don't."

"No, because you got everything you needed from the Terwilligers."

Not everything. Love, he'd never gotten that from the Terwilligers. He'd realized early on that he and his brothers and sisters and cousins were little more than pawns in a cruel self-absorbed adult game revolving around money and power.

"There I was, without a pot to pee in, pardon my French." She fumbled in her red leather purse for a handkerchief. "I gave everything I had to the Lord. It wasn't for me that I wanted money, it was for Him. To continue His work, which is my work."

"Well, I believe in separation of church and estate," he said.

"It's hard for me to understand what you believe in, Terry. You always were so selfish with your things."

"No, I'm just careful," he said. "I can spot a scam a mile away."

The kitchen door slammed. Billy stormed in. "That fucking bitch Cassandra!" Wheeling into the living room, he saw Cornette and zipped his lip. Turned to Terry for an explanation.

"This is my cousin, Cornette," Terry said.

"I live right next door." Cornette rapidly scanned Billy's unkempt appearance, trying to place him in Terry's meticulous world. "And who might you be?"

"This is William Bird," Terry said.

"Are you a friend of Terry's?"

Terry answered for him. "He's my—uh—helper."

Cornette smiled. "Oh? I thought you did everything yourself. What does he help you with?"

"The house," Terry said. "The yard. And things."

"You mean a houseboy. I didn't know you could still find good white help. God knows I never could in Dallas."

Terry hustled Billy out of the living room before he could open his mouth again. "Go somewhere," he whispered.

"Where? I ain't got no money." Billy tried to peer around the kitchen door at Cornette but Terry blocked his view. "Issat the Jesus bitch?"

"Here." Terry drew ten dollars out of his wallet, thought better of it, and pulled out a five instead. "Go down to Twenty-third and have a latte or something."

"You mean walk?"

"I told you, you're not using the car. It cost me two grand to get those scratches repainted."

"That wasn't my fault," Billy whined. "Anyway, you said your insurance covered it. And you said you'd buy me a new car."

"I said a used car. Maybe."

Cornette, who'd been silently moving closer to the kitchen and had heard every word, peeked around the corner. "That tea—I can almost smell it. Oh, are you leaving, Mr. Bird? I don't want you to fly away on my account. I didn't interrupt anything, did I?"

"No, he was just leaving," Terry said, nudging the recalcitrant youth towards the door.

When Billy had gone Terry stirred the tea in his mother's silver teapot, arranged two thin china cups on one of her silver trays, and carried the tea service into the living room. Cake or cookies would only prolong Cornette's visit. He could feel her eyes on him, sense her feminine curiosity about Billy. Leonora had been the same way when she first met Billy. Instantly suspicious. Why? Just because Billy was forty years younger? "He seems to have the run of the place," Leonora had remarked disapprovingly.

"Well, here we are," Cornette said, twitching her stiff wings as she settled on the sofa. "Five years older, five years wiser, five years closer to that heavenly kingdom." She let out a contented sigh. "Just think, Terry, after all these years we're finally neighbors. Having real tea instead of pretend. A power tea for two."

He was dying to ask her how she and her husband got the money to buy Delmont's house. Ripped off her "ministry" no doubt. "One lump or two?"

"One, please." She laughed. "Gracious, I just remembered sitting with you when we were kids and having you ask me that very same question. And how I always said 'One, please' when I really wanted two."

"Why didn't you ask for two then?"

"I thought Auntie Irene would think it was selfish. She had such stiff notions about everything. Sort of made us feel like beggars when we came to visit." She paused, smiling. "You know what, Terry?"

"What?"

"I think I'll have two lumps." She perched forward on the edge of the sofa, knees touching, and accepted her cup.

He could still see the little girl in her. Behind that thick coat of make-up lurked the same obedient little numbskull terrified of doing wrong, cowed into submission by the sudden pounding rages of her father and the see-sawing emotions of her mother. When Cornette came to his parents' house she came as a despised hostage, and Terry treated her as such. Made fun of her, mocked her Texas twang and gawky, graceless ways.

"Go play with your cousin," his mother would bark, "but don't let her touch anything."

Little did they know. There was a whole secret world that the grown-ups, endlessly drinking and bickering downstairs, knew nothing about. There was the big closet under the stairs leading up to the third floor, for instance. Cornette was frightened of it, but Terry would coax her in, promising candy and cokes. She was so docile, so passive! Once he got her into that stuffy closet that smelled of camphor and old cardboard, he'd make her pull down her underpants. He'd do the same. "Touch it." And she would. "Lick it." And she would. Afterwards, when she'd ask for the candy or the coke, Terry would jeer at her for being so stupid. The only time he was nice to her was when he needed someone to play 'tea party' (up in his room so his father wouldn't yell at him).

He wondered if she remembered any of that.

She did. It was the feeling of dirtiness she remembered. Not just the dirtiness of what went on in the closet, but the dirtiness unfairly and so often ascribed to her that it took root at the deepest and most vulnerable level of her quavering adolescent self-perception. A poisonous seed, dumped into the pristine waters of innocent girlhood, taking root like those dirty invasive cottonwoods in the scum of her pool. Once she overheard Aunt Irene say, "That child belongs in a pigsty." Aunt Irene was forever making Cornette show her hands. "Go right upstairs and wash them and don't touch anything on the way, they're filthy." They weren't filthy, but Cornette came to believe they were. It was immaculate Terry who was really the dirty one.

If Terry's mother was suspicious, it was for a good reason. Expensive little curios were always missing from the house after the Texas Terwilligers packed into whatever beat-up luxury car they were driving and headed back south. "Pearline, Cameron,

Cornette—it could have been any one of them," his mother would rage. She never suspected that it might have been her own son.

"You must be doing pretty well now if you can afford that house next door," Terry said.

"The Lord's been generous. I suppose you knew the person who lived there before us?"

Terry nodded.

"Did he have a family?"

"No."

"Divorced?"

"No."

"Wife passed away?"

"No."

She looked chagrined. "Are you telling me that a bachelor, one single man all by himself, lived alone in that great big five-bedroom mansion?"

"Is that so hard to believe?"

"It just seems kind of queer. The realtor told us that this was a family neighborhood."

"Sissy Parker told you that?"

"She said, I quote, 'Everyone here's just like one big happy family.' I just assumed that went for our place, too. But come to think of it, I haven't seen one happy family, not one child, not one parent, not even what looks like a parent, since we moved in."

"People in the hills tend to keep to themselves," Terry said grandly. "We don't just drop in unannounced."

"In Dallas we always had a Welcome Wagon for new families, to help get them acquainted with all their neighbors."

"There are no Welcome Wagons in the hills," Terry said frostily.

"Well, maybe they're just a little overawed at the idea of Ron and Cornette moving into their neighborhood."

"I doubt it. We don't awe easily."

"I did meet that little Chinaman across the street," Cornette said.

"Ito? He's Japanese."

"Well whatever he is, he's not very polite."

"Ito happens to be the most famous landscape designer in Portland," he said.

Cornette cracked her cup down on its saucer. "Him? Oh Lord! The most famous, you say? The one who lives in the house on stilts? Well, I never. I guess I'd better go over and introduce myself to his wife then. I just hope she's more gracious than he is."

"He doesn't have a wife."

"What? Did she pass over? I know I would if I had to walk up all those stairs every day." With elaborate ladylike precision she sipped her tea again. "How about this person on the other side of us, Terry?"

"Jay Zucker?"

"He doesn't seem very friendly either."

"He's from New York."

She sipped and nodded. "That would explain it."

"Explain what?"

"His wild accusations. Hysterical! Says we let our dog run loose and terrorize people. We don't have a dog, Terry. We were temporarily taking care of a dog but it wasn't our dog. And this fellow from New York says we should pay him for a new curb, too. I never heard of such a thing."

"What, curbs?"

"Being so unChristianly to new neighbors! And I'd never even seen the man until he came over and started screaming and calling me a liar!"

"I think you saw him one night when you ate at his restaurant, Chez Jay." The night this whole unsettling change in Queer Corners first materialized.

She sucked in a breath. "He owns that darling little place with the yummy french fries? Oh Lord." She stared into some deep private revery. "Well maybe I should talk to his wife then. Or is he a bachelor, too?"

Terry nodded.

So did Cornette. Cleared her throat. "Mm-hm. And I suppose that colored boy I saw driving away from the house directly across the street from us one morning at eight a.m. in a luxury car works for the family that lives there?"

"No, that's Peter Love. It's his house."

"He owns it?" She was slack-jawed with amazement, her eyelashes beating furiously. "Well, you know I am not prejudiced but Sissy Parker could at least have mentioned there was a colored man in the neighborhood. I suppose his wife is a white girl."

"Doesn't have a wife."

"Lives there alone, I suppose, like the Japanese man and the restaurant-owner. And you."

"No, he shares the house with John-Don Webster."

A moment to ponder, to collect and transform her anger, then a bright red forgiving flash of smile. "Well, I can see I've got my work cut out for me. Once we get back on the air I'm going to have to start up my Christian singles dating service again. Introduce all you lonely single men to Christian single ladies."

Terry was mortified. "You mean you're going to start another show? Here in Portland? On television?"

"Why yes, that's part of the whole plan. Different format, though. More politically active. Using Christ's message to make a change in government. And more talk-showy. Ron and I are going to do it together. He's more the politics side, I'm more the prayer side."

The kitchen door opened. "Terry?" Cassandra's angry voice carried into the living room. "Terry, I've got to talk to you!" She barged in, saw Cornette, and stopped in her tracks. "Oh."

Cornette's eyelashes framed and locked on the young woman as if she were a target at the end of a firing range. Was it a girl? Dressed like a splattered housepainter? With a ring in her nose and a cap turned backwards on her head? The suspicious litany of questions that arose every time Cornette was confronted by something she couldn't immediately classify rose to an unspoken roar.

Terry didn't introduce Cassandra. "What's wrong?" he asked, using the coldly dismissive voice he reserved for store clerks.

"It's um—it's about him, you know, *him*, but maybe this isn't the right time to, um—but anyway I do have to talk to you about it, about him." She backed away, reduced to mush by the concerted artillery of their eyes. They were the same eyes, Terwilliger eyes, cold unimaginative eyes that saw nothing but what was in front of them and not even that.

"Who in God's name was that?" Cornette asked after Cassandra had left.

"She lives in my carriage house."

"You rent out your carriage house to someone who looks like that? Terry, she's got Satan written all over her. Did you see that ring in her nose? That's how they identify themselves. A devil-worshipper right next door!" The strain was too much, she had to get up, move, felt the compulsive need to pray, to scour the polluted air with the solvent of the Lord. "Oh Jesus!" she cried.

"Cornette, she's just an artist," Terry said.

"An *artist*! As if I couldn't guess. And what kind of art is she making, I'd like to know, up there in that carriage house of yours? Images of the Devil. Painting with blood from dead babies. Urinating on crosses. That's how they do it, and the U.S. government gives them money to encourage their mockery."

"She paints landscapes," Terry said, enjoying his cousin's discomfort.

Cornette's holy pilot light had been fed its gas and now snapped into flame. She was powerless to control it. Didn't want to control it because once the fire was lit, she started cooking. Seared by the hot flames of the Holy Spirit, basted with the juice of Jesus's blood, the love of God oozed out of her like fat dripping from a pig on a barbecue spit. When she was in this state nothing could stop her. Possession was nine-tenths of the law of Christ. The sad old confines of her personality, bruised by doubt and shadowed with guilt, vanished, burned away by God's exhilirating truth. No more filthy Cornette, no more frightened Cornette, no more despised Cornette.

And no more childish fear of her cousin Terry.

"Terry, I want you to pray with me," she cried.

"Now? It's three in the afternoon."

"Get down on your knees, offer yourself up to Him."

"Him who?"

"To Our Lord Jesus Christ. He loves you, Terry. I love you, too. I've forgiven you for all those violent sexual acts you forced me to perform. Oh Jesus. I've forgiven you for all the pain, suffering and confusion you brought me." Her eyes swam in a quivering pool of tears.

"I don't know what you're talking about," he said.

"Oh yes you do, Terry. You know. And you're going to be a prisoner of those sins for as long as you deny them."

It was grotesque, the sight of her in that dress, so agitated and emotionally uncontrolled. No different and no less frightening than the sight of his Aunt Pearline, Cornette's mother, in one of her sudden manic states. In the wink of an eye the sullen, silent, slack-jawed Pearline would disappear and a raging, hyperactive harpy would take her place, terrorizing the damply sedated emotions of the Portland Terwilligers.

"Don't you see now why the Lord brought me here?" Cornette cried, lifting her arms in exultation. "He brought me here, right here, right next door to you, Terry, so I could guide a member of my family into the arms of Christ. So I could reveal to you and everyone around you, all your neighbors, all your friends, the workings of Our Saviour Jesus Christ. And He's telling me, He's telling me, Terry, that you're going to help me with my mission. You're going to be there, right at my side, helping me. Redeemed as I was by the blood of Christ." Her face turned up in a glaze of rapture, oblivious to the tears now pouring out of her eyes and cutting a streaked, shining path down her cheeks.

"I can't help you, Cornette." No one but a psychiatrist could.

"Yes you can. You *can*, Terry, and you *will*. You'll see the light. You'll want to help. You'll want to introduce us to everyone in the hills, all your important friends, all the people who want to see Christ restored to His throne. You'll want to help us support our new ministry and everything it stands for. You'll want to help us with our new campaign to bring God back to government and government back to the people and the people back to God."

"No," he said, "I won't."

"Yes, yes, yes you will! Because I've forgiven you, Terry. The Lord says to forgive, to love the sinner no matter how great the sin. In my heart, where all those secrets've been hidden for all these years, I've forgiven you. I haven't told anyone because it was my shame, too. But now—"

His stomach turned over. "Now?"

"Now I may have to go public, Terry, to let the world know that you can survive the worst life has to offer and still end up a role model. Unburden myself so that others can do the same. Get everyone to pray with me, pray for you, pray for all the molesters and devil-worshippers who hold positions of power, so that they can be unmasked, and look into the forgiving eyes of Jesus Christ!"

His hair implants contracted, sending a tingling fuzz of sensation down his skull. His breath grew shallow. Warning. Terry: trapped. Terry: in danger. He looked blankly at his Rolex watch. "I have an appointment."

"Yes, you do, Terry. You have an appointment with the Lord. And I'm going to see to it that you keep it."

CHAPTER 13

FOR A WEEK WELLFLEET HADN'T DARED TO APPROACH THE TABLE, BUT it called to him like some unstoppable confrontation in a nightmare. The table, covered with leaflets, clipboards, and an enticing platter of cookies, was set up every day in the student commons. It was attracting considerable interest. Taped to the front of it was a banner that read "Christian Students for the ACA." An enlarged, airbrushed photograph of smiling Ron Labonne, the new trustee, greeted passing students and faculty. The table was usually manned by Mimi Strang and Tina Pedersen

Passing by, Wellfleet would see Mimi in earnest conversation with cookie-nibbling students. She fastidiously brushed crumbs from the table as she pointed to things in the leaflets and urged them to sign a petition of some kind. It wasn't until one afternoon when Tina sat alone at the table that Wellfleet summoned up the courage to find out what his former students were advocating.

Tina, shifting nervously in her chair and avoiding eye contact, was obviously embarrassed to see him. She'd dropped her private voice lessons with the lame excuse that she had too many other commitments. For a moment, Wellfleet felt his usual urge to humiliate and browbeat her into submission—all for her own good, of course.

"Hello, Tina," he said. "What are you up to?"

She smiled but wouldn't look at him. "Oh, well, we're collecting signatures for the ACA's new ballot measure." Her voice was a self-conscious mumble.

"So you're into politics now," Wellfleet said amiably, his eyes pulled towards the photograph of Ron Labonne. "What is this ballot measure?"

Tina handed him a leaflet. "This tells all about it."

Wellfleet scanned the paper. His eyes stumbled on certain words: bestiality, pedophilia, unnatural, abortion, homosexuality, sadomasochism, transvestism, perverse, classroom, school. There was some sort of linkage between them but his rational mind could not accept it. Nor could he accept the irrefutable fact that the words he saw blazing before him formed any part of the vocabulary used by the timid, sweet-natured, overweight farm girl from Yakima, Washington, sitting behind the table. None of them could possibly be in the lexicon of her virginal personal experience. So why would she spend her time worrying about perversions she knew nothing about?

Phrases leapt out at him: *there shall be no special class status, no special minority status, no quotas, no classification based on immoral behaviors, such behaviors are to be actively discouraged.*

He looked at Tina, tried to see her behind the wall of her enormous glasses. "Why don't you tell me what this is about?"

"It's all in the leaflet," she murmured.

"I can see that but I want you to tell me in your own words."

She licked her lips, tugged at her sweatshirt embroidered with a procession of smiling trunk-to-tail elephants. "Well, it's about right and wrong. Values. Values in the public schools and what kids are being taught."

He frowned. "You think homosexuality, abortion and transvestism are being taught in the public schools?"

"Well. Yes. I guess so. He says they are." She nodded in the direction of Ron Labonne's photograph.

"Were they taught to you in school?"

"No. I mean maybe. They could have been, and I didn't know it."

"Didn't know it?"

"Sometimes they plant suggestions," she said. "Hypnotize you."

He let out an exasperated sigh. "Tina, what's the point of all this?"

"The point?"

"The goal!" he snapped. "What are you trying to do?"

"We're trying to collect enough signatures to make this into a ballot measure that people can vote on. We're helping the ACA "

"Helping them what?"

"Helping them recover the morals of America," she blurted out. "Helping them bring God back into people's lives."

"Putting civil rights to the vote, is that what you're trying to do?"

"Yes. No. There shouldn't be any civil rights for certain people."

"What people?"

"The ones—the ones who do what's in the brochure."

He gave her a withering smile and reread the leaflet. "Mm-hm. I see. You're making your version of morality the basis for all civil rights. In other words, you're rewriting the Constitution."

"You're twisting around what it says." A hostile glow surfaced in her eyes.

"No, Tina, *you're* twisting around what the Constitution says."

She was visibly shocked when Wellfleet crumpled the paper and flung it down in contempt. He had just turned to leave when Fletcher Davis, a cup of coffee in his hand, casually sidled up to the table.

"Wailfleet, how are you today?"

"At the moment I'm completely disgusted," Wellfleet said, walking away. He idled at the nearby bulletin board, watching Fletcher out of the corner of his eye.

"What is this?" Fletcher said. He put down his coffee and stuffed a cookie into his mouth while he read a leaflet. "Amen, it's about time."

"Have another cookie, Mr. Davis," Tina said, pushing the plate towards him.

"I will, thank you kindly. Did you make these yourself?"

She nodded, blushing. "We're collecting signatures. Are you a registered voter in Oregon, Mr. Davis?"

"I most certainly am."

"Well, we're helping Mr. Labonne get this on a ballot measure."

"That man is gonna be a hero," Fletcher enthused. "He is going to go down in history as a great Christian leader." He scanned the list of signatures. "Didn't Mr. Stipple from my music department sign?"

"No," Tina whispered. "He said it was twisting around the Constitution."

"He did, did he? Well, the only Constitution I know is the Holy Bible."

"That's what Mr. Labonne says." With a look of triumph, Tina slid the clipboard towards him as Fletcher took out his pen and clicked it several times in anticipation of signing.

▼ ▼ ▼

They were closing in. It was too ridiculous, too frightening for words.

In his Catholic boyhood Wellfleet had thrilled to tales of the Christian martyrs. He felt their pain because he was often in pain himself. Much of his childhood was spent clamped into orthopedic devices that were like medieval instruments of torture. Pain, when offered up to God, was ennobling. Otherwise it was just pain, and all the more horrible for being meaningless.

In those lurid stories that had been circulating for two thousand years there was no question of who was right and who was wrong. The Christians, a persecuted minority defying the pagan politics of Rome, were the heroes. As a boy, Wellfleet put himself into their camp. He was ready to accept death without a fight. Tied to a stake in the Coliseum, he heard the roars of the hungry lions pacing back and forth in their subterranean lairs. Watched his fellow Christians as they were gored, slashed, burned, tortured for the insatiable amusement of the crowd. Waited stoically, armed with nothing more than faith in God, for his appointment with the executioner. Knew his reward for death was eternal life.

And now, by some ironical twist of fate, the historical continuum had doubled back and tied itself into a knot. The persecuted Christians had become the persecutors. The oppressed had become the oppressors. The victims were now the victimizers.

He didn't believe in their God. He was queer. His days were numbered.

Wellfleet had kept his sexual preferences so well-hidden for so many years that he was surprised he still had them. His homosexuality had always been a source of shame and embarrassment to him, another painful disfigurement to be carried through a life already weighted down with more than its share of burdens.

Maybe being queer—or his life in general—would have been tolerable if he was attractive, but he wasn't. He was ugly, and he knew it. He limped because one foot was slightly shorter than the other. His face, like his spine, was slightly crooked, and his compressed features looked as though they'd been squeezed in a vice. His hair was thin and oily. He had absolutely no interest in clothes. He'd found his one and only refuge in music, that sacred temple of art where his own outcast personality was subsumed and made irrelevant by the majestic genius of others. If he lost that, what was left?

In a world based on appearances, he wasn't even a runner-up. Sexual predators ignored him, avoided him, dismissed him, relegated him to some distant point in their peripheral vision. He was exiled to the darkest, remotest corner of the gay jungle, an outcast amongst outcasts, left to stare hungrily at the luscious, tantalizing fruits forever dangling beyond his reach. The only way he could find sex was to pay for it. That added a nice sordid fillip to his sub-zero self-esteem.

Which was why being fired from the last college where he taught still stuck like plaster in his craw. He was fired for being gay and he'd never even been able to enjoy his perversity!

His sexuality was never mentioned as a reason for dismissal, of course, but Wellfleet knew why he was ousted from the pack. He wasn't married, had no children, kept to himself, avoided the old boys' network. It happened so conveniently, just when he was coming up for tenure, so he'd had no legal recourse. The whole affair, and what it revealed to him, was as frightening as it was infuriating.

He'd taken the Portland job because no other offers came his way. In the wake of citizen-led tax revolts, schools nationwide had instituted fiscal slash-and-burn policies. Arts programs were always the first to go. Teaching jobs were scarce.

Some people were lucky. They fit in effortlessly, or adapted and disguised themselves so successfully that the world accepted them at face value. But Wellfleet, the ugly gimpy grumpy little queer, was a stranger to the world and always had been. Over the years he'd even become a stranger to himself. It wasn't until he moved to Queer Corners and met Delmont that he felt even a nominal attachment to other same-sexxers. Delmont became his first true gay friend.

Now, without Delmont, there was no one to help him strategize his defense against the advancing hordes. He was no longer the passive boy with a prayer on his lips and martyrdom in his heart. He wanted to fight back. But how? The forces working against him were overwhelming.

He tried to submerge the gut-grinding reality of his situation in the churning, impersonal waters of history. Tried to place his puny individual suffering in a larger context of shared, ongoing struggle. It was his only way of feeling less alone. But all he could see, in the sweeping flow of history, was that he and people like him had always been denied their life jackets. The water was full of drowned queers.

Alone with his dread. With that panicked sense that the waters were closing over his head and the end was near. Culture, always a tenuous and reviled commodity in America, was in its death throes. Rational discourse had given way to paranoid hysteria. Delmont would have understood. His house had always been a welcoming resort, an emotional spa where outcasts could drop their straight-world defenses and luxuriate in a queer bubble-bath.

"Love thy neighbor, darling," Delmont once said, "but never as much as yourself— or your Limoges china."

Good advice, but since Wellfleet found it impossible to love himself, he could hardly be expected to love his new neighbor. This particular neighbor, Ron Labonne, was his enemy. Wellfleet hated him even more than he hated himself.

CHAPTER 14

RUN, RUN, RUN. UP THE WINDING STREETS, ALONG THE RIDGE WITH ITS changing views of downtown, the Cascades, the Willamette River with its bridges, ships and grain elevators, past sedate old mansions and the garish new McMansions springing up everywhere a tree was left to be cut down.

Run, run, run. Breath steady, deep, smooth.

The houses fascinated John-Don. On his nightly runs up the hill and into Forest Park, he passed examples of every major style of American domestic architecture in the last seventy years. All of them uniquely adapted to the steep terrain, all of them in mint condition, all of them charter members of the Northwest Order of the WASP: two immaculate foreign cars in every garage, a Brink's Security System sign on the front lawn, an imported woven-willow or pine-bough wreath on the door, two-wheeled garbage containers neatly aligned at curbside next to the neatly sorted recyclables in their special yellow bins.

Run, run, run. Calves starting to tingle. Sweat on the brow.

He hated the McMansions but felt an affinity for the old houses because he'd grown up in an old house himself, over on the east side. Nothing so grand as a house on the hill, of course, but exuding its own mesmerizing, working-class, emotional tug. John-Don liked the hauntedness of old houses, the way they were storehouses of lives and emotions played out generation after generation against a changing backdrop of social history. Over time, starting with Delmont's Queen Anne, the houses in Queer Corners had accrued their own special hopes, dreams, and aspirations. He and Peter would add the emotional content of their lives to the house they shared, just as the family before them had left theirs. All part of the continuum.

Run, run, run. Filling his lungs with clean, cool air saturated with the smell of earth and trees. Leaping over a puddle just for the hell of it.

Paradise! That's what Portland was to him. It took him fifteen minutes to get from his front door to the traiihead for Forest Park, and he had a view of the entire city and its surrounding landscape along the way. He loved the place and had never wanted to live anywhere else. Of course moving to the hill with Peter had given him a whole new outlook on the city of his birth. He'd never imagined himself living amongst such wealth. Or with a man like Peter, for that matter.

He felt blessed, loved, extraordinarily healthy, privileged to be alive, a little guilty that he was sometimes so happy in such beautiful surroundings when so many were not.

He'd also come to appreciate the subversive irony of having a black lover wealthier than he was and living as an interracial gay couple on the all-white and predominately heterosexual hill. Queer Corners was proof that gay America, disenfranchised in so many ways, could at least partake in one aspect of the American Dream. Economics, unfortunately, was the key to assimilation. In a capitalist market economy gays would never be taken seriously until heterosexuals realized how much money-power homosexuals wielded as a group. And conversely, gays would never garner the political clout they needed to win full equal rights until they made their economic power known. In the end, all Americans respected was money.

John-Don lifted his arms as he ran, stretching out the tensions of the day. He was doing a four-miler tonight. There was just enough time before the sun set and the forest trails became too dark to see.

His pace was easy as he headed down Cumberland Terrace towards the trail that began at the end of the street.

Then he was in the forest, with the wind hissing high overhead in the firs and cedars. Darkness was being sucked down into the understory of alder, maple, and stunted hemlock. There was just enough ebbing light to see the dark red berries of the native hollies and the glistening green shag of moss on the tree trunks. Sword ferns everywhere, row upon row, tier upon tier, hardy, primitive colonizers that hid the old scars of logging. John-Don spread his nostrils to take in more of the dense wet woody smell.

The trail threaded along the side of the hill for about a quarter-mile before the first switchback. That was where his run really began. For the next mile or so it was all uphill.

Endurance. Stamina. The ancient endorphic high of the athlete in complete physical control of his body. Pushing beyond the limits. Working with himself and against himself. Unable to stop until the goal was reached.

The trail, as usual, was deserted. It never ceased to amaze John-Don how few people used the park. He liked it that way. A seven-mile-long living, breathing semi-wilderness right in the middle of the city and fifteen minutes from the overly designed environs of Queer Corners. His theory was that most people were basically afraid of nature. Hated it, in fact, because it was so alien and abstract from their techno-pumped version of reality. They couldn't see the forest, only the price-tags on the trees. But for John-Don, entering the forest was like entering a vast but familiar old house, where a second generation was carrying on the traditions of the original inhabitants.

Its primeval virginity was gone but it was still a dense "working" forest. As recently as a year ago a bear had terrorized an unsuspecting hiker. Mountain lions had been spotted, had even prowled down into the nearby residential streets to hunt fat housecats. Red and Douglas squirrels chittered and scrambled in the conifers, enormous raccoons trundled through the ferns and ivy, red-tailed hawks soared on the air currents above the forest canopy.

As he huffed to the end of one switchback and started up the next, John-Don heard a loud howl. Where? He didn't want to break his stride, but neither did he want to confront a hungry scavenging mountain lion or wild dog.

He heard the sound again, a low mournful baying that echoed from somewhere deep in the darkening brush. In pain? Separated from the pack? John-Don scanned the hillside and deep ravine ahead of him but saw nothing. He increased his speed by pushing himself harder than usual. Felt the tug of gravity in his knees and ankles.

The path wound up to the top of Imperial Heights, a thousand feet above the city, where he had to skirt around the panoramic grounds of Pittock Mansion, an enormous French Renaissance Revival house completed on the eve of World War I. The rich family that once lived in the place, and the harried servants who kept it going, had been replaced by a transient stream of tourists.

He wound past the gatehouse that had been turned into a summer tea shop and picked up the southern extension of the trail. All downhill now. Water from swollen underground streams seeped and trickled onto the path, creating oozy pockets of mud. It was almost dark. The wind was picking up. John-Don, wearing running shorts and a sleeveless t-shirt, felt the sudden, bracing change of temperature on his naked skin.

He slowed down and squelched his way around a soggy bend, keeping his eyes on the path. When he looked up he saw a young girl—or what he presumed to be a young girl—sitting on a fallen fir tree about a hundred yards in front of him, at a point where the trail split off in two different directions. She was bunched over like a rag doll, her blonde hair spilling down and nearly touching the muddy earth in front of her. Blue jeans, sneakers, a purple jacket that looked too thin for January.

Hearing him, she jerked her head up with a look of alarm. Their eyes met. He saw that she'd been crying. More than crying. Sobbing. Her face was puffy and red and miserable.

She leapt to her feet, wide-eyed with panic. John-Don smiled to reassure her that he meant no harm. But as he approached, she bolted down the path.

It happened to be the Wildwood Trail, the path he was taking. The girl evidently thought he was following her for when she looked back over her shoulder her face convulsed with terror. She ran on, flat-footed, uncertain of the path, clumsy with fear.

John-Don could have easily overtaken her, but he didn't want to frighten her any more than she already was. At the same time, he didn't want her to think that he was some kind of woodland predator. "Hey!" he called.

She ran on, slipping in the mud, scrambling to get her balance.

"Hey wait!" Maybe she was lost. What private teen-age anguish had driven her here in the first place? John-Don, who taught teenagers, who always made himself available to his students, knew first-hand the emotional nightmares that plagued her generation.

Now it was dark. He knew every twist and turn in the trail and could have run it blindfolded, but the girl, flailing her arms and gasping so loudly he could hear her, was in danger of hurting herself. She raced around a bend and he lost sight of her.

Okay, let her go. Let her live with this distorted memory of a sex-fiend chasing her through the forest when all he really wanted to do was help.

John-Don rounded the bend and nearly crashed into her. She'd slipped in a patch of mud and fallen. Stunned and silent, she sat beside a bank of sword ferns.

"Whoa!" He braked his downward descent and stood in front of her, panting, his breath puffing out in vaporous clouds. "What's wrong? Are you all right?"

She was terrified. Breathing hard, with difficulty. Stared up at him like a frightened animal caught in a trap. He could see the tears on her cheeks, the mucus running down from her nose like a trail of snail slime.

"Here, let me help you up." John-Don extended his hand.

That was when she screamed. Screamed so loud that his damp hair bristled.

"I just want to help you!" He reached forward and grasped her wrist to pull her up.

She screamed again. Screamed and screamed, the thin, horrible sound slicing through the night. Jerked her arm away and scrabbled frantically towards the bank of ferns.

And there, in the dark forest, John-Don suddenly feared—what? Someone hearing the scream and running in and seeing him looming over her, misinterpreting his actions, turning him into a sweating pervert menacing a young girl. "Be quiet!" he said. "I only want to—"

But as he leaned towards her she screamed again and began shaking her head back and forth. John-Don wondered if she was insane or on drugs. There was no way to break through to her trust. She screamed as if she couldn't stop, as if she didn't know any other way to communicate. It was frightening. It was dangerous.

He turned and walked away. Left her there, screaming in the sword ferns. Picked up his pace. Wanted to get away from that pathetic hysteria. Hoped no one would see him. Began to run. Ran the rest of the way in the dark, urged on by his desire to escape that accusing sound.

▼ ▼ ▼

Dove Labonne stopped screaming when the man ran away. She was safe—for the moment.

Scared, covered with mud, alone in a forest darker than any in a fairy tale, she shakily got to her feet and tried to frame a prayer of thanks.

But couldn't. She was too overwhelmed, and when she was overwhelmed she couldn't think straight. After one of her fits—her mother called them "tornadoes"—it generally took about three hours before her emotions slipped back into place and everything was neat and tidy again.

But now the trouble was, even if things slipped back into place they would still be awful. Disordered. Unkempt. Frightening. Like this ugly forest. She hadn't escaped anything. She still had to go back to that house, in this new city, return to her new stepbrother and her new stepfather and the mother who had become a stranger, who no longer took Dove's side, who seemed to give all her attention to the two strangers they now lived with. She had to go back to a life with no friends, to that snotty new school where they were already laughing at her.

She began to cry. A black cloud of hopeless misery enveloped her. There was no-where to go where she wanted to be. She wished she could die, right there in the forest, have it all end. That would show them. It was all so unfair! She hated them—*hated* them—and that made her feel even worse because it meant she was cut off from God's grace.

Her soul was as black as tar, coated with hatred and fear. That's what it felt like. No one loved her. Well, God loved her, but then why wasn't He answering her prayers? And why couldn't she, no matter how hard she prayed, ever get back that feeling of closeness she used to have? Maybe she was praying for the wrong things and that made Him angry? But when she prayed that God would strike Ron and Lester Labonne dead, she knew that God understood her predicament and sympathized with her motives.

She was hungry and wanted to go home, but her old idea of home had been completely erased, leaving her with nothing more than a vague smudge as a memory. She thought of her stepbrother's angry, acne-covered face, of the smirking dangerous undercurrent he gave off like a bad smell. She heard her stepfather's harsh terrifying voice, barking out orders, demanding that she obey, criticizing everything she did no matter how well she did it. They hated her as much as she hated them. And her mother, sweeping everything under the rug, told her that she had to love them!

"You've got to make an effort, Dove," her mother kept saying. "A Christian family has to be harmonious. We have to set an example for others to follow."

"They're not my family!" she'd whimper. "They scare me."

"I don't want to hear you saying that anymore, young lady. They are your family. You should be proud and grateful to have a new daddy and an older brother."

Why? Just because she'd jumped at the chance to marry again? Her mother, before she quit drinking, once confessed that she was as lonely as a spider without a web. "A woman needs a husband and a girl needs a daddy and if there was any rich worthwhile Christian man within spitting distance I'd lasso him and drag him to the altar so fast his head'd spin."

Dove, who was terrified of spiders, didn't care for the spider and web analogy. She'd never known her real daddy and from what her mother said, they were both better off without him. She'd had her mother almost entirely to herself for most of her fourteen years and liked it that way.

So, she thought, did her mother. Because she took care of her mom just as her mom took care of her. She was a perfect daughter, a shining example, cleaning the messy house in a dreary subdivision of Dallas without being told, washing the dishes, mopping the floors, scrubbing the toilets, even shopping for food when her mom became too busy with her television show. Dove, the watchful, comforting, orderly, smiling daughter. When she broke down and had one of her "tornadoes" her mom would rock her, sing to her. When her mom broke down and hit the bottle and cried and said she was miserable and couldn't go on alone, Dove would rock her, sing to her. Together, they'd turn to the New Testament for help and consolation.

All that was gone now. Even the Bible had changed. Ron used it so differently. He emphasized the Old Testament, the parts about what you weren't supposed to do. Everything was about obeying.

For as long as Dove could remember her mom had warned her about how awful men were and yearned for one to make her life complete. And though she knew God had created woman to serve man, Dove selfishly prayed that her mom would never meet anyone. When it finally happened, when her mom went up to Oregon and met Ron, everything changed overnight, just as Dove had always feared it would. Now they both had to serve men and pretend that they liked it.

"He's the man of my dreams!" her mom gushed. "Dove, honey, you're gonna just love your new daddy." Her mom certainly did. Suddenly she had eyes for no one else. Certainly not for Dove, who was bumped out of the picture.

The crying jag ended. Dove blew her nose and tossed the tissue into the ferns. She was filthy, unbearably filthy, she'd never been so filthy and cold and hungry in her life. The mud was caked all over her freshly washed jeans, in her fingernails, on the sleeves of her jacket. She'd have to sneak up to her room via the back entry. That's what her life had turned into: sneaking around, trying to avoid them, trying to avoid everybody.

It was so dark. She wished Pharaoh was with her. She ached for Pharaoh, her protector, her friend, her one link to her old life. The dog had run away weeks ago but Dove was still determined to find and bring him home. That's why she was in the forest. No one else cared if Pharaoh ever came back.

Fighting back another wave of panic, she slowly started down the path. What if he was waiting for her—the tall man—waiting in the darkness ahead? Waiting to grab her, stuff a rag in her mouth, throw her to the ground and stick his thing in her . . .

She had to go home, but what would her mom say if she caught her coming in all dirty and dishevelled, having been out alone after dark? What would Ron say?

What would Dove say?

She'd tell the truth. She'd say she'd been out looking for Pharaoh and a man tried to attack her in the forest.

PART THREE

CHAPTER 15

IN THE HANDS OF THE LABONNES, DELMONT'S BEAUTIFUL QUEEN ANNE house seemed to be undergoing a malignant transformation. Soon after their arrival, thick rubber-backed curtains went up in all the windows. Permanently drawn, they lent a closed, suspicious, sinister air to the place.

"Honey, those people have obviously never heard of window treatments," Peter said to Susan Bark when he ran into her at Starbucks on 23rd. "They're still living in the Sears' Drape Age."

"At least we don't have to look at those huge, hideous lamps in their windows anymore," Susan said.

Even more offensive, they both agreed, was the clutter of junk spilling out from the front door and garage to form a trail of debris around the house.

It was hard to identify what, exactly, all this stuff was. It looked like the litter of a disorganized home handyman who started one project without completing or cleaning up after the last. It also had something to do with cars. Car parts, or what looked like car parts, were heaped about on the oil-stained driveway. Ron Labonne's wide, lumpy ass was sometimes seen protruding from the engine of whatever truck, camper, or car he was rooting around in.

Nobody in Queer Corners worked on their own cars. That's what auto dealerships and mechanics were for.

"It's bad enough having to look at those junk heaps they drive," Peter complained. "Now they're turning the place into a repair shop as well."

"Poor darling," Susan sympathized, "and you right across the street forced to *stare* at that mess. At least Corbett and I have some shrubs to shield us from the worst of it." She dumped three Sweet 'n Lows into her double-tall-flat-skinny vanilla latte, gave it a brisk whisk, and sucked up a bit of foam. "There must be some kind of law we could use to bring those idiots to task. Can't we get them on a code violation?"

Peter shook his head. "Bad taste is the price we pay for democracy."

"Yes," Susan agreed, "it's absolutely appalling. With enough money anyone can move in anywhere." And at one time, she remembered with a twinge of guilt, it was Peter Love himself that she'd objected to as a neighbor. The Labonnes had put that silly prejudice in a whole new perspective. "Of course I knew something like this would happen the moment I heard they were heterosexuals."

"Honey, there are other heterosexuals on the hill," Peter pointed out.

"Darling, they're everywhere," Susan said. "In the hills, in the dales, on the mountains and at the sea shore. And if *we* didn't set the standard I daresay they'd drag everything down to their level of mediocrity."

Just then Sissy Parker, fresh from showing a new high-end loft condominium, popped into Starbucks on her way back to Sarah Sue Seagull Realty. When she saw Peter and Susan, Sissy smiled and gave a tentative wave of her hand. They snubbed her with such vehement hostility that Sissy was forced to turn her appalled gaze to the pastry case for consolation.

The transformation of the stately Queen Anne continued.

"They're wrapping Delmont's house in Saran Wrap!" Peter cried one night when he returned home and saw the Labonnes' next phase of design heresy. "Look at that! Just look at it!" He stared in disbelief, his face stricken, his stomach roiling.

The Labonnes had stapled up plastic "storm windows."

John-Don had seen this kind of cheap insulation before. It was used a lot on the east side, in the lower-middle-class neighborhood where he came from. And though he vigorously applauded all attempts, however unaesthetic, to cut down on wasteful oil consumption by reducing energy loss, this was too depressing for a single clap. Suddenly those hand-blown panes of glass that lent such a charming, old-fashioned twinkle to Delmont's house were gone, hidden behind reflective sheets of plastic that sagged and rippled in the wind.

"I can't stand it!" Peter howled.

He howled even more when the painting began. Everyone in Queer Corners howled. The lovely, subdued, discreet exterior of the house, a combination of warm grays and muted greens with just a touch of ochre for accent, was blasted with a single insipid shade of baby blue. Delmont's house, which had blended in so pleasingly with the surrounding trees and garden, now stood out like a bassinette in a wood pile. Drifting paint blasts from the spray-gun had stained all the shrubs under the casements blue and left a powder-blue haze on the grass. The plastic storm windows puckered where the paint splattered them.

There was nothing anyone in Queer Corners could do because there was no civic legislation that applied to house colors. Galling and embarrassing as it was, they had to live with the fact that Delmont's regal Queen Anne had been stripped of all dignity and was now a cheap-looking commoner.

And then there was the noise.

Jay Zucker was awakened early one Saturday morning—a morning he'd specifically scheduled for some extra sleep—by the blasting drone of what turned out to be a leaf blower. Except for Jay, who avoided gardening altogether, the residents of Queer Corners always raked their leaves. Jay liked the pleasant, methodical scratch-scratch-scratch of a rake. It was natural. This was not. It was unbearable. More than that, it was pointless. Jay peered angrily out his front window and watched as Ron Labonne, lugging some heavy gizmo with a hose attachment, tried to blow up wet leaves from the sidewalk. They stuck, of course, so Labonne merely blew longer and louder.

Straight men and their toys, Jay thought. And why even bother with the leaves when the garden was becoming such a weed patch? The grass in front of the baby-blue house shot up in thick rank clumps. The garden beds, always so meticulously tended, were black and overgrown.

Another time it was the sputtering roar of a chain saw that shattered the early-morning peace of Queer Corners. The younger Labonne, perched precariously on a ladder, was slicing through limbs on the horse-chestnut tree while his father stood below him, yelling.

"Can they do that?" John-Don screamed as a huge arboreal arm came crashing down to the street. "I think we should we call the police. They're murdering a tree!"

Peter got nothing but a set of inapplicable options when he dialed the Portland police number.

Alarming as all these events were, they were, in comparison to what happened next, no more than pebbles tossed into the decorous pond of Queer Corners. In February the first rock was thrown.

▼ ▼ ▼

It was nothing more than a small story in the Religion and Ethics section of the Saturday paper, and Ito Kudomono was the first person in Queer Corners to read it.

Since it was still difficult for Ito to get up and down his stairs, John-Don had helped him rig up a basket on a long nylon cord that extended from the top landing of Ito's house down to his mailbox some sixty feet below. The papergirl obligingly put Ito's paper in the basket every morning, and Ito hauled it up soon after to read with his breakfast of herbal tea and rice cakes.

He leafed impatiently through the news—strife, scandal, murder, political chicanery, corporate deal-making, racist bombings in Germany, anger over Japan's refusal to open its markets. He paused in relief when he came to the marriage announcements. Two pages of smiling Caucasian couples about to tie the knot. Even the ugliest of them looked happy, which just went to show you that love could strike anyone at any time, regardless of genetic makeup.

It had struck Ito, too. But of course a photo of Ito and his beloved would never appear in the local press.

Ito smiled and chewed his rice cake, shifting slightly on his chair to ease the persistent throbbing ache in his lower back. Bedridden for almost a month after his fall, his spine was still whacked out of alignment. He had to walk as carefully as a fashion model balancing a book on her head. If he sat down too hard or rose too quickly or tried to turn to the side, a spurt of stinging breathless pain shot up from his coccyx to his jaw, sending his entire body into a spasm.

Woven into those frantic jolts of neurosensory pain was a memory of Cornette Labonne. Ito was convinced that she was responsible for blowing the final fuse that shut down his system. When she clapped her hands on his back, she'd transmitted the malevolent pain-karma that now pulsed and boiled in his spine.

Ito hated the pain, but recognized that it had also brought him great happiness. One joy dispels a hundred cares, as the proverb said.

He carefully rose and shuffled over to the windows that looked down onto the tiled roof of the Mediterranean house next door. Meditated. Exhaled pain and judgment. Inhaled the dark tender silence of an early Saturday morning before sunrise, the floating blue-gray mist that blurred outlines, the peace that was always so peculiarly alive to him at this hour.

Looking down at the house, he imagined John-Don's thick blonde hair mussed on the pillow. Imagined John-Don's lean, naked body under the blankets. Envisioned himself next to John-Don.

Ito had never had a lover. On a purely physical plane, he was, in fact, a virgin. On the spiritual plane, however, Ito's sexual history wasn't quite so simple.

In his thirties, at a time when he was intensely involved in his meditation practices, Ito had some strange experiences. He didn't know what to call them because they didn't fit in with the Zen notion of enlightenment through quiet detachment. They were, in essence, states of total rapture, when it felt as though his entire body was an open conduit for a powerful energy force that surged through every fiber of his being. It was like an orgasm, only there was no seminal discharge and no sexual object.

He'd experienced what he later discovered to be kundalini, a self-feeding objectless sexual energy that flowed up from the base of the spine to the third eye, flooding the soul with a bliss akin to madness. In yogic iconography it was pictured as a snake, and only the strongest and wisest of yogis could control it. Kundalini was so intense, so mind-altering, that the "real" world paled in comparison. That was kundalini's attraction and its danger.

After several unforgettable appearances, Ito's sexual-energy-snake gradually slipped back into its hiding place at the base of his spine. There it had lain, coiled and dormant, until his violent fall on the stairs.

It emerged again, transformed, in the midst of Ito's excruciating pain. This time, however, it had an object. This time he could identify it. It was not kundalini, it was sexual desire, and it was awakened and aroused by the touch of John-Don's hands.

After his accident, everyone in Queer Corners except for Terry Terwilliger and the Labonnes, had come to Ito's aid. He was both touched and appalled by their helpfulness. At first Ito hated the intrusion. He was accustomed to doing everything for himself. His house was a sanctuary, he was its celibate priest. But the truth was, in the first weeks after his fall he couldn't even get out of bed by himself.

Ignominious as it was to rely on his neighbors for help, Ito gradually got used to them. Jay Zucker and Cassandra brought him gourmet macrobiotic meals. Susan sat and pumped him for city-wide gardening gossip while Carolyn cleaned and did his laundry. Wellfleet drove him to the acupuncturist and Chinese herbalist. But it was John-Don that Ito waited for.

John-Don came over every evening to check on him. He shopped for Ito, ran errands, answered his phone, took messages, raked the gravel in Ito's Zen garden, watered his orchids, even cooked for him. When Mrs. Hill called to inquire about the status of her new garden, John-Don quietly explained to her what had happened.

"I'm real sorry to hear that," the ancient millionairess said, "but please tell Mr. Kudomono that we need to get going on my garden as soon as possible because Helen's threatening to have me declared incompetent."

As John-Don and Ito slowly got to know one another their friendship blossomed in a way it never had before. Ito dropped his habitual reserve. John-Don lost the awe that had always made him feel shy and awkward in Ito's presence. And once they started turning the soil of one another's personality, loosening the surface crust, they couldn't stop digging. Gradually they began to talk of the things that mattered most to them. Touched intimate nerves. Found that they shared an intense love of the natural world and an equally intense rage at the way it was systematically being destroyed.

One evening John-Don said, "Why don't you let me give you a massage?"

The idea of foreign hands on his body, of poisonous hands like Cornette Labonne's, touching him and disrupting the delicate vibrational balance of his body, made Ito wince. He respectfully declined.

"It might do you some good," John-Don said. "I wouldn't hurt you. I used to study massage, you know. Reiki and shiatsu, too."

Well, the acupuncture hadn't alleviated Ito's agony, nor had the Chinese herbs that gave his tea such a bitter aftertaste. Eventually he gave in.

The moment John-Don laid hands on him, Ito got an erection. He was on his stomach, so it didn't show. Now he got an erection just thinking about those strong tender stroking hands. Now he couldn't wait for John-Don's visits. Ito's serene emotional landscape had exploded. His peace was shattered.

He didn't know what to do about it because he'd never been in such a situation before. He couldn't graft his sexual desire onto John-Don. For one thing, Ito doubted that John-Don felt any reciprocal sexual attraction for him. For another, John-Don had a lover.

No matter what Ito did, no matter how often he detached himself through meditation, this physical desire for John-Don remained disconcertingly alive. Once it took hold it couldn't be uprooted. Ito could feel it coursing like sap through his veins, a mysterious, tumescent force welling up from the bowels of nature, from life itself. He'd devoted himself to making things grow and flower for others. Now it was his own life, a garden sprouting with so many weedy new emotions he couldn't name them all, that he had to tend.

With a sigh Ito returned to his rice cakes and the paper. Flipped the page to Religion and Ethics. They should have called it Christianity and Ethics, he thought, since no other religions were ever mentioned. He was about to turn to the gardening section when a small headline caught his eye: American Christian Alliance Seeks Protective Pro-Family Legislation.

The group, Ito read, was launching a grass-roots effort to collect signatures for a new ballot measure initiative called "The Non-Special Rights Status and Child Molestation Protection Act." Ron Labonne, director of the ACA, was quoted as saying, "This ballot measure is necessary if parents want to protect their children from the increasing power of homosexuals to make over society in their image. These vicious perverts are preying on the minds and bodies of our young."

In his agitation, Ito shifted too suddenly on his chair. He cried out in agony as the pain—a pain he could trace back to the moment he first saw the Labonnes' moving van running into his cypress tree—shot through him.

▾ ▾ ▾

The Non-Special Rights Status and Child Molestation Protection Act was a constitutional amendment intended to prohibit homosexuals from claiming "special rights" under the law. It would prevent them from teaching in public schools, it would ban all books with homosexual themes from public libraries, and it would deny public funds for any activity that "promoted or expressed approval" of homosexuality.

In the classroom, family values were to be promoted, abortion was to be considered murder, and homosexuality was to be condemned as a "deviant lifestyle" along with pedophilia, necrophilia, sado-masochism, transvestism, and bestiality. Employers and landlords were to be protected from prosecution for discrimination in the hiring and housing of homosexuals.

In order to get this constitutional amendment on the November ballot, the ACA had to collect signatures from six percent of the registered voters who had cast a ballot in Oregon's last gubernatorial election. That translated into roughly 97,000 people.

And in their zeal to get the voters behind them, the ACA volunteers started their state-wide grass-roots anti-gay-rights canvassing campaign right in Ron Labonne's neighborhood, which happened to be Queer Corners.

CAROLYN COULD ALWAYS TELL WHEN HER LOVER WAS UPSET. THERE WAS an emotional semiquaver in Susan's normally brusque voice that only Carolyn, with her long practice of eavesdropping on Susan's telephone conversations, could hear.

Susan was in her first-floor study just off the living room, talking long-distance to her father in Brighton, England. Her mother was gravely ill. Mrs. Bark had been bedridden with undiagnosable "feminine complaints" off and on for her entire life. According to Susan, who was just the opposite, her mum was an insatiable hypochondriac who regarded everything, including her menstrual cycle, as a debilitating disease. "She'd play up her bloody periods for every cramp they were worth," Susan complained. Even worse, Mrs. Bark tried to instill in her daughter's vagina the same sour resentment that inhabited and inhibited her own. Susan, so buoyantly physical, in love with hockey fields and hockey mistresses, refused to cooperate.

But this time it wasn't *une malade imaginaire* that had taken hold of Mrs. Bark's nether regions. It was ovarian cancer and the last operation had been unsuccessful in stopping its malignant advance into her lymph nodes.

"Daddy, stop crying!" Carolyn heard Susan say. "Tell me how long the doctors give her."

Sympathetic tears welled up in Carolyn's eyes. Rather than slurping them back in, as the stoical Susan always did, she put down her knitting and let her emotions flow out in a soft, snuffling exhalation. Poor Susan. Poor Mrs. Bark, too—even if she was a phantom. Carolyn had never met Susan's mother and, given Susan's exasperated descriptions of her, wasn't sure she wanted to. Now she'd never have the chance. It was too late.

And as in life, so in death: Carolyn knew she wouldn't be asked to stand beside Susan at the gravesite or to participate in any of the family grieving. She'd remain outside the emotional periphery of her lover's deepest and most difficult private moments, just as she always had.

It made her guiltily think of her own parents. Seventeen years earlier, when she'd run off and become a member of the Bruderschaft cult, she'd been forced to disavow them. She'd done this in a letter she now regarded as so monstrously cruel that she couldn't bear to think of it. When she came to her senses and escaped from the Bruderschaft it was, oddly enough, her family that she wanted. But it was impossible to go home. She was on the lam, a traitor to the revolution, totally paranoid that a fanatical cult member would catch and kill her. If she returned home, she'd put her parents in danger. Or so she believed.

When she moved to Portland Carolyn re-established telephone contact with them. Her parents begged to see her, but she said no, she couldn't face them. They sent money that allowed her to get a degree in library science and begin assembling a life for herself.

And then, suddenly, they were both dead, hit broadside by a semi on their way to Disney World. She didn't even know until a month later when she called and found their number had been disconnected. Her younger brother, when she reached him, was cold, to say the least. He sent Carolyn her share of the inheritance but made it clear he had no desire to see her.

She had no one left. She'd disconnected them all, even her son, who now wandered somewhere out of her reach. She had only Susan.

Carolyn softly called to Lady Caroline, wanting to comfort herself by giving the dog a pat and a kind word, but Lady Caroline, swollen to grotesque proportions, merely eyed her with exhausted chagrin from her new whelping basket.

Though she felt alienated from Susan's private life, the impending death of Susan's mother had brought Susan closer to her than ever before. Now it was Susan who was the needy one, the emotional one. It was Susan who, without being asked, came and rested her head in Carolyn's lap, let Carolyn brush her hair, curled up in Carolyn's arms at night. Carolyn the Comforter was thrilled with this unsought physical intimacy. She liked being the strong one. Susan hadn't been so vulnerable since the death of Byron, the ancient Sheltie she'd bought as a pup when she first came to America.

"Yes, daddy," she heard Susan say, "of course you can come and stay here with me afterwards. If that's what you really want, of course. But let's settle on a plan for now, darling."

Carolyn felt a chill run through her. The constant reconfiguration of life. Just when you thought you'd achieved a moment of stability, of repose, death banged on the door and sent all your emotional china crashing to the floor. Of course they'd talked of this, of the possibility that when Susan's mother died her father would come to spend some time with his only daughter. It was Susan's house, after all, paid for with the huge settlement she'd received from her divorce. But where did that leave Carolyn? What was her actual "status" in Susan's life?

Lately Carolyn had been pondering this question from various hypothetical angles. If she and Susan had been free to marry, for instance, and live their partnered life the way heterosexual couples did, Carolyn would have visited the Barks in Brighton long ago. She would have gotten to know them, become a part of the family. And, consequently, because she'd be a co-owner of the house, she wouldn't now feel so threatened by the idea of Reginald Bark, a total stranger, coming to stay with them for an indefinite period of time.

If love between two women was legal, and (somehow, miraculously) accepted by society, there'd be no need to explain or hide her relationship with Susan to Mr. Bark or anyone else. She'd feel secure in her own home because it would *be* her own home. She'd inhabit it with the firm, grounding status of spouse. Legally, as matters now stood, she floated around in an unattached state of limbo, relegated to the non-status of "roommate."

Such a small thing to ask for, really, and so infuriatingly unjust when you started to think about it. It was the age-old bind shared by all committed, same-sex lovers condemned by society for immoral promiscuity and then denied all means to legalize their relationship. Economic punishment meted out by the Establishment. And all because *they* didn't like it. Because it didn't fit in with *their* limited notions of love and family. In the end, of course, it was nothing more than sexual apartheid: blatant, time-honored discrimination based on a prejudiced notion of heterosexual superiority and entitlement. As though the ability to procreate gave you special economic rights and somehow made you a better person! As though there were some "official version" of life that everyone was supposed to adhere to!

The Goddess Women knew better. They knew the ancient foundations of authoritarian penocentric capitalist society were crumbling. They knew the male god was losing his hard-on. They knew the Goddess, clubbed unconscious by the patriarchy so many centuries ago, was reawakening after her long coma. It was just a matter of time before She reclaimed everything that had been stolen from her. But sometimes even a patient Goddess Woman got tired of waiting.

Carolyn's ego pricked up when she heard Susan speak her name.

"Caroline? She's fine."

And for one moment, Carolyn was fine. Elated. Susan was actually admitting Carolyn's existence to Mr. Bark. The Atlantic had been crossed. Carolyn was being allowed into the British Bark family. Or so she thought until Susan went on:

"No, she hasn't whelped yet."

Carolyn sighed and picked up her knitting, trying not to resent the dog resting in its pretty new basket.

"I'll settle things at the kennel this afternoon," Susan said from her study, "and then fly over straightaway. They have direct flights from Seattle now. No, darling, not Gatwick, Heathrow. The train connections are easier from there."

Susan was leaving. Right when Lady Caroline was ready to whelp.

The doorbell rang. Lady Caroline groaned, lifted her head, and let it drop again. Carolyn, peering cautiously through the living-room window, saw a man and a woman, clutching leaflets and clipboards, huddled under a dripping umbrella. Probably collecting money for some needy cause. Or religious fanatics. Lady Caroline let out an annoyed half-hearted bark when they rang again. The two strangers moved closer to the door and tried to peek in through the curtains.

Carolyn quickly opened the door, surprising them in the midst of their snoopy curiosity. Startled, the man and woman stepped back. Carolyn, fierce guardian of the household that wasn't hers, pulled her handknit cardigan tightly over her stomach, crossed her arms, and gave them a disapproving stare.

"Hello, ma'am, my name is John Davis and this here lady is Helen Hill," the man said. He was middle-aged and bony, a tall skeleton with thin lips, pale close-set eyes and close-cropped hair. "How are you on this rainy Oregon morning?"

"I'm rather busy at the moment," Carolyn said coldly.

"Well, we won't stand here and take up no more of your time than we got to, then. Let me just ask you this, ma'am: Are you a registered voter here in Oregon?"

She noted the ungrammatical double negative and wondered what they were after. "Yes."

"And did you vote in the last gurberna—gurverna—"

"Gubernatorial," prompted the woman.

"Thank you, Helen, my tongue seems to be half-froze today, gubernatorial election?"

Carolyn nodded. What was he leading up to?

"Now let me ask you this, ma'am: Do you believe in God?"

So that was it.

"No," she said. "I worship the Goddess."

She laughed inwardly at their consternation. The woman, as fat as the man was thin, with flabby jowls and a humorless face, eyed her with a gluey mixture of suspicion and disapproval. She was buckled into a navy-blue coat, wearing a white plastic rainhat and matching white plastic boots.

"Well, fine," the man said dubiously. "I'm not exactly sure what you mean by that, but—"

"But what?" Carolyn demanded, glowing with hot, confrontive Goddess power.

"Well, we understand the reverence you Catholics feel for Our Lord's mother," the man said placatingly, "and that's fine."

"I'm not a Catholic," Carolyn snapped, "and I don't care if you think it's fine or not."

Nervously shifting his weight from foot to foot, the man narrowed his eyes and stared at her for a moment before switching gears. "Well, whatever. What we come to do, ma'am, is collect your signature for an important new state constitutional amendment that we want on the November ballot."

"I like the constitution just the way it is, thank you," Carolyn said, stepping back inside. Before she could close the door the woman said in a loud, accusatory voice:

"Aren't you even concerned about the safety of your children?"

The question sliced into Carolyn like a scalpel, exposing her tenderest and most vulnerable secret. The source of the guilty pain that never went away.

"You do have children, don't you?" the woman said.

Carolyn didn't answer.

"You don't want them endangered by child molesters and sexual perverts, do you?"

"What are you talking about?" Carolyn asked in a faint voice.

"We're talking about all the homosexuals that teach their filth to our children," the woman said contemptuously. "They're in the schools, they're on the playgrounds, they're everywhere you turn, and now they're trying to get special rights to protect themselves and make everyone accept their disgusting lifestyle. They're trying to put themselves above the law of God."

The man took over. A tag-team. Hitler and Hitlerina. "The ACA, that's us, the American Christian Alliance, we're going to stop these perverts in their tracks. We've had enough of their corruption. We're gonna pertect our children. That's why we need your signature, so we can get our ballot measure to the voters. It's the Christian voters of Oregon, ma'am, who're going to lead the way. We're going to show the nation that we refuse to give special rights to degenerates."

Carolyn heard ordinary human voices unable to hide the anger and hostility that lay just below the surface of their lives. Voices trying to make contact with her not through common standards of decency and justice but through bigotry and fear. Trying to recruit her into their homophobic fold. Two gay-bashing strangers in her own home, and she couldn't even muster up the courage to tell them that she was one of the enemy.

"I'm sure you want to sign," the woman said with conspiratorial coziness, holding out her clipboard. "You're a mother, you know the danger your children are in. You believe in upholding Christian standards of decency, I'm sure."

"Get away from here," Carolyn said in a dull voice.

They stiffened but didn't move.

"Get away from my house!"

"Well, how about we just leave you some information," the man said, thrusting a leaflet into Carolyn's hand. "Look it over, ma'am, and you'll see how important this legislation is. You can send a donation if you want. It's your own neighbor, you know— Ron Labonne, lives right down there in the pretty blue house—that's head of the ACA. You should feel real proud to have a man of such strong Christian principles right here in your midst."

Carolyn slammed the door in their faces. A shudder ran through her. She looked out the window to see where they were headed next. Up Santavista Terrace towards Wellfleet's. She raced into the kitchen to call and warn him. Dialled. Heard Susan's peeved voice on the extension: "*Excuse* me, I'm using the telephone."

A querulous male voice with a high-pitched English accent said: "Who is it, Susan? Is there someone there with you? Do you want to ring me back?"

"No, daddy, it's just some interference on the line."

Carolyn quietly hung up, berating herself for disturbing Susan in the midst of her family crisis. Yet this was a crisis, too. She was furiously alert and aware, like a mother who realizes her children are in danger. Pumped full of protective adrenalin, ready to lift cars, swim icy rivers, climb mountains in order to save them. It translated into a need to warn her neighbors. But she couldn't. She had to be here for Susan. Susan's crisis took precedence over everything else.

Anxiously chewing her fingernails, a bad habit she thought she'd cured by taking up knitting, Carolyn returned to the living room. Her thoughts, rippling out from the point of impact, wouldn't settle.

Two ordinary-looking human beings out on a mission of persecution. Two anti-homo homo sapiens trying to collect signatures, in Queer Corners of all places, for a campaign of hate spearheaded by her own neighbor.

She'd met Lester, his teenage son, but Carolyn had never actually seen Ron Labonne. Delmont's house was just far enough away, and Carolyn's vision just near-sighted enough, to keep the faces of the new owners a blur. She was curious, of course, but once the house had been painted blue, she'd instinctually avoided looking in that direction. If she looked, she'd have to face the bitter galling truth: They'd absolutely ruined the neighborhood. They'd turned a beautiful house into a pigsty, an eyesore, a laughing-stock.

Definitely not people you wanted to get friendly with or encourage in any way.

Carolyn stared through the oriel window that looked down onto Skyview towards the house she'd been avoiding. There were two extra cars and a pickup parked outside of it.

Susan, her face unusually pale, her brisk stride reduced to a preoccupied shuffle, emerged from her study. Carolyn thought she was going to berate her for picking up the phone, but Susan came over and embraced her instead.

"I have to go, darling. They don't think she'll last more than a couple of days now.'"

Carolyn nodded, fighting back her tears. "What can I do to help?"

"Nothing, pet. Really."

"I want to help you," Carolyn croaked. "There must be something I can do."

"No, I can manage. I'm fine, really."

"Let me help you!" Carolyn began to sob. "You're my partner! I want to help you. You're all I have."

Susan drew back and looked at her. "Darling, what *is* the matter?"

"Nothing. I'm sorry. It's inappropriate."

"What is?"

Carolyn told her about the two strangers at the door and what they, with the backing of Ron Labonne, their new neighbor, were trying to do. Her voice rose in fury. She waved the orange leaflet she'd been carrying around. "They gave me this before I slammed the door in their stupid faces."

Susan scanned the pamphlet. "Unbelieveable. It's the same old rubbish as Section Twenty-eight."

"What's that?" Carolyn asked.

"The British Parliament passed a ridiculous act in 1988 to restrain local authorities and schools from 'promoting' homosexuality. This covers the same tired old territory."

"They did that in England?" Carolyn the romantic Anglophile was aghast. "I thought they were so civilized over there."

Susan sniffed. "They like to think so, too. It was that Tory cunt Thatcher, of course, and all the Conservative MPs hiding behind her skirts. Morons!" she spat. "The whole bloody country going down the tubes and all they can think of to do is pick on lesbians and gay men. Pathetic!"

"And it actually passed?"

"Yes, darling, it passed."

"What if it passes here?" Carolyn said anxiously.

"Darling, it won't."

"But it passed in England."

"Yes, love, but that's because no one hates sex more than the English. I'm surprised they haven't put a tax on it. Americans may be stupid and illiterate, but at least they don't hate sex."

"Of course we hate sex!" Carolyn cried. "We're Puritans, aren't we? From England?"

Susan, easily exasperated when she was short on time, glanced at the 19th-century French ormulu clock her father had given her as a wedding present. So much to do before she flew off to say a final goodbye to her mother. She didn't have time to soothe Carolyn's ruffled emotional feathers over some bloody queer-bashing crackpots. At the same time, she could see the agitated panic it had caused. Poor sweet darling, she thought: takes everything so personally.

Carolyn's mind was racing through the rapids of paranoia. "So if we're Puritans and we hate sex and we're from England where they passed the same kind of legislation," she said with breathless logic, "what's to prevent the people here from doing the same?"

"Oregon's a liberal state, darling." Susan kept her voice sternly calm, the way she did when handling a high-strung dog. "There are plenty of idiots and crackpots, of course, including our delightful new neighbor, but I can't believe there are enough of them to get this nonsense on the ballot. It's unconstitutional. The legislature will see that and throw it out." She crumpled up the leaflet. "We'll just put this in the rubbish, where it belongs, shall we?" She smiled and kissed Carolyn. "Now, love, I've got to get cracking and book my flight."

Carolyn calmed down. "I'll make some tea," she said.

"Yes, lovely. I'll have a small brandy as well."

Carolyn took the crumpled leaflet and headed into the kitchen.

"You will be all right, won't you, pet?" Susan called to her. Carolyn turned and saw her crouched over Lady Caroline's basket. The sight aroused a sweet flood of tenderness. "Yes, darling, I'll be fine."

"I know you're worried about Lady Caroline," Susan said, "but you do have the vet's number in case anything goes wrong."

Yes, there was that to contend with, too: the possibility that the purebred Ruby English pups Susan had already sold would turn out be worthless mongrels.

"I doubt it will, though," Susan said. "Our girl's a healthy little bitch, isn't she?" She stroked the swollen dog between its bulging eyes and gave her a final once-over. "Don't forget to massage her nipples with mineral oil, will you darling?"

"I won't forget."

"And make certain that she eats up all of her placenta, like a good little girl."

Carolyn shuddered at the thought. "I will." She tossed the ACA brochure into the bin under the sink but then thought better of it and fished it out again. Later, after she'd calmed down, she'd read it for herself. Annoying, but nowadays a citizen had to remain well-informed on all the poison circulating through the veins of society.

She stretched out the crumpled orange paper and smoothed it over the side of the kitchen counter. There was a photo on the front. Carolyn glanced at it as she filled the electric kettle with water.

The crinkled photo was badly reproduced and covered with grease from the garbage bin, but something in the stained image immediately caught her eye, tugged at her attention, pulled her deeper into its repellent gaze. She forced herself to look away, to attend to the kettle, but the image on the countertop drew her back with a power that was as inescapable as it was inexplicable.

Carolyn slipped on her glasses for a better look. Her hands were trembling. She looked at the photograph and then up, slowly, until she was staring blindly out the kitchen window, into the gray drizzle that seemed to absorb her stunned senses.

It couldn't be. No, it was impossible.

She looked again. Closed her eyes, drenched in a wave of cold, nauseous dread.

It said Ron Labonne. It was a photograph of the neighbor she had never seen.

And yet she had seen him. He'd had a different name then. So had she.

Standing in the kitchen, Carolyn suddenly felt as though her guts were about to spill out onto the floor.

CHAPTER 17

OKAY, SHE WAS OUT OF THERE. THEY'D WON. TERRY WANTED THE carriage house for Billy Bird, Billy Bird wanted it for himself, and she, the resentful Cassandra, didn't have any claim on the place except the insanely possessive love she felt for it.

Living in the carriage house had been like a honeymoon for her. If she'd just had a honey to go with it, it would have been perfect. It was more than just a space to live in. It was her. Like a patient lover it had waited for Cassandra Taylor to come and claim it as her own. She'd never felt such an emotional affinity for a place, such a strong desire to put down roots. As if she finally belonged somewhere.

Terry, with all his goddamned money, could never understand what those two rooms above the garage meant to her. In them, her art had undergone an almost miraculous transformation. She'd dropped the violent stuff—the bitterly ironic "Glamor Queen" series (slashed, mutilated women overlaid with "glamorous" rhinestone-graffiti that spelled out *bitch, whore, cocksucker*), and the series she called "Cuntries at War" (screaming women with knives, guns, and barbed wire grotesquely sprouting from their vaginas). A series of serene watercolor landscapes took their place.

Cassandra had never bothered with landscapes before. She didn't know if the ones she'd completed in the carriage house were good or not. All she knew was that, living there, her vision had shifted and expanded to take in something new, something antithetical to the secret raging anger that had been feeding her ideas and images. Moving from dump to dump, living in squalid inner-city neighborhoods where rents were cheap and life was dangerous, she'd developed a keen, despairing sense of urban blight, fucked-up human relationships, and her own perennial vagabondage. It wasn't until she moved into the carriage house in Queer Corners—and looked out at that view every day—that she began to see the relentless force and impersonal splendor of the natural world.

She was a little embarrassed by her new subject matter. "Nature" seemed so contentless, so meaningless, when compared to the shocking, emotionally charged images she'd been feverishly working on before. But the desire to capture the eternal, elusive common ground shared by all life grew stronger than any intellectual concerns about making an angry feminist statement.

Painting the landscapes was the closest she'd ever come to escaping the boundaries of her self. She slipped out of the fretting, anxious, lonely, penurious confines of her life and floated free, in the clouds, over the trees, above the mountains. The trouble was that she always had to come back. Face the shrapnel of hate and abuse and inequality that made all life, but especially gay life, such a endlessly frustrating struggle.

Like that crap the ACA was distributing. She'd found a stack of their blood-boiling brochures in Terry's kitchen. On top was a note written in a loopy scrawl: "Terry, you can help us by pasing these on to youre freinds in the neborhood. Yours in Jesus. Cornette."

"I don't believe it," Cassandra gasped as she read through one of the pamphlets. "This is fucking insane! Terry, how can you let your own cousin get away with this shit? Doesn't she know you're gay?"

"That's none of your business," Terry said, his voice sharp.

"Christ, have you actually read this?"

"Yes. And I don't necessarily disagree with everything they say."

"What? You've got to be kidding." She laughed in disbelief, dumbfounded by his indifference. "Terry, this applies to you as a gay man. It's an attack on you and all your gay neighbors."

"It doesn't apply to me," he said.

"Why? Just because you pretend you're not gay doesn't mean you aren't."

His dyed black eyebrows shot up in annoyance. She was getting personal, confronting him, and that was not allowed. The fact that she saw him differently from the way he saw himself made her dangerous. "I don't pretend to be anything," Terry snapped. "I don't label myself."

"That's just an excuse to stay in the closet."

"I think it's about time for you to find another place to stay," he said coldly.

Still she hung on, waiting for a final eviction notice. She knew exactly why she was being ousted from her nest. Terry desperately wanted to keep his young stud-muffin close at hand, but he couldn't stand having Billy Bird in the house with him. Billy was an embarrassment. His whorish presence mocked the hetero-pretensions of Terry's Mock Tudor. Billy was a trashy pig, and since Cassandra refused to clean up after him, and Billy refused to clean up after himself, and Terry refused to live with a mess, what choice did Terry have? He had to stable Billy, as he'd stabled all his other "houseboys," in the carriage house.

Blackmail briefly crossed her mind. She could tell Terry that she'd out him to his cousin, Cornette Labonne, unless Terry let her remain in the carriage house. But much as she loved the place, she couldn't sink that low to keep it.

Then one night she came home unexpectedly and caught Billy Bird in her studio. He was looking at her violent paintings of violated women, the "Glamor Queen" series.

"What the fuck are you doing in here?" she said angrily.

"I come up to see your art gallery."

"It's not a gallery, it's my studio. How did you get in?"

"Through the door," he said casually.

She remembered locking it. "I never gave you permission to come in here."

"Yeah," he said, flipping through the canvasses, "and now I know why. You didn't want no one to see this shit."

"Get out of here." She slammed the row of stacked canvasses back into place, catching his finger between two of them.

"Ow! Son of a bitch!" Billy yanked his finger out and glared at her. "Better watch it, cunt."

"No, prickface," she said, "you'd better watch it."

"Better start packing your dildos cuz you're outta here."

"I said get out and I mean it."

"What're you gonna do, tell Terry?" He let out a snort of laughter. "You think that old queen gives a shit about you? He told me this place is mine."

"It's not yours yet," Cassandra said. "Now get out before I call the police."

"Terry wouldn't like having the police comin' around."

"I know what you're up to," she said. "I know you're just using him."

"Oh, and you ain't?"

"I work to stay here. Fair trade."

"I'm all the trade he gets," Billy said. "You don't do nothin' around here."

"Yeah? And what do you do? Outside of his bedroom, I mean."

"Watch it, tunafish, or I'll turn you into Chicken of the Sea."

"You try anything with me, cocksucker, and I'll cut your dick off."

"That's all you fuckin' dykes really want, ain't it? To get your hands on a man's dick and slice it off."

"A cock in the hand is worth two in the tush," she said. It was a Bobbitt joke that Jay had told her. But Billy didn't get it.

"Yeah," he said, grabbing his crotch and moving towards her, "this is what you fuckin' muff-divers really want, ain't it? Hmm? You want it, baby? You want me to show you what a man can do?"

There was angry, boozy, unfocussed danger in his eyes, a macho threat in his body. She remembered the time she'd been raped at gunpoint. The joy the man took in her fear. "Take one more step, pigbrain, and I'll kill you." She grabbed a pair of scissors from her worktable.

Billy lunged. She caught him on the wrist with the scissors. He howled and backed away in disbelief.

"Fuckin' cunt!" he gasped. "Fuckin' maniac cunt! Look what you done to me!" A thin line of blood was oozing out of the shallow cut.

"If I ever see your ugly face in here again I'll put this baby right up your ass," she growled.

"Cuntsucker! You are outta here!"

War. Greedy male usurpation of female territory. The peace of her studio destroyed. The fact that it was two gay men who were putting the screws on her made the situation even worse. Of course closet cases like Terry and petty hustlers like Billy were the most dangerous kinds of queers. Self-hating, afraid to admit who they were, cut off from their emotions, unable to love, they were the puny descendents of Killer Closet Queers like Roy Cohn, Joseph McCarthy, and J. Edgar Hoover.

The next evening she came home from Chez Jay and found a letter shoved under her door. From Terry. Telling her to vacate the premises within a week. "I don't know what to do," she moaned to Jay.

"You'll have to move in with me," he said.

She demurred, Jay insisted. "You can have the downstairs. There's enough room for a studio and a living space. It looks right out onto the garden."

"Jay, it would be great but I can't afford it."

"You can't afford free? Hey, I owe you. You know damn well I couldn't have kept the restaurant going without you."

That was true. As the customers dwindled, and other staff was laid off or quit, she hung on, tenacious as a tick, until she and Jay were almost singlehandedly running the place, like a mom and pop store—or, as Jay put it, "like rats on a sinking ship." She couldn't bear to see his defeat. Wanted to stand by his side, like a loyal spouse. Well, she was the patron saint of lost causes. What else could you call a lesbian in love with a gay man?

Then it was over. Chez Jay said adieu, closed its doors, became Portland history. The last night, she and Jay sat together at their favorite corner deuce and Yvor cooked them a fabulous meal and the three of them got so drunk they couldn't stand straight. For the first time, she and Jay touched—lingering commiserative strokes and squeezes. Jay gave her a big sloppy kiss of gratitude and it was all she could do to keep her tongue from Frenching into his mouth. Now, exhausted but desperate, Jay was talking about starting a new gay bistro and scouting around for a space on 23rd.

And she was going to live with him.

Too utterly weird, the way things worked out.

In exchange for his basement, she was going to be his unpaid, noninvesting business partner in the new bistro. "My ideas person" Jay called her.

"If we can make a go of it on half a shoestring," he said, "I'll set you up with a profit share and something under the table."

"Of course it'll go," she said.

"You think?"

"I believe in you, Jay."

"You do?" Her declaration, coming in the midst of his hollow-eyed anxiety and preoccupied grief over losing Chez Jay, surprised and touched him.

Well, it was true. She did believe in him. It was more than sexual infatuation. Jay was the first man she'd ever meshed with. She adored his sexy "older man-ness," that layer of experience and sophistication missing from every other man she knew. He was hip, knew what was going on, and he actually listened to her. She was credible in his eyes, a real artist, and, unlike Terry, he didn't look down on her because she was poor and a woman.

▼ ▼ ▼

Okay, everything was boxed and ready for the move. She'd added them all up: it was the eighteenth time she'd changed residences in twenty-five years of life. She looked around the studio one last time, said goodbye to the rooms, to the mesmerizing view out over Portland to the Cascades. Gathered up an armful of paintings and brought them downstairs. Pulled out the little red wagon she stored in the garage behind Terry's Mercedes. She'd use it to haul everything down to Jay's.

Terry was peeking at her from the kitchen window as she piled the paintings into the wagon. God but he looked pathetic. Like a vain old woman desperately trying to stay young: pinched, tucked and dyed into a state bordering on mummification. He opened the side door and said peevishly, "Well, I guess this is goodbye."

Cassandra ignored him.

"Where are you going?" Terry asked.

"What difference does that make to you?"

"Well, pardon me," he said snippily. "After all I've done for you you might at least say thank you."

"You haven't done a goddamned thing for me, Terry," she said wearily. "I'm the one who did everything for you, and I never once got so much as a thank you."

"You got the carriage house, didn't you?"

"No, I never even had that because the minute that slimy little two-bit hustler arrived you both did everything you could to get me out."

"I believe this is my property," Terry said. "I believe I am free to do with it whatever I want. I believe that is how the capitalistic system works."

She nodded. At this point she had nothing to lose by telling the truth. "I feel sorry for you, Terry. You're being conned by that little shit and you don't even know it. All he wants is your money."

"He works harder than you ever did to earn his keep."

"That's a lie and you know it."

"You're calling me a liar?"

"You're so out of touch with reality that your whole life is a lie," she said. "You know what you really are, Terry? You're a cheap, selfish, miserly old queer with a bad facelift and dyed hair. No wonder you don't have any real friends. You know what everyone around here calls you? Terry the Turd."

He stood uncomfortably transfixed in the doorway, staring at her with a look of angry bewilderment.

"Go back into your closet, Terry," Cassandra said, hoisting up her canvasses. "Maybe you'll realize one day how empty it really is."

Billy appeared and craned his head over Terry's shoulder. "Get a load of her, Big Buddy," he whistled. "Are them your moving clothes or are you just going out to walk the streets?"

Cassandra ignored him.

You better have all your shit out by tonight," Billy called. "And you better not take nothin' that don't belong to you, either."

"Go fuck yourself, Billy Birdbrain," she said.

Back and forth between the carriage house and Jay's, all morning long, her red wagon piled high with her belongings. She was certain that the Labonnes were watching her. Every time she passed their house—their "unreal estate" as Jay called it—the heavy curtains were pulled open just enough for someone to peer out. She couldn't make out actual faces behind the plastic sheeting, but she knew they were there. Creepy.

Of course she'd had a feeling that this would happen. And it was true that she wanted to provoke them. Ever since reading their homophobic brochure in Terry's kitchen she'd been wondering how she could further incite their sexual hysteria. That's why she was wearing her tight fake-leopard-skin jump suit, dark glasses, and little shortie jacket. It was the sort of outfit Jayne Mansfield wore in the Fifties, only Jayne wouldn't have worn it for hauling stuff in a red wagon.

Cassandra, raised in regulation housing on army bases, had always appreciated the subdued stateliness of the houses in Queer Corners. She'd particularly liked Delmont's house, its quiet humming air of wealth, generosity, and hidden treasure. Now she could hardly bear to look at it. There was a blasted, desolate look to the house and grounds, as if the Labonnes, determined to eradicate everything that made the place special, had detonated a megaton of bad taste right in the middle of Queer Corners.

On one of her trips Cassandra noticed Ron Labonne standing in the darkness of his garage pretending to do something but really looking at her. Ugh. Like a gorilla ogling her from its cage. Still, this was her opportunity to infuriate the homophobic sex-hating asshole. She hesitated, daring herself, then opened her jacket to give him a shot of her tits and pushed out her fanny, swinging it with an exaggerated va-va-voom as she walked by.

Ron Labonne's eyes practically fell out of his head.

Fucking hypocrite, she thought; if you only knew. Her exhibitionism was a game, yet she couldn't deny that it gave her a tingling thrill of power. She felt like an agent provocateur.

Ron Labonne nodded. She pretended, on that trip, not to see him.

On her next haul she saw that he'd moved closer, from the garage door to the side of the red Cadillac parked in the driveway. He was inspecting it, polishing it here and there with a rag. "Looks like you're moving," he called.

She stopped and looked at him. What a laugh. Those long Sixties-looking side-burns and that droopy handlebar mustache. Hair parted just above his ear and care-fully combed over the top of his head. The bullish heft of his body, his belly straining against the lower buttons of his checkered shirt Little piggy eyes. Definitely from Lower Slobolia.

"Need some help?" he called.

"I can manage." But one of her toiletry boxes tipped over as she started down the hill.

He was at her side before she knew it. "That's a mighty big load for such a little gal to carry," he said, smiling, crouching down beside her. Hands the size of steaks.

"I'll do it," she said, quickly scooping up bars of scented soap, free samples of perfume from Saks, and a box of tampons before he could touch anything. His sudden proximity frightened her. She was hurriedly winding up a roll of toilet paper when she saw, with alarm, that "Jay," her vibrator, had tipped out on the grass and was lying beside one of Ron Labonne's enormous shoes.

"I don't believe we've met," he said. "You're the little lady with the pink VW bug, aren't you?"

She nodded, caught in her own trap.

"Sixty-nine, isn't it?"

"Mm-hm."

"I know that because I'm an old car buff. My Caddie there's a fifty-nine El Dorado. Isn't she a beaut?"

"Classic," Cassandra said.

"You know how they say people are like their dogs? I think people are like their cars. You can always tell what a person's really like by the car he drives."

"Yours reminds me of a big hungry shark," she said.

He chuckled, taking it as a compliment. "Does it? Yours looks like an old hippie Love Bug." He picked up the vibrator and examined it. "What does this thing do?"

"That?" She grabbed it from his hand and stashed it in the box. "It's a lip stimulator."

He stared at her. "I've been so busy since I moved in that I haven't even introduced myself to my neighbors. Ron Labonne."

"Oh, we all know who you are," Cassandra said. "We've all seen your picture on those little pamphlets."

He grinned, pleased. "You're gonna see my picture all over town pretty soon," he said proudly. "The campaign's just beginning. Did you sign the petition?"

"No."

"Why not?"

The time had come. "Because I'm a lesbian."

He leaned back on his heels and began to laugh. "That's a good one. I like a girl with a sense of humor."

Just then Cornette Labonne, her white-blonde hair braided into two stiff pigtails, stuck her head out the front door. "Ron, sweetheart? Could you come here, hon, and help me with something?"

"Yeah," he barked over his shoulder, "be right there." He turned back to Cassandra and said in a low voice: "Where you moving to?"

A perverse instinct told her to play along. She could be a spy, like Mata Hari. Provide useful information to the panic-stricken gay groups that were already mobilizing throughout the city. "Right down there," she said, nodding towards Jay's.

"That crazy guy from New York lives there."

"Jay Zucker," she said. "He's not crazy. Do you know him?"

"No, but you'd think he was a Jew, the way he carries on."

"He is a Jew," Cassandra said, stacking her box on the wagon.

Ron took this as another joke. His eyes darted appreciatively over her body and fastened on her breasts. "Yeah, right, and you're a lesbian."

"That's right. And I'm going to be living right next door to you."

His guffaw was cut short by another wheedling wail from Cornette. "Ron, honey, I need your help."

"I'll see you around," he said. "I hope."

CHAPTER 18

AS THE EARTH DUTIFULLY SPUN ITS LOAD OF FIVE AND A HALF BILLION confused human souls through the heavens and around the sun, giving them the only certainty they would ever know—that night follows day and spring follows winter—a group of citizens banded together on the Pacific west coast of the North American continent, about midway between the Bering Strait and the Gulf of Panama, in a place with two mountain ranges, thirty-six counties, and just under three million inhabitants on 97,003 square miles of land, and began to preach a gospel of hate.

The place was called Oregon.

The group was called the American Christian Alliance.

As storms whipped through the Cascades and the Coast Range, blanketing the highest peaks with record snowfalls, the first spring flowers opened in Queer Corners. Winter aconites shivered in the moist winds that blew through the valley and across Terry's pool patio. Twenty-year old clumps of snowdrops in front of Wellfleet's adobe wall glowed with the ferocious brilliance of maturity. Bright huddled patches of gold, white, and purple crocuses blossomed in Susan and Carolyn's cottage garden. The fat buds on the camellias in front of Jay Zucker's burst into pink and white flower. Tiny yellow narcissi and enormous black Queen of the Night tulips selected by Peter and planted by John-Don the previous October speared up through the soil. Ito's steep hillside was embroidered with rare alpine plants from the Himalayas, tough little irises from Siberia, early flowering Japanese quince, and glory-of-the-snow.

The only bare spot in this blossoming enclave was the Labonnes', where the old shrubs that graced the street facade of Delmont's Queen Anne had, for some mysterious reason, been levelled by an electric buzz saw. Their stumps now guarded the house like a set of twisted, discolored teeth.

Spring in Oregon. Fragrant, balmy winds. Sunshine after a long, wet, gray winter. Such a rich, lovely, hopeful season. The ground was warm, ready, waiting. It was a perfect time for the American Christian Alliance under the leadership of Ron Labonne to begin planting the poisonous seeds that would soon burst into bloom throughout the state.

With apostolic fervor, minions of the ACA took to the road, preaching in small towns. The ACA's grass-roots ministry fared best and collected the most signatures for the proposed Non-Special Rights Status and Child Molestation Protection Act in depressed rural communities.

But important as it was for the ACA to enlist the rear-flank support of rural and small-town voters, the real battle for the hearts, minds, and pocketbooks of Oregonians was going to be waged in the larger urban centers and their surrounding suburbs.

Portland was the homosexual power base, according to Labonne. There, in Sodom on the Willamette, the homosexuals were masterminding their devious plans for eventual world domination.

It was imperative to funnel the vital resources of the ACA into the big city. Eager volunteers set up tables in the airport, on downtown streets and college campuses, in parking lots, shopping malls and in front of supermarkets, collecting signatures, distributing brochures, inveigling donations. They went from church to church, house to house, assembling data for their computer records, noting with equal care those addresses where they were welcomed and those where they were turned away.

At first, despite a barrage of PR kits, the mainstream media mostly ignored Ron Labonne and cast a leery eye on the ACA. This, according to the ACA, was to be expected. It was part of the conspiracy to keep Christian values and Christian leaders out of the entertainment-saturated public eye. And who, after all, controlled the media? Homosexuals, with their anti-Christian agenda. So Ron Labonne claimed, anyway, in interviews that appeared in the *Springfield Gazette*, the *Medford Herald*, and the *Coos Bay Courier*. He reiterated the point on talk-radio shows in Grants Pass, Roseburg, Pendleton, and Salem.

He didn't get any television exposure until *On-Air With Jesus* premiered on a local cable channel. In its eleven-thirty p.m. time slot, wedged in between *The Gospel Truth* and *The Light of the World*, it was hardly prime-time viewing. *TV Host* merely called it "Paid Program." It had to compete nationally with Rush Limbaugh, locally with a transvestite preacher named Sister Rita, and with the restless ten-second attention spans of channel-surfers whizzing through sixty-three other late-night possibilities. But at least it was on the air, spreading the message.

In a small studio where ACA volunteers had constructed a talk-show set with donated materials, Ron and Cornette Labonne prayed, tried to do some Regis and Kathy-type banter, welcomed their first guests, all of whom fervently agreed that the ACA ballot measure was necessary, and exhorted their unseen viewers to call in and participate in what Ron called "a politically active interface with God."

"Remember," Cornette said, as organ music swelled at the show's finale, "our ministry belongs to you. We are part of your loving family. And all of us are part of Christ's family here on earth. Praying together we can change the world."

"It's your prayer offerings," Ron added, as an address and phone number flashed on the screen, "that allow us to translate the word of God into direct political action. We'll look forward to hearing from you. And remember—your politicians will be hearing from us."

"God bless," Cornette cried, blowing a kiss, "and bye-bye for now!"

▾ ▾ ▾

"We've got to do something," John-Don said, restlessly pacing back and forth through the living room.

"Honey, would you please sit down?" Peter flipped through a book of fabric samples, comparing textures, combining colors. After three months of schmoozing, he'd nearly landed the job with Katrina Parsons, an ice-princess executive who'd moved up from Phoenix to become a vice-president at Nike. She'd just bought a half-million dollar house near the Pittock mansion. Peter had to do one last presentation, and if all went well, the contract would be signed. "I've got to sell my ass tomorrow and you're making me nervous."

"You *should* be nervous," John-Don said. He took a quick swig from his bottle of generic spring water. "They're after you. They're after us."

"They're morons," Peter muttered.

"Yes, but they're smart morons."

Cerise and ochre for the dining room? That was the Nineties. Katrina was in marketing, she wasn't afraid of color. Peter had a sudden vision of Katrina's fabulous new house, filled with guests, the rich-snotty-hip-corporate Nike crowd. There they were, pretending not to be dazzled by the eye-searing brilliance of the interior. "Who was your designer?" they'd ask. "Peter Love," Katrina would say. "Let me introduce you."

He'd have to replenish his wardrobe, of course. Maybe a shopping trip to New York was in order—a visit to the design showrooms and Barney's men's store. John-Don had never been to New York. They could stay at the Paramount, that was hot. See "Angels in America." A rejuvenating dress-up honeymoon in a sophisticated city where queers could be queers.

"Did you hear what I said?" John-Don asked.

Peter looked up from his revery. "You said they're smart morons and they're after us."

"And?" Now John-Don was challenging him.

Peter's voice rose irritably. "And what?"

"And what are we going to do about it?" John-Don shouted. "For Christ's sake, are you just going to sit there with those goddamn color chips while these maniacs across the street are out collecting signatures to have us branded as pedophiles and perverts?"

"Yeah." Peter gave him a stubborn look. "That's exactly what I'm going to do. Sit here with my faggoty little swatches and ignore them the best I can."

"I guess that's about what I'd expected," John-Don said under his breath.

"What the fuck's that supposed to mean?"

"Just what I said." John-Don went to the window and looked across the street. With the heavy curtains you could never tell if anyone was home or not. But there were always extra cars and pickups out front. It was beginning to look like a compound.

"I suppose you're implying that I'm not an active activist."

"You're not," John-Don said. "And I'm not either. Not the way I used to be. That's the problem. I've become too comfortable."

"God forbid you should be comfortable."

"Too complacent. Bourgeois home owner on the hill. I've moved too far away from my old radical center."

An old radical center, he might have guiltily added, that had never fought for gay rights. He'd demonstrated for the freedom of others but never for his own. His sympathy was there, of course, but not his actual presence. When it came to the environment—the Trojan nuclear reactor spewing contaminated waste into the Columbia or the lumber companies clear-cutting the last virgin forest in North America—he was on the front lines, with his family, agitating against the entrenched profit-motivated power system that was turning the earth into a polluted cesspool. He'd always taken the global view: everyone shared the earth and if the earth was to survive you had to preserve it for future generations. He wouldn't personally be adding to those future generations, but that didn't mean he shouldn't fight on their behalf. But now that global view had shrunk to what he saw from the front window of his own house. A different battle, one that called into question his personal honor and integrity, was being mounted right across the street.

Peter joined John-Don at the window. Put a hand on his shoulder. Wanted to calm him and calm himself and calm the two of them together.

"The worst thing is," John-Don said, "that what they're doing is perfectly legal. No one can stop them because it's their right as citizens. But we're citizens, too. We pay taxes to support the system that allows them to take away rights we don't even have. The illogic of it is breathtaking."

"Not to mention their hideous taste," Peter said. "Poor Delmont must be turning over in his grave."

"I don't know what to do," John-Don said anxiously, "but I've got to do something."

"Maybe we should sell the house."

"No!" John-Don barked. "I'm not going to let those maniacs chase us out of here. It's our house. This is our neighborhood. They're the intruders."

Peter squeezed his lover's shoulder. A surge of emotion ran through him. John-Don had said "our house." And for Peter, who was just a simple homebody at heart, a perfect house shared with a perfect lover was what he'd always dreamed of. A life suitable for framing, as photographable as anything found in the upscale glossy magazines stacked on his Memphis coffee table. *Architectural Digest* meets *Inches*, that was the general idea. And on the surface, that was what he had: a beautiful house and a hunky cream-in-your-pants-just-looking-at-him lover.

But John-Don, his fantasy Don Juan, remained infuriatingly elusive when it came to real intimacy. The horrible truth was that since the Labonnes had begun their anti-gay rights crusade John-Don had gone from cold fish to dead fish. It was affecting him in ways that left Peter even more sexually frustrated and emotionally isolated.

"Everything was so perfect until they moved in," Peter said wistfully.

"Just because they moved in doesn't mean we should move out."

"Hey, I was joking about the house. We couldn't sell it if we wanted to. With that piece of shit across the street no one would even give us the price we paid. We'd have to take a loss."

"For Christ's sake," John-Don said, pulling away. "Is that all you can think about—property values?"

"Honey, in case you didn't know, that's what this house is. A piece of shared property. It's our financial future."

"We're not going to have a future. Not if they win."

"They aren't going to win."

"How do you know? We're not talking about rational discourse here. We're talking about a witch hunt. We're talking about people looking for someone to punish for their own miserable lives. Do you know how deeply ingrained that is in human nature?"

"Hey, I'm a black man, remember? A nigger queer in a racist homophobic society. I've seen the best America has to offer."

"Then why aren't you terrified?"

"Because terror is a victory for them. That's what my father always said. Your fear increases their power."

"So what do you do? You act, right? You do something."

"You do your work. You go about your bidness, as my grandmother used to say. You accept the fact that in some people's eyes, no matter what you do to prove yourself, you're always going to be considered a degenerate queer, or a welfare-cheating nigger, or a conniving Jew. You find your happiness despite every obstacle they put in your way."

"No," John-Don said, "you fight back."

"I am sick of fighting," Peter said, returning to his fabric swatches. "I hate politics. I just want to be left alone to do my work and live my life and be with you and make a million dollars before I'm fifty."

"That's all you want?"

"Okay, two million."

"Can't you get it through your skull that it's not just *us* that I'm talking about. This is about trampling the civil rights of every gay person in Oregon. Maybe you can sit back and pretend it's all going to disappear like a bad dream, but I can't. We're talking about my job. We're talking about my state. We're talking about my people."

"'My people?'" Peter snickered. "Where did you get that, from one of your old Peter, Paul and Mary records?"

"Yeah, go ahead. Make fun of them all you want, but Peter, Paul and Mary were committed to doing something more constructive for society than sniffing horse tranquilizers and going to discos to dance all night and fuck in orgy rooms."

"Ouch!" Peter cried, flicking his hands up as if he'd been burned. "I've got the ACA right here in my own house! I've married into the enemy camp."

"What's that supposed to mean?"

"It means, girl, that when you say things like that you're no different from them." John-Don stiffened in indignation. "Me? How?"

"Judgmental. Moralistic. Anti-sex." Peter whipped off his round tortoise-shell glasses and spun them around like a propeller. "A gay homophobe, girl, that's what I sometimes think you are."

"How the hell can you say that? And stop calling me girl."

"Why don't you just admit it? Being queer embarrasses your masculinity, your nice-little-boyness. Intellectually you're cool with it, but physically you're a prude who still thinks queer sex is dirty."

"Hey! We have safe sex at least once a week."

"You see? You can't even say 'sex.' It's got to be 'safe sex.' It's got to be so fucking safe that it's hardly sex at all."

John-Don turned away. "I'm sorry if I bore you in bed. I guess I'm just not as experienced as you are."

The implication stung Peter to the quick. "I know you're afraid of my butt-fucking cock-sucking past. But you know what, baby? I'm not sorry about what I did. I loved it. I still do. I love sex. You don't. End of conversation." There, let Mr. Boy Scout mull over that.

"Christ." John-Don blew out a deep guilty breath and ran his hands through his hair. "I try."

"Try? After four years you won't even put your tongue in my mouth. The minute you come you jump into the shower and scrub yourself with Lysol."

"I do not use Lysol."

"Okay, so it's Mr. Clean. How do you think that makes me feel? Like Mr. Unclean! When I fuck you with a dildo, you make me put a rubber on it!"

John-Don was mortified. Sex talk. His inhibitions, out in the open. "Then I can pretend it's you," he said.

"It ain't me, honey. You wouldn't let my cock enter that holy hole of yours if I was wearing a ten-inch-thick armored plate. And God forbid you should ever fuck me. You'd have to wear a spacesuit."

"I've got to be careful!" John-Don shouted. "You might not like it, but I've got my health to consider. It's my body, isn't it?"

"It sure is," Peter said. "And it's a body that's scared shitless to feel anything for another man's body."

"That's bullshit."

"Is it? Then why don't you ever touch me? Why do I always have to be the one to instigate sex? Sometimes I think you're afraid of me because I'm black."

"How can you say that?"

"Because that's what it feels like. It makes me wonder if you really love me or if I'm just some fucking symbol you live with."

John-Don stared at him, his mouth open, incredulous.

"Maybe I'm just a foil for all that white liberal guilt you carry around. It would be so politically correct for Mr. Socialist to have a black lover."

"You think that's all you are to me?"

"I don't know!" Peter cried. "All I know is that I don't want to be another cause. I don't want to be condescended to, and that's how you make me feel."

John-Don was very quiet. For a moment the entire house was very very quiet. "Are you saying you want to split up?"

"No!" Peter yelped, lurching out his chair and lassoing John-Don in his arms. "No, honey, no, that's not what I'm saying. I'm just telling you what it feels like sometimes."

"Okay, I'm a prude, I admit it. I didn't come out until I was thirty. I've lived my entire adult sexual life with this fear of AIDS." John-Don stomped back to the window. "And that's another thing. It pisses me off that those idiots are using AIDS as part of their scare tactics. It's perfect. They couldn't have chosen a better time, when everyone's so depressed and demoralized by the epidemic. That's really hitting below the belt," he said bitterly. "That's real Christian compassion."

"Honey, they're straight. Get it through your noggin. They operate in a very limited sphere. They think they're masters of the universe. They've been pulling this God-shit on us since day one. It doesn't matter what you do, or what you say, or how you behave, you ain't gonna change their minds about it."

"But they're wrong!"

"Of course they're wrong."

"I'm not a pederast, I'm not a necrophiliac, I'm not fucking animals and I'm not preaching to schoolkids."

"Honey, it's straight people doing this. So let the straight people fight for us for a change."

"They won't," John-Don said bitterly. His face turned grim. "You know damn well they won't. They never have and they never will. It's up to us."

Peter knew that was true. Everything in his experience as a gay man, a gay child, a gay sibling added up to one inescapable truth: in the cozy heterosexual scheme of things, his life, the reality of it, was seen as having no real value.

So what did you do? You either accepted their version of you or you didn't. If you accepted it, you lost every last ounce of joy in your heart and self-respect in your soul. If you rejected it, as he had, you went your own way, lonely maybe, but at least true to the promptings of your own inner nature. He wasn't going to beg for crumbs of understanding from their formica tables. He wasn't going to grovel in guilty fear and abasement before his accusers. Nor was he interested in trying to change their attitudes. It wasn't fatalism so much as sheer disgust. Let them prove to him, for a change, that they were worthy of being considered *his* equal. "Those who judge without mercy shall be judged without mercy," as his hypocritical mother used to quote from the New Testament.

John-Don glanced at his watch and headed for the front hall.

"Where are you going?" As if he didn't know.

"To check up on Ito."

The sour nightly pang of jealousy. "I'm beginning to think you two have a thing going."

John-Don didn't answer. He opened the door but didn't leave. Peter's heart began to race. Suddenly he was terrified that he'd hit upon a truth he didn't want to acknowledge. John-Don was going to tell him that . . .

"I've never cheated on you," John-Don said.

"Honey, I know that. I was joking. It was stupid of me."

"Look," John-Don said, his voice low, "I know that I don't always show it the way you'd like me to, but I do love you."

A cool, sweet February breeze wafted into the living room, bringing with it the irritating tinkle of distant windchimes.

"You believe me, don't you?" John-Don asked. "Even if I'm—crummy in bed?"

Peter nodded, sitting tight, trying to hold on to some semblance of respectable masculine composure as his feelings for John-Don slipped out of their habitual orbit and shot into a new emotional trajectory. I've escaped death, he thought, and I've found love: I am blessed. The man standing in the doorway of this house is my redeemer. Everything is nothing without someone like him to share it with.

"You make me very happy," he croaked. "Even if you do spend every goddamn night with Ito."

"So come and kiss me goodbye."

"What?"

"Come here and stick your tongue down my throat in front of our neighbors." He looked defiantly across the street. "I want them to see."

Peter threw down his designer sample books and got up from his chair. "Is this love or a political statement?"

"Same thing."

"What if we start a civil war?"

John-Don pulled him into his arms. "Then Queer Corners is Fort Sumter."

▾ ▾ ▾

Cassandra loved her new home. She had a separate entrance, down and around the back at the ground-floor level of Jay's house. Outside her door there was a brick patio, covered with emerald-green moss. The overhang of Jay's back deck formed a long, verandah-like porch above her south-facing door and windows. From the patio she looked out into a dense, overgrown thicket of trees, bushes, and ferns. Her basement studio was darker than the carriage house, and had a lingering earthy mustiness that she couldn't quite eradicate, but it was quiet and it was free.

Jay had obviously never set foot back here, but Cassandra could see, as she scraped the moss from the patio bricks and hacked away at the invasive ivy and blackberry vines, that at one time this lower level had been carefully tended. Now that the weather was turning warm she spent as much time outside as she could. She liked hard physical work, liked the idea that she was reclaiming a bit of wilderness.

An old path—a memory of more congenial days—wound between and connected the two adjoining properties. Cassandra's view of the Labonnes' back yard was partially obscured by a holly tree and the large shrubs that formed a boundary line, but with artful positioning she had a pretty clear shot.

Not that there was anything pleasant to look at. The shockingly blue house towering above her was bad enough. Below it, Delmont's beautiful garden had for all intents and purposes vanished. The Labonnes ignored the garden, using it primarily as a dump site for their seemingly endless cache of junk.

There was one new addition, however: a rickety-looking rabbit hutch.

And once that went up, Cassandra began to catch glimpses of a young girl, evidently the Labonnes' daughter. The girl spent part of each afternoon by the hutch. She fed the rabbits, cleaned their cage, and wandered aimlessly around the back yard, usually holding a rabbit in her arms. Gradually the girl became aware of Cassandra's presence.

Cassandra could tell that the girl was watching her and passively trying to get her attention. She was like a shy curious deer, coming close and then darting back into the forest when it was startled. The girl looked harmless enough. Nerdy, immature, and lonely. But Cassandra, predisposed to loathe all the Labonnes, ignored her. She wanted nothing to do with the family behind the awful Non-Special Rights Status and Child Molestation Protection Act.

One warm February afternoon as she was busily tilling up an old flower bed near the property line, Cassandra felt a shiver creep down her back. She looked up and saw the girl standing a few feet away, staring at her.

The girl offered a tentative smile. She was cradling a white and black rabbit in her arms. As Cassandra watched, she lifted the rabbit to her face and rubbed her cheek against it. Cassandra wondered if perhaps the girl was retarded.

"That's a pretty rabbit. Does it have a name?"

The girl slowly nodded, obviously afraid of Cassandra but fascinated by her as well. Her eyes nervously jumped from Cassandra's short spiky hair to her earrings, nose ring, and paint-splattered bib overalls. "Speckles," she said in a faint voice. "Do you live in that house?"

Cassandra said she did. "I know your rabbit's name, but I don't know yours."

The girl twisted in what looked like shy, delighted agony. "Dove," she said. Then suddenly: "Do you want to see my other bunnies? I've got six of them."

Cassandra couldn't bring herself to step across the property line. "Some other time maybe."

The girl looked crestfallen. Her shoulders slumped, her mouth dropped, and she turned and shuffled away.

In the days following, as Cassandra hung a bird feeder, pulled a rake through Jay's weedy grass, and tried to prune back the laurel that was partially blocking her stairway, Dove Labonne was never far away. Cassandra waved but stayed close to the house and made no further effort to get to know her.

Then one fine, breezy afternoon she opened her door and heard someone crying. She stepped out onto the patio and saw Dove sitting on a stone bench, her body racked by convulsive sobs. Cassandra couldn't help it: she felt sorry for the miserable girl.

"Dove?" She walked over to the property line. "Dove, are you okay?"

Dove lifted her miserable face, shook her head, and burst into another explosive fit of sobbing.

The sound of her anguish was so naked, so heartbreaking, it roused a tender protective nerve. "What's the matter?" Cassandra asked.

Dove looked miserably towards the rabbit hutch. "Speckles is dead."

"Oh. I'm so sorry."

"He killed Speckles," Dove sputtered. "He's going to kill *all* of them."

"Who is?"

"Him. My stepdad."

"Why?"

"To *eat* them," Dove moaned. Holding her stomach, she collapsed in another flood of tears, bent double on the stone bench.

Cassandra pondered what to do. She glanced up at the blue house. The curtains were closed. "Is there anyone home at your house?" she asked cautiously. Dove shook her head. "Well listen, I've got some chocolate cake. Would you like a piece?"

Dove stopped crying. She wiped her nose on her sleeve. "You mean come over to your house?"

"Just for a minute. Just for some cake."

Dove considered for a moment. She peered up the dark windows.

"Okay."

Cassandra got the feeling that Dove was feeling as conspiratorial as she was. "Can I bring Fluffy? He's my favorite now."

▼ ▼ ▼

As Cassandra listened to the story she thought, Don't get involved. Don't react. But it was difficult not to.

The facts, according to Dove: When her stepfather built the rabbit hutch and bought six beautiful Belgian rabbits, Dove thought they were for her. She adored the bunnies. She played with them and took care of them. The day before, she'd come home to discover that Speckles, her favorite, was missing. Her mom was at a prayer meeting so Dove had asked Ron to help her find Speckles. She was horror-stricken when Ron told her he'd killed the rabbit. "That's what rabbits are for," he said. "Eating. You're gonna love my famous rabbit stew." She'd almost thrown up when Speckles' stewed carcass appeared on the dinner table, cooked up by Ron himself. Ron laughed and refused to excuse her from the table. "You're gonna learn to eat what's put in front of you," he said. She watched as her stepfather and stepbrother hungrily sucked Speckle's tender flesh from the bones.

Now, fiercely cradling Fluffy in her arms, Dove said she couldn't bear to think that all the bunnies were going to be slaughtered, one by one. "I won't let him," she moaned. "But I don't know what to do."

Quite a talker. There was no stopping Dove once she got started. As she wolfed down a piece of chocolate cake she told Cassandra how frightened she was of Ron and Lester. Then she began to reveal to her new friend other strange, tantalizing secrets about the Labonne household. And as Dove talked, Cassandra kept quiet. She carefully listened and nodded encouragement.

CHAPTER 19

STRAPPED TO A GURNEY, WHEELED THROUGH A DARK LABYRINTH OF corridors, Carolyn pleaded with her captors to let her go, that she wanted to give birth outside, on her own, away from them. There were grim faces and guns everywhere she looked. She caught a passing glimpse of Susan, watching, her shocked, disapproving face pressed to a grimy window. A syringe. Carolyn fought, screamed. An injection. Labor. Intense pain. She looked down over the heaving mound of her belly, through the V of her stirruped legs, her body stretched beyond endurance, pushing, straining. One last contraction . . . and then mind-gibbering horror as a huge black dog slipped free of her bloody loins.

She gasped and bolted upright in bed, her heart racing. Stared blankly at the soft pearly light of dawn nuzzling the curtains. Her pelvic bones throbbed with the psychic residue of her dream. Sleep, when it came, was as exhausting as consciousness.

There was no need to pull on her favorite robe. She was wearing it. And a flannel nightie. And a hand-crocheted bed jacket. And thick woolen socks. There were two blankets and three comforters on the bed, and the thermostat was pushed up to a heretical seventy-five degrees, but she still felt cold.

She resisted the temptation to crawl back under the covers. Fumbled for her glasses, got out of bed. Went immediately to the window and blearily peeked out. The chickadees were starting their early-morning twitter in the Japanese maple. Chick-a-dee-dee-dee. She'd always loved to wake up to that buzzy, cheerful sound. Now she hated it.

Another morning. Another day closer to Susan's return.

What would Susan say? How on earth would she tell Susan?

She groaned and began to cry. Panic plucked like a vulture at her entrails.

She plodded miserably downstairs. Went to Lady Caroline's whelping basket. Looked at the six enormous black puppies sleepily guzzling from the pumps. Lady Caroline nudged them away from her swollen nipples. With a slow savory lick she slid her tongue across their tiny sphincters and, good mother that she was, slurped up their spurting excretions. Then she climbed out of the basket, her nails clicking against the hardwood floor as she stretched and yawned.

Six squirming, squeaking puppies, so adorable in their sweet helplessness, so threatening—like everything else just now—to Carolyn's relationship with Susan. The puppies couldn't help it if they were mongrels, just as Lady Caroline couldn't help it that she'd conceived them with the Labonnes' now-vanished dog. It was nothing more than the blind force of nature, seething, dripping, gestating, haunting the body of every creature on earth, working ceaselessly to reproduce. The quality of life outside the womb meant nothing to nature. Life was life. An open raffle.

Susan wouldn't agree, of course, which is why Carolyn, in her transatlantic conversations, had conveniently neglected to reveal the identity of the puppies' sire. In Susan's eyes, Lady Caroline's value lay solely in her breeding capabilities. The dog was a worthwhile investment only so long as she produced purebred puppies for the marketplace. She was nothing more than a conduit for a selective bloodline.

But Carolyn had been there like a midwife at their birth. Watched the whole messy magnificent process. Saw at once that the puppies were bastards, stains on the royal Ruby English line, infiltrators from an enemy gene pool. Susan wouldn't accept them, but Carolyn had to. They were her responsibility. She would have to suffer the consequences of Lady Caroline's blind biological urges as if they were her own.

"Are you a hungry mummy?"

The dog twitched her tail and with swinging pendulous dugs followed Carolyn into the kitchen.

Lady Caroline was ravenous, but Carolyn had no appetite. Food had become repulsive to her. She'd dropped ten pounds in the last week. The Anxiety Diet.

▼ ▼ ▼

Carolyn peered out the oriel window. She looked at her watch. It was almost eight. She would be late for work if she didn't leave within three minutes.

Five minutes later Ron Labonne stepped out from his front door. He was wearing a rust-colored suit and carrying a briefcase. He got into his red Cadillac, backed out the drive, and headed down Skyview Boulevard towards Burnside.

Carolyn snapped into action. She slipped on her new dark glasses and snatched her bag from the table. Her Volvo was parked directly outside the front door so she could dart from house to car within seconds.

"Good morning,"

Startled, Carolyn dropped her heavy ring of keys. Wellfleet, her closest neighbor, stood beside his open car door.

"Morning," she said. "Can't talk. Late for work. Bye." She scooped up her keys and unlocked the car.

"Have you seen them in the library?" Wellfleet asked.

"Who?"

"The ACA," Wellfleet said. "They have spies going through the shelves now, you know. Looking for dirty books."

Carolyn froze. "Who told you that?"

"Half of my students have joined the ACA. They do everything they're told. And our dear neighbor is telling them to infiltrate all the public libraries. I thought maybe you'd seen them."

"No," she said, sliding into her car, "I haven't."

"Well, I guess you wouldn't since they're incognito. Except for their halos and hard-ons they look just like everyone else."

Carolyn waited for Wellfleet's old Datsun to sputter down the hill before she backed down Santavista herself. She had to go almost as far as the Labonnes' before she could shift into first and start down Skyview to hook up with Burnside. This was the most frightening part of her morning journey. She kept her eyes straight ahead, refusing to look at Delmont's mutilated house and gardens.

Once on Skyview she heaved a momentary sigh of relief. Then sucked in a terrified breath when she saw the red Cadillac turn off Burnside and start back up Skyview.

The street was narrow. Their cars passed within inches of one another. Carolyn averted her face as the red Cadillac slowly slid by. Her heart was hammering and her perspiring hands stuck to the steering wheel. She resolved never to take this easy route again. From now on she would drive up Santavista and around the hill.

Carolyn's coworkers at the library didn't know what to make of her behavior. She said she had an eye infection and kept her dark glasses on. When people came to the information desk she spoke in a mumble, as if she were afraid to raise her voice. Later that day they discovered that she had requested a transfer to the telephone reference section in the basement. It seemed so odd that friendly, outgoing, gregarious Carolyn Corbett would want to sit in an underground lair, out of sight and away from the general public.

▼ ▼ ▼

Cassandra got the call at 10:30 that morning. It was Carolyn, agitated and obviously in no mood for small talk.

"I'm at work so I'll make this fast. Didn't you tell me once that you worked as a beautician's assistant?"

Cassandra said she had.

"So you know how to cut hair?"

"Sure. Why?"

"I want you to cut off mine and help me dye it black."

Cassandra laughed. "You're joking, right?"

"No, I'm not joking. Can you come over tonight, around six? Please?"

At six o'clock Cassandra rang the doorbell of Bilitis Cottage. It was a warm, fragrant evening, with a soft golden light still lingering in the sky, but all the windows in Bilitis Cottage were closed and the curtains drawn. Carolyn peeked out, then unlocked the door and cracked it open just enough for Cassandra to slide through and enter the dark, stuffy house. Only one small lamp was on in the living room. The living room was stifling.

"I've got everything set up," Carolyn said. She'd just washed her hair and wrapped it in a towel. Her face, devoid of makeup, looked thinner, flushed but strangely lifeless. She wore a threadbare terrycloth robe and woolen socks. "Do you have a scissors?"

Cassandra held up her bag of hair-cutting equipment and followed Carolyn into the kitchen. Here, too, it was dark and uncomfortably warm. The wooden Venetian blinds—all the rage now in the hills—were closed. The room smelled like cigarette smoke. Carolyn was not a smoker. Had she received a secret visitor before Cassandra? "Why's everything so closed up?"

Carolyn snapped on the light. "I mostly live downstairs when Susan's not here."

"Did Lady Caroline have her puppies?"

"Yes, she had them."

"Oh, can I see, can I see?"

"Maybe later," Carolyn said. "She doesn't like anyone coming near them. Want a drink?"

Cassandra noticed a wine glass and a half-empty bottle of a cheap California chablis on the kitchen counter. Now that she was living at Jay's Cassandra had grown accustomed to drinking fine vintages, private reserves. The stuff Carolyn was drinking was rotgut. "I'll have a Coke."

"It'll have to be diet." Carolyn said.

As she watched her clumsily fumble for a glass, Cassandra realized that Carolyn was slightly drunk. Alcohol usually loosened Carolyn up, made her funnier, sharper, and/or sentimental. The rotgut, or whatever else she was drinking, seemed to have the opposite effect. She was glum and oddly withdrawn. She must be lonely, Cassandra thought. Her lover's gone and she doesn't know what to do with herself. Then another possibility occurred to her: Maybe Carolyn had designs on her. "When's Susan coming back?"

Carolyn dug out a diet soda and popped the lid. "Couple of weeks. Her mother died. She's got to help her father settle the estate." She handed Cassandra the soda and poured herself a glass of wine.

"Well—cheers," Caassandra said. "Or, blessed be, as the Goddess Women say."

"Come on," Carolyn said, seating herself in a kitchen chair. "I want to get this over with." She pulled off the towel and shook out her hair.

Cassandra opened her bag—the one she'd filched from Betty's Snip 'n' Curl, the Spokane salon where she'd briefly worked before coming to Portland—and was laying her implements out on the counter when the doorbell rang.

Carolyn stiffened in her chair. "Ignore it!" she snapped. "It's probably Wellfleet. I don't want any interruptions."

It was all so mysterious. What had happened since the last Goddess Women meeting? Cassandra had entered into the spirit of the ceremony with raucous, uninhibited frenzy. She'd danced, moaned, chanted, rattled, and embraced a joyously weeping Carolyn. She wanted to make a good showing to impress Carolyn and the other Goddess Women. A flicker of apprehension ran through her. Maybe Carolyn thought she, Cassandra, was simply using her, Carolyn, to gain entrée to a group of rich, wellconnected professionals. Maybe she, Cassandra, had been too obvious when she said afterwards, practically rubbing her hands together, "They look like the kind of people who buy art."

"I can't wait until the summer solstice ceremony," she said, sipping her soda and trying to sound nonchalant. "The last one was such a blast. I loved being possessed like that."

Carolyn took a gulp of wine but remained silent.

"I love that song. 'Oh Great Goddess, blessed be,'" Cassandra sang, off-pitch, "'loving, caring, you are me.'"

Carolyn, plainly annoyed, turned to look at her. "Are you afraid to do this or something?"

"No, but I'm not a professional. I can't guarantee results."

"I don't care. Just start cutting." Carolyn draped a dry towel around her shoulders.

"It's just—I thought you were into looking natural," Cassandra said.

"I want a change. I'm sick of the way I look."

"But your hair's so beautiful as it is." Cassandra appreciatively fingered Carolyn's thick, wet, shoulder-length curls. Even the gray strands running through the rich auburn tresses were as lovely as seams of silver.

"I want a different look, that's all."

"What's Susan going to say?" Cassandra asked.

"I don't know."

Still Cassandra hesitated. "What will the Goddess Women say?"

"Sweetheart, the Goddess can change her hair color at will. She can turn it into hissing snakes if she wants to. Changing the way she looks is a woman's perogative."

"But the way you look is so you," Cassandra argued. "Why do you want to look like someone else? Doesn't Susan love you just the way you are?"

Carolyn took another sip of wine. "Susan thinks I'm a frumpy old hippie," she said. "She likes glamour."

So that was it. Carolyn wanted a makeover so she could rekindle Susan's waning interest. "Okay," Cassandra said. "I'll do it on one condition. You let me keep the hair."

"Why?"

"I've had this idea ever since the Goddess Woman ceremony." She tipped Carolyn's head forward and began to comb out her wet, fragrant tresses. "I want to do a series of goddess paintings using women's hair. Sort of like incorporating the magical part of us." Her plan was to ask each of the women to donate some of her hair, then try to interest them in buying the finished painting.

Carolyn sighed. "Okay, it's a deal."

As she cut and bagged Carolyn's hair, Cassandra gossiped about the Labonnes. "I really feel sorry for their kids," she said.

Carolyn shifted in her chair. "Why?"

"He's so hard on them. I can hear him yelling and ordering them around. I think he beats them—well, I know he beats the son."

Carolyn flinched. "How do you know that?"

"Dove told me. That's the daughter."

"You've talked to her?" Carolyn was incredulous.

"She's the enemy's daughter, isn't she?" Cassandra said. "What better way to get information about those assholes?"

Carolyn bit her lip. "What else has she told you?"

"Well, she's afraid of both of them—her stepfather and her stepbrother. Especially the stepbrother. Thinks he might do something to her."

"Like what?"

"Carolyn, wake up! What do you think?"

"I don't know. I don't know anything about their private lives."

"Get this—the son was in a reform school before they moved up here."

"Why? What did he do?"

"What didn't he do? Lied, stole, took drugs, beat up kids. Sounds like a psychopath to me."

"I don't think it's a good idea for you to get involved with that girl. You don't know what it might lead to. Those people are dangerous."

"I think I should seduce her," Cassandra said.

"Cassandra!" Carolyn said sharply. "You wouldn't! She's just a girl!"

"Relax, will you? Did you think I was serious?" Cassandra smiled as she quietly clipped. "You have to admit it would be great negative publicity, though. Get that homophobe's daughter to fall in love with me, turn her into a dyke, and then—"

"And then what? Expose her? She's not a pawn to play games with," Carolyn said, anxiously kneading her hands. "She's probably just a sweet little confused girl who wants a friend."

"A sweet little fourteen-year-old girl who's just dying to know about sex," Cassandra said. "I was sexually active at her age, weren't you?"

"No," Carolyn said firmly. "You were? With women?"

"Sometimes, but mostly with men. Until I was raped." She'd told Carolyn about this harrowing event after the Goddess Women ceremony, when they were both emotionally woozy and in the mood for confidences. Carolyn had pulled Cassandra to her warm, comforting breasts and wept with her. Now she reached up and silently stroked Cassandra's arm.

Cassandra, afraid of another emotional scene—something that might get out of hand—instinctively drew back. "Ever happen to you?" she asked.

Carolyn closed her eyes and solemnly nodded. "Let's not talk about this right now," she whispered.

They both sighed. Cassandra resumed her snipping. "Okay, have a look." She handed Carolyn a mirror. "Is that sort of what you had in mind?"

Carolyn looked into the mirror, turning her head back and forth. She put the mirror down. "Take off some more. It's too smooth. Make it look more—angry."

The phone rang.

"I'll get it," Cassandra said.

"No!" Carolyn jumped out of the chair to stop her. "Just let it ring."

"But maybe it's Susan."

The answering machine beeped into action. "Carolyn, it's Wellfleet. Turn on Channel Five. The bastards."

Carolyn raced over to the small television on the kitchen counter.

Amanda Drake, the local evening news anchor with the wide, permanently startled eyes and weirdly immobilized face—a pretty Barbie doll perennially at odds with the horrors she was forced to report—was just finishing up a segment on the ACA.

". . . held a victory rally this morning to celebrate their new anti-gay rights initiative. ACA president Ron Labonne said the group had collected the ninety-seven thousand signatures necessary to put the initiative on the November ballot."

A clip of smiling Ron Labonne standing at a podium, his wife beaming at his side, accepting cheers and applause. "This ballot measure is going to put political power back in the hands of the people it belongs to," he thundered. "We're going to reclaim our children from the hands of deviants who want us to believe their perverted lifestyles give them special rights under the law. We're going to fight for the Christian family values that this country is built on. We're going to fight—and we're going to win."

"You scum-sucking liar!" Cassandra shouted at the television. She stabbed the air with her scissors. "Man, I am going to get something on that bastard. Just wait."

▾ ▾ ▾

Carolyn's new hair was short, jagged, crow black, dykily punkish and completely at odds with her flowing Earth Mother wardrobe of natural fibers and rich muted colors. She went shopping. Bought lots of black clothes with severe lines, clothes completely inappropriate for someone with heavy thighs and a wide forty-two-year-old butt. She didn't care. She was grimly determined to erase the nice Carolyn Corbett of the sweet smile and easygoing acquiescent grace. A new Carolyn emerged, hard-edged and more in tune with the angry side of the Goddess.

She was constantly looking at herself in the ornate Victorian mirror Susan had bought at an auction soon after they met. Stared, trying to see the essential kernel of who she was. The mirror had always reminded her of the Tenniel drawings for *Alice in Wonderland*. And, living with Susan, she'd gradually created a gentle, stable, respectable image that fit in and looked at home in the old-fashioned looking glass.

Now that reflection was gone. She'd fallen through to the other side. She'd entered, once again, a dangerous world of shifting identities and violent possibilities. Back to disguises. Going underground again, but this time a fugitive in her own house— or, rather, in Susan's house, which made it even worse.

▾ ▾ ▾

John-Don, his lean face covered with a foamy white beard of shaving cream, studied his reflection in the bathroom mirror. It was still his face. He was still John-Don Webster. But he knew that others would not see the same image that he saw. He saw a dedicated teacher and solid, hard-working, well-respected, community-minded citizen. In their eyes he was something else entirely: a dangerous pervert, someone who could not be trusted with children, someone who was always searching for new prey.

He'd never regarded himself as abnormal in any way, and certainly not immoral. He'd never had a problem with self-esteem. In fact, he thought rather highly of himself. In all these respects John-Don knew he was lucky. Unlike Peter, he'd never been rejected or made to feel unworthy. Throughout his life he'd been supported by his parents. They were as livid about the ACA's ballot-measure proposal as John-Don was.

But now this strange, antithetical image of himself as a threatening pervert—a fantasy dreamed up by the ACA—hovered about him like an evil twin. He didn't accept it but it dogged his steps anyway, as if it were waiting for him to falter or crack. He was particularly aware of it when he was in bed with Peter. In the midst of their lovemaking, John-Don would suddenly see himself through a second set of eyes. *Their* eyes. He'd stand outside himself and watch as he committed acts regarded as sinful and disgusting.

It added an illicit thrill to sex and actually made him into a better lover. He and Peter had never been so close sexually.

He positioned his new Dunhill razor, one of many annoyingly extravagant Christmas gifts from Peter, and cut a smooth, clean trajectory from his left sideburn down to his chin. The razor was heavier than his old one and still didn't feel quite right in his hand. Ouch. This time he nicked himself. A bright bead of blood welled up. John-Don cursed the razor and pressed a piece of toilet paper on the cut.

The truth was, it had nothing to do with the razor. He was nervous. In an hour he'd make his pitch to Bill Lonsdale. In two hours he'd have to stand in front of his second-period American Government class and look at Lester Labonne.

With Lonsdale he envisioned success. And there was no reason to assume that the sullen, slouching, anti-social Lester even knew that John-Don was his neighbor. But since Lester was the son of Ron Labonne, and Ron Labonne was behind the ACA, and the ACA was persecuting gays, John-Don couldn't help but feel that Lester was watching him carefully. Waiting for some slip-up (but what?) which he could then report to headquarters. And this Lester would certainly do if Lonsdale agreed to the proposal John-Don had been diligently putting together.

Peter, in his new navy-blue crepe suit, came into the bathroom and kissed John-Don on the neck. "I've got a breakfast meeting with Katrina. Gotta go."

"Okay, I'll see you for dinner."

"No, I'm taking her to the theatre tonight, remember? Should be home by eleven, unless she wants to go dancing afterwards."

"Dancing?"

"Yes, dancing. You know—" Peter did a quick hip-hop routine.

"Does she think you're straight?"

Peter snatched the towel from John-Don's waist. "I don't know. We're so busy fucking we never have time to discuss it." He cast an adoring glance at his lover's body. "Mm-mm, you are one sexy honky. How about you save some of that white meat for me later on?"

"You just had some last night."

"Mmm, and tonight too, and tomorrow night, and the night after that. Let's not be stingy."

When Peter left, John-Don finished scraping off his whiskers, hopped into an ice-cold shower (good for the immune system, he believed), and prepared himself mentally for his meeting with the school principal.

It was a glorious morning. Majestic white clouds drifted slowly through the blue sky. Birds sang. John-Don sniffed the air appreciatively as he wheeled his old 20-speed racing bike from the garage. Now that the weather was fine, he rode the bike to school. He slipped on his trouser clips, positioned his backpack, fitted on his helmet, and set off. The ride was almost entirely downhill. He flew down Burnside, the wind slicing through his hair, his eyes watering. Spring in Oregon. How he loved it.

A half-hour later he was in Bill Lonsdale's cluttered office. Studio portraits of Bill, his wife Nina, and their four children smiled down at John-Don from walls and shelves. Books, manuals, and stacks of file folders were heaped everywhere. Bill put down his coffee mug and swiveled away from his computer to greet him. His bald head, ringed with a fuzz of short gray hair, gleamed in the overhead light.

They shook hands. "John-Don, how are you? Sit down. What can I do for you?"

John-Don got right to the point. "I want to get my American Government classes interested in the ACA's ballot measure."

Bill Lonsdale, the weary principal of Hamilton High School, sat forward and clasped his large hands on his desk. "Oh. Why?"

"Well, it's a lesson in the workings of democracy and the state's ballot-measure initiative process. And it's current events, so the kids could follow it closely." He pulled a manila folder from his backpack and handed it to Lonsdale. "Here. I've outlined the discussion and possible report topics."

Lonsdale glanced over the typewritten pages. "Mainstream Media Misinformation, what's that?" he asked.

"Just what it says." A media junkie, John-Don had been monitoring the situation, searching in vain for an outraged public response from the state's political leaders. The mainstream newspapers, radio and television stations, either through disinterest, embarrassment, or lack of gay spokespeople, never reported on the gay side of the issue. "How the media controls and directs public opinion. How it purports to be fair, when in fact it's one-sided. How citizens make uninformed decisions because they're only given half of the story."

"So you'd have your students read these homosexual newspapers?" Lonsdale said, scanning the report. "The Blade, The Advocate, The Pink Triangle?"

"I'd have them look at all forms of media. For balance. They'd see that the gay papers have a very different take on this issue."

"Obviously." Lonsdale closed the folder and shoved it aside. "John-Don, I'm going to be completely upfront with you. I don't think it's a good idea."

"Why not? It could be a special learning unit. The kids could use it for one of their contemporary affairs credits. They could track it from now until November."

"The issue's too volatile," Lonsdale said.

"Why? Because it's about freedom of sexuality?"

"John-Don, let's be realistic here. You know as well as I do the pressures we're under. Remember the stink we had when we tried to expand the human sexuality portion of the health curriculum? The minute parents got wind of it, the minute they saw that homosexuality was going to be discussed as an ordinary component of sexual experience, they hit the roof."

"Okay, parents don't want their kids to know anything about sex. They'd rather keep them blind and ignorant about teenage pregnancy and AIDS and everything else. But the fact is that these kids *are* having sex, whether their parents want them to or not."

Lonsdale glanced at a photo of his sixteen-year-old daughter and fifteen-year-old son, both dutifully smiling. "How do you know that? Do they tell you?"

"Come on, you know as well as I do. Sex interests them. And here we have a group of people who've made sexuality into a political issue. A constitutional issue. I think the kids could really get into this."

"I'm in complete agreement with you on that point. The kids would eat it up. But the minute you start talking about homosexuality in the classroom some religious fundamentalist like Ron Labonne is going to accuse us of teaching kids that's it's all right to be gay."

"It is all right to be gay," John-Don said with quiet exasperation.

Bill Lonsdale looked at him, wondering for the first time if John-Don Webster was gay himself. "Of course it is," he said cautiously. "But that's for everyone to decide for himself."

"How can anyone ever decide if they're never told the truth?"

"No, wait a minute, we're getting into personal values here. And personal values are not to be taught in the classroom."

"Unless they're heterosexual," John-Don countered. "Heterosexual values are taught every day, but that's okay because it's presumed that everyone is heterosexual. Well, not everyone is. Bill, I've got gay students in my classes."

"How do you know that?"

"I just know, that's all. Why should they have to sit through an obligatory Marriage and Family class when they're not allowed to get married and probably will never have children?"

Everyone knew that Bill Lonsdale, an old liberal who over the years had become completely fed up with American education, was now counting the days to his retirement. He smiled and nervously scratched his neck. "John-Don, I know you're a reasonable man. You're one of our best teachers. But you know damn well what would happen if you brought this issue into the classroom."

"Yeah, it would get kids to think about it. To ask themselves questions. To look at fundamental issues of discrimination."

"And sexuality."

"Bill, this is government I'm talking about. This is how their country works, and they should at least be exposed to how the system can be misused."

"Well, there you are. You couldn't really be impartial, could you? You'd be guiding them towards your viewpoint."

"Wait a minute. Are you saying I couldn't be impartial?"

Lonsdale frowned. "You want the honest truth, John-Don? Knowing you as I do, no, I don't think on this issue you could be impartial. Neither could I. Neither could most of the teachers at Hamilton High."

"So we're all going to let ourselves be bound and gagged because we're afraid of a group of religious fundamentalists?"

"It's not just religious fundamentalists that are supporting this ballot measure."

"No, all the Republicans in the state legislature seem to be behind it too."

"Yes, and the Republicans happen to control the legislature. Don't you realize what they could do to education funding if they heard about this? They've already cut our budget to nothing. We're understaffed, we don't have enough textbooks or classrooms." He shook his head in disgust. "I could go on and on."

John-Don leaned forward in his chair. "Bill," he said urgently, "they're trying to rewrite the Oregon constitution. This is serious stuff I'm talking about. It's dangerous."

"I know it is. If you start talking about it in the classroom it's dangerous for you, for me, for the entire school. But my hands are tied."

"No, they're not. If they are it's because you've tied them yourself."

"I've got to think about my school. I've got to consider what's best for the students—"

"I don't think it's the students you're thinking about," John-Don said. "It's your retirement package."

Lonsdale shot him an angry, aggrieved, and slightly guilty glance. "John-Don, I just don't think the kids or their parents are ready for this."

"Look, I can tell that you don't want to hear what I'm saying. But listen to me."

"I'm listening, I'm listening," Lonsdale said wearily.

"No, you're not," John-Don said heatedly. "You're refusing like everyone else to understand the importance of this ballot measure. It doesn't affect you personally so you can afford to ignore it."

"Why in God's name are you so interested in this one particular issue?" Lonsdale suddenly asked.

John-Don knew if he said "because I'm gay," the simplest answer, it would invalidate the force of his argument. Lonsdale would then have "proof" that John-Don was pushing forward a "personal agenda." He had to proceed cautiously, but his anger was rising.

"Because basic civil rights are at stake," he said, trying to keep his voice calm. "Because I'm supposed to be teaching kids about the workings of government. Bill, this ballot measure is based on complete misinformation. It's discriminatory, inflammatory, and unconstitutional. It puts the rights of some people—"

"Homosexuals," Lonsdale said, watching him.

"It puts the fate of gay people in the hands of people who disapprove of them. You can't ask a biased majority to vote on the civil rights of a minority group they don't like, can you?"

"This is Oregon," Lonsdale said. "Like it or not, we've got a system that allows for public ballot-measure initiatives to go to the voters. The ACA collected enough signatures, they've followed the rules."

"Do you really mean to sit there and tell me those rules are fair? That the validity of lives can actually be put to the vote?"

"Fair or not, they are the rules. If the ballot measure's unconstitutional it's up to the state Supreme Court to say so."

"Right, as if any gay person has ever been fairly treated by the courts. I guess you didn't read the story about the judge in Texas who recommended leniency for a killer because his victim was gay."

"You're getting way off the track here."

"Well, if you'd actually *look* at my outline, if you'd actually *read* it, you'd see that's one of the discussion topics: Can the courts be fair and impartial when they're protecting a legal system that excludes gays."

"I think you're overstating your case." Lonsdale looked away, as if John-Don's intense expression was too much for him to deal with this early in the day. "Look, I understand that this is obviously something you feel very strongly about, but—"

"The answer is no."

Lonsdale spread his hands. "Yes. I'm afraid the answer is no."

John-Don left in a rage. He was short-tempered for the rest of the day. He reamed out his second-period class for not reading their assignments. He took delight in repeatedly calling on Lester Labonne to answer questions. When Lester couldn't, John-Don looked at him with withering, impatient contempt.

Riding home later that afternoon he was still angry. He swore at drivers who changed lanes or made turns without using their blinkers. He pedaled furiously, weaving dangerously in and out of traffic. When he saw his first ACA bumper sticker—"No Special Rights for Perverts"—he pulled up to the side of the car and peered in. Who were these people?

The driver was a pleasant-looking older woman. She nervously waved at John-Don. He wanted to shout, but what good would that do? The wheels were set in motion.

On the surface, of course, nothing had changed. He saw Portlanders going about their daily business. They smiled and said hello to one another. They gulped down coffee and commented on the beautiful spring weather. He passed cherry trees blossoming in frothing clouds of pink.

No, on the face of it nothing changed. But John-Don could sense the dark, irrational power growing beneath the polite crust of society. What to do, what to do, what to do? He felt as though he were racing down a strange new highway towards a destination he wasn't sure he wanted to reach.

CHAPTER 20

"LOOKIT THIS," BILLY BIRD SAID, FAST-FORWARDING THE VIDEO.
At high speed, the flesh in *A Hole In One* looked like frantically pumping engine parts. Billy slowed down at his favorite segment.

Lester, his eyes glazed from smoking pot and drinking Terry's premium Russian vodka mixed with Jolt, lurched forward on the sofa. "Holy shee-it!" he giggled nervously. "That's fuckin' impossible, man!"

"Pretty hot, huh?" Billy inhaled and passed the joint back to Lester.

"Makes me wannna fuckin' *puke* when I see a nigger with a white chick." Lester pounded his fist into his palm, his eyes glued to the screen.

"Chicks can't suck cock good," Billy opined. "They're too afraid of 'em. They're too fuckin' dainty and their mouths ain't big enough."

"They got big mouths for everything else, though," Lester observed.

"You ever get a chick to blow you?"

"Sure, lotsa times."

"You're a fuckin' liar, man," Billy laughed.

"No, I swear, this retarded chick down in Medford used to give head for five bucks."

"That don't sound retarded to me. That sounds like a whore."

"That's what she was—a retarded whore. Gave head to everyone else cuz she didn't have one herself." Lester let out a high-pitched cackle that ended in a supersonic belch.

They were sprawled out in Terry's darkened "media room," curtains pulled tight to ward off the bright sunshine of an afternoon in May. The room was littered with an assortment of dirty plates, overflowing ashtrays, empty bottles, sticky glasses, and greasy food wrappers. Terry, off in Palm Springs, had left Billy in charge of the "big house."

He'd meant only that Billy, now ensconced above the garage, was supposed to keep an eye out for burglars. He did not mean that Billy was supposed to enter the manor whenever he felt like it, drink his best liquor, sleep in his bed, use his pool, drive his Mercedes, eat his non-perishable foods, use his VCR, or bring strangers in to smoke dope and sniff PCP.

But as far as Billy was concerned, Terry's Mock Tudor and everything in it was at his disposal. A treasure trove of possibilities. It occurred to him that he could sell off half the shit in it and disappear, but the comfort of the place had a certain long-term appeal. He liked to pretend the house was his, just as he liked to pretend the Mercedes was his. Terry had pointedly taken the car keys with him, unaware that months earlier Billy had had copies made. The fact that he'd finally made a new friend in the neighborhood also made Billy reluctant to split.

▾ ▾ ▾

It wasn't a sexual thing with Lester, just a guy thing. Billy was lonely for a like-minded buddy. Life with Terry was comfortable, but it was also a big fucking drag. The other neighborhood faggots he'd met at Thanksgiving wouldn't even look at Billy. They were all too rich and too smart. If there was anything Billy hated it was a bunch of suspicious tight-ass faggots who made him feel like a loser. That went double for Cassandra Taylor.

What a laugh: a neighborhood of queer dykes, kikes, gooks and niggers who thought they were better than he was. They didn't know or seem to care that youth made him a star, accustomed to the adulation of lonely fairies in resort enclaves like Palm Springs and Key West ("trade shows," as they were called by the hustlers Billy hung around with). Okay, maybe at twenty-five his best years were already behind him. In the youth market there was always a younger prettier face ready to nudge you out of the picture. Maybe Billy Bird wasn't the hot commodity he'd been at sixteen, a runaway freshly dropped out of high school. But he was still younger than *they* were, and he was still able to land a rich sucker like Terry. If that wasn't a noteworthy accomplishment, what was?

Lester, at seventeen, was more on Billy's mental wavelength.

For weeks Billy'd seen Lester hanging around next door, usually working halfheartedly on various house projects under the supervision of his old man. Then one day he ran into Lester down on 23rd, sitting glumly by himself on the sidewalk in front of Coffee People, halfheartedly begging for change. Billy struck up a conversation and bought Lester a triple-espresso Velvet Hammer.

With only Terry to tell him how wonderful he was, Billy was in need of a little hero-worshipping. A kid like Lester needed someone to look up to, someone older and wiser, someone who understood that even though life was a bitch always ready to drag you down there were still a few punches you could pull to make yourself feel better.

Lester, revved by the triple espresso, was eager to talk. He said he was new to Portland and didn't have any friends. He hated school, hated Portland, hated his old man and hated his old man's new wife and daughter. When Lester boasted to Billy of his stint in reform school, it added a certain dangerous luster to his personality.

They had shitloads in common. The whole fucking world, they agreed, was a shithole. They didn't want to fit in because they never had and knew they never would.

Lester was incredibly unobservant. When Billy told him they were neighbors Lester couldn't believe his ears. And when Billy asked him if he'd like to come over some time, Lester eagerly agreed.

On one of his first visits to the carriage house, loosened up by some of Terry's filched vodka, Lester showed Billy the tattoos on the soles of his feet: two screaming skulls with nails pounded into their heads. Cool, Billy said, but why on his feet? Lester said it was so his old man wouldn't see them.

Billy asked if Lester was pierced. "I wanna be but I can't," Lester said dolefully. "The old man would see the holes right away."

Billy told him how he could fake it. A couple of days later he obligingly took Lester down to a grungy head shop that sold clip-on nose and ear rings. Lester was excited but said he didn't have any bread. Billy did. He periodically rifled through Terry's wallet while Terry was in the shower. He bought Lester a heavy nose-to-ear clip and some other stuff, then let Billy stash all his forbidden gear in the carriage house. He even gave Lester his most treasured possession: an old Mega-Death t-shirt stolen from a concert two years earlier.

Their friendship really took off when Terry left for Palm Springs and Billy moved into the "big house." Billy persuaded Lester to sneak out of the house and meet him at a Smelly Farts concert. Lester wanted to, but didn't know how he could manage. He had to be careful because his old man beat the shit out of him for any infraction. To sweeten the offer Billy said he'd pay for the tickets and mentioned that he'd scored some good acid.

Lester, popeyed with fear and excitement, met him. They dropped acid and bonded like real buddies.

"Come on over to my pad tomorrow," Billy said. "I've got something you'll really get off on."

▼ ▼ ▼

"You know any sexy chicks here in Portland?" Lester asked, feeling his cheeks for ripe pimples, his eyes glued to the pumping, sucking, moaning action on the screen.

"Ain't had time to meet any," Billy said evasively.

"How'd you meet the guy who lives here? I told you he's my old man's wife's cousin, right?"

"Yeah." Billy got up to pour them both another vodka. "I just met him someplace. He needed someone to take care of his house."

"Is he a fag?"

Billy shrugged. "Terry? I dunno."

"He looks like one. He acts like one. I'd say he was definitely a fag, except that he's putting money into the old man's anti-fag campaign, and no fag would do that. But this still looks like a fag house to me."

"How would you know what a fag house looks like?"

"Shit, man, I can smell a fag a mile off. And the minute I see one, I just wanna bust their fuckin' skull wide open. Roadkill, man. Like my old man says, the only good fag is a dead fag. You ever bash any fags?"

"No, just niggers. Have you?"

Lester grinned. "Shit yeah. There was this fag picked me up once when I was hitch-hiking. I beat the shit out of him."

"What for?"

"Shit, man, you don't need no reason for bashing a fag. They can give you AIDS just by breathing on you. They're sick motherfuckers. You know what they do for sex?"

"What?" Billy asked, curious to hear what Lester knew about gay sex.

"They shit and piss on one another."

"Bullshit," Billy said. "How the fuck would you know that?"

"You don't believe me? Just wait." Lester rose unsteadily and stumbled towards the door. Billy could see that he had a hard-on from watching the porn. "My old man has a video. I'll go get it. Show you."

"Your old man's got a gay porn video?"

"Just wait. They ain't home. Be right back."

When Lester was gone, Billy collapsed on the sofa and began furiously chewing on his fingernails. His head felt like one of those skulls with nails pounded into it on the soles of Lester's feet. What was this "anti-fag campaign" Lester had mentioned? He'd have to be careful about what he said to Lester. Didn't want to make his new buddy suspicious. He'd have to deflect all that faggot shit away from himself.

'Cause I'm not a fag, he thought. There was a difference between being a fag because you wanted to be and being a fag for profit. And Billy Bird was always the top man, always the one who controlled the situation and made them beg for his favors. That meant he wasn't a fag.

He told himself Rich Fag World was just something he'd fallen into, an easy way to grab some otherwise unobtainable luxury. He could leave the fag world anytime he wanted. He'd stolen from his tricks, double-crossed them, taken what he wanted and then split. That meant he wasn't a real fag. He didn't get emotionally involved. Plus he liked straight porn—even if it was the men's cocks that got him hot.

There, in Terry's media room, stoned and drunk, a vision of the future suddenly opened up before him, like a big-screen teevee in his head. He could almost hear the announcer saying, "It's The Billy Bird Show!" and the excited applause. He dimly tried to put himself into it, to see himself later on in life, doing something, but couldn't. He couldn't see a fucking thing. The screen was empty. Fuck it. He reached for the vodka.

"Here," Lester said, returning with a video. "You wanna see how sick those fucked-up faggots are? Stick this fucker in."

The video was put together, Lester said, by his old man's group, the ACA. They were going to send out hundreds of copies, all over the state, to show people just how dangerous faggots really were.

"They pretend to be normal," Lester said, "but that's just so people won't know the truth about how fuckin' sick they really are."

It was the biggest load of crap Billy had ever seen. Even a moron could see that. He watched, uncomfortably fascinated, as a series of straight "experts"—all of them ugly dudes wearing glasses—described in detail the disgusting sexual habits of homosexuals. They had statistics to prove that 85% of homosexuals practiced "mutual defecation" while another 68% indulged in "fisting."

"You hear that?" Lester shouted. "Those fuckin' perverts stick their hands up one another's buttholes and smear shit on one another! I say kill 'em. Kill the fuckers or send 'em all to concentration camps."

Billy remained silent. This stuff wasn't true. The fact that he knew from his own experience that it wasn't, yet saw it being presented as though it were, was worrisome but he couldn't say why. It wasn't that he all of a sudden wanted to defend the queers he'd spent his life reviling in one way or another. No. It was more like realizing for the first time in his life how people made up "information" and used it for their own weird ends.

He glanced over at his buddy, watching as Lester excitedly picked at his pimples, his face an acne-smeared picture of angry disgust. Something in the video seemed to hypnotize him, but what? The dudes in polyester describing the meaning of "golden showers"?

"Here, watch this, watch this," Lester said excitedly.

It was footage from an old Gay Pride parade in San Francisco. It looked to Billy like something really ancient, like from the early Eighties, maybe even the Seventies, which Billy knew from reruns of the old television sitcoms that formed his earliest childhood memories.

The street was full of drag queens—"viciously mocking a woman's sacred femininity," according to an off-screen voice—and gym clones wearing skimpy shorts. One of them turned around, bent over, and spread his cheeks for the camera, peeking through his legs.

"This group of homosexuals has openly dedicated itself to a life of perverted sadermaserchistic acts," the voice sternly intoned. The film jumped to a group of leather queens marching down Castro decked out in their S/M regalia. "Torturing one another with pins, clamps, whips and chains, these devil-worshippers are so desperate for new converts that they frequently abduct children for use in their satanic rituals. Recent statistics show that seventy-eight percent of the missing children on milk cartons are the victims of their deranged and insatiable lust."

Billy laughed. Lester, startled out of his mounting rage, shot him a hostile, suspicious look.

Man, he really takes this shit seriously, Billy thought. It's like a red light to a bull.

"Flaunting their decadence, these so-called gay libbers are now demanding special rights to protect their immoral lifestyle," the off-camera voice said. "The choice is up to you. Vote yes on Ballot Measure Three if you agree that the last thing America needs is special rights for homosexuals. Vote yes on Ballot Measure Three to keep the moral fabric of America family life safe for democracy."

The camera zoomed in on a flower-covered float strewn with an assortment of half-naked men writhing around to an old disco song. Definitely Seventies, Billy thought. The men were pumping it up for the crowd and for the camera, which moved closer.

"Holy shit!" Billy exclaimed.

"I told you. Look at those queers! It makes me want to go bash some right now. Come on, let's go riding around in that Mercedes of yours and find some."

"I don't believe it," Billy said. He excitedly backed up the film, replayed it, and froze the image of a black man on the float. "Yeah, it is. It fucking is."

"What?" Lester asked.

"It's that rich nigger from across the street," Billy said.

There on the Gay Pride float, dancing for the camera, dressed in a pair of cut-offs and cowboy boots, was a young Peter Love.

▼ ▼ ▼

Cassandra didn't encourage Dove Labonne's visits but neither did she discourage them. It seemed like the moment she picked up a paint brush, or sat down to read, or was about to wander upstairs to get cozy with Jay in the hot tub, Dove's furtive, expectant face would appear at the door of her basement studio.

Annoying, but Cassandra, against her better judgment, had become fond of Dove. She saw in Dove something of the girl she'd been at that awful age. Confused, on the verge of young womanhood, body changing, emotions being tugged loose from the eroding shore of adolescence and sucked out into the treacherous, terrifying waters of adulthood.

Dove's vulnerability brought out emotions Cassandra would have preferred to lavish on Jay. But harried, preoccupied Jay, though he was always telling Cassandra how much he *appreciated* her, treated her more like a daughter than the lover she wanted to be. She couldn't get him to respond to her as a woman, with deep passionate desires. When she went out to the lesbian bars and attractive women made eyes at her, Cassandra couldn't respond to them—maybe because she feared they'd interrupt her non-existent affair with Jay. So that left Dove, who sucked up attention like a sponge and provided Cassandra with at least one outlet for the frustrated tenderness in her heart.

Dove's presence in her studio also allowed Cassandra to enjoy an illicit sense of revenge. There was a delicious irony in allowing the daughter of her homophobic neighbors to develop a crush on her. More importantly, Dove was an excellent, if unwitting, source of information about the Labonnes. When the time was right, Cassandra planned to use what she'd learned. She didn't know how, and until she had something tangible she could only fantasize what her revenge might be. Thinking about it gave a strange and rather exciting double edge to her life. She, after all, was the only one in Queer Corners who had access, via Dove, to the inner workings of the Labonne household.

With Dove, Cassandra carefully avoided any mention of her own sexuality. The Labonnes had no doubt indoctrinated the girl into believing their twisted "facts" about homosexuality. One careless remark and Dove would see Cassandra as an evil enemy and bolt. That would ruin everything.

Since Dove never mentioned her parents' political vendetta against gays, Cassandra kept mum on the subject herself. Queer demons seemed to play little or no part in Dove's imagination. But that sexual demons of some kind were afoot Cassandra had no doubt. They skittered and flew about, a dark, gibbering legion of them, just beneath Dove's virginal, good-girl demeanor. Perhaps they were figments concocted from her sin-laden, fire-and-brimstone upbringing. Perhaps they were fed by the hormones in Dove's maturing body. Or perhaps they were real.

Why was Dove so frightened of her stepbrother and of Ron himself? Why couldn't she couldn't bring herself to say what was so obvious to Cassandra: that at least part of the fear was sexual?

Instead, Dove implicated an unnamed man in a weird on-going sexual plot. It had to do with a frightening experience she'd had in Forest Park months earlier. She hadn't told her parents about it, Dove said, because then they wouldn't let her go out. She could tell Cassandra because Cassandra was like a big sister: Cassandra understood men, or so Dove thought.

But what Cassandra understood was that each time Dove talked about this "attack," new details were added, or embellished, or altered. It apparently excited Dove to cast herself in the role of a helpless victim. Cassandra suspected that she was consciously dramatizing the story to gain more sympathy and attention. It stirred up memories of her own rape, years earlier, but Cassandra didn't want to frighten Dove by telling her about that.

She wondered if Dove was hiding something truly awful. It wasn't uncommon for sexually abused girls to dissociate. If Dove was being molested by her stepfather or stepbrother, she might be transferring all her fears onto the shadowy, malevolent figure in Forest Park. It wrenched Cassandra's heart to think of it. She didn't want to know, yet she did. For if she found out and could actually prove that the author of the Non-Special Rights and Child Molestation Protection Act was molesting his own stepdaughter, she could ruin him.

As spring slipped into early summer, Dove's visits grew more frequent. Cassandra worried that the girl might become too reckless. Because for all her seeming innocence, there was definitely something frightened and frightening buried in Dove's personality. It came out in sudden bursts of furious resentment, mostly about Ron, Lester, and the way they all treated her. Being a robotically good "nice girl" obviously wasn't easy for her. Cassandra could sense the anarchic pressures waiting to break loose and wreak havoc. She understood those pressures all too well.

▾ ▾ ▾

At first she snuck over only when her mom and Ron were away. That was happening more and more now that they had their television show. They were out a lot with their ACA ministry, giving talks and holding prayer meetings. But then she began to sneak over to Cassandra's even when they were at home, holed up with their friends, "talking strategy," as Ron said.

The rabbit hutch at the bottom of the yard offered a convenient excuse for Dove to leave the house. From there, she could quickly reach the path that lead through the trees and over to Cassandra's studio. She usually brought a bunny rabbit with her. If they ever caught her, she could say that a rabbit had escaped and she'd gone to find it.

Each visit was a breathless, thrilling adventure. She'd never actually been *forbidden* to visit Cassandra, but that was because she kept it all a secret. She knew her neighbor was off-limits because her mom had nothing good to say about Cassandra.

"My mom said you're a devil worshipper," she'd blurted out once, in an agony of confusion. If it was true, what would she do? She watched Cassandra closely, fearfully, half-expecting a viper's tongue to dart out of her mouth.

But Cassandra only laughed, as if it were a silly joke. "Really? Why on earth would she tell such a terrible lie?"

"It's a lie?" Dove was breathless and wide-eyed with anxiety. She believed Cassandra. So did that mean she couldn't believe her mom? It was so confusing. Who was telling the truth?

"Of course it's a lie," Cassandra said. "Why would she say such a thing about a person she doesn't even know?"

"She said people who wear rings in their noses worship Satan."

"Well, you know better, right?" But then her eyes grew sharp and accusatory. "Or do you think I'm a devil-worshipper, too? Because if you do, I think you'd better leave my studio right now and never come back."

"No, I don't believe it," Dove insisted. "Not in a million years. Not *you*."

It was such a relief, because Dove fervently loved her new friend. Cassandra could do no wrong. Dove had never known anyone who lived in a "studio" or made art. In her fascinated eyes, Cassandra's basement apartment was an alluring, magical world stuffed with fascinating treasures. Cassandra was like a kind, tattooed sorceress presiding over it.

If Cassandra was a witch she was a good witch. She served Dove herbal teas poured out into little porcelain cups and offered her delicious, exotic foods Dove had never heard of, much less tasted. She burned incense and lit candles. She introduced Dove to k.d. lang, Enya, and Sting. She let Dove try on her clothes and experiment with makeup. She taught Dove how to work in clay, let her dabble with watercolors, draw with charcoal.

At first Dove wrestled with a vague, troubling sense that what she was doing was terribly sinful. Cassandra, with her tattoos and nose rings, was sinful. She, Dove, was sinful for wanting to spend every minute with a sinner, and because she enjoyed it all so much. But she couldn't for the life of her understand why it was sinful. There didn't seem to be anything wrong with it. Cassandra was the only person who really paid attention to her, who took an interest, who *listened*.

Dove was elated when, in June, Cassandra said she wanted to do a portrait of her. She sat in a chair, holding Fluffy, and they talked while Cassandra made preliminary sketches.

Cassandra was so nice. She understood how hard it was to be uprooted from everything you knew and thrown into a new house in a new city with a mean new stepfather and a creepy new stepbrother and rich snotty kids at a new school who laughed at your clothes and accent.

"We moved every two years," Cassandra told her. "My dad was in the army, so I grew up on military bases. Every time I'd make a new friend and feel settled, we had to yank everything up and go someplace else."

"Was he mean, your dad?" Dove asked.

"Mean! Everything had to be just so. If it wasn't, we'd get the tar beat out of us."

"That's how Ron is. Especially with Lester."

"We weren't allowed to be kids," Cassandra said as she sketched. "You know, when you're a kid you're curious about things, you question things, you want to know more than what they tell you about. Right?"

"Right," Dove agreed.

"But in the army you're not supposed to question anything. It's like a religion," she said. "You're just supposed to obey orders."

"That's how Ron is. Do this, do that. He gets so mad. You should see what he does to Lester when Lester doesn't obey." She described a recent fight, heaping on the gory details until Cassandra winced. "But Lester deserves it," she added. "He's bad. He's really bad." Her voice rose. "Sometimes I just hate him. Ron, too. I just hate him. They're so mean. It's like they hate me, but I never did anything to them. Never!"

Cassandra was silent for a moment. "Dove, does he—your stepfather—does he ever—touch you?"

"You mean hit me?" Dove shook her head.

"No," Cassandra said quietly. "Not hit you. Touch you. Where you don't want to be touched."

"You mean like that man in the park?" Dove tried to remember what she'd told Cassandra about her attacker, and then tried to connect it somehow to Ron. "No," she said carefully. "But I think he wants to." Seeing Cassandra's look of alarm, she settled back more comfortably in her chair.

▾ ▾ ▾

Ito hadn't realized how much he wanted the Hill commission until he lost it.

When he finally felt well enough, he called Mrs. Hill to set up an appointment to resume work on her garden. Helen, her daughter, answered the phone. She seemed to take malicious delight in telling Ito that the garden project, for which (she implied) Ito had bilked her mother out of twenty thousand dollars, had been cancelled. Now that her mother had been declared incompetent, Helen had taken over all administrative responsibilities for the Hill estate.

"Of course you do owe me twenty thousand dollars worth of services," Helen Hill said, "so I want you to draw me up a plan for a different kind of garden."

She was wrong, he owed her nothing, but Ito didn't argue the point. During his convalescence he'd turned down several smaller offers so he could concentrate his feeble energies on Mrs. Hill's lucrative large-scale project. Helen Hill was rude, but Ito agreed to meet with her because he needed the money. He also felt a deep hungry need to reconnect with the earth. The question was, what kind of garden did she now have in mind?

As he drove through the secluded, winding streets of Dunthorpe, Ito wondered about old Mrs. Hill. Eccentric? Yes. Incompetent? No. What had happened to her? It troubled him, the way Americans always seemed so eager to get rid of their parents, banishing them to rest homes the minute they were no longer considered "useful." Ito, a second-generation Nisei, had been raised to revere his elders. In Japan, the elderly were considered living treasures. Here they were unceremoniously junked like old cars.

He turned onto Military Road and slowed down as he approached Hillmount, Mrs. Hill's estate. Stretching along the entire length of the brick wall separating the grounds from the street were large red signs, "We Agree With Three!" printed in bold black letters.

Seeing them, Ito stopped his car.

"Three" referred to Ballot Measure Three, the anti-gay rights bill being pushed by Ron Labonne and the ACA. John-Don ranted about it every time he and Ito were together. Ito, trying to view the ballot measure with his habitual Zen detachment, had at first dismissed it as unworthy of reflection. It was too idiotic to be taken seriously, he said. That was exactly why it did have to be taken seriously, John-Don said: "You can't underestimate the stupidity of people when it comes to sexuality."

If it weren't for John-Don, Ito would have ignored Measure Three and tried to meditate away its emotional effects. Because, as John-Don rightly pointed out, it appealed to just that—emotions. And what were emotions? The false, fretful, worldly debris of ego, eternally chafing and distracting the soul from its true path: the Eternal.

"You live such a sheltered life, Ito," John-Don said. "You're like a monk. You don't realize that there really is evil out there. Evil masquerading as good."

Which was not true. It was precisely because he did know there was evil "out there" that Ito preferred to live like a monk. Evil, he had always believed, was firmly rooted in emotion, ignorance and mediocrity. Particularly mass emotion, mass ignorance and mass mediocrity. Democracy was supposedly government by majority but as this ballot measure made abundantly clear, democracy was always in danger of devolving into the lowest form of mob rule. And what mob had ever done anything wise or useful for humankind?

If it weren't for John-Don, Ito thought, staring at the red "We Agree With Three" signs, I wouldn't be sitting here thinking about emotions. And perhaps I would be better off without them.

But that wasn't true and he knew it. What was love if not an emotion? And what was his feeling for John-Don if not love? And what would his life be, now, without his love for John-Don? A barren wasteland . . . of sorts. Just thinking about John-Don made something in him rejoice. His body jangled with excitement. It felt as though a strong, luxurious vine was shooting up through his spinal cord and tickling his heart with new sensations.

Well, at least go up and see what Helen Hill has in mind for her new garden, he thought. No harm in talking to her.

Driving up to the house through the barrage of signs made Ito uncomfortably aware of other painful emotions that he tried to ignore. Hadn't the emotional hysteria that led to his family's internment during World War II been created with signs, slogans, words? That experience, which had poisoned his parents' lives and scarred the landscape of his own childhood, was something Ito avoided thinking about whenever possible.

Now he remembered his bewildered pain when schoolmates began calling him a "dirty Jap." He remembered seeing his parents huddled over a newspaper, nervously whispering in Japanese, which they reserved for only the gravest situations. He couldn't understand why the headline—OUSTER OF ALL WEST COAT JAPS NEAR!—frightened them so much. Or why, suddenly, on every telephone pole, there were signs instructing all people of Japanese ancestry to prepare for evacuation. Or why his mother, in the middle of the night, burned all her Japanese family mementos. Everything that connected her to her past, to her ancestors, to her traditions, she reduced to ashes, "so they will not think I am a traitor." His mother, a traitor? Ito saw panic in eyes that were usually calm and steadfast. Why? What happened? What had they done wrong? Why had everyone turned on them?

And then there was the camp itself. The barbed wire. The filthy conditions. The military personnel, armed guards with rifles. The punishing desert heat, undulating up from the cracked earth in snakelike waves, and the freezing desert cold. So different and so awful and so incomprehensible after his father's leafy green apple orchards, which he'd been forced to sell at a loss.

Ito muttered a short mantra to clear his racing mind. Remembered what the Buddha said: "Hatred does not cease by hatred at any time, hatred ceases by love."

Several cars and pick-up trucks were parked in the driveway of Mrs. Hill's huge white neo-colonial house. Near a side entrance, two heavyset men were bundling together stacks of the "We Agree With Three!" signs.

Leave, Ito told himself. Back up and go. Get out of here. Something's really screwy.

But it was too late. A young man, prematurely bald, wearing an ill-fitting brown suit with a wide red tie and a "We Agree With Three!" button on his lapel, rushed down from the porch and stuck his head in the window of Ito's Landcruiser.

"Are you Mr. Kundamoto?" he asked.

"No, I am Mr. Kudomono."

"Sorry, yeah, Miss Hill's waiting for you inside. I'm Bob Sayles, administrative assistant and director of merchandising." He pumped Ito's hand and led him inside.

The interior furnishings were the same, but everything had been moved around, destroying the meticulous order he remembered from Mrs. Hill's tenancy. The house was apparently being used as an office.

There were people everywhere—all of them Caucasians, Ito noticed, and all of them wearing "We Agree With Three!" buttons. Boxes were stacked in the front hallway. An overweight woman sat at a computer in the living room, chewing gum as she entered data from a stack of forms. A sunken-cheeked man and a tiny woman sat on the sofa, talking and scribbling notes on yellow legal pads. At another table a young woman with a bouffant hairdo and a pleased grin on her face slit open envelopes, extracting checks and cash.

Ito, uncomfortably aware that he was being scrutinized, followed Bob Sayles through the house to what had been Mrs. Hill's study. The young man rapped on the study door and a voice said, "Come in."

When Ito entered and saw a dumpy, middle-aged woman in a plain navy-blue dress sitting behind the desk he knew at once that it was Helen Hill. She had the humorless severity and the grim fashion sense of a prison matron. Seated to one side of her, in matching wing-back chairs, were Cornette and Ron Labonne.

Ito stopped in his tracks. The sight of Cornette Labonne, who'd refused him help after he'd fallen, whose hands had transmitted so much pain, sent a warning flash of anger through his backbone. There she was, a pair of enormous eyelashes under a pile of stiff silver-blonde hair, smiling at him with puffy orange lips weirdly outlined in black. She was dressed in a white ruffly concortion that made her look like a Spanish Madonna about to be paraded in a religious procession—or maybe one of those frilly-skirted dolls used to disguise spare rolls of toilet paper.

And there was Ron Labonne, the nemesis of Queer Corners, who had turned Delmont's house into a devalued eyesore and was now spreading anti-gay propaganda. His black suit, tight in the thighs and pinched in the shoulders, had the reptilian sheen of indestructible manmade fibers. He looked stiff, uncomfortable, but self-consciously powerful, sitting like a Pharaoh with his clenched hands resting on his knees.

All three of them were wearing "We Agree With Three!" buttons.

"Good morning," Helen Hill said, her jowly face unreadable behind enormous glasses. "I think you know your neighbors, Ron and Cornette Labonne."

Ito did not move. He couldn't move. He stood there, his hat clasped in his hands, like a schoolboy called to the principal's office.

Nor did Ron Labonne budge from his chair. He nodded, his eyes glinting like fish scales.

Cornette was more animated. She waved her fingers in greeting like a coy little girl. "I surely am glad to see you up and about again!" she cried. "I've been praying for you ever since you collapsed on my front porch."

Helen Hill looked puzzled. "Since he what?"

"Oh," Cornette laughed, "he took a little tumble one day, didn't you, Mr. Kutahara, and he came over to ask for help."

"That is not strictly true," Ito said. "Your movers had destroyed my cypress tree. For which I have still not been reimbursed."

"Well, I told you we weren't responsible," Cornette said. Her friendliness vanished as quickly as a magician's hanky. "You'll have to take that up with the moving company."

Ito pressed the point. "The moving company says the drivers were acting on your orders."

"What orders?" Ron Labonne asked his wife.

"Oh, nothing, hon, nothing." She turned back to Ito. "Maybe we can deduct the cost of that darn tree from the garden you're going to make for us. We could do that, couldn't we, Helen?"

"I beg your pardon?" Ito said. "I was not aware that I was going to create a garden for you."

"Well, that's why you're here," Helen Hill said.

"Is it?"

"Yes, it is. Now, as you know," Helen said, pretending to be lawyerly, shuffling through some papers, "I'm in charge of my mother's estate. And my mother, as you also know, was not competent to enter into any contractual obligations when you got her to pay twenty thousand dollars for this garden scheme at Hillmount."

"Your mother was perfectly competent," Ito said. "She came to me, I did not force her to do anything."

"A sick eight-two-year-old woman who asks you to design a garden that's going to cost hundreds of thousands of dollars is not in her right mind," Helen insisted.

"My contract with Mrs. Hill will stand up in any court of law," Ito said.

"That remains to be seen," Helen said. "I asked you here today so we could discuss a fair settlement."

"There is no settlement," Ito said. "I provided Mrs. Hill with a landscape design. She paid me for that phase of my services."

"Twenty grand for a lousy garden design?" Ron Labonne muttered out of the side of his mouth, just loud enough to be heard.

"Excuse me," Ito said, turning to him, "it was not a lousy garden design. I do not create lousy garden designs."

"For twenty grand, I hope not," Ron said.

"That's a lot of money," Cornette added, blinking so rapidly it made Ito's head spin. "That's money that could be put to a really useful cause."

"Like your own, I suppose," Ito said. For he understood now what was going on. Helen Hill was turning over all or part of her mother's estate to the ACA.

"All right, Mr. Kudomono, I'm aware of your reputation," Helen Hill said. "But I've checked around, and no landscape designer in Portland charges that much for a garden design. The people I talked to were shocked—*shocked*—when I told them how much you got."

"Perhaps they were not professionals," Ito said.

"Oh, they were professionals. They were Christians, too."

"Professional Christians or professional landscape designers?" Ito asked.

Helen Hill stiffened. "I can take this matter to court, if you like," she said, "but wouldn't it be better to save the cost of lawyers and courts by settling this between ourselves? All we're asking for is another garden design."

"Well, two, really, Helen," Cornette said. "Yours and ours."

Ito remained silent.

"What we want," Helen continued, "is a whole new garden with a Christian theme."

"I beg your pardon?" Ito said.

"A Christian theme garden," Helen repeated. "Stories from the Bible, with lifelike statues. With some kind of a walkway that connects them. It would start with the Garden of Eden. Then maybe maybe you could have a couple of little pools, one that shows Moses being found by Pharaoh's daughter, and another one that shows Jesus walking on the water in the Sea of Galilee."

"Oh praise Jesus!" Cornette cried. "That would be just beautiful, Helen."

For the first time, Helen Hill smiled. It looked difficult for her. "It would all lead up to the final tableau," she said to Ito. "Golgotha—Jesus nailed to the cross."

"Amen!" shouted Cornette. "That would be truly inspirational. Oh, I can just see it, Helen—that's just what I want for our garden, too. And maybe, you know, there could be blood dripping from his wounds—you could do that with a recirculating water pump, couldn't you, Mr. Kutahara? Dye the water red so it looks just like blood."

"That might be a little excessive, Cornette," Helen said.

"Excessive?" Cornette laughed. "People need to see the *symbols*, Helen, or they don't understand the *pain*." She turned to Ron. "Don't you think it would be a good idea, hon? Blood dripping out his hands and head?"

"The point is to make the place as popular as we can," Ron said to Helen. "If we're going to charge admission, they're going to want something special."

"You know, like at Disneyland you can see Cinderella and Mickey Mouse," Cornette said. "So here they'll see people dressed up like the Apostles. Wouldn't that be a cute idea, Helen?"

"Excuse me, I must leave now," Ito said.

Cornette grabbed her husband's thick wrist and checked his watch. "Gracious, hon, we've got to go, too. We're going to be late for our show."

Helen Hill nodded and rose from her chair. "So you do understand who we are and what we're after, Mr. Kudomono?" she said.

"Yes, perfectly," Ito said. "You're a group of bigots and you want free work from someone who has no intention of giving it to you. Good day."

His spine was aching as he took his leave. He half-expected them to come rushing after him, to call one of their minions to detain him. But the only thing that happened was that Bob Sayles offered Ito a "We Agree on Three" pin for a five-dollar donation.

He looked hurt when Ito refused. "You don't want one? Well, I put a free bumper sticker on your car anyway."

Ito gasped when he saw it. "I did not ask for this! Take it off immediately!"

"What?" The young man couldn't believe his ears. "I told you it's free, courtesy of the ACA."

Ito tried to tear the red "We Agree With Three!" from his rear bumper. It wouldn't come off. Finally he gave up. "You people are wicked!" he shouted to the startled young man.

Before he got into his Landcruiser, Ito saw someone looking down at him from an open second-story window. It was Mrs. Hill. The old woman shook her head sadly and raised her hand in recognition.

CHAPTER 21

SUSAN, ULTRA-CHIC, WEARING A BEAUTIFUL CREAM-COLORED TROUSER-suit she'd bought in London, her hair freshly styled, finally came out of the jetway at Portland airport. Carolyn, standing behind the crowd at the gate, nervously waved at her. Susan stopped in her tracks, a shocked look on her face, before cautiously proceeding.

"Darling!" She gave Carolyn scathingly quick up-and-down appraisal. "What have you done to yourself?"

"Don't you like it?" Trying to look sexy and calm.

"Not particularly," Susan said, brutally honest as always.

"It's the new me."

"I think I liked the old you better. Why didn't you tell me?"

From the perfunctory peck and tepid embrace Susan gave her in the privacy of the Volvo, Carolyn knew just how much her lover disapproved. Susan didn't seem particularly glad to see her. It cut Carolyn to the quick, but she kept up a stream of nervous chatter.

Susan warmed up a little on the way home. "Well, I must say, it's going to take some getting used to this new you. It wasn't those tiresome goddess creatures putting a hex on you or something, was it?"

"Of course not. I've lost twenty pounds."

"Really? I couldn't tell from those clothes."

After a month in England, Susan's accent was noticeably stronger. Her emotional reserve was more impenetrable than ever. When she relayed the devastating news that she'd been cut out of her mother's will, there wasn't a crack to be seen in that superior, self-contained facade. She looked so sophisticated, so English-countryside-cosmopolitan, in comparison to everyone else in casual, grungy Portland. Carolyn felt like a ratty drab beside her.

But Susan's English cool erupted into hot Vesuvian fury when she got home and saw Lady Caroline's bastard brood.

Carolyn was forced to tell her how Lady Caroline had escaped and been impregnated by the Labonnes' dog. Susan was livid, infuriated as much by Carolyn's ongoing evasion of the truth as by the genetically inferior outcome. All that money down the drain! If she'd known about the mongrel mating she could have had the litter aborted.

"They're worthless, goddamn it!" Susan screamed. "Absolutely bloody fucking worthless! I'm going to kill the lot." And to Carolyn's cringing horror, Susan angrily scooped up a puppy in each hand and ran to the bathroom, where she threw them into the toilet.

Carolyn grabbed Susan's hand before she could flush. "You can't do that!" She shoved Susan out of the way and fished the frantically dog-paddling puppies from the toilet bowl.

Susan tried to get them away, clawing at Carolyn's hands. "They're mongrels and I'm going to get rid of them!"

"Over my dead body!" Carolyn faced her lover's wrath with a sudden wrath of her own.

"What am I going to tell the people who've already paid for them? I've already spent their money! They paid for purebred Ruby English, not Spam! This is going to ruin my reputation as a breeder!"

Carolyn, crying, dried off the squirming puppies and carried them back to their mother, hovering protectively over the whelping basket as Susan, like a predatory hawk, tried to push her away and get at them. Carolyn pushed back. Lady Caroline gave her squealing offspring a suspicious sniff but seemed more interested in the battle taking place above her. Her bulging eyes darted nervously from one mistress to the other.

It went on from there. A shrieking, screaming, vein-popping shouting match that came dangerously close to blows. Carolyn stood her ground. She accepted full responsibility. She said she'd refund the potential owners and pay for Lord Nelson's stud service and find homes for the puppies. But, in the end, it all came down to "home," and that meant Susan's home, where Carolyn, tossed in the wake of Susan's explosive anger, felt she was no longer safe or even wanted.

"I don't know you anymore!" Susan bellowed. "I go away to see my mother before she dies, I find out I've been axed out her will, and then I come back to find you looking like some bloody ridiculous punked-out dyke and lying about the puppies."

Oh, Carolyn thought bitterly, that's not the half of it. "I was trying to make myself more attractive for you," she whimpered, instinctively begging for a crumb of sympathy.

"Well, you didn't. Why didn't you *tell* me for Christ's sake?"

"Because I wanted to surprise you."

"I'm talking about the puppies, stupid!"

It was like a blow. Susan had never called her stupid before. "I didn't want to upset you any more than you were already upset. Your mother had just died."

"That didn't upset me. Being cut out of her bloody will is what upset me. And now *this*." Susan pointed towards the whelping basket. "Why did you lie about it? What else have you lied about?"

"Susan!"

"How can I ever trust you?"

"I guess you can't," Carolyn cried. And the awful truth was, Susan had every right not to trust her.

"I could never trust mummy," Susan ranted, "but I did think I could trust you. But it's like coming home and finding a stranger in my house! A mongrel stranger and her six mongrel puppies."

Carolyn was too upset to respond. It was an apt description of how she felt herself.

▼ ▼ ▼

Once again the word "homosexual" never came up as the true reason for his dismissal. After examining his students' evaluation forms, the administration and the Board of Trustees had decided that Wellfleet Stipple did not represent the best Christian interests of the college.

Wellfleet demanded to see the evaluation forms. Refused. He demanded to have his dismissal considered by a faculty review board. Refused. Such coercive political tactics might be used at elitist universities but they had no place at a private, non-unionized religious institution.

It wasn't Wellfleet's teaching *per se* that was at fault. Willard Lansgaard, the grim, white-haired president, actually said that. It was Wellfleet's "personal values as perceived by the students" that were in error.

Wellfleet didn't inculcate the highest Christian principles in the classroom. He showed neither love nor respect for God, country or family. He had been heard to laugh at the idea of creationism (from this Wellfleet knew that Mimi Strang had denounced him). He had told a voice student that she should be prepared to forego marriage and family in order to pursue her career (from this Wellfleet knew that Tina Pedersen had betrayed him).

Infuriated, Wellfleet tried to garner student and faculty support by starting a petition of his own. To his surprise, dozens of students actually signed it. It was less of a surprise that no one on the faculty, and specifically no one in the music department, did.

"In all good conscience, Wailfleet, I can't sign your petition," drawled Fletcher Davis, the dandruffy head of the department.

Wellfleet, detecting a victorious sparkle under Fletcher's false solemnity, exploded. "That's because you've wanted me out of here since the day you arrived, you lousy piece of mediocrity."

Fletcher pulled himself up with a look that was both aggrieved and aghast. "Lord, Wailfleet, whatever put that uncharitable thought into your head?"

"Do you think I'm blind? It's always the same with losers like you, Fletcher. You don't have any real talent so you protect yourself by sucking up to power."

"The only thing I suck on, Wailfleet, are the reeds for my bassoon," Fletcher said.

"Well, you better start sucking on something else, Fletcher. And fast."

"Just what do you mean by that obscene remark?"

"I mean," Wellfleet said, "that when I tell Lansgaard about your extracurricular and extramarital student affairs program, Fletcher, you won't have a reed left to suck on."

Fletcher's glow of spiritual superiority suddenly vanished. His face hardened into a mask of corn-pone-and-grits hostility. "You got nothin' on me, Waillfleet."

That was true, in an evidential sense, but Wellfleet was beyond caring about such niceties. "Don't I?" he taunted.

"You're just desperate, that's all. Like a coon trapped up a pine tree."

"It's the desperate ones who change the world, Fletcher. Christ was pretty desperate towards the end, wouldn't you say?"

"There you go," Fletcher cried, "mocking Our Lord's message, the same way you mock it in the classroom!"

"What message is that, Fletcher?"

"Obey thy Lord God for the Judgement Day is at hand."

Wellfleet smiled. "It certainly is, Fletcher."

"Christ wudn't desperate. He died willingly, to save mankind from its sins."

"Didn't work, did it?"

Fletcher was stunned. "You are a dangerous man, Wailfleet. I knew that the first time I saw you."

"You're such a hypocrite, Fletcher, I suppose you prayed for me."

"Get out of my office, Wailfleet. You're polluting my air."

"Your air's always been polluted, Fletcher—you stink of hypocrisy."

It was a small campus, and though gossip was censured as an uncharitable activity nothing of interest could actually be kept secret for long. When the administrators got wind that Wellfleet was trying to stir up trouble, that he wasn't going to tuck his tail between his legs and skulk away like a beaten dog, they whistled him back into the administrative fold. Charity and redemption, that's what they were most concerned about after all. Perhaps, they suggested, Wellfleet should be given one more year, as a trial . . .

One more year, he thought, breathing a secret sigh of relief. I've won. They've backed down.

. . . *if* he would sign an oath of Christian loyalty. The document created by the Citizens for Educational Reform and instituted at the college by Ron Labonne was presented to him.

"What is this?" he cried. "The Inquisition?"

The administrators were not amused when Wellfleet stormed out saying he was going to file a job discimination suit. His termination papers were in his campus mailbox the next day. Wellfleet packed up his office and left to the sound of hymns being sung in the college chapel.

▼ ▼ ▼

The ACLU lawyer was sympathetic, but his hard-pressed, overworked organization was lacking funds to tackle all but the most important constitutional test cases. Wellfleet's was not the first case of job discrimination based on religion. Similar cases built on separation of church and state were crawling through the overburdened court system at this very moment.

The difficulty came from the fact that the employer was a private, non-accredited religious institution specifically set up to teach a set of religious principles. Its right to do so, and to require its employees to sign an oath of Christian loyalty, was protected under the Constitution—freedom of religion.

"But the religion itself violates constitutional principles," Wellfleet said. "It's exclusionary, don't you see? Like every other organized religion."

182

The lawyer said more research would be needed. It would take time. They had so much to do right now with Ballot Measure Three, which they were trying to get thrown off the November ballot.

Wellfleet left feeling like a faceless statistic, a pin that had been pulled loose from the machinery of society and was now slowly being ground to dust. He realized with wincing clarity just how expendable he truly was. A court case would take years. And he didn't have years to wait.

▼ ▼ ▼

Jay, wearing dark glasses and designer t-shirts that showed off his magnificent biceps, zipped around town with the top down on his Mercedes 190 roadster. In the warm, breezy June sunshine, under cobalt-blue skies and pink and white blossoming trees, everything looked so fresh and full and clean and hopeful that he seemed to breath it in by osmosis. This was Portland at its glorious best, with Mt. Hood gleaming in the distance, day after day, like some genial, beneficent deity.

After a long, dull, sexless winter and spring Jay Zucker was in business again, getting and giving the eye. A buck in mating season, his antlers growing larger by the day. So much energy. The sweet fragrance of the air. The birds raucously singing as they made their nests. The ripe aura that seemed to emanate from everyone's winter-weary crotch. Too bad there was no time for sex. Work was his sex.

No looking back. Chez Jay was now trés passé, a forlorn empty space with a For Lease sign in the window. This was a whole new era. Everything was coming up Too-Too.

Jay was originally going to call his new gay bistro "Twenty-Two" because the address was 22 N.W. 23rd Avenue. "Why not Too-Too instead?" Cassandra suggested.

He'd known immediately that she was right. "Hey, that is simply . . . Too-Too."

Cassandra, his new housemate, was right in a lot of things. Decor, for instance. They'd spent an evening carefully watching black-and-white movies from the Thirties, the kind where Americans spoke with quasi-English accents and were always going off to Art Deco nightclubs. The next day Cassandra produced a sketch that encapsulated exactly the kind of sleek Too-Too interior Jay was looking for. More importantly, penniless schemer that she was, Cassandra knew how relatively glamorous effects could be quickly and cleverly fudged.

Except for Terry Terwilliger, who avoided contributions of any kind, Jay's gay neighbors in Queer Corners pitched in and did more than their share. It touched him, the way they were willing to put their personal problems aside in order to help him.

Because there were problems. Wellfleet had lost his teaching job. Ito, after his long convalescence, had lost a big gardening project. Something was going on between Carolyn and Susan, but no one knew what. And hanging over everyone's head, like a black toxic cloud detonated by their neighbor, Ron Labonne, was Ballot Measure Three.

But disheartening as things were, queer life went on as it had for decades past and would for decades to come, whether Ballot Measure Three won voter approval or not. And if Portland queers were not feeling particularly patriotic, they were definitely feeling gaytriotic. In this sense, Too-Too was just what everyone needed: a new gay-friendly project that brought out every queer's creative, scavenging, cost-cutting best.

Jay, with his good looks, organizational skills, and never-say-die manner, knew how to inspire and direct people. Sometimes it took nothing more than a kiss, a wink, or a pat on the butt. He bolstered spirits sickened and demoralized by the sight of "We Agree With Three!" bumper stickers and yard signs. He told his cohorts that Too-Too was going to be for them—yes, finally, a chic gay bistro right in the heart of yuppie straightsville 23rd Avenue, the hottest new part of town. Gays were not going to vanish, they were going to increase their visibility quotient.

So the lighting and set designer from The Mousehole theater troupe conferred with Peter Love, who had a trade discount on just about everything, on lights and construction plans. They built a small stage, covered it with black linoleum, and draped yards of sheer white gauze along the sides. Wellfleet Stipple, who'd inherited Delmont's Boesendorfer, contributed his old black Steinway. Susan Bark, though rarely seen, sweet-talked a lumber baroness dyke-friend into contributing wages and materials for a group of home-handydykes to sheetrock walls and hammer up a second tier for seating. Carolyn Corbett found twenty rolls of shiny green vinyl and spent hours devising a way to cover old banquettes. Ito was contributing orchids: exquisite and bizarre, each would sit on its own pedestal in a tightly focussed spotlight. The bar, hauled over from Chez Jay, was already in place. The kitchen was old, but serviceable, and could handle the limited menu Jay had in mind.

Using a quasi Art Deco style, Cassandra frescoed the freshly plastered walls with famous figures from homo-history. They were all out on the town at a place that was, well, Too-Too. Sappho sat with Gertrude Stein and Alice Toklas, Hadrian with Antinous, Lytton Strachey with Harvey Milk, Edward II with Shakespeare and Marlowe, Cole Porter with Natalie Barney, Virginia Woolf with Vita Sackville-West, Rock Hudson with Danny Kaye and Laurence Olivier, Oscar Wilde with Noël Coward.

Jay, working eighteen-hour days, was exhausted but happy. Happy, he realized, because for the first time in his public life as a restaurateur he was letting himself be queer. He felt strangely liberated, as if he'd come out of shadows into bright sunlight to claim his real life at last. The charming, sexy, funny, hard-working, middle-aged gay man he'd recently met was none other than himself.

When he ran into old Chez Jay patrons and they asked about his new place, he told them it was a gay bistro and said he hoped they'd stop by. When he received newspaper coverage, he made certain that it described Too-Too as "gay-oriented." When John-Don asked if opening night could be a kick-off fund-raising benefit for the new No on Three campaign, Jay said yes even though it would put a big dent in his take.

He'd always let Chez Jay be used for liberal causes. For years local politicians and community organizers had gathered there for meetings and fundraisers and Jay hadn't charged them a cent. Where were those politicos now that he had come out and gone Too-Too? Nowhere to be seen. So Jay, even in the midst of construction, opened his doors to John-Don and other gay groups involved in mounting a counter-offensive.

It was going to take lots of money to fight the ACA. Estimates ran as high as a million dollars. Media costs would take up the bulk of it, but funds were also needed to set up community outreach programs outside of Portland, in the smaller towns where the pro-Three activists were most obnoxiously vociferous. And irksome as it was to have to funnel hard-earned money into a political campaign to battle unconstitutional legislation, everyone knew there was no option.

Democracy was based on money.

It was especially infuriating because for years charitable gay money had been put to constructive, compassionate use. Gays always helped gays. But now that the ACA had backed queers into a corner, queer money had to fight back. To mount a counter-offensive a massive influx of funds was required. The entire state-wide gay community, not just segregated parts of it, had to be tapped for money.

▾ ▾ ▾

The single greatest irony of the anti-gay rights campaign was that it emanated from the heart of Queer Corners.

Delmont's distinguished Queen Anne was the victim of endless ongoing assaults. The huge horse-chestnut tree in front had been so badly butchered by the Labonnes that only its highest branches sent out a few meagre leaves. Concrete had been poured over most of the front lawn, and a new cyclone fence surrounded it. Plastic deer and chipmunks had been set up near the sawed-off rhododendron bushes. A snarling American eagle soared on plastic wings over the front porch. A happy family of dressed-up pigs—four of them, Momma, Poppa, Sonny and Sis—cavorted on either side of a tombstone-like marker embossed with the Labonne family name. Worst of all was the proliferation of "We Agree With Three!" signs.

▾ ▾ ▾

"We already know they're pigs, so why do they need to broadcast the fact?" Peter Love said late one afternoon when several Queer Cornerites had congregated at the unfinished Too-Too. "The four little pigs! It's too weird."

It was cocktail hour so Jay opened a bottle of his best Pinot Gris and began pouring.

"I've looked into all the housing codes," Peter reported, "and there's nothing we can do about the pigs and the concrete and that hideous blue paint job short of burning the place down."

"Anyone got a match?" Carolyn asked. Everyone laughed.

She really did want a match, though. To their surprise, Carolyn had taken up smoking. But this was the new Carolyn—thin, hollow-eyed, silent—very different from the talkative Earth Mother Carolyn they'd known. In her leather jacket and perennial dark glasses, her short hair dyed black, she almost looked like a wild biker chick. And though everyone noted the change in her, no one—not even Cassandra—knew what accounted for the transformation. These things happened. Carolyn and Susan were rarely seen in one another's company.

"The other day I saw the Labonne son out in back firing a gun," Jay said, lighting Carolyn's cigarette with an experienced flourish.

Carolyn, inhaling too quickly, started to cough. "A gun?" she choked.

"That's illegal!" Ito cried. "Did you report it to the police?"

"I think it was a b-b gun," Jay said.

"Labonne has a whole collection of guns," Cassandra announced. "Dove told me."

"Paramilitary mentality," John-Don nodded. "I knew it. The whole place is starting to look like a compound."

Wellfleet, who'd been standing off to one side near his recently delivered piano, spoke up. "Maybe we should all get guns."

Jay thought of the unloaded revolver sitting in a drawer beside his bed.

"Honey, I am not going to start carrying no gun!" Peter exclaimed. "If you need to carry a gun to be queer in Oregon, I'm all for setting up a separate state in Key West."

"Someone should kill the bastard," Wellfleet muttered.

It was a shocking statement—but no one was shocked. What was clear to everyone by then was that without Ron Labonne there would be no Ballot Measure Three. If he was gone, there would be no anti-gay rights campaign. The ACA buzzed around Ron Labonne like flies around a piece of rotten meat. He was the maniac leader, the skewed pivot, the focal point of their hate-blurred vision. He was forceful, decisive, someone who was not afraid to lie in the name of God and family values. The locus of this new and growing homophobia was centered directly in him.

Jay sighed. "Where are the assassins when you need them?"

"The worst thing we could do would be to make him a martyr," John-Don said.

"Right," Peter said. "Remember when Dan White assassinated Harvey Milk and George Moscone? Who became the straight-folks' martyr? Dan White, honey. The murderer! The fact that Dan White shot Harvey because Harvey was gay didn't mean bo-diddly to that straight jury. They let that homophobic scumbag off because he was under family pressure and had been eating too many Twinkies. But if a gay person assassinated Ron Labonne, it would be a different story. Then we wouldn't just be pedophiles, animal-fuckers, and corpse-lovers—we'd all be murderers, too."

"Bad public relations," John-Don agreed. "The backlash would tip people towards voting yes on Three."

"Someone has to kill him," Wellfleet said, his voice frighteningly matter-of-fact. "That's all there is to it."

No one spoke because no one knew what to say. They'd all, in one way or another, wished Ron Labonne would vanish. They also knew that he wouldn't. Since he wouldn't, idle thoughts of assassination had briefly crossed all their minds.

"Did you hear about the two gay guys who got beat up last week?" Cassandra asked.

It happened right in front of a gay bar on Stark Street. The assailants used baseball bats. One of the victims was going to be blind in one eye.

Horrifying, infuriating reports like this were trickling in from all over the state. You didn't hear about them from the mainstream media, of course, but word traveled through the gay pipeline. Lesbians living on isolated ranches in southern Oregon chased and shot at by men in pickup trucks. Lesbians on the coast who came home to find their beloved fir trees cut down. An outspoken lesbian veterinarian in Salem, the state capital, whose favorite horse was stabbed to death. It was really truly happening. The homophobic rhetoric of the ACA was escalating into violence. The only thing missing was news coverage that linked the two.

"All those in favor of assassination raise their hands," Wellfleet said, playing a few bars of Chopin's Funeral March.

"Stop it!" Carolyn screamed at him. She covered her ears and turned away. Everyone looked at her, and at one another. "Please," Carolyn said, her voice softer, "just stop it, Wellfleet."

"I'd love to," he said. "I'd love to stop all of them, the same way they've stopped me. I'd love to put a bullet right between Ron Labonne's eyeballs. Because it's thanks to him that I won't be teaching next year." It was Wellfleet's first public announcement that he'd been fired. "First me. I'm an easy target because it's a Christian college and there's no union to protect me. But who's next? You are, John-Don. Because you're a gay high school teacher. And then you, Carolyn. You're a lesbian who works in a public library filled with dirty books. And then maybe Jay will be next—maybe they'll revoke liquor licenses for gay bars."

"Look," John-Don said, "I've been thinking. The one thing we haven't done is confront Labonne directly."

"What good would that do?" Ito asked.

"Well, for one thing it would let him know that all his neighbors are queer."

"You don't think he's figured that out already?" Jay asked.

"No. They avoid us as much as we avoid them."

"With one big difference," Wellfleet said. "We're hiding from them because we're afraid."

"The woman is stupid, but the man is frightening," Ito nodded. "I saw the whole organization when I went to Mrs. Hill's. There's a strange flatness in all of them, you can see it in their eyes. They're impenetrable, but they're cunning as well."

"Okay," Cassandra said, "I didn't tell this to any of you, but the day I was moving over to Jay's, Ron Labonne tried to make a pass at me. So I told him I was a lesbian. He just laughed. He didn't believe me. Because he doesn't *know* any real queers."

"So what if we all go to their house—I mean all of us—and we tell him that we're gay and we're sick of what he's doing and we're going to do everything in our power to defeat the ballot measure." John-Don scanned their faces for some small sign of agreement. "Shouldn't he at least know that his neighbors are the very people he's persecuting?"

"Why should he care?" Wellfleet said. "He's in this for the money. baby. He's figured out a way to make money off this issue and he's going to do everything he can to protect his source of income. You're crazy if you think Ron Labonne's going to listen to a bunch of faggots telling him to have a heart. The man doesn't have a heart. A heart would get in his way. And he's not going to change his mind no matter how rationally you confront him because he's locked into the whole irrational idea of Biblical punishment for all sins except his own."

"His heart is cement," Ito agreed. "Like his front yard."

"Haven't you heard their shtick on television?" Cassandra said. "Their official line is, We love homosexuals, we just hate what they do."

"That's just another cozy Christian lie," Peter said. "They hate faggots but they can't just come out and say so because the Bible says, Thou shalt not hate."

"In other words, we're okay if we're neutered," Jay said. "If we renounce our sexual lives and live the way they want us to, they'll forgive us."

"Yuck," Cassandra shuddered, "can you imagine anything worse than wanting to live like them?"

"I still think it would be useful to let Labonne know that he's surrounded by queers," John-Don said. "That we exist. That we're everywhere, even next door. And that we're not going to let him get away with this."

"Let's say we do identify ourselves," Jay said. "We go over there and he opens the door and we all scream, 'We're queer!' All that does, John-Don, is put *us* at risk. Then he knows who we are, he finds out where we work, and God only knows what the man or his stormtroopers might do then."

"Goddamn fucking son-of-a-bitch!" John-Don slammed his fist down on the bar, then quickly stuffed his hands in his jeans pockets as he paced angrily around the room. "Christ Almighty, are we going to run around like scared rabbits for the rest of our lives? It's visibility that's going to change things. We've got to put our asses on the line! That's the only thing that's going to work in the end. Here we are, we're queer, we're your sons and daughters and mothers and fathers and cousins and aunts and uncles and grandparents! We're queer and it doesn't matter how or why, we just are, and we deserve to live our lives with the same protections as everyone else and without the fear of being clubbed or shot or voted into extinction. Goddamn it!" he shouted. "Talk, talk, talk! It's time for some action out in the real world!"

A tinkling melody floated in from the street. The tune was unfamiliar, but the sound reminded Jay of the Mister Softee ice-cream trucks that used to cruise through his neighborhood in New York. He went to the front door to see what it was.

"Oh no," he groaned.

The others joined him. Outside, an enormous van was slowly moving down 23rd Avenue. Fixed to the top was a huge sign that read HOMOSEX KILLS. The sides were plastered with "We Agree With Three!" bumper stickers. A biblical quotation from Leviticus was painted on the back.

For a moment the group stood in stunned silence.

"Who's driving?" Cassandra asked. "Can you see?"

"It must be Ron Labonne," Peter said, squinting out into the street.

"No," Jay said, "it's his son."

Carolyn burst into tears and ran from the bar.

"What's wrong with her?" Jay asked Cassandra.

Cassandra shrugged. "Nerves? I don't know."

CHAPTER 22

ONCE AGAIN CAROLYN WAS A FUGITIVE SECRETLY INHABITING TWO worlds. She was afraid to go outside. She no longer puttered in the lovely garden of Bilitis Cottage. Neighborhood strolls were out of the question. She avoided Skyview Boulevard entirely. To get to and from the library she devised laborious routes up and around the backside of Queen's Heights. Anything to avoid a possible chance encounter with Ron Labonne.

And yet she couldn't take her eyes from the Labonnes' house. Using her new high-powered binoculars she kept them under obsessive surveillance, noting the arrival and departure times of each family member and timing her own furtive departures accordingly.

The pitch of Carolyn's anxiety was so intense, so constant, that she wanted to howl. Nerves? It sounded so ladylike. How about a frantic, full-blown nervous breakdown, complete with screaming, frothing, and a strait-jacket?

The delicate balance she'd worked so hard to achieve was shattered. Her life was spinning out of control. She seemed not to be living in the present at all. Everything *now* was a black, bubbling nightmare oozing up from the past. She had tried so hard and for so long to put it all behind her. But it was like building a new house on rotten foundations. The slightest tremor and it would come crashing down around her.

Home. What did that mean when Susan refused to acknowledge her existence? Carolyn was in the doghouse, and a doghouse was not a home.

She and Susan had been avoiding one another for weeks, sleeping in separate rooms, eating at different times. It was a tense, unspoken war of wills. Who would break first? Who would take the first step to heal the breach or conclude that it was irreparable?

Susan completely ignored Lady Caroline and the puppies. She made cruelly certain that Carolyn overheard her making dates with Flavia Billingsley and her other rich single friends. Carolyn shuddered to think of what Susan was saying about her. She was haunted by the old paranoiac fear of being humiliated behind her back.

Sometimes Susan would come home early in the morning, sometimes she wouldn't come home at all. Was she sleeping with her adoring girlfriends? Carolyn dared not ask. If she asked, it would lead to yet another fight, or worse mockery than she'd already endured.

And still she loved Susan. Now, more than ever, she needed her support. The question was, did Susan still love her? And if she did, what would Susan do when the next round of revelations appeared? It was all bound to come out sooner or later. Things couldn't go on this way much longer. Eventually the dyke would burst.

So alone. There was no one she could confide in. No one knew, and no one must ever know, the soul-shredding torment that turned her days black and her nights into sleepless agony. She looked at other people and envied what she imagined to be the boring ordinariness of their lives.

Carolyn prayed to the Goddess for aid and succor. But all the Goddess seemed to say was, "You're on your own, baby. You got yourself into this mess, now you have to get yourself out of it."

How could fate be so pitiless? So mocking? How could it be such a cruel joke? In bed, at work, sitting on the toilet, Carolyn anxiously paged through a little book called *Recovering Spirit*, hoping to find a comforting phrase or thought to calm the psychic maelstrom that threatened to engulf her. One ancient, anonymous aphorism caught her eye: "Coincidence is God's way of performing a miracle anonymously."

It made sense only if she substituted Goddess for God. Then she could begin to imagine that all these years, completely unknown to her, some powerful, impersonal, Nornlike force had been patiently knitting together the skeins of her fate. She, Carolyn Corbett, was woven into a pattern as inexorable as it was inescapable. She, in fact, had unwittingly provided the design.

Maybe the Goddess, through this "coincidence," was giving her a second chance. The Goddess was telling her: you can redeem yourself, you can heal the wounds you've inflicted on yourself and others. But you can only do that by confronting the truth of your past and accepting the consequences of your actions. You are a coward and you can choose not to act, but if you don't act you must forfeit all claims to future peace and happiness. If you do act, your life will be changed forever, in ways you cannot begin to imagine. Act wisely, Carolyn Corbett, for you will never be given this chance again.

Through it all she kept working. She'd finagled the transfer to the telephone reference section of the library. She was now an unseen voice emanating from an underground lair, a faceless oracle answering the endless questions posed by others. How high is Multnomah Falls? Who was the fourteenth president of the United States?

Between calls she ran book searches, trying to glean information on her own predicament. *Emotional Development, Women and their; Life Stages, Women*—see Female Psychology; *Inner Spirit, Healing your*—see New Age; *Goddess, Your Personal*—see Archetypes under Psychological Theory; *Crisis, Handling Your Own*—see First Aid, Trauma Intervention, Domestic Medicine.

Danger everywhere she looked. Never a moment's peace. Always the terrifying possibility that she would finally be caught and unmasked. Stand naked in judgment. The only alternative was to unmask herself. Doing that might loosen the stranglehold she was caught in now. But it could also lead to something worse: permanent banishment and exile from Susan, Queer Corners, and everything she held dear.

Finally the day came when she knew she must set the wheels of her fate, whatever it was to be, in motion.

She asked if Susan wanted her to move out. Susan waffled, which meant "no" but was as bad as a "yes." At least it was a starting place. Carolyn swallowed her non-existent pride and held on in self protection. She had nowhere to go, and the idea of actually separating, of breaking up the charming, comfortable home they'd created together, was more than she could bear. Nor did she want to give up her proximity to the Labonnes.

The puppies were the next order of business. By now they had lost their infant adorability and were rapidly growing into ugly, wolfish hounds. All they'd inherited from Lady Caroline were bulging eyes and long silky ears. When the puppies were fully weaned, Carolyn guiltily brought them over, one by one, to say goodbye to their exhausted mother. Lady Caroline didn't have a clue that her mongrel brood was about to be carted off to the Humane Society. But Carolyn looked upon this final separation through a haze of guilty, anthropomorphic dread. She had watched the puppies being born, she felt responsible for their very existence. Now she was casting their fates to the wind. If they weren't adopted within a few days she knew they would be given a lethal injection and incinerated.

The one puppy left behind was the runt of the litter and Carolyn's favorite. She had other plans for it. One evening when Susan was out judging a dog show in Vancouver, Carolyn put the runt into a box and with trembling hands tied a note around its neck. "This puppy belongs to you. Your dog was his father. Take good care of him." She closed the box and trained her binoculars on the Labonnes' house, waiting until the red Cadillac backed out of the driveway and disappeared down Skyview.

When it was dark she turned off the lights, slipped out of the house, and made her way down to Skyview Boulevard. It was a windy June night. Massive broken clouds moved in a slow caravan across the sky. The alders, in full, luxuriant leaf, whispered below the giant Douglas firs. Flowers in a bank of rhododendrons glowed in the light of a street lamp. Alyssum bruised by a recent shower sent out a sweet, heady fragrance.

The lights were out and the curtains drawn in the Labonnes' house. The street was deserted. Carolyn hurried up the driveway, carrying the boxed puppy. She froze, rooted to the spot, as a sensor-light snapped on and flooded the front of the house with blinding incandescence. The plastic deer and chipmunks, the eagle, the dressed-up pigs— they all looked like evil toys suddenly startled awake and ominously watching her. Behind them there was a blinding red row of "We Agree with Three!" signs.

No time to hesitate. She unlatched the gate in the cyclone fence. It swung silently open. She half-expected the weird, immobile menagerie to spring to life and lunge for her. She took a deep breath and darted up to the front porch, laid the box by the door, and ran back home.

▼ ▼ ▼

Her mom and Ron were going out, as usual. Dove couldn't wait. The minute they were gone she would dash over to Cassandra's. But before they left, Ron told her he needed some clean clothes by tomorrow. That meant going down into the basement. The thought filled Dove with terror. When she tried to wheedle her way out of it, Ron silenced her with that look. "If you're gonna live in my house you're gonna work for your keep," he said.

Dove ran upstairs to her mom, but Cornette wasn't sympathetic either. "Dove, honey, I'm just so busy with the Lord's work I don't have time for housework. I thought you liked to do the washing and ironing."

"Our stuff," Dove sniffed, "not theirs."

"Get a move on!" Ron hollered up the stairs. "We're gonna be late!"

"Oh Lord, late for Senator Peckerwood's fundraiser and here I am with only half my face on." Peering into the bathroom mirror, Cornette hurriedly fluffed up her hair, closed her eyes, and let loose with a blast of hairspray.

"Do I have to?" Dove pleaded, carefully watching her mother. Cornette's glamorous transformations never ceased to amaze her. The minute she had her "face on" she was a different person.

"Well, honey," Cornette said, stretching her lips and applying her lipstick, "you have to learn how to wash and iron for a man sooner or later." She blotted her lips with a tissue and began the intricate positioning of her eyelashes. "One day you're going to be married and you'll have to take care of your husband." She turned and smiled at her daughter. "And your children."

"I'm never getting married," Dove muttered. "Not if it just means doing their stupid laundry."

"Dove! You are being just plain silly, young lady. Cleanliness is next to godliness, you know that."

"His clothes stink," Dove whined. "So do Lester's."

Cornette's face, even with only one set of eyelashes glued on, was stern. "What do you mean by that?"

"They smell icky. Like b.o."

"Then it's your job," her mother said firmly, "to march down to the basement and put them in the washer, and then put them in the dryer, and then iron them. Now march."

It was an order, but fear kept her from automatically obeying. "But I hate it down there. It's scary." Her voice rose. "It's haunted."

"Haunted?" Her mom let out a hoot of laughter. "Dove, you're too old to be afraid of bogeymen."

"There's a ghost," Dove whimpered.

"Stop it! I've been putting up with that nonsense of yours since you were four."

"But there is! I've seen it. A man." One day while she was doing laundry she caught a glimpse, out of a corner of her eye, of a dark silent shape. When she raced upstairs and breathlessly reported what she'd seen, they didn't believe her. They said it was "just a shadow." When her mom tried to calm her down, Ron pulled Dove out of her arms. "Ignore her," he shouted. "How long are you gonna put up with her lame excuses to get out of doing some work around here?"

Only Cassandra believed her. "I think ghosts are left-over energy," she told Dove. "They're connected to a place for some reason. Either they loved it or hated it. They can't leave until things are put right."

"Dove," her mom said softly, staring at herself in the mirror, "there is no such thing as a ghost. When people die they go to heaven or hell. They sing or they scream. That's all there is to it."

"But I *saw* it. And what about Satan? You said he prowls the earth."

"Yes, but Satan is real, honey. He's not a ghost. And he sure as heck doesn't prowl around this house."

"How do you know?"

"Dove, enough. If you're frightened you can ask Lester to sit down there with you."

"No!" That would be worse than seeing the ghost again.

"It's time you got all this scaredy-cat nonsense out of your system. Ask the Lord to help you confront your fears. Now skedaddle."

Dove shuffled away fighting back a hopeless surge of anger. When she was almost at the door her mom peeked out from the bathroom. "While you're at it, honey, you can do up my blouses, too. Delicate cycle, no bleach, one capful of fabric softener, you know how I like them." She winked and went back to her mirror.

Dove stalled for as long as she could. Watched with panicky foreboding as her mom and Ron backed out of the driveway. She hadn't seen Lester, but assumed he was upstairs in his room pretending to study. The big old house, with its yawning air of secrecy and menace, was as silent as a tomb.

"Dear Lord Jesus, please don't let the ghost get me," Dove prayed. She opened the door to the basement and stared down into a funnel of black. She flicked on the meager light and slowly started down, hot with anxiety. If only Pharaoh hadn't run away. He would protect her. She'd always taken him down to the basement with her, to guard against the devils and demons that lurked underground waiting to snatch the unwary.

There weren't any basements where they'd lived in Texas. This one was huge, filled with shadowy corners and a musty, earthy smell. There were dark rooms she'd never dared to enter. Who knew what was quietly waiting for her behind all those closed doors? There weren't enough lights, just bare, dim bulbs hanging down from cords in the cobwebby ceiling. From the bottom stair she ran to the laundry room and began her work. She never let her eyes wander far from the pool of light over the ironing board.

She finally finished her mom's blouses. Each ruffle was starched and pressed to perfection. Not one burn mark. She looked down at the laundry basket. Ron's shirts, Ron's handkerchiefs, even Ron's underpants and t-shirts still had to be ironed. Lester's stuff, too. It was so unfair. She gave the basket a resentful kick.

The steam hissed and spluttered as she set the iron back on its cradle. She wearily picked up one of Ron's white shirts, sniffed it, sprayed it with water, and stretched the collar out on the board. The iron stuck to the synthetic fabric. No matter how hard and carefully she pressed, the wrinkles never disappeared.

A stair creaked. Then another. Her heart began to flutter. A long black shadow slid down the basement stairs from the kitchen.

"You down there?" Lester called.

Her voice caught tight in her throat. "I'm ironing," she squeaked.

"Did you see that ghost again?"

She let out a shrill laugh. "There's no such thing."

"Oh yes there is," Lester said, his voice low.

"You're just trying to scare me."

"I've seen it too."

"I'm not scared," she said, her voice cracking.

"Well, I am. It was the scariest thing I've ever seen. A humpbacked man with green eyes and a knife. One night I saw him looking into your room."

"Liar, liar, pants on fire!" she cried, prickles racing up her back.

"He was just standing there, staring at you with those green eyes. He had a big bag in his hand. Big enough to throw you into it. Then he thump, thump, thump, slooowly walked down to the basement and went into the pantry—right next to the laundry room."

Her eyes flittered over to the door of the pantry.

"That's where he lives," Lester said, lowering his voice. "He's down there right now. He's just waiting for me to lock the door up here, so you can't get out."

"Don't!" She smelled something burning and looked down in alarm. She'd left the iron sitting on the front of Ron's shirt. It stuck when she frantically tried to pull it off. "I'll tell my mom!" she moaned.

"What good'll that do? You'll be dead of fright!" Her stepbrother laughed, flicked off the lights, and slammed the door above her.

"No!" she shrieked, knocking over the ironing board as she bolted for the stairs. She heard the iron crash to the floor, turned and saw sparks. A fire, and she wouldn't be able to get out. "Lester!" she screamed, frozen in terror. She reached out into the darkness, clumsily groping her way back towards the ironing board. Cried out as she rammed her hip against a cupboard, but kept going. "Ow!" She burned her hand on the hot iron. Sobbing, she yanked the cord from its socket and then began feeling her way back towards the stairs.

"Oh my God! He's coming!" Lester called from upstairs. "I can hear him! What are you gonna do when he throws that bag over your head?"

In blind panic, crawling on her hands and knees, she looked over her shoulder. And saw him. Staring at her. His eyes weren't green. Like the rest of him they had no color at all. She screamed as he slowly extended a hand. Picked herself up and ran for the stairs, up the stairs, pounded on the door. "Let me out! Let me out! He's trying to get me!"

When Lester finally pulled the door open she fell onto the kitchen floor.

"What's the matter with you, birdbrain?" he said contemptuously. "The door wasn't even locked, stupid."

Dove's legs were still on the basement stairs. She was certain that a hand, his hand, was going to reach out and grab her. Pull her back into the darkness where she'd be lost forever. She scrabbled to her feet, gasping for breath, and shoved Lester out of the way. Heard him laughing as she ran through the living room. Go where? Not upstairs. She could be trapped up there, too. Where? Cassandra's. Cassandra would help her.

She unlocked the heavy oak door and yanked it open. She was racing out when her feet crashed into something. She tripped, lost her balance, and went sprawling to the floor of the porch, landing on top of a cardboard box. A loud frightened yelp came from inside it.

Sniffling, she rolled onto her side and opened the box. A black squealing puppy leapt out and began excitedly licking her face.

▼   ▼   ▼

Hiding up in his room, Lester heard Dove's high, gibbering, hysterical voice. He knew she'd squeal. She had to save her own skin. She'd committed two major offenses:

scorched a shirt and dropped the iron. But she claimed it wasn't her fault.

"And then he said there was a ghost and then he locked the door and turned off the lights and I couldn't see and the shirt got burned and I dropped the iron and—" She went on and on in that snivelling, whining voice of hers.

He heard a shrill exclamation from Cornette. Heard his father roar his name. No escape. He should have taken off when he had the chance. He'd started to. He went over to tell Billy his plan, but Billy wasn't home. And Lester didn't have any money. So he went back and tried to sweet-talk Dove out of telling. She was by then engrossed with the puppy that had mysteriously appeared on the doorstep. She ignored his entreaties. "You're bad," she spat at him. "You're gonna get it."

"Lester!" his father bellowed again. "Get your ass down here!"

Feigning innocence, pretending he'd been asleep, Lester came down to see all three of them standing in the living room. Dove, clutching the puppy, was sobbing in her mother's arms. Cornette glared at him with a mixture of disbelief, contempt and revulsion. She started to say something but Ron flung up an arm to silence her. "Get down to the basement," was all he said. Lester didn't move. His old man jabbed him in the chest. "Move!"

It was an old ritual, but Lester never knew exactly what form it would take. First the lecture. Then the punishment.

His sense of strength vanished. Once again he was a meek little boy about to get the bejesus whipped out of him.

His old man closed the basement door behind them. Breathing heavily, he slapped the back of Lester's head to keep him moving. Hands clenched, jaw tight, body rigid, Lester stumbled down the stairs to the basement. Saw the evidence against him: the overturned ironing board, the scorched shirt, the iron. Evidence of the little idiot's terror.

"Pick up the ironing board."

As Lester did so, he saw his old man examine the iron. It popped when he plugged it in.

"Take off your shirt." When Lester didn't respond, Ron slammed a fist into his back. Grunting, Lester lurched forward on frozen legs. He peeled off his t-shirt and stood next to the ironing board, his mind racing. Anything to escape what was coming. No way to escape what was coming.

His old man's voice was low, flat, unforgiving. "You've got the mark of Cain on you, Lester. Always have and always will." The iron clicked several times and began to exhale a soft splutter of steam. "There's something rotten in you. You were born evil, just like your rotten mother." The iron hissed, as if in agreement.

"Spread your arms out on the board."

Lester obeyed. Floating in the suspense of imminent pain, his mind went blank. Sweat dripped down his side. He could smell the stink of his fear. He heard the soft whisk of Ron's belt being pulled free.

"It was just a joke," he stammered.

"A joke, huh? Here's a good joke for you " The belt whipped through the air and landed on his shoulders. "How's that for a joke?" The lacerating sting was familiar. Lester lifted his head and sucked in his breath, tightening his fingers on the edges of the board. "Here's another one." The belt came whistling down again, harder. "Is that funny?" Lester moaned and bit his lips, refusing to cry out or beg for mercy, the way he'd once done. "I don't hear you laughing." Another lash. "I'm gonna keep this up until I hear you laughing at your stupid joke."

No, he wouldn't. His pride wouldn't let him. His face twisted and rose every time the belt struck his flesh. His father kept at it with silent fury, enraged by Lester's refusal to give in. Lester panted, grimaced, gasped, but he refused to laugh. It wasn't until his father threw down the belt, crushed Lester's face flat against the board, and pressed the steaming iron to his back that Lester finally screamed.

It released something in him. His strength. His indignation. His hatred. No more silent shame. No more humiliation. The whimpering little boy was suddenly dead. Lester the man emerged.

He rose up to his full height, hurling over the ironing board, and spun around with a snarl, nostrils flaring, snot running down his face, eyes bulging with pain and outrage. He made a fist, drew back his right arm, and cried, "Touch me again, fucker, and you're dead!"

Startled, his old man instinctively backed up, holding out the iron like a shield. "What did you say to me?"

Lester said it again. This time it gave him pleasure. He kept his arm cocked. He wasn't afraid to use it. And he knew, finally, at last, that his father knew it.

"Go up to your room."

This time he did laugh. Right in his old man's face. A crazed, choking gargle shot up from his bowels to his throat. "You crazy fucking son-of-a-bitch! I'll beat the shit out of you if you ever touch me again. Understand? I'll kill you!"

And before his old man could answer Lester ran upstairs and locked himself in his room.

▼ ▼ ▼

The next night he was still up there, only now he was locked in.

After his outburst the old terror returned. He fought it, battled for courage, refused to become the little boy again. But he was afraid to leave his barricade. If he stepped foot outside he knew his father would be waiting. He'd crossed a line. He could never go back. Go back where? he asked himself. There was no place to go back to, no place that he wanted to be. Not in this house.

All day he stayed in his room. No one bothered him, no one said anything. He could hear them walking along the upstairs hallway. He didn't even dare unlock his door to go to the bathroom. So thirsty. He'd drunk up his secret stash of Jolt. He held his bladder until it was ready to burst, then peed out the window. His bowels were in an uproar. His stomach was growling.

He thought of possible escape routes. Out the window? It was a twenty-foot drop down to the stone terrace behind the house. What if he broke a leg? The only way was to open his door and make a run for it.

He was mulling over this plan when, early that evening, he heard noises outside his room. The clunk and rattle of his old man's tool box. The whine of a drill. The squeak of screws turning in wood.

"What're you doing?" he finally asked.

There was no answer.

Later, listening by the door, he made out that they were leaving for a Christian rally and taking Dove was with them. When they left, he cautiously unlocked his door. Pushed. It didn't move. He rattled, shoved, finally threw himself against it. The thick old door held firm. His old man had installed some kind of locks on the outside. They were going to starve him into submission.

He paced around his room, wearing an old pair of military fatigues, his torso bare. He couldn't bear to have anything touch his back, which was covered with a fretwork of hot, throbbing welts and a fiery red burn. The mark of Cain, branded onto his flesh. "Crazy fuck!" he shouted.

He looked at the phone. That was a lifeline. But he only knew one person who might help. He dialed Billy's number. A thin, nasal voice answered. Lester asked to speak to Billy. "Who is this?" the voice asked suspiciously.

"Please. If he's there can I talk to him? It's important."

"I'm afraid not." The phone clicked off.

Trying to remain calm, he laid down on his stomach and idly riffled the pages of *Hunting World* and *Soldier of Fortune*. Why hadn't he thought to grab one of his old man's guns? He could see the rifles, all cleaned and polished and neatly lined up in their cabinet. With a loaded rifle he could do anything. He could shoot his way out. The thought excited him.

He pulled out his secret copy of an old *Hustler* and sat on the edge of the bed to jerk off. But the big-titted girls spreading their legs no longer invited him into their arms. They seemed to be looking at him with disdain. Why would they want someone like Lester Labonne, a scarred, pimply teenager locked in his room?

He suddenly realized how tired he was. On red alert, he hadn't slept all night. He was exhausted. Parched. Hungry. In pain. He crawled back onto the bed and tried to find a comfortable position.

He was just being tugged down into a deep black sleep when the phone rang.

"Hello?" Silence on the other end. Lester coughed and licked his parched lips. "Hello?"

Someone sucked in a breath. "Lester?" A woman.

For a moment he thought it was Cornette. "Whudayou want?

The woman was taking in short, shallow breaths. "Is this Lester Labonne?"

"Yeah, who is this?"

"Lester," the woman said. "This is your mother." Her breath grew ragged.

"What?"

"Your mother," the voice stammered.

He figured it was some kind of weirdo playing a game. "Right. Fuck you, too."

Another sharp intake of breath. "Don't hang up. Don't hang up, Lester. Don't be afraid."

"Who is this?" he demanded.

"I told you."

"My mother?" he said incredulously. He tried to conjure up an image of a phantom he'd never seen.

"Listen to me, Lester. Don't hang up. What I have to say is very important."

His brain was turning somersaults. He couldn't speak

"Listen, I know how you must feel. You're shocked. But listen to me. This is as hard for me as it is for you."

Now his breath was as short and anxious as hers.

"I don't expect you to understand," she said. "Not now anyway."

"Not ever," he panted, unable to catch his breath.

"You don't know. You don't know." She began to weep. "You don't know."

"Is this a joke?" he asked.

"No," she sniffled. "No, it's not a joke. Oh, there's so much I want to say to you."

"How do I know you're telling the truth?"

"You're my child," she moaned. "You have to believe me."

"You're crazy," he said angrily.

"No, I'm not crazy."

"You run off and disappeared. You run off and left me so you could drink and take drugs and screw around. He says you're a rotten whore."

"That's not true."

"That's what he said."

"Lester, you don't know what happened. You don't know. I wanted to take you with me. I tried but I couldn't."

"Why not?"

"I'll tell you that when we finally meet."

"I don't want to meet you!" he shouted. "You're roadkill as far as I'm concerned."

She whimpered, fighting for control. "You're angry, you're angry, I know you're angry. But don't you even want to see me? Just once? Aren't you curious?"

"No, I ain't curious. I'm fuckin' pissed off is what I am."

"I can understand that."

"No!" he shouted. "No, you can't understand that. How could you? You run off and left me with him."

"I've never forgiven myself." Her voice rose tremulously. "Never. But at the time it was all I could do. I had to get away."

"Why?"

"Because—oh—because—oh, I'm so sorry," she wept. "Lester, I'm so sorry."

Another long silence. Lester was crying, too. He hated himself for being such a wimp. He didn't know where the tears came from, or what they meant. They just suddenly welled up like blood from a wound. He'd never believed in all those miracles Cornette was always yakking about and trying to make happen. His life was and always had been the opposite of a miracle. Black and bleak and hopeless, with a past he didn't want to remember and no future worth thinking about. From the beginning his father had taught him to expect nothing. He was, for reasons he never understood, tainted by *her*, this disembodied voice on the telephone, the mother who'd fucked and run. It was the ultimate insult, an unforgivable betrayal. So why was he crying with what felt like relief?

"I don't expect you to forgive me," she sobbed. "What I did was unforgivable. I've lived with the consequences every day of my life."

"What about my life?" he bawled. "You wanna talk consequences? He's broke my arm, he's whipped me, he's made me stand in the cold without no shoes on. Last night he shoved a hot iron on my back. Now he's starving me."

"Oh God no. Oh, Lester."

"There wasn't no one I could ever go to, was there? 'Cause if I ever told he'd kill me. And you were off somewhere screwing around."

A pause. The voice was firmer. "I won't let him harm you anymore."

"Yeah?" he mocked. "How you gonna do that?" Silence. He wondered if she'd hung up, if he'd lost her again. "He's gonna shit bricks when I tell him you called."

"No!" she cried. "No, don't tell him. No. That's not a good idea."

"How come?"

"Because—because I'm afraid of him. Of what he might do. I'm as scared of him as you are."

"I never said I was scared," Lester rebuffed her. "I can handle myself. And the minute I turn eighteen? I'm outta here, man. And no one can do nothin' about it. Not you, not him, not nobody."

"Your birthday is July fifteenth," she said.

How could she know that unless—? "Yeah?"

"That's not too far away. How about we meet on your birthday?"

"Why should I?"

"If you're going to leave, you're going to need money. I'm not going to stop you, Lester. All I want now is to help you. Believe me."

"Why should I?"

"You meet me on July fifteenth and I'll give you enough money to get out of town."

He considered this for a moment. "How much?" he wanted to know.

"Two thousand dollars. That's all I've got right now."

"You'll give me two grand?" Maybe there were fucking miracles after all.

"All you have to do is meet me."

"Where?"

She named a park on the east side. Told him how to get there. "There's a picnic shelter, in a grove of Douglas firs. Meet me there."

"Two grand in cash? No strings attached?"

"Just one. You can't tell him I called, or that you're meeting me. You've got to promise me that."

"You ain't gonna stop me from going?"

"No, I'm going to help you get away. That's all I can offer you. But you've got to promise. You can't tell him or anyone. No one."

He tried to mull it over but was too excited to think clearly.

"Do you promise?"

Two grand. He'd be out of there and on his way. He didn't know where, but it didn't matter. "Yeah," he said finally. "Okay."

▼ ▼ ▼

Ron Labonne obviously had no idea that Dove was sneaking over to see Cassandra. And Dove Labonne obviously had no idea that her stepfather's sexual radar was tuned into Cassandra's frequency. But Cassandra knew.

It was a deliciously warm June afternoon and she was out sunbathing on her patio. She heard a twig snap and saw a flash of movement in the next yard. She looked over, expecting to see Dove. What she saw was Ron Labonne lurking behind the huge satellite dish he'd recently installed near the rabbit hutch. The dish now sat like a monstrous growth, its one giant black metallic petal turned up towards the heavens, where a bank of Delmont's bed of prize-winning roses had once delicately scented the air.

She did it on a sudden dare to herself. Why else would she make a split-second decision to tease the interest of the most repulsive man in Oregon? "Picking up signals from another universe?" she playfully called.

Labonne sheepishly emerged from his dark hiding place and squinted in the sun. "Yeah, this baby lets me tune into eighty channels." He gave the satellite dish an affectionate pat. "You should see how clear my reception is."

"I heard those things give you cancer of the brain," Cassandra said from her chaise, lifting a shapely leg and slowly rubbing sunscreen onto it.

Labonne moved closer, casting furtive glances back towards his house. "Yeah? Well, I heard that sunbathing gives you cancer of the skin."

"Not if you block it." She sat up, pulled down the straps of her flimsy bikini top, and slowly slathered oil on her on her partially exposed breasts. Now the hard part. She turned to him. "Would you mind helping me, like a good neighbor should?"

He tripped on some ivy. Nervous. "How?"

"Rub some of this on my back. I can't reach."

The property line was like a magic barrier he couldn't cross. He stood by the holly tree a few feet away, stiff and uncomfortable, staring at the tattoo above her breast. Cassandra smiled. "Do you want me to get skin cancer?" Her eyes locked into his, she could see his desire and his fear. "Scaredy-cat," she mocked. "Never mind. Sorry I asked." She turned her face away and picked up *Atlas Shrugged*, the novel she'd been trying to read for the last six months..

The taunt brought him closer. "Hey, little lady, I wouldn't want you to think I'm unneighborly."

"No, never mind," she said, dismissing him with a wave of her hand. "Better go back to your satellite dish. I'm sure *it* knows how to pick up signals."

After that, on hot afternoons, he'd sometimes hang around the rabbit hutch as Cassandra, innocently humming, puttered around in her bikini or shorts and a halter top. His own hot-weather attire was something only a straight man at the lowest rung of the fashion ladder could dream up: frayed cut-offs with white knee-length athletic socks, running shoes, a t-shirt emblazoned with a race-car, and cheesy fake Porsche sunglasses. Mr. Cool.

He'd never spent so much time fiddling around in his back yard. Day after day, at a time that just happened to coincide with Cassandra's. This used to be Dove's time, just after school, but she never came outside when her stepfather was there. A couple of times, looking up the blaze of sun, Cassandra saw a shadowy figure peeking out from an upstairs window. Was it Dove? Or maybe Cornette?

Labonne tried to make small talk. B-o-r-i-n-g! But she responded with just enough pert, teasing suggestiveness to keep his libido piqued, his masculinity in question, and her own availability a distinct possibility. The vixen in heat: it was a time-honored feminine role she despised but played with a certain relish because her neighbor had no idea that she was really a fox in vixen's clothing.

Or perhaps he did know, and that added to his intrigue. She had, after all, once told him that she was a lesbian.

One day he suddenly called out, "You like rabbit meat?"

"I don't know," she shrugged.

"If you want, I'll slaughter one and skin it for you."

How romantic. "No thanks. I'm basically a vegetarian."

Another afternoon he said, "I'm getting rid of these roses back here. You want them?"

The last of Delmont's rare roses. She did want them. Suddenly she desperately wanted them. But she couldn't bring herself to accept a gift from Labonne. It would make her feel like she was collaborating with the enemy. It would blur lines that she had to keep in sharp focus. There was no room in her heart for mercy. She had to remember that. She couldn't take something without giving something back. It wouldn't be fair.

PART FOUR

CHAPTER 23

"ONE? TWO?" JOHN-DON ASKED.

"How many is everyone else putting up?"

"We're putting up four, Jay and Ito two, and Carolyn said they'd put up one."

"What about Terry?"

John-Don frowned and hitched up athletic socks that were slipping down into his hiking boots. "Zero. He says he never puts up political signs. Doesn't want holes in his lawn."

"Why not? They'd match the ones in his head."

"I think it was the price. We're asking five bucks apiece as a contribution. You don't have to pay, of course, since you're unemployed."

"I'll take three," Wellfleet said. "And I'll pay."

John-Don pulled three of the black-and-white "No on Three!" signs from his bundle. "Want me to help you put them up?"

"No, I can do it. What else do you have?"

John-Don showed Wellfleet the buttons and bumper stickers he was hawking to raise funds. Wellfleet looked at the goods but cast a few furtive glances at the other wares on display. It was hot. John-Don was wearing hiking shorts and a sleeveless t-shirt. His strong leg muscles and smooth, broad chest made Wellfleet light-headed.

"I'll take a button and two bumper stickers." He shaded his eyes and glanced towards Bilitis Cottage. "Did you actually talk to Carolyn?"

"Nope. Telephone tag. Why?"

Wellfleet shrugged. "I never see her anymore."

"No one does," John-Don said. "Susan either. Carolyn hasn't been back to Too-Too since that day she ran out crying."

"Maybe she's depressed," Wellfleet said.

John-Don was not sympathetic. "Half the queers in Portland are depressed or terrified or both. If they'd get off their butts and get involved maybe they wouldn't be."

Wellfleet nodded. It was another grim reminder that the ACA was steadily gaining power. Ron Labonne, initially ignored by a mainstream media as crackpot, was now a man in the news. Republican politicians were taking notice of him; many had already pledged their support for the ACA-sponsored ballot measure. In the gay community there was a mounting sense of panic and urgency. No one was prepared for and no one really knew what to do about the plague of homophobic sentiment spreading throughout the state. It was every gay person's worse nightmare come true. And there it was, in the collective front yard of Queer Corners, emanating from the very house that had once drawn them all together.

"I suppose no one knows what to do because nothing like this has ever happened before," Wellfleet said.

"Okay, but it's happening now," John-Don said. "What does it take, for God's sake, to get gays politically motivated? Half of them can't see beyond the discos. And everyone else seems to be running in different directions. Everything's so goddamned polarized."

He knew what was going on because most of his time was now devoted to the newly organized No on Three campaign. There were other, smaller gay political organizations in the city but thus far they refused to band together under the larger umbrella of No on Three. Long-simmering tensions between gay men and lesbians, assimilationists and separatists, moderates and radicals, whites and ethnic groups, between all the haves and have-nots of the "gay community" were surfacing. "We don't have the luxury of apathy," John-Don said heatedly. "And in-fighting at this stage will kill us."

"Well, you know I'll do what I can." Wellfleet fished in his wallet for a twenty dollar bill. There goes a week's worth of lunches, he thought.

"You're coming to the gala fundraiser, aren't you. It's the opening night of Too-Too. Jay's donating all the profits to the No on Three campaign."

"Er—I'd like to, but—"

"Wellfleet, you don't have to pay," John-Don said.

Wellfleet blushed. "Why not? Everyone else is paying. I don't want be the neighborhood charity case."

"No, look, I've got an idea. I'm in charge of this shindig, It can't be just political, it has to be *fun*, too." He said "fun" with barely concealed disdain. "So I'm lining up all sorts of acts and performers between the speeches and fund-raising."

"You want me to perform? What would I do? No one wants to hear an old fag playing 'Claire de lune' on the piano."

"I thought maybe you could accompany Sid Charisse.'"

"Who's that?"

"He's a famous drag queen. Jay knows him from The Mousehole. He's offered to impersonate Cornette Labonne singing 'Getting to Know You.'"

Wellfleet was aghast. "You want me to accompany a drag queen dressed like Cornette Labonne singing 'Getting to Know You'?"

"I know it's not the sort of classical thing you're accustomed to, but—"

"Love to," Wellfleet said. He smiled up at tall, handsome John-Don. "Maybe I should go in drag, too. As Ron Labonne."

"You do that," John-Don said, clapping him on the shoulder. "See you."

Watching John-Don stride off like a gay peddler with his load of signs and merchandise, Wellfleet was suddenly flooded with a keen yearning for his own lost manhood. His lost life. If only he'd been born twenty years later, grown up in the post-Stonewall age when queers—some queers, at least—could finally be brave and open and unguilty about who they were. Facing the same bigotry, yes, but marching ahead and demanding their place in the world.

As a gay man coming of age in the closeted McCarthyite Fifties, Wellfleet had donned a hairshirt tailor-made for self-hatred. He'd lived his life as a ghost. Why had he done that, he wondered now? *Because he'd passively accepted all the lies straights told him about his own homosexuality.* By never speaking up, by never confronting what he knew to be lies, he had participated in his own destruction. Annihilated his very soul. Aided the oppressor. It was a dumbfounding revelation for a man pushing sixty.

The thought stayed with him as he angrily pounded in his "No on Three!" signs. He couldn't shake it. When he'd finished with the signs he went inside and looked at himself in the bathroom mirror.

"Queer." He said it aloud, introducing himself to his haggard, unshaven reflection. "Faggot. Pansy. Sissy. Homo. Cocksucker. Sodomite." Trying, for the first time in his life, to wear the words like a proud badge of honor instead of a shameful one.

With Delmont dead and Carolyn mysteriously incommunicado he felt cut off from the queer life of the neighborhood. There was no one he was close enough to to call for simple, friendly gossip. They pitied him because he'd lost his job, but they couldn't know what it was really like. The long, empty hours that had to be filled, the gnawing fear that he'd never find work again, the choking anger over the way he'd been dismissed.

Later that afternoon he drove downtown and picked up a copy of "Getting to Know You" at the sheet-music store. On his way back he drove past the Labonnes' house—Delmont's house—and counted the number of "We Agree with Three!" signs. Ten of them, forming a solid red line in front of the hacked-off rhodies under the front windows.

Rage left a bitter taste in his mouth. As he was slowly reconnoitering up Skyview, passing Terry's house, he saw the Labonne boy and Billy Bird dart up the stairs to the carriage house. What were those two numbskulls up to?

As soon as it was dark he went to bed, tossing restlessly as raccoons noisily trundled through the shrubs outside his window.

The goddamned raccoons had a better life than he did! Plenty of garbage to eat, no mortgage payments, no lonely sense of rejection or wasted life to keep them awake at night. Animal instinct, that's what they had. When they were attacked, they fought back. Underneath their cute playful exterior they were tooth-and-nail survivors.

Well, he had his instincts, too. His furious sense of desolation was so intense that it demanded an outlet. But what?

▼ ▼ ▼

The next morning, as he stepped outside to pick up his paper, Wellfleet noticed that his "No on Three!" signs were gone. He looked up and down the quiet street. A dull shiver of dread ran up his spine as he stood there in the early-morning light with the birds twittering around him. It hadn't been raccoons that he'd heard outside his window.

He scuffled over to Bilitis Cottage in his bedroom slippers and rang the bell. Carolyn peered out the window before cracking open the door.

"Wellfleet. I'm not dressed."

"Did you put up your No on Three sign?" he asked.

Carolyn looked bleary-eyed and disheveled. "I put it up last night, why?"

"It's gone," Wellfleet said. "So are mine."

"Gone?" She peered around the door, fright dawning on her face, and retreated back inside. "Who would do that?" she whispered.

"Who do you think? Our vigilante neighbors. They've obviously got their eyes on us. Don't want any opposition."

Carolyn stared at him, her mouth open. Blinked as if rousing herself to attention. "Listen, I'm late, I've got to run. Sorry." She closed the door.

Everyone's signs had vanished. John-Don, fuming, brought over new ones the same day. This time Carolyn did not put hers up. She missed the next round of desecration. That night someone sprayed swastikas on the signs with black paint.

▼ ▼ ▼

"You heard what happened to John-Don, didn't you?" Cassandra's noisy pink VW raced along the curves of Skyline Boulevard. It was the twenty-first of June. She and Carolyn were on their way to the Goddess Women's summer solstice potluck.

Carolyn, staring out of the car window, shook her head.

"On the last day of school, Lester Labonne called him a faggot. Right in the classroom." She glanced over at Carolyn, looking for a reaction. Nothing. "John-Don says it's because he gave Lester an F."

"Pull over," Carolyn said. "There's another one."

Cassandra swerved onto a gravel driveway. Carolyn darted out, looked around, and uprooted the "We Agree with Three!" sign next to the mailbox. She slipped into the backseat with the others.

"I see some more up there," Cassandra said, starting off again. "We should have taken your Volvo. There's more room."

If it hadn't been for Cassandra, they wouldn't be going to the summer solstice potluck at all. Cassandra had been looking forward to it for weeks but she never received an invitation. She couldn't go unless Carolyn invited her. When Cassandra finally called and asked if Carolyn was going, Carolyn said no. It was a shock. But, then, Carolyn had changed, as they all had changed. Her voice was flat, sucked dry of emotion. No one saw much of her anymore. Cassandra had to use all her powers of persuasion to talk Carolyn into a boogie with the Goddess.

It was Cassandra's idea to pull up every "We Agree with Three!" sign they passed. "They fuck with us, we fuck back." She'd been doing it herself until Carolyn finally said, "Let me do this one." Now they were conspirators. Ripping up her first sign had snapped Carolyn out of her emotional coma.

"Why would Jeanine want to live out here anyway?" Cassandra said. "It's infested with ACAers."

"She didn't know that when she moved in. She was just looking for a peaceful rural area close to the city. She didn't meet any of her neighbors."

"I suppose this wouldn't be a good time to go around and introduce herself. 'Hi, I'm your Goddess Woman-lesbian neighbor and I live just up the road.'"

"It's so beautiful out here, though." Skyline Boulevard snaked along a high, forested ridge just west of Queen's Heights. Above them, struck by the sun, the tops of the giant Douglas firs rearing up on either side of narrow road were glowing like candle flames.

"Yeah, it's pretty," Cassandra said, "but I'd still be afraid to live out here. I don't trust places with long driveways and houses you can't see." She slowed down and stopped beside another pair of signs. Before Carolyn could open the car door a snarling German Shepherd came bounding out of the underbrush. Cassandra took off. "See what I mean?"

"I don't think we'd better pull up any more signs," Carolyn said. "We're getting too close to Jeanine's."

They drove on. Once again Carolyn seemed disinclined to talk. Cassandra didn't get it. They were in the middle of a war. Queer Corners was turning into a battle zone. How could Carolyn be so uninvolved? It was as if she didn't want to know what was happening right under her nose. "You heard that Terry's tires were slashed, didn't you?"

Carolyn shook her head. "When?"

"Couple of nights ago. He thinks it was Lester Labonne."

"It was probably that horrible boy he lives with," Carolyn said.

"Billy? I wouldn't put it past him."

They lapsed into another silence. Finally Carolyn said, "Are you still talking to that little girl? What's her name?"

"You mean Dove? She's got a new puppy."

"Oh?"

"Ugliest thing I've ever seen. But she says it was the Lord answering her prayers. Someone left it on their doorstep. I hope it has rabies and bites Ron Labonne in the dick."

"Does she still tell you about the rest of them?"

Cassandra nodded. "All sorts of juicy stories. It's mostly stuff about her brother."

"Like what?"

"Well, the last thing was that he got into some sort of fight with Ron. He got whipped for it and then Ron locked him in his room for two days without food or water."

"That's child abuse!" Carolyn cried. "Someone should turn him in."

"Yeah, I thought of that. But I can't do it without proof. I can't just take Dove's word for it."

"You mean you can't trust her."

"I don't know. Living in that family would drive anyone nuts."

"The son's probably acting out of rage against his father," Carolyn said.

"Aren't we all? The bastard's set off a witch hunt. And we're the witches."

Carolyn stared out the window.

"Maybe we should all try to cast a spell on Ron Labonne," Cassandra suggested. "Give him incurable ringworm, or cancer of the prostate, or make him accidentally shoot himself in the head."

"That's not what the Goddess Women are about," Carolyn said quietly. "Unfortunately." She pointed ahead. "It's the next driveway."

Cassandra slowed down and turned onto the long unpaved driveway leading to

Jeanine Rotter's estate. The drive wound up and through an almost primevally thick stand of forest. As Cassandra carefully started up the steep slope, a man with a video-tape recorder suddenly appeared in front them, blocking their path.

"What the hell is he doing?" Cassandra said.

"Maybe Jeanine's taping the ceremony for her Goddess archives."

His face hidden by the camera, the man slowly walked towards the front of the VW. Cassandra and Carolyn smiled nervously. They exchanged a quick glance as the man silently came around to the side of the car, crouched down, and continued filming through the car window.

"I don't like this," Carolyn whispered. "Let's just go ahead."

Cassandra shifted into first and slowly inched forward. She gasped and lurched to a stop as a small, screaming mob of men and women rushed out from the thick undergrowth and surrounded the car. They waved Bibles, crosses, and signs that read "WITCHES KILL BABIES" and "GOD HATES GODLESS WITCHES." The forest reverberated with the flurry of their enraged voices.

"Jesus Christ!" Cassandra shrieked. "Lock your door! Roll up your window!"

"The signs!" Carolyn, trapped by her seatbelt, scrabbled to pull the blanket Cassandra had brought over the "We Agree with Three!" signs.

The ambushers pressed their livid faces to the windows and screamed. "Witches!" "Baby killers!" "It's a cult of the devil!" "Pray for forgiveness!" "Murderers!" "Daughters of Saaaaatan!"

Before Carolyn could roll up her window a crazed-looking woman wearing a green polyester pants-suit thrust in a cross. She waved it in Carolyn's face as if she were a vampire and brayed, "Baby killer!"

Pushing the woman's hand away with one hand, Carolyn frantically rolled up the window with the other. The woman fought back, hitting her in the forehead with the cross. Carolyn kept rolling until the flailing hand was trapped. The woman pressed her face to the window and screamed to the others as if she were possessed. "She's got me! The witch's got me!" The cross dropped into Carolyn's lap.

Her shrieks galvanized the crowd. They pressed in and began rocking the tiny car back and forth.

"OhmyGodwhatdowedowhatdowedo?" Cassandra gabbled. They were trapped. The crowd was looming over them in front, behind, and on both sides. A hurled stone twanged against the windshield. "They'regonnakillus, they'regonnakillus."

"Go forward," Carolyn urged. "Start moving forward!"

"But I'll drag that crazy bitch with us!"

"Just start moving! Honk your horn!"

The horn sounded like a beeping child's toy. Cassandra shifted and began inching forward again. The woman panicked. Carolyn wound down the window just enough for her to pull her flailing hand free. "You tried to kill me! I'm suing you! I've got your license number! I'm suing you!" the woman screamed.

The crowd stood its ground, refusing to move until Cassandra closed her eyes, gunned the motor, and shot forward. The car jolted up the steep, rocky drive amidst a hail of stones.

At the top, near the house, they saw several Goddess Women clustered in an anxious knot around tall Jeanine Rotter. Clad in a long shimmering robe of black and silver, her horns of Hathor headpiece knocked askew, the high-priestess was trying to calm everyone down, including herself.

"I've called the police," Jeanine panted as Cassandra and Carolyn joined the group. "This is private property. I told them I'd have them arrested if they didn't leave."

"How did they find out?" someone asked.

"They must have gotten hold of one of the invitations."

"That's impossible," Jeanine said.

"Maybe we've been infiltrated by a spy from the ACA."

The Goddess Women looked at Cassandra.

"We mustn't succumb to paranoia," Jeanine insisted, drawing a sleeve across her perspiring face.

"But we're all on videotape," another woman cried.

With trembling hands, Jeanine repositioned her headdress. "We are not breaking the law, Sierra. They are."

"Well, I for one am leaving," Sierra said. "This is too scary. As soon as the police come I'm going home. I think we all should."

There was a general murmur of assent.

"And where do I go?" Jeanine asked. "This is my home."

"And what about the solstice ceremony?" Cassandra said.

The excuses came fast and thick. Mostly they had to do with fear of exposure. Several of the women were married. Many of them had important jobs. No one wanted her secret life as a Goddess Woman revealed. As their fears gathered momentum they cried, moaned and wrung their hands like a regiment of deafeated Walkyries. They didn't stop until a commanding voice rose above the din: "I think you're a bunch of cowards!"

It was Cassandra, daughter of the military. Her face flamed with defiance. "The Goddess isn't about being scared like a bunch of little girls. She's supposed to help us reclaim our strength as women. That's what I thought, anyway." An admiring glance from Jeanine Rotter gave her the courage to go on. "This isn't just play-acting for fun or an excuse to get away from your husbands and kids for a night. If that's all it is to you, you should pick up your skirts and go."

The women were silent.

"Don't you get it?" Cassandra shouted. "We need to fight, not surrender! And here you are, waiting to be rescued by the police. By big strong men in uniforms. You're not real Goddess Women, you're a bunch of sniveling babies."

"What do you suggest we do?" asked Jeanine.

"I think we should march out to the meadow and have our ceremony."

She was as inspiring as Boadicea on the battlefield, but many of the Goddess Women were still not prepared to fight. Violence was not their thing. Those ACA people were extremists, they could have guns. The would-be goddesses dithered around, huddling close to Jeanine's house, until a squad car finally arrived. The two officers reported that they had searched the entire length of the drive and found no trespassers. From the amused looks on their faces, it was obvious that they treated the matter as a joke. "Is this an early Halloween party?" one of them asked. When they left, several Goddess Women packed up their wands and rattles and followed them.

"I want to go, too," Carolyn whispered.

But Cassandra was adamant. "No, Carolyn. We're going to stay here and fight. Are you a woman or a mouse?"

Flushed with exultation, Cassandra led the small but grimly determined band of remaining Goddess Women to All-Mater Meadow. Jeanine, her golden horns glinting in the light of the setting sun, plodded heavily by her side. Carolyn, her forehead bruised, carried a platter heaped with Oregon strawberries and asparagus lightly sautéed in olive oil. They chanted, sang and gamely shook their bells and rattles as they progressed through the tall, dry grass. The warm air was refulgent with the promise of a bountiful summer. Insects buzzed and clicked. Off the to the west, stretching as far as the Coast Range, the vast, fertile cradle of the Tualatin Valley, with its vineyards, farms, and mushrooming suburban housing developments, glowed in a soft purple haze.

When they reached All-Mater Meadow the Goddess Women formed a circle. Jeanine took her Havilland platter from Carolyn and raised the offering-feast to the sky. She invoked the blessings of Astarte, Ceres, Cybele, Demeter, Gaia, Inana, Ishtar, Isis, and all suppressed and forgotten Great Mothers of the Gods. "We will not be driven underground like our foremothers," she vowed.

The air was suddenly filled with the sound of flapping wings and hoarse, gargling caws. A flock of crows flew out from Jeanine's sacred grove of alders, maples, and fir trees. "It is a sign from the Raven Mother," Jeanine said with a reverent smile. "She has sent her children to bless our feast and tell us not to be afraid."

Was it a blessing, a warning, or a curse? For just then a fervent brigade of screaming ACAers raced out from their hiding-places in the trees and stormed the sacred grounds of All-Mater Meadow. That was when all hell broke loose.

▼ ▼ ▼

The police were called. Some of the Goddess-crashers were apprehended and charged with trespassing. Unfortunately, that was just what they wanted. Dutiful publicists for Christ, they made certain that their civil martyrdom received significant press coverage. Christians fighting witches: it made a sensationally good story. But the story destroyed the anonymity of the Goddess Women and raped their sense of private sacred purpose. Jeanine disbanded the group until further notice.

▼ ▼ ▼

Terry was getting suspicious. It was nearly July. He knew Too-Too was scheduled to open on the first of the month. He'd heard that there was to be a fundraising gala on opening night. Some of his older gay friends were in a real twitter about it. They said it was going to be *the* gay dress-up event of the summer.

So why hadn't he received an invitation? Terry Terwilliger, not on a guest list? Or— hideous possibility—*crossed off* the guest list? Once again the ugly thought crossed his mind: he was being forced to give up his entire gay social life because of Billy. It was jealousy, of course. But that didn't make it any easier.

Finally he gave in and called Jay Zucker to glean details of the opening-night gala. Jay told him John-Don Webster was in charge. When Terry called John-Don, he was told that of course he and Billy could attend—but there were only $250 tickets left.

"You mean I have to pay *five hundred dollars* to get in?" Terry sputtered. "As a neighbor, I should be able to get in for free."

"It's a No on Three fundraiser, Terry. Nobody gets in for free. We have to raise as much as possible to fight that sick cousin of yours."

"I'm not responsible for what she does," Terry protested.

"Look, you're either with us or against us on this. If you're with us, put your money where your mouth used to be. I've got two tickets left, do you want them or not?" John-Don sounded as hard as nails.

"Well, you're not making it sound like much fun."

"Being gay is more than just having fun, Terry. We're fighting a battle and we need money."

"Oh, money, money, money," Terry grumbled. "That's all politics is nowadays. What do I get in exchange?"

"Dinner, two glasses of champagne, and a chance to kick Labonne in the balls."

"I simply don't understand why you're all becoming so hysterical about this silly issue!"

"Because we live in the real world, Terry. I'm in a rush. Do you want the tickets or not?"

"Two hundred and fifty a piece? How about—"

"I'm not going to give you any special discounts, Terry. Yes or no?"

"Well, you don't have to be so—"

"I take it the answer is no, then." And with that John-Don hung up on him.

In a funk, Terry accepted Leonora's invitation to a boring but free cocktail and dinner party in the Heights that evening. For once Billy didn't seem to mind, even seemed eager to get him out of the house.

CHAPTER 24

ON THE FIRST OF JULY A GIANT SPOTLIGHT, THE KIND USED AT MOVIE premieres and rarely seen in Portland, swept the warm evening sky above Too-Too with its powerful beam. Shining cars and hired limousines cruised up and down N.W. 23rd, looking for parking spots. A gawking crowd had already gathered around the cordoned-off entrance to watch the glittering proceedings. There was air of excitement and festivity all along the street.

Jay hadn't slept for two nights. He wouldn't allow his thoughts to dwell on the failure of Chez Jay. Everything was riding on Too-Too. His new venture had to make a fabulous first impression. He'd poured everything he had, and then some, into the place. If Too-Too didn't take off, his life as an independent restaurateur would be over.

The evening promised to be entertaining as well as politically useful. So why did he feel such *spilkes*? The doors would officially open in less than half an hour. The gala queer crowd already gathering outside was here to fight back against the ACA. But they were also Jay's future patrons. He'd done all this for them. As they murmured and laughed on the sidewalk Jay raced around in his Cerruti tuxedo checking last-minute details. Cassandra, dressed in a white floor-length Fifties evening gown and red shoulder-length gloves, swished along behind. She held a clipboard in one hand and stroked Jay's tense back with the other.

The employees and crew of volunteers, amused by Jay's high-voltage nervousness, were lined up for the general's final inspection and pep talk. "Okay, everyone, this is the big night," he said, scanning their crisp white jackets for stains. "I want all of you to be real professionals tonight. People are paying a lot of money. They're here to have a good time. I want the service to be smooth and fast. Too-Too isn't just a reflection of me,"—though it was, of course, and he glanced at his reflection in the mirror behind the bar to make certain he was gorgeous—"it's a reflection of all of us. Every gay man and lesbian in Portland. This is our place. And tonight we're committed to raising as much money as possible to fight Labonne and those assholes from the ACA. So are all of you ready?"

Yes, they shouted, humoring him.

From the bar Jay and Cassandra made their way through the candlelit dining room. Jay's experienced eyes checked the placement of cutlery, glasses, salt-and-pepper shakers. Everything had be perfect. He bent over to snatch a scrap of paper from the floor. "You've made sure that everyone has a place card, right?"

"Right," Cassandra said, pretending to consult her clipboard.

"We're booked solid." Jay began nervously rubbing his hands together. "How does it look?" he asked.

"It looks wonderful," Cassandra said.

He beamed and cast an admiring glance around the room. "It does, doesn't it?"

"Really, Jay. I'm so proud of you."

He kissed the top of her head. "Couldn't have done it without you."

"No, no, *no!*" came a booming, irritated voice from the stage area. "The curtain opens and bang! the spotlight hits me *center stage*. I do my opening shtick and the spot *stays with me* as I skip over to the piano. Is that really so difficult to remember?"

"Sid Charisse," Cassandra whispered. "He's been giving hell to the stage crew all afternoon."

They looked over and saw Wellfleet sitting in the dark, at the piano, as a spotlight tracked enormous Sid Charisse around the stage. The drag queen, wearing a garish sequined dress, mile-long eyelashes, and an enormous white wig festooned with "We Agree with Three!" buttons, was an instantly recognizable parody of Cornette Labonne.

"Poor Wellfleet." Cassandra couldn't help laughing. "He must be in agony."

John-Don slipped away from the stage area and joined them. "I never really knew what a queen was," he whispered, "until I had to deal with him."

"La-la-la, I stand here, then you follow me over to the piano player. What's your name again, darling?"

"Wellfleet," came the low, miserable voice.

"Wellfleet? My *Gahd*, darling, isn't that a brand of enema? All right, boys, keep him in the dark but track me over to here, and then widen the spot so you can see both of us." The spotlight grew to reveal Wellfleet in his pasted-on mutton-chop sideburns and handlebar mustache. "I'll say something like, 'I'd like all you loverly folks to meet my darling hunk of a hubby, my big fat stud Ron the Con, I mean Labonne. Ron, as you may know, is the head of the ACA. I can never remember what that stands for, hon. Is it Anti-Cocksucking Alliance?"

Wellfleet shook his head.

"Anti-Clitoris Association?"

Jay looked at his watch. "Okay," he called up to the stage, "we're ready to open. Break a leg."

Sid Charisse hurried off to the dressing room he'd commandeered. A perspiring Wellfleet joined Jay, Cassandra, and John-Don.

"Jesus," he moaned. "She's terrifying." He peered at a placecard. "Where's the Queer Corners table? Is everyone coming?"

"Susan had to fly back to London," Cassandra reported, "and Carolyn's pretending to have a migraine. The truth is she's been scared shitless ever since the ACA attacked us at the Goddess Woman ceremony."

"Terry won't be coming either," John-Don said. "The cheapskate objected to the price."

"No loss there," Wellfleet said. "What about Peter and Ito?"

"Here we are!" a voice called. "Bearing gifts." Peter, carrying a bottle of Veuve Cliquot, and Ito, with a huge bouquet of flowers, hurried towards them.

"What is this?" Jay said as they all kissed him and pressed the wine and flowers into his hands.

"It's from all of us," John-Don said. "A little thank you for what you've done."

"With our congratulations and best wishes for your success," Ito said with a ceremonial bow.

"Our success," Jay said. He cleared his throat and blinked his suddenly moist eyes. "Okay, everyone hang around afterwards and we'll drink a toast. But right now it's time to open the doors."

He fiddled with his bow tie as he made his way towards the entrance. Ran his tongue over his teeth and practiced his dazzling smile. Flung open the doors of Too-Too, beamed at the crowd, and made his long-anticipated announcement: "Too-Too is now officially open."

He heard music. And then saw the van, with its blazing HOMOSEX KILLS placard and "We Agree With Three!" bumper stickers, turning the corner. Its new sound system was blaring hymn tunes. As Jay and the crowd watched in stupefied silence, the van pulled up and double-parked right in front of Too-Too.

One of the van's two occupants—whom Ito later identified as Bob Sayles, marketing director of the ACA—jumped out and began passing out ACA literature. The driver harangued the crowd through the van's loudspeaker, denouncing Too-Too as a den of homosexual vice and iniquity.

Losing his tuxedoed cool, Jay barged through the crowd and pushed the leafleteer away. "Get out of here." Sweat was pouring down his bright red face.

"You see how he's trying to silence the truth?" the frightened Bob Sayles squealed to the bystanders. "He's trying to silence Christ's message about the sin of homosexuality! These people are all homosexuals and they want you to believe their perverted lifestyle is—"

"If you don't get your ass out of here," Jay threatened, grabbing Sayles by the collar, "I'm going to take these leaflets and ram them down your throat!"

Cassandra stopped Jay from punching him. But by that time the angry crowd of formally dressed gay men and lesbians had surrounded the van. The terrified driver locked the doors so Bob Sayles had to pound to get back in. The crowd swarmed, blocking the van's exit, hammering on it with their fists, kicking it, clawing at the "We Agree With Three!" stickers. A man and woman in fancy evening dress were hoisted up to the roof. They kicked over the HOMOSEX KILLS placard and hurled it into the street.

That was the opening of Too-Too.

▼   ▼   ▼

Ito watched the melee from the door of Too-Too. He tried to remain detached and uninvolved, but it was finally too much for him. He slipped away before he could be sucked into the fracas.

He walked quickly through the neighboring streets, trying to quell the nausea that was suddenly wreaking havoc with his stomach.

Hatred. Violence. How quickly they could blind the heart, overtake reason, and cast a shadow on the soul. In the blink of an eye a human could lose his humanity and revert to his most primitive instincts. Terrifying, the lightning-speed at which people could cast off their thin shells of individuality and hatch into a raging mob. He'd witnessed this sort of transformation as a boy, only then it had been Caucasians banding together against the Japanese. Now it was Christians against queers and queers against Christians.

What was most disturbing to him was his own desire to join in the fray. There'd been a moment when he, Ito Kudomono, a quiet, orderly, principled landscape designer, felt the hot tug of mob madness. He'd wanted to rush in and add his own burning outrage to the fuel igniting that hammering, kicking crowd.

He hadn't realized until then how angry he was. Anger had burrowed into him like a larva stealthily chewing its way into a tree. He'd tried, through his daily meditations, to transcend the nightmarish reality of the ACA. Tried to project loving goodwill towards the Labonnes. Told himself they were not "enemies," only misguided fools. It was Ito's habit to extract spiritual lessons from every manifestation of human behavior, no matter how brutal. How else could he reconcile mankind's endless cruelty to his own Taoist vision of life? Maybe the ultimate value in all this hate, he'd recently suggested to John-Don, was to jolt hearts numbed by fear and isolation into a greater awareness of compassion, love and concern.

To which John-Don replied, "Bullshit." Logic, reason, compassion—none of that did any good, he argued, in an illogical, unreasonable, hate-filled world. "Queers have to realize once and for all that their rights will never be freely given to them. Human rights never are. They're taken—by force if necessary."

Over the past weeks Ito had watched John-Don hardening before his eyes. It caused him great pain. John-Don was demonizing the ACA just as the ACA was demonizing homosexuals.

The nausea was getting worse. I am sick, Ito said to himself. But it was a spiritual sickness as much as a physical one. He was literally at war with himself.

He turned dizzily down the side street where his Landcruiser was parked. Before he could reach it, a wrenching pain seized his gut. He jack-knifed forward and spewed an acrid stew of rice cakes and green tea into the gutter. Waited for the next heaving spasm. One more.

Too-Too was only five minutes from Queer Corners. The air turned cool as he drove up the green, leafy corridor of Burnside towards Skyview. Home. He yearned for his bed.

He saw the flames as soon as he pulled up in front of his house. Something was burning in front of John-Don and Peter's house. When he realized what it was, a cold, malevolent hand suddenly seemed to be choking the breath out of him. Someone had thrust a crude wooden cross into their lawn and set it on fire. Through the flames he could make out the words "Kill Nigger AIDS Faggots."

He raced over to see if their house was in danger. Scanned the street. Looked at the Labonnes' house. Barricaded in darkness.

Split-second decisions. The house was safe. Something told him not to put the fire out. A line had been crossed that had never been crossed before. People must see it, recognize it. He only wished it wasn't Peter and his beloved John-Don. There was no telling what this would do to them.

He sprinted back to his Landcruiser and sped back to Too-Too.

▼ ▼ ▼

Fifteen minutes later John-Don and Peter pulled up in front of their house and were met by police cars and a fire truck. The charred cross was still smoldering on their manicured front lawn. The Labonnes' house was dark but the action on the street kept activating their sensor light.

John-Don knew that any visible reaction—especially fear—would be a victory for the other side. He absorbed his initial shock by taking it in, recognizing it, and spitting it back in the unseen faces of his enemies. It was a way of detoxifying their poison before it destroyed him. But when he saw the effect the burning cross had on Peter, he realized that his lover's psychological immune system wasn't as strong as his own. That was when his rationality recrystallized into pure, primal, implacable hatred. He wanted to destroy "them" not for what they had done to him, but for what they had done to Peter.

From the stricken look on Peter's face, John-Don knew that he could never begin to comprehend the full impact that message—"Kill Nigger AIDS Faggots"—had on a black gay man.

He gripped Peter's hand as they sat dazedly in the car. "Peter, look at me." It was like talking to a person struck by lightning, someone whose entire personality had been rearranged by a sudden, searing shock.

Peter stared vacantly at the cross, slumping lower and lower in his seat as if his life were visibly draining away. John-Don put his arms around Peter, tried to squeeze him back into reality. "Peter!"

Outside the car there was a disorienting flurry of noise and activity. Red and green lights flashed across the lawn. Firemen with hand-held canisters were spraying the flames with a thick foam that looked like hair mousse. The clicking, bristling static of radio messages—"no immediate danger," "situation under control"—and the appearance of news vans racing up Skyview added to the sense of swarming hysteria.

"Peter." He lifted Peter's drained, haggard face, turned it towards his own. "Listen to me. We can't let this frighten us. We can't let it destroy us."

Peter was hyperventilating, literally panting for breath. "They want to kill me," he choked out.

"Nobody's going to kill you."

"They're going to kill me," Peter insisted.

"I won't let anyone hurt you."

"I hate it here!" Peter cried. "I want to go home."

"You *are* home."

"This whole fucking state is *crazy*. They hate blacks, they hate queers, they hate everybody—what kind of home is that?"

"It's our home," John-Don said. "*Ours*, remember?" He, who had so much difficulty readjusting his beliefs before he could move into a house in upper-middle-class Queer Corners with Peter, now felt an urgent, almost patriotic need to convince his lover that it was worth fighting for.

"Yeah," Peter said, staring out towards the house, "homo sweet homo." He sucked in a shuddering breath, trying to control himself, then broke down and began to sob on John-Don's shoulder.

A policeman rapped on the car window and bent down to peer inside. He stared uncomfortably at the two men embracing in the front seat. "Are you the homeowner?" he asked John-Don.

John-Don thought the officer said "homo-owner." He glared furiously at the officer. "What did you just say?"

"I asked if you were the homeowner."

"We both are."

"Would you mind getting out and talking to us?"

John-Don kept his arm protectively around Peter as they made their statement to the police. He tightened his grip as the hungry news teams swooped towards them with a blinding barrage of lights. Who had called them? How had they gotten here so quickly?

Peter froze in alarm. "Don't let them see me," he pleaded, turning away, covering his face. "I don't want anyone to see me, it's too humiliating."

"Goddammit, we're going to stand out here together and let them see us," John-Don said.

"No, honey, I can't, I just can't."

"Do you want them to see that you're afraid?"

"Afraid? I'm scared shitless!"

"We're not going to run inside like a couple of hysterical queens. We've got to face this, head on, together."

"You can stay," Peter moaned, "you can be butch about it. But I'm going to run inside like an hysterical queen because that's just what I feel like."

John-Don wouldn't let him go. "You're going to stand out here at my side and we're going to tell them exactly what's going on. Come on, don't let me down. Don't let yourself down." He looked into Peter's frightened, bloodshot eyes. "Come on. I love you."

"Oh baby, I love you, too. But now they're all going to think I have AIDS. Katrina, the whole Nike crowd. It's going to ruin my career."

Race, sexuality and disease—the message had tied all three together in a noose that Peter was slipping over his own neck.

More and more people were stopping, rubbernecking as they slowly drove by. Frightened white faces gaping from Mercedes and Land Rovers, horrified when they heard what had happened. The Klan? Here in the hills?

Neighbors they'd never seen before straggled down from the surrounding streets. They stared, shivering and awestruck, at the goo-dripping cross and the two men glowing in the hallucinatory white lights. John-Don spotted Ito, Wellfleet, Cassandra, and Jay standing in an anxious knot near the front door of the house. In the surreal atmosphere, their faces were familiar and reassuring.

And through it all, John-Don knew that he had to turn this nightmare around, put his rage to constructive use. The news media, which had yet to draw any parallels between the growing number of hate crimes and Ballot Measure Three, finally had a perfect example of it right before their eyes. He wouldn't let them look away this time, or call it a "childish prank." He'd smear their faces in it. He'd make them see exactly how the ACA was putting their cherished symbol of Christian redemption to use.

He pulled Peter with him to the cross. Its acrid smell floated on the air like a sickening incense. John-Don wiped away the foam so the news crews and the gaggle of neighbors could see the charred message.

"Take a good look!" he shouted. "And if you think this doesn't affect you, think again. Because this sends a dangerous message all across America. It says that racism and homophobia are on the rise. It says that unless we get off our butts and do something to stop them, reactionary, right-wing hate groups like the ACA are going to turn all of us against one another. Make us afraid of one another. Is that your vision of America? A land of hate where everyone works against one another?"

Silence. A captive crowd standing before an orator.

John-Don pointed towards the Labonnes' house, flattened by their high-intensity sensor light into what looked like a false-fronted stage set. "If you really want to know who's responsible for this sick and malicious act, ask our neighbors right there across the street. Ask them, because they're the ones behind the ACA. This is their message to us, their neighbors, and to all the gay people in Oregon. But it's also their message to you. Because hatred is what's really behind Ballot Measure Three. And if you quietly sit back, out of fear or apathy, and you let this ballot measure pass, then you're just as guilty as they are. And tomorrow a symbol of right-wing hate might be burning in your front yard."

A nervous, uncomfortable, palpable air of emotion rose from the crowd. No one was prepared for this extempore indictment that drew attention to what they'd all tried so hard to avoid. Peter, who'd been standing with his head bowed, looked up at John-Don with glowing eyes. Wellfleet, Ito, Jay and Cassandra were squeezing one another's hands. Cassandra was weeping.

Then, all at once, the news teams surged forward. They wanted more. They began shouting questions. John-Don, suddenly exhausted, told them he and Peter would make a statement in the morning. In the midst of his anger he felt a mysterious glow of power, as if he'd passed through a wall of flames and come out charred but alive.

▼ ▼ ▼

When Dove, jangling with excitement, appeared at the studio door the following afternoon, the mere sight of her threw Cassandra into a fury. She didn't see Dove, she saw one of *them*. Dove was no longer neutral territory, she was part of the enemy camp. With icy contempt she told Dove that she didn't want to see her anymore.

Cassandra's sudden coldness threw Dove into a panic. She fluttered aimlessly about, desperately wanting to sit, to stay, to talk. "What about my portrait?" she asked, close to tears.

"No way. I'm too pissed-off to paint."

"Pissed-off with me?"

"Yes, with you. And with everything your parents stand for."

"But I'm not like them!" Dove insisted.

"How do I know that? Maybe you are. Have you ever thought about it?"

"About what?"

"About what they're doing! About the way they're picking on gay people. Telling lies. Burning crosses."

"They didn't burn it, they weren't even home. I was with them."

"If it wasn't them, it was their ACA people. Do you think that's right, Dove, doing something so malicious—so hurtful?"

"Why would they do it if it wasn't right?" Dove said. "They're doing it because it says in the Bible—"

"Oh shut up about the goddamned Bible!" Cassandra cried. "The Bible tells people to love their neighbors, not hate them."

"But those people are bad," Dove insisted. "God destroyed Sodom and Gomorrah because—"

"This isn't Sodom and Gommorah, it's Portland, Oregon, and someone burned a cross on my friends' lawn!" Queer Corners, as they had all known and loved it, was dead. She'd never forget the anguish on John-Don and Peter's faces, or her own stunned, sickening fear and disbelief. Today her gut was throbbing with anger. It was bad enough that the ACA had tried to tried to disrupt the opening of Too-Too, but burning a cross was unforgivable. That obscene act was an open declaration of war. "Don't you get it? They did it because of the hate your parents are preaching. And if you accept that, then you're as evil and stupid as they are." Furious, she stamped around the studio, wishing the girl would leave. "Just get out of here, will you?"

Dove started to cry. "Can't I come over here to visit you anymore?" she whimpered.

"No."

"Why not?"

Cassandra whirled around. She wanted to lash out, destroy Dove's sniveling innocence. Just how innocent was she anyway? Cassandra had always treated the girl's exalted, virginal notion of herself with tenderness and respect. Now it enraged her. Why should Dove be spared knowledge of the real world when Cassandra and her neighbors were being attacked, undermined, and demoralized on a daily basis?

"Because I'm—" She caught herself. "Just get out of here."

Dove let out a wail and began pulling on her silky blonde hair as if she wanted to rip it from her head. "But we're *friends*!"

"Not anymore. If your parents found out, they'd probably burn a cross on my lawn, too."

Dove covered her face. Like Eve, she was banished from the Garden of Eden.

▼ ▼ ▼

On that same afternoon Wellfleet was waiting anxiously for the story to appear on the local television news. "A burning cross ignites terror among residents of a peaceful west-side neighborhood," the news anchor dramatically announced. "That and other stories coming up next."

"We're not terrified," Wellfleet grumbled, reaching for the telephone. "We're pissed-off." He dialed Carolyn's number. No answer, as usual. The answering machine clicked on. Susan's voice asked callers to leave a message. "Carolyn, where the hell are you?" Wellfleet said irritably. He knew she was home because her car was parked out front. "Turn on the news." He hurried back to the television. The story was beginning.

"Two Portland residents returned to their home in Queen's Heights last night and found a cross with racist and anti-homosexual sentiments burning on their front lawn," said wide-eyed Amanda Drake. There was a shot of the foam-covered cross. A hand—John-Don's—wiped it off and a camera zoomed in. The words couldn't be seen clearly. Then the night footage switched to day. John-Don and Peter, interviewed that morning, appeared on the screen. Flanked by John-Don's parents, they stood with stricken faces near the front door of their house, John-Don's arm protectively around Peter's shoulder. John-Don explained the circumstances of their return from the No on Three fundraising rally the night before. "The ACA had already disrupted that event," he said.

"How did you feel, seeing a cross burning on your lawn?" the reporter asked. The camera focused on Peter, who silently looked at John-Don.

"As gay people we live with discrimination every day," John-Don said. *Right, good*, Wellfleet thought. "When we saw the burning cross we knew this was another form of persecution by the ACA—only this time they were using the tactics of the Ku Klux Klan."

"Do you have any proof that the ACA was behind this?" the reporter asked.

Trying to keep his voice reasonable, John-Don looked directly at the camera. "We hold Ron Labonne and his right-wing bigots directly responsible for this racist homophobic attack. Now the citizens of Oregon can see what's really behind the ACA's message of hate. This is the real truth of Ballot Measure Three. It's an attempt to deprive gay people of our most basic humanity. Can you imagine what that feels like?"

Yes, yes, yes, Wellfleet thought, watching John-Don, captivated by his looks, his courage, his charisma—*finally someone is telling the truth!*

His excitement was short-lived. Ron Labonne, Cornette clinging to his arm, was next seen being interviewed on the set of *On-Air With Jesus*. He was cool, low-key, unperturbed. "I can personally assure you that the ACA had nothing to do with it," he said. "If anything, I think it shows the lengths that homosexuals will go to to discredit us and gain sympathy for their special-rights agenda."

He was asked if he believed, then, that gays were responsible for the cross burning.

"I think it's more than likely. These people are sick and they'll stop at nothing to advance their deviant lifestyle."

"We've *never* advocated violence against homosexuals," Cornette blurted out. "We *love* homosexuals, it's their sins we can't stand."

"Are members of the Ku Klux Klan involved with the ACA?" she was asked.

The question appeared to unnerve Cornette. She blinked rapidly and turned to Ron. "The Ku Klux Klan? Why that's just plain ridiculous."

"I'd like to clarify a point here," Labonne said. "At that so-called fundraising rally, which, by the way, was held at a new homosexual bar on Twenty-third Avenue, where neighborhood children pass every day? What happened was that those animals attacked two unarmed Christian men who were exercising their rights to free speech. Why? Because homosexuals can't stand the truth! The truth that is in the Bible, for anyone to see with their own two eyes."

"Two of the nicest Christians you'd ever hope to meet," Cornette added.

"Terrified by a mob of homosexuals who attacked their persons and their property," Labonne cut in. "Was that truthfully reported in the press?"

CHAPTER 25

ON A BLAZING HOT JULY AFTERNOON, TWO DAYS AFTER THE CROSS-burning incident, John-Don and Peter watched from their living-room window as an ACA work crew hoisted a twenty-foot flagpole into the center of the Labonnes' concrete front yard.

"What are they going to do next, string me up from that thing?" Peter groaned. "I feel sick. I can't watch anymore." He wandered listlessly into the kitchen. When the phone rang he ignored it, a sure sign that something was seriously wrong.

It was an excited Wellfleet. "John-Don, did you happen to watch On-Air With Jesus last night?"

"I never watch that crap."

"Well I do. I watch it *religiously*." Wellfleet cackled. "Anyway, they said they were going to film a special fourth of July segment in front of their house. That's tomorrow. They're on the defensive, baby. They're scared. Ever since you got on the news."

"Yeah, but so did they. They denied everything."

"Doesn't matter. You got a gay sound-bite in. Now they have to deal with negative publicity. Bad public relations. This could bring the bastards down if you play your cards right."

"So what are they planning tomorrow?" John-Don asked.

"Some sort of patriotic bullshit in front of Old Glory. God, country, and family, that sort of thing. At five o'clock. They've invited the media to attend. Don't you think we should do something?"

"Yeah," John-Don said, scratching his chin as he watched the ACA crew busily at work across the street. "Yeah, I do."

He immediately called an emergency meeting of his neighbors. Everyone but Terry and Carolyn showed up. John-Don outlined his counter-attack plan. There was no time to waste. "Get on the phone. Call everyone you know who supports us. Tell them all to show up here tomorrow by four with rainbow flags."

Ito asked what rainbow flags were.

"Queer flags," Cassandra said. "Our flags. Come on, I know a shop that sells them."

When they'd gone, Peter told John-Don he wasn't going to take part. "Honey, I know it's heresy but I hate those Rainbow Diversity flags. They're so tacky. I object to them on the grounds of bad taste."

"They may be tacky, but they're all we have and we're going to put one up in front of the house."

"Well, you go ahead. I don't think I'll be feeling up to it."

"Peter, what's wrong with you?"

"I just don't have any energy. I'm so sick of all this fighting."

"Fighting? You're not fighting. You've been moping around like a—"

"Like a scared faggot," Peter cried. "I'm scared, all right? I'm afraid or what they might do to me."

"That's why you should join us," John-Don urged. "You can't go through the rest of your life cowering behind Venetian blinds, can you?"

"What life?" Peter said. He turned and plodded away.

The next day Peter stayed upstairs in the bedroom. John-Don stopped trying to coax him out. There was too much to do. People started to arrive at three-thirty. By five, when the Labonnes showed up with their television crew, a contingent of about fifty men and women was assembled and ready.

They waited until Ron, Cornette, Lester, and Dove filed out of the house and solemnly took their places by the new flagpole. "Look at that," Cassandra whispered. "They think they're the First Family!" As the American anthem blared from loudspeakers set up beside the house, the flag was raised and the four Labonnes raised their hands in a military salute.

"Okay, let's go." Following John-Don, the gay and lesbian brigade streamed out the front door and laid five Rainbow Diversity flags on the front lawn, where the cross had burned. A contingent then marched to Jay's, Ito's, and Wellfleet's, hanging flags from each of them.

Wellfleet, who'd never taken part in a public demonstration, was simultaneously elated and terrified. When he stumbled, a young man with a ponytail and an earring took his arm and helped him on.

The rest of the group silently lined the street and sidewalk in front of the Labonnes' house, holding up rainbow flags and signs that read: "No on Three," "Equal Rights Are Not Special Rights," "The ACA is UnAmerican and UnChristian," "Hate is Not a Family Value," and "American Gaytriots."

There was consternation, confusion, fear, anger among the ACAers. Were they in danger? They pressed back, looking to Labonne for guidance. As the anthem played, the Labonnes grimly held their salutes, only it now looked as if they were saluting the queer demonstration in front of them. Dove, catching sight of Cassandra, darted behind her mother so Cassandra wouldn't see her. Lester, meeting John-Don's steely gaze, froze and looked off into the mid-distance. Labonne, his eyes narrowed, scanned the crowd on the other side of his cyclone fencing.

"What are they doing, hon?" Cornette, dressed in red, white, and blue, and still saluting, had to shout to be heard above the national anthem.

"Ignore them!" Ron bellowed to his camera crew and the assembled news teams. "They're desecrating a private ceremony. They're trespassing on private property!"

But they weren't, and he knew it. John-Don had told everyone to stay on the street and sidewalk. There were to be no repeats of the battle in front of Too-Too.

The anthem ended. The two groups silently faced each other.

"I'm calling the police!" Helen Hill cried, her eyes riveted on Ito.

Ron stopped her as she started for the house. "No, Helen, that's just what they want us to do."

Cornette, peering anxiously over her shoulder, grabbed her husband's arm. "Ron—why are they doing this?"

Dove, suddenly exposed to view, felt like she was caught in a whirlpool, spinning around and around, being dizzily sucked down into the middle. For there, in the crowd, standing next to Cassandra, she saw the man who'd attacked her in the park. A friend of Cassandra's! Both of them, all of them, attacking—for that was how she saw it—her mom and Ron. And attacking her, too, since she was on her mom's side. What would they do? Why were they against her mom and Ron and the ACA's ministry? Stupid and evil, Cassandra called them. But Cassandra was with *him*. Dove sidled away so he wouldn't see her, then slipped back into the house.

Labonne extricated himself from Cornette's grasp and took a threatening step forward. "I know what you're trying to do!" he shouted. "Perverted degenerates mocking our sacred flag!"

The tense silence that followed was broken by the sound of Wellfleet's pitchpipe. He moved in front of the group and raised his arm.

"Oh say can you see, by the dawn's early light . . ."

John-Don, who'd been raised to distrust blind patriotism, stood in front of Ron and Cornette Labonne with fifty queers and sang "The Star-Spangled Banner." He hadn't sung it since being forced to in grade school. Patriotism, his father always said, quoting Dr. Johnson, was the last refuge of a scoundrel. There was no gay anthem to sing, or the group would have sung that. This was a calculated media gambit and a symbolic way to claim America as theirs, too. John-Don watched with delight the God Couple's squirming discomfort, their disbelief, their visible anger at the way the news teams turned their attention away from them and towards his group. He sang louder, fueled by a sudden surge of power. He, John-Don Webster, leading the queers, was as newsworthy as Ron Labonne. He and Labonne represented two opposing armies.

Cornette, in a bid to win back media attention, dramatically spread her arms and tried to take charge with a prayer. "Oh Lord!" she cried. "You see before us a group of America-mocking devil-worshippers!"

"What so proudly we hailed, at the twilight's last gleaming . . ."

"Shine your loving light down on these wicked, unAmerican souls!"

"Whose broad stripes and bright stars, through the perilous fight . . ."

"Show them the way to the truth! Show them the light of your merciful heart! Lead them away from their sinful ways!"

"Oh say does that star-spangled banner yet wave . . ."

Cassandra, holding aloft her "Hate is Not a Family Value" sign and singing along with the rest, saw Ron Labonne's eyes trained on her. Her gaze wandered over to Cornette, who'd carefully fallen to her knees in the concrete pen of the front yard and was continuing her entreaties to the Lord. The woman looked insane. They all looked insane. But no one looked more insane than Lester Labonne, who suddenly appeared on the front porch with a crooked smile on his face and a rifle in his hands.

"O'er the land of the free! And the home—"

"He's got a gun!" Cassandra screamed.

The singing stopped. Time stopped. Everyone turned to see Lester raising the rifle. In the terrified silence they clearly heard him say, "Want me to pick off a few queers, dad?"

Pandemonium. Screams. A convulsive surge of movement. The gays threw down their rainbow flags and ran for cover. Only there wasn't any cover. They were all open targets. They scattered in all directions.

Labonne rushed over and wrenched the gun from his son. "What do you think you're doing?"

Lester crumpled back, flattened by the fury in his father's eyes. "Hey, it wasn't loaded or nothin'. It's just my b-b gun. Thought we should give those queers a scare is all."

"Get in the house," Labonne hissed through clenched teeth, "and don't open your mouth again or I'll bash your head in. They *heard* you, you stupid moron!" He turned back to the crowd with a bland, cajoling grin. "Relax, everyone! He wasn't serious. It's just his toy b-b gun." He heard the clicking, whirring shutters of the cameras. Realized they were taking pictures of him holding the gun. "Hey!" he called. "Let's everybody go inside and calm down. Cornette's cooked up a real fourth of July feast!"

The story appeared in the paper the next day with the headline: "Gay Group Disrupts ACA Flag Ceremony."

▾ ▾ ▾

The shop was down on Fourth Avenue, between an XXX-rated movie arcade and a boarded-up restaurant. It sold hunting equipment mostly, but also used handguns. Wellfleet passed several times before he got up the nerve to enter.

As he nervously approached the counter, a lanky man about his own age, wearing blue jeans, a plaid shirt, and cowboy boots, slowly approached him from the back of the store. "Howdy. What can I do for you?"

"Yes, I'd like to look at a gun, please."

"What kind?" the man asked, tucking a wad of tobacco in his mouth.

"What kind?"

"What are you gonna use it for?"

"Use it for?" Wellfleet dumbly repeated.

"Deer? Elk? Or your wife?" The man laughed, showing a mouthful of brown teeth, and began to cough.

Wellfleet politely laughed too. "I just want it for some target practice," he said. His eyes roamed among the handguns laid out behind the counter and the long guns hanging on the wall. "How about that one?"

The man unlocked the counter and withdrew the handgun Wellfleet indicated. "Yup, she's a beaut." He handed the gun to Wellfleet. "Feel the balance in her."

To Wellfleet, who was a virgin when it came to firearms, the experience of handling a .38 was fraught with a dark, forbidden excitement. The sturdy weight of it in his palm, the way it fit in his hand, its perfectly engineered beauty—it was like caressing a beautiful musical instrument built to play just one deadly note.

"Can I use this at a firing range?" he asked.

"Shure," shrugged the gun dealer. "Don't see why not."

The procedure for buying the gun was unbelievably simple. All Wellfleet had to do was fill out a form in triplicate. The form went to the city police, who tracked down verification. Since Wellfleet had never been convicted of a felony or violent misdemeanor, this would present no problems.

"There's a five-day waiting period before you can take possession," the shopkeeper said.

"Right. Yes. I understand."

"You wanna apply for a concealed weapon permit while you're at it?"

"Oh—uh—do I need that?"

"Depends on if you're gonna conceal it," the man said.

"I beg your pardon?"

"On your person. The gun. Are you gonna conceal the gun on your person?"

Wellfleet cleared his throat. "Oh. Conceal it on my person? No. I mean, I don't think so. I mean—"

"It takes longer and requires more paperwork."

"No," Wellfleet said. "I don't think I'll bother with it then."

The shopkeeper shrugged. "Just thought I'd ask."

When Wellfleet went back to pick up the gun he noticed a "We Agree With Three!" sign tacked up behind the counter. Seeing it there among all the hunting paraphernalia—guns, ammo, knives—he had a dark vision of himself as a frightened animal hounded and chased by grinning bloodthirsty killers. But when he put down his cash and picked up the .38, he was suddenly flooded with a strange, lightheaded sense of power. The animal could now take aim at the hunters.

Returning to the perpetual twilight gloom of his decaying adobe, he sat quietly in the dark with his new gun on his lap, petting it like a cat. Thought of just how hopelessly threadbare his life had become. The naive aspirations of his youth had vanished long ago. He was a voice teacher without a voice. He was an ugly, gimpy, unemployed fifty-eight-year-old homosexual choral director sitting alone in the dark daydreaming about murder. Violence: the aphrodisiac of the dispossessed. All he had left was his futile rage.

Wearing his "No on Three" button, his beat-up Dodge Dart plastered with every anti-ACA bumper sticker he could find, he felt, wherever he went, that he was a moving target. So it was always a relief and a pleasure, especially when he returned from the firing range, to sit in the dark stroking his new gun and envisioning Ron Labonne's face in the middle of a bull's-eye.

▼ ▼ ▼

On July 15th Carolyn withdrew two thousand dollars from her bank account and drove across the Burnside Bridge to the east side of Portland. A band of pain throbbed around her temples. Her entire body was tense with a sense of impending disaster that she was powerless to stop.

It was unusually hot. The sky looked like a dirty gray sponge. Pollution warnings. Dribbles of rain. A stale gray fog blurred the outlines of buildings. The most ordinary events seemed charged with portent. Carolyn nearly got into an accident. Her car stalled on Martin Luther King Boulevard. She saw a three-legged dog loping down the street.

She drove through her old neighborhood and pulled up on one side of the park where, before she met Susan, she'd played in so many lesbian softball games. The great expanse of lawn was deserted.

Clutching the thick, sticky wad of bills in her raincoat pocket, she trudged through the wet grass to the picnic shelter. Lester was supposed to meet her there at four o'clock. Five minutes to go.

Scenes from her life passed through her mind in an unending, accusatory stream. Mistakes. Bad judgment. Cowardice. Fear. Poverty. Loneliness. Who was she? A forty-two-year-old woman standing in a deserted park waiting for the son whose life she had ruined.

Then she saw him. Wearing blue jeans and a t-shirt, with a huge backpack rearing up behind him, he slowly crossed the lawn. Carolyn kept her eyes on him. Lester kept his eyes on her. The fog turned to rain. It hammered down on the corrugated roof of the picnic shelter. Lester kept his same, steady pace.

As he got closer she saw that one side of his face was covered with a swollen, purply-yellow bruise.

He stood for a moment, rain dripping down his face and soaking his clothes, just outside the shelter. Looking at her. Seeing himself in her. His bruised, disfigured face taut, wary. She watched his Adam's apple slowly move up and down.

Carolyn felt naked. So emotional she couldn't speak. She put out her hands, offered them to him.

Lester didn't move. "It's you?" he said in a low incredulous voice.

"It's me."

"I don't believe it." He looked away, confused, then nailed her again with those hard blue eyes. "All this time you were there, in that house across the street?"

She nodded. "I had no idea when you moved in—"

"How'd you find out?"

"I recognized him. Your father."

"Must of been a shock after all those years."

"Yes. It was a shock."

"Yeah, it's a shock for me, too." He quickly backed away when Carolyn took a step towards him. "Don't touch me." He gently prodded his swollen cheek and twitched his face.

"All right," she said, trying to keep her voice calm. "But come in here, out of the rain. You're getting soaked."

"You sound just like a mother," he mocked.

"Come in here. We need to talk for a minute. Before you go."

He glanced suspiciously around the park. "You ain't gonna try to keep me."

"No. I said I wouldn't."

He stepped into the shelter, his face grim, keeping his distance.

"Where are you going, Lester?"

"That's none of your business."

"I want to help you, you know that. In any way I can."

"It's too late for you to help me. All you can do is give me that money so I can get the fuck out of here."

She pulled the wad of bills from her pocket and held it out. "Here. Happy birthday."

He kept his eyes on the money as he approached her. When he took it, Carolyn suddenly, without thinking, grabbed him by his wrists and tried to pull him into an embrace. Her hands wanted to stroke, fuss, fondle. Furious, Lester shoved her away.

"I said don't touch me and I mean it. I don't want your dirty hands on me."

"Lester—"

"I hate you," he said, his voice cracking. "Fuckin' bitch."

Carolyn wheeled around, covered her face, and began to sob. The spasms that shook her body came from somewhere so deep, so long buried, they seemed to burn her heart. Suddenly she was afraid he'd leave her there, walk away when her back was turned and she'd never see him again.

But he was still there, rigid as a board, held upright by his backpack. Staring at her, a stony, unforgiving look on his lumpy discolored face.

"I'm sorry," she gasped, wiping her eyes. "This is harder for me than it is for you."

"How do you know what it is for me?" he said.

"I don't, I couldn't know."

"That time you picked me up in your car? I thought something was weird that day."

"Did you? So did I. But I didn't know then who you were." She stared, trying to absorb as much of him as she could, a close-up snapshot to be developed and printed on her heart. But all she could take in was that bruise. His swollen, tender, assaulted flesh. She lacked the courage to ask where it came from. She knew.

"You had red hair," Lester said.

"Like yours." She tried to smile. "It's still there, underneath, the same color as yours."

"I never thought—never thought in a million years—" He turned away. "It's just too fuckin' weird."

"Maybe coincidence is God's way of performing miracles."

"Don't talk to me about God," he spat. "I've had enough of that bullshit to last me the rest of my life."

"It's just a phrase," she said.

"This God everyone's always yakkin' about. The son-of-a-bitch is never there when you really need him."

"It seems that way, doesn't it?"

"When your arm's broke or you're freezing in the cold or you've had the shit beat out of you so bad you can't—" He gingerly touched his face again. "I used to pray that you'd come back and help me. That you'd come back and get me out of there."

His words were like bullets exploding in her heart. "He would have killed me," she whispered.

He locked his eyes on hers. "And you would of deserved it. Bitch. Cause you left *me* there to get killed instead "

Carolyn clutched her stomach and bowed her head.

"I'm going."

She nodded and tried to find her voice. It had evaporated almost to nothing. "Lester, you know where I am now. You can come to me for help at any time. I want you to know that."

"Don't hold your breath," he said. Then he turned and walked away.

▼ ▼ ▼

Money and media. That's what politics was all about. John-Don had no illusions about the necessity for both. What he hadn't counted on was the third factor that crept into the equation: the blurring intoxication of power.

The cross burning catapulted John-Don into media visibility. Since Natalie Notale, the head of No on Three, and her steering committee remained annoyingly invisible, John-Don felt that he was justified in acting as an official spokesman.

Why not? He was educated, eloquent and "presentable"—the all-American queer. He thought of himself as a leader. In his mind, the brief flare of visibility allowed him to step directly into the ring with Ron Labonne. No one else from the No on Three campaign was doing it. Labonne and everything he stood for evidently struck terror into their hearts. Labonne was the bogeyman hiding in every queer's closet, under every queer's bed: *if I close my eyes and don't move, he won't get me.*

John-Don wasn't afraid of the bogeyman. He'd been raised to question authority and act on principle. And, though he was loathe to admit it, he secretly enjoyed the limelight.

He'd foolishly thought that the organization would be pleased when he publicly identified himself as a member of No on Three and denounced Labonne and the ACA. Instead, his comments on local television and in the paper unleashed squabbling within the organization. No on Three was in danger of splitting into opposing factions: lesbians vs. gay men. The women were mostly behind Natalie, the men were forming resistance around John-Don.

Trouble had been brewing for some time. The growing consensus among the men, who began hanging around John-Don more and more, was that Natalie didn't know what she was doing and was taking too long to do it. John-Don, who'd joined the organization because he wanted to help in some way, sensed that the anti-Natalies wanted him to foment a rebellion and take over No on Three.

He was no stranger to political intrigue but he was a novice when it came to gay politics. He hadn't expected divisiveness in the No on Three campaign. Until he started working on the campaign he'd always thought of himself as a left-of-center liberal. Now he was encountering so many new and contrary viewpoints in the lesbian and gay community that he no longer knew what was politically correct. His fear was that No on Three, at the most crucial moment in its existence, would lose sight of the larger picture and break down into a welter of rigid and politically impotent ideologies. He didn't want to set himself up as Natalie's rivial. Splintering off to form another group would be time-consuming and counter-productive. But he was so intent on winning the battle, at whatever cost, that he began to resent Natalie, doubt her strength, and question the direction of the campaign. He wanted some kind of no-holds-barred showdown with Labonne. Direct confrontation rather than what he perceived to be sidestepping apprehension.

He heard rumors from the men that Natalie Notale was jealous of the attention he was getting. Since Natalie never confronted him directly, John-Don ignored the rumors. But then she summoned John-Don to her office.

The very sight of Natalie had always irritated him. Perhaps it was because he wanted or expected the woman in charge of No on Three to look and act "powerful." Labonne, her political opponent, was big and mean and a dirty fighter. Natalie, a thin, plain, soft-spoken woman with a shag haircut and frameless glasses, simply did not inspire confidence—at least in John-Don, who towered above her and thought he sensed the intimidating force his own masculine energy had on her.

Natalie was never alone. Today she was surrounded by her usual cadre of advisers. When John-Don sat down she said, without preamble, that she wanted him to stop making statements to the press unless she had okayed them in advance.

It was a touchy situation. John-Don was surprised by the vehemence of his resentment. Why did he feel so bitterly angry? Because she was a woman, a lesbian, telling him what to do? Because she was less politically experienced than he was? Because she was silencing him, when he knew he could be such an effective spokesperson? It was all of that. But most of all it was because she sat on the power side of the desk. Natalie was making the decisions and John-Don wasn't.

"We have to be very careful in what we say and how we present ourselves," Natalie explained. "I don't want you to identify yourself as a spokesperson for the No on Three campaign."

"Why not? No one else is saying anything. Isn't it about time?"

"We're forming a Media Committee to—"

"Oh great," John-Don angrily cut in, "another committee. You don't need a Media Committee to tell you you should have been on the tube months ago, Natalie. Nobody even knows who's running this campaign."

"I'm running it," she said firmly. "In my own way. That's what I was hired to do."

"Well, you're running it all wrong," John-Don snapped. He felt bold and reckless, ready to start fires. "What the hell have you done? What's happening to all the money that I've raised? No one even knows how it's being spent. All we know is that you've spent tens of thousands of dollars on a useless survey."

She was starting to bristle. "You don't think it was useful?"

"What did it tell you?"

"It told us that a majority of Oregon voters aren't in favor of general discrimination."

"Yeah, but the same poll showed that a majority of Oregon voters didn't believe in 'special rights.' So the campaign has to be marketed in a way that emphasizes the discriminatory aspects of Ballot Measure Three and downplays any idea that gay rights are 'special rights.' I could have told you that."

She sat back and looked at him. "I'm sure there's a lot you could tell me. Or would like to tell me."

"There should be people going door to door to talk to voters. There should be a phone bank of volunteers calling voters. There should be public demonstrations every week. Guerilla warfare if necessary. Disruptions. And you should be demanding media coverage, however you can get it."

"You seem to have taken that on yourself," Natalie said.

"Someone has to. How can we get our message across when the head of No on Three is invisible?"

"She's not invisible," one of the women said. "Maybe you just can't see her because of your own blinding radiance."

John-Don stiffened at the affront. "Media, Natalie. Essential. The biggest paper in the state reports only on the straight side of the issue, but *we're* the ones who'll be affected. What *we* think about our criminalization is never discussed."

Natalie tapped the ends of her fingers together. "But it doesn't do us any good to get headlines like 'Gay Group Disrupts ACA Flag Ceremony.' People see that and get frightened."

"Good! I think they should be frightened. I think they should know we're not taking this like passive wimps. They should know we're angry."

"No," she said, shaking her head. "We have to present ourselves in a positive, non-threatening light."

"There is no positive light when you're queer. Don't you get it? The straight media doesn't want that. It's our visibility that's threatening to them." His leg was starting to jiggle. "We're being silenced, and your job is to give us a voice. You should be visiting editors, pounding on tables, making them hear what's going on. That we're being terrorized. That our humanity's being stripped away. They don't want to see or hear that so it's your job to make them see and hear it."

"Look," she said, keeping her annoyance in check, "I just don't want you organizing demonstrations that aren't approved by—"

"The Demonstration Committee?"

"—me. And I don't want you to identify yourself as some sort of official No on Three spokesperson. You're not."

"Why not?"

"You're not—careful enough in what you say. Or do."

"I'm impulsive."

"Yes, John-Don, you're impulsive."

"I'm sick of being careful. Being nice isn't going to get us anywhere."

"You're pushing the envelope too far too fast," Natalie said. "You act like you're speaking for everyone and you're not. We can't just lash out, okay?" Natalie took a deep breath and sat forward in her chair. "Please," she said. "I want you in the organization. I need your support. You might not like my decisions, or agree with them, but they're my decisions and I'm in charge."

The old power struggle. She was in charge and he wanted to be. He threatened her autonomy, just as she threatened his. He could leave or stay. If he left, how would he fight? He needed to fight. If he stayed, it would be on her terms. He could not work against her. His conscience would not let him. Solidarity was everything at this juncture.

In the end he swallowed his resentment and agreed to stay on as Director of Campaign Fundraising. Renouncing his secret desire for total control over the campaign was more difficult. For the first time in his life John-Don admitted to himself that he craved power.

▼ ▼ ▼

In the midst of his own flurry of activity, John-Don didn't see that Peter was sinking into a deep depression. He didn't want to see it. At first he assumed Peter's listlessness was an emotional aftershock of the cross burning, that he'd spring back to life once he'd had time to recover. In fact, Peter was canceling business appointments and rarely left the house. He looked drained, seemed barely able to drag himself from one room to the next. He was often asleep when John-Don returned at night.

Peter kept saying that he wanted to get away. "What good would that do?" John-Don asked.

"I wouldn't have to look at their house and wonder when someone was going to shoot me."

As that hot, hateful summer sped on, John-Don grew more anxious and concerned about Peter. Peter was drinking. Peter was shutting him out. He'd lost all interest in sex—just when John-Don was finally loosening up enough to enjoy it.

John-Don had never been able to understand depression. He regarded it as a self-indulgent weakness, an inability to face and grapple with reality head-on. Peter had alluded to depression before. He'd said there were times in San Francisco, after most of his friends had died, when he'd thought about suicide. But that was before he met John-Don. And now John-Don, who'd "saved" him once, who wanted to think of himself as Peter's protector, saw his mate slipping into an impenetrable emotional prison.

He hadn't realized how much he missed the old Peter, the sexy light-hearted party boy experienced in camp, frivolity and all the pleasurable things John-Don was no good at, until he was gone. And with the old Peter gone, their intimacy evaporated, and without intimacy they were nothing more than strangers sharing a house.

"I don't know what to do," John-Don confided to Ito. He now spent more time with Ito than with Peter because Ito, to everyone's surprise, had thrown himself into the No on Three campaign. "He won't let me in."

"You want the relationship to continue?" Ito cautiously asked.

"I love him, Ito. But seeing that cross changed him."

"It changed all of us," Ito said.

"It just knocked the life out of him. I mean, I can see why it would. But if you don't fight back, if you just crumple up—"

"Do you want me to have a talk with him?" Ito asked.

"I don't know what good it would do."

"It might not do any good," Ito said. "But then again—"

CHAPTER 26

DOVE WAS VACUUMING. THE BIG OLD AIR-CONDITIONERS LUGGED UP from Dallas were rattling in the windows. A television was blaring upstairs. And still she could hear them as they progressed from room to room, upstairs and down, Ron tailing her mom like an angry shadow.

"You didn't know?" Ron shouted at Cornette from the kitchen.

"No, hon, of course not. How could I?" Cornette lurched around the corner of the living room, grabbed the vacuum cleaner from Dove, and frantically began to push and pull it across the new orange carpeting.

Without the roaring vacuum cleaner Dove felt naked and exposed—a helpless bystander forced to watch her mother extricate herself, yet again, from one of Ron's tirades. The tirades had become more and more frequent since Lester's disappearance. More frightening. With a threatening menace in them that made Dove sick to her stomach. She had to control herself, though, because Ron wouldn't stand for any of her emotional "tornadoes."

Dove's life had changed. The way she thought about things had changed. The way she thought about *them*—about Ron and her mom—had changed.

They pretended to be one thing, but they were something else. Even her mom. All that blathering about how wonderful Ron was—it was a big fat lie. Her mom was scared of Ron. Everyone was scared of Ron.

Dove was glad that Lester had run away, but he'd run away because of the way Ron treated him. It served Ron right. But Ron didn't show any of the pained paternal remorse Dove thought he should. No, he was just afraid that someone might find out. So was her mom. Dove had heard them telling lies, making up stories, and they'd told her to lie, too. Lester was supposedly off at a special Bible retreat.

The two of them didn't care about her, either. They only cared about themselves. It made her sick, the way they pored through the papers to see if their names were mentioned or their pictures had appeared.

That changed after the cross burning. People accused them of doing it. Cassandra accused them of doing it. Dove knew they hadn't, but she enjoyed watching their discomfort. Something in her had grown cold and hard.

She blamed them for making her lose Cassandra's friendship. That was maybe the worst of all, being cut out of Cassandra's life because of them. Having Cassandra think she was like them was horrible. Not being able to go to Cassandra's was agony. There was no one to listen to her. No one to talk to. Now, when Ron started picking on her, her mom ignored it or looked the other way. Without Cassandra's sympathetic ear,

Dove was forced to endure Ron's cruelty in silence.

When Lester was around, he received the brunt of Ron's perpetually simmering anger. Now that Lester was gone there was no one for Ron to pick on and bully except for Dove and her mother.

Dove winced and backed away as her stepfather stalked into the living room. "Please, God," she fervently prayed, "strike him down right now. Let him fall over dead and *leave us alone*." But her prayer went unanswered.

"You said you knew this neighborhood!" Ron bellowed.

Cornette's vacuuming grew more agitated. She zoomed off in another direction.

"You said it was the best neighborhood in Portland!" He jabbed the air with his finger. His face was red and the veins in his neck stuck out.

With trembling hands, but careful not to break any of her long red nails, Cornette affixed another attachment to the hose and began skimming the heavy, perpetually drawn drapes.

Suddenly the vacuum cleaner gave a hollow, dying wheeze. Cornette turned and saw that her husband had yanked the cord from the outlet.

"Heavens, hon, how can I clean without power?"

"Isn't that what you said?" he demanded, slapping the cord against the palm of his hand. "The best neighborhood in Portland?"

"Hon," she whimpered, "I don't remember what I said."

"Well, I do. I remember every word. You said this was a ritzy family neighborhood."

"That's what Sissy Parker told us, remember? I only said—"

"You said you knew this neighborhood from visiting your cousin here."

"Well, hon, I did visit him here, and at the time it seemed like such a nice peaceful place."

"He didn't tell you this nice peaceful place was loaded with *perverts*? Why didn't that cousin of yours mention that, I wonder?"

"Dove, sweetheart, why don't you go outside and feed the bunny rabbits?" Cornette suggested.

Dove couldn't bear to look at the rabbits. Fluffy had recently appeared on the supper table. "I don't want to," she said.

Ron was on her immediately. "You don't want to? That's your job, isn't it? That's about the only thing you do to earn your keep around here."

"Oh, Ron, Dove does plenty of work around the house." Cornette brushed her daughter's pale face. "Why don't you take the puppy for a walk then?" she said tenderly. "You can feed the bunnies later."

Dove knew her mom wanted her out of the house because they were going to have another fight. A really big one. And that was why she didn't want to leave. She was afraid if she left Ron might do something to hurt her mom. He hadn't yet, but there was always a first time. She'd seen what he'd done to Lester.

"Go on, honey," Cornette whispered. "Later on you can help me sew up that pretty new party dress "

"What party dress?" she asked.

"Why, the one you're going to wear to all those dances and parties."

"Nobody ever invites me to no dances or parties."

"Well, I bet they will once you start high school and they find out your daddy's one of the most important men in Oregon."

"He's not—" But seeing Ron looming above her, Dove clenched her lips and slowly shuffled towards the back door. Ron made her keep the puppy, which she'd named Dumbo because of its big floppy ears, on a heavy chain just outside.

"And stop sulking," Ron called after her, "or I'll really give you something to sulk about."

▾ ▾ ▾

When his stepdaughter left the house, Ron hitched his pants up over his gut and turned back to Cornette.

She saw that he was gearing up to resume the battle and tried to disarm him by saying, "Hon, I wish you'd be a little gentler with her."

"Nobody was ever gentle with me when I was a kid," he shouted. "That's the trouble nowadays, everyone's so soft."

"She's just a girl. She's at a vulnerable age. It hasn't been easy for her, moving up here, away from her friends and her school."

"Stop protecting her. She's spoiled rotten and you know it."

"She's my daughter, Ron, I've got to protect her. I don't want her running away, too."

"What's that supposed to mean? Are you saying Lester ran away because of me?"

Cornette answered by saying nothing.

"It wasn't me," Ron insisted. "It was her—his mother. It was her bad blood. She had the devil in her. I couldn't get it out of him, no matter how hard I tried."

"I know that," Cornette said placatingly. "I just hope nobody else finds out that he's gone. Helen was asking me about him yesterday. She said it was important for all of us to be seen together, as a family. For the campaign to be truly effective, she said, people have to see us as Christian role models."

"Speaking of family, what about that cousin of yours next door? He's one of them, isn't he?"

"One of them?"

"One of the perverts who've taken over this neighborhood that you just had to live in."

"If Terry was a pervert, hon, why would he be contributing so generously to our cause?"

"Generously!" Ron guffawed. "All he's shelled out is two lousy grand. Peanuts! That's not even enough for one mortgage payment on this house that you had to have."

"Well, hon, it's more than most of our people have contributed."

"It's not enough! You said he was a millionaire. And right now we need some real money. Big bucks, not nickels and dimes. We've got to fight like never before because these sick faggots are raising money like crazy. They're like Jews when it comes to money. They control the banks—"

"Who does?" Cornette asked, confused, as always, on this point. "The Jews or the perverts?"

"Both," he snapped. "They've got it all figured out. They're selfish and greedy. That's one of the reasons why they choose to be homos. They don't want to spend money on raising families, they want to spend it all on themselves. And that's what they're doing right now. They're outspending us five to one."

Cornette hated facts. And the fact was that despite their repeated pitches for money, hardly enough was coming in to pay for air-time, let alone mortgage payments, property taxes, and Ron's improvements on the house. There was a whole new round of expensive mailings that had to go out, not to mention statewide distribution of the official ACA video, *Homosexuals on the March*.

The ACA, after all, was a family-run business, dependent upon the faithful to keep food on the table and righteousness in the soul. Cornette had contributed the downpayment for the house on Skyview herself, using up every last penny from her Terwilliger inheritance and the sale of her place in Dallas. Ron, full of promises, said once they got their foot in the door, as it were, the ACA would take care of everything else. But if it weren't for Helen Hill, whom they cultivated with the desperate acumen of penniless nobility, bestowing upon her the title of Campaign Director, the ACA would be in hock up to its ears.

For one horrible moment Cornette saw the entire ACA edifice come crashing down in an avalanche of unpaid bills and tax liens. She, who'd given up everything to help Ron in his noble crusade, would be no better than a penniless queen. Ron, who'd selflessly dedicated his life to the moral rejuvenation of his country, would be a king without a throne. It was so darned unfair.

"The Lord will provide," she said. "He knows our cause is just. He won't fail us, hon. It's right there in Matthew: 'Therefore, I say unto you, if ye have faith and doubt not, whatsoever ye shall ask in prayer, believing, ye shall receive.'"

But Ron wasn't so sure. He strode around the living room, eyes narrowed, cracking his knuckles. "The endorsements aren't coming in the way they were supposed to," he said.

"They will!" Cornette cried. "Look at all the endorsements we've got already. The Hamster Breeders Association of Oregon. The Sons of Lumber. The Federation for Family Growth."

"It's not enough. Those stinking faggots are getting all the important endorsements."

"What about Senator Peckerwood? You said he's on our side. If he'd just come out and say so publicly—"

"He wants more money for his re-election campaign."

"You mean he won't give us a public endorsement unless we pay him more? I thought he was a public servant."

Ron looked at her, exasperated. "Peckerwood's a politician. He serves the people who pay his bills."

"Well, what about the polls? They show that half the people in Oregon are behind us."

"It doesn't cost anything to give a stupid opinion," Ron spat. He swept his hand up and over his carefully arranged hair. "Anyway, the poll was taken before that goddamned cross burning. We've got to do more damage control. Run more prime-time ads. And we've got to get Bob Sayles' new book out double-quick."

He meant *Pink Nazis,* a history exposé that clearly showed how homosexuals were responsible for the rise of Nazism in Germany. For some reason, despite years of painstaking research and writing, Bob Sayles still couldn't find a publisher for it. He told Ron that if the ACA would pay for printing, he'd donate all the proceeds to the ACA. When he heard that, Ron was suddenly convinced that *Pink Nazis* was going to be a national bestseller.

"That cousin of yours needs to fork over some more cash."

"Oh, hon, I don't know if he will."

"He will," Ron said, "if he knows what's good for him. Get him on the horn."

"Now? I don't know if he's—"

"I said call him!"

He gave Cornette the harrowing look that made her insides quiver with fear. With the fear came resentment. With the resentment came guilt. With the guilt came the Lord, bristling with anger at her secret, stubborn, unwifely rebelliousness.

It was true: recently there were moments when the faith that had sustained her seemed to vanish, sucked up in an arid whirlwind of doubt and confusion. At such moments she felt like a dry leaf torn from the Tree of Life.

She watched as Ron stomped back into his cluttered den. Through the open door she saw him take a rifle from his gun rack, pull aside the draperies, and stare out into the sun-glazed back yard as he meditatively polished the barrel. He did this often. At first she'd thought it was his way of clearing his mind, giving himself a respite from the heavy load of responsibilities that weighed him down. Then, one day, from an upstairs window she saw what he was really looking at. It was the girl next door. The little devil-worshipper was sunbathing in a bikini that was little more than two strings. Since then Cornette grew suspicious every time her husband stood by the window.

"What are you doing, hon?" she called nervously. As if she didn't know.

"Waiting for you to call your cousin."

She wanted to go in and confront him but wifely intuition told her not to rile him up when he had a rifle in his hands. The longer she delayed, the longer he'd keep on looking. Well, Ron was an attractive man with a man's normal desires, she couldn't blame him for that. It was obviously the girl, so deliberately provocative, who was to blame. The evil little slut had been a part of that godless contingent on the fourth of July. She'd marched, her face glowing with vicious glee, with all her neighbors, who'd turned out to be flag-mocking homosexuals. She was probably a homosexual herself. *So why was Ron always looking at her?* Cornette wrung her hands as the fires of jealousy raged in her heart. She had to get Ron back, had to reclaim him from the devious snares of that she-devil.

A nightmare! They were surrounded on all sides by the very deviants whose satanic power it was their mission to disarm and destroy. It was the Alamo all over again, only instead of Mexicans they were battling homosexuals.

And what was the point? Cornette sometimes caught herself wondering. It was her crusade only because it was Ron's crusade. If it weren't for Ron, she'd be doing what she'd always done: healing souls by casting out fear. Leading the halt, the sick, and the lame into Jesus' corral. She hadn't known a thing about the homosexual menace until Ron entered her life. Now she wished she'd never heard that word—homosexual—or any of the other sexually disgusting words that had taken over her entire life.

They were trapped in this house, too, because if they moved it would be a sign of defeat. That was exactly what the sodomites wanted them to do. Her faith had been sorely tested in the past, but never like this. She felt her soul was being eaten alive by a plague of queer locusts. She generously included the homosexuals in her prayers, begging God to make the miserable creatures of darkness see the light before it was too late. But their hearts were obviously as hard as stone. They'd rather perish in the flames, like those Waco Branch Davidians, than give in.

Of course Ron was right: they had to be stopped before they brought down the entire world. It was a commandment from God. But Cornette, even in her wildest dreams, hadn't imagined their family crusade would meet with the kind of resistance that it had. Nor had Ron. He'd said it was going to be a sure-fire win, an issue that would easily garner such massive popular support that it would elevate the two of them into the highest echelons of political power. The way he talked, they were headed for the White House.

And things had been going pretty well until the cross burning. With one strike of a match, the entire campaign had taken on a hellish new glow. Since then, public opinion—and, more importantly, contributions—had taken a nose-dive. She stood by Ron when he said that the homosexuals had devised the cross burning as a publicity stunt to gain sympathy for their cause. But secretly Cornette didn't believe that for a minute. She was convinced, despite her better judgement, that Lester was behind the whole thing. Lester's disappearance, just when the police were stepping up their investigation, wasn't exactly coincidental. And though she never said so, she was glad that he was gone.

There were times when she simply wanted to pack up and move back to Dallas. Take Dove and run. Maybe down there, away from this moral cesspool, among normal folks who revered her powers as a healer, she could regain some of the spiritual equilibrium she'd lost by entering politics.

But what about Ron? He wasn't one to admit defeat. That's what had attracted her to him in the first place: his powerful sense of purpose. His manly determination to do the right thing. They'd seemed so compatible in the beginning. He'd talked so sweetly. She'd been so eager to get married, to have a strong man at her side, that she believed everything he said. The joy they'd share. The prominence they'd enjoy. The good life that would be theirs. Ron hadn't said anything about the insults, bullying, and financial strain that went along with it.

In the lovemaking department Ron was disappointing, but she tried to inspire him by faking dramatic orgasms to coincide with his own. Marriage, after all, was more than just sex. It was a shared partnership of spirit. Still, she desperately wanted to give Ron the one precious gift that would cement their relationship and bring out the tenderness she knew he had. She was supposedly too old to have a child, but miracles were always possible. She'd been over forty when she had Dove. And hadn't Sarah given birth to Isaac when she was ninety? And those were the days before fertility clinics.

Cornette was leaning on the vacuum cleaner, lost in thought, when Ron quietly slipped back in and laid a hand on her shoulder. She froze, her body instinctively trying to decipher his intent. To her relief, his hand was gentle. She turned and gazed up into his eyes, hoping to erase all visions of their bikini-clad neighbor from his own. She put her arms around him and squeezed. "Oh you big grumpy papa bear, you! Did you come back to give mama bear a big kiss?"

But it didn't work. Ron was tuned in to a different channel. "I've got an idea," he said, rubbing his hands together. "Did you call him yet?"

"No, not yet, hon. But I will. Don't you worry, I'll get some more money from him."

"Look, let's face facts. Your cousin's got to be a homo. You said he's never been married. You said he's got a statue of a naked boy on his bookshelf."

"He said it was art, hon."

"That's what they all say. Face facts, Cornette."

Facing the facts of Terry's sexuality always made her uneasy. Ron didn't know the ploy she'd used to wring that contribution from Terry. Ron didn't know what Terry had done to her as a child. Terry certainly hadn't been a homosexual back then! And in the society column his name was always linked with someone named Leonora Halsey. Then there was the other thing: the stigma attached to her if Terry, her cousin, did prove to be a a homosexual. She'd feel even more contaminated. "Hon, I know you think that Terry's a fairy, but I know him better than you do. He's got a girlfriend."

"Come on. He's just been hiding because he's got enough sense to be ashamed. Alot of them are like that. They hate their lives, but they're trapped by all the gay libbers who tell them they can't change themselves."

She couldn't help but admire Ron's superior knowledge. He knew every ugly trick in the homosexuals' handbook.

"So here's what I've been thinking. What we need now—besides money—is some homosexual who's willing to take a stand and say, 'I've been brainwashed. The gay lifestyle is sick and degenerate, and I'm here to tell you how terrible it really is.'"

Cornette batted her eyelashes, trying to understand. "You mean get Terry to say that?"

"That's all we need—just one homo on our side. Just one homo willing to tell the truth. Think of it, Cornette. Just one ACA endorsement from a homo would demolish all their arguments, all their lies, and the press coverage would be fantastic. People would see that we're telling the truth because a homo would be backing us up." He let out a trimphant cackle and smiled at his wife.

"But what if he won't, hon?"

"You'll have to persuade him. You can do that, can't you?"

"I guess I can try."

His eyes hardened. "You *guess* you can *try*? This is war. In war the means justify the ends. Understand?"

Yes, she understood. She didn't want to, but she did.

▼ ▼ ▼

Terry had always liked to think that the lovely stucco wall surrounding his pool shielded him from his neighbor's covetous glances. Now, sitting under an umbrella beside the sparkling, chlorinated water, he saw his walled patio in a different light. A pen, that's what it was. It didn't keep others out, it kept him in.

He sighed and sipped an icy strawberry daiquiri as the hot August sun beat down around him. Merciless sun. Withering, dessicating sun. His dermatologist told him if he didn't stop bathing in its harmful rays he'd develop even more of the terrifying little proto-cancers that were popping up all over his body.

But what was a man without a tan? A tan was as essential to his attractiveness as money. Or hair.

Or youth.

Now that Billy was gone he'd have to find someone else. And frankly, he was tired. Tired of young men he couldn't trust. Tired of always giving, giving, giving, and never getting anything in return. What good was generosity when it was repaid with deceit and destruction?

On the night of the cross burning, while Terry and Leonora were attending that boring West Hills party, Billy had stolen everything he could, trashed the house and disappeared. As the extent of his loss became clear—his mother's antique silver was gone as well as his own gem-encrusted jewelry, rare coins, credit cards, and over a thousand bucks in well-hidden (he'd thought) cash—Terry's panicked hysteria turned to anger. He was not only angry with Billy, he was furious with himself. Hadn't he known, somewhere in the depths of his desperate infatuation, that he was courting disaster? Was it coincidence that just a few days earlier, when he'd refused to let Billy use the Mercedes, the tires of the car had been mysteriously slashed?

His neighbors had seen Billy for what he really was. They'd seen it instantly. But Terry's proud, headstrong refusal to hear the ugly truth under their mockery only made him idolize Billy even more. The insinuation that he'd purchased Billy's affections was simple jealousy. But even if it were true, what was wrong with appreciating Billy like some expensive object in the home?

Now this. The expensive object had made off with other expensive objects and gone on a needless rampage of destruction. It was like a horrifying rape, and it exposed Terry to the withering we-told-you-so scorn of the neighbors he'd been snubbing on Billy's behalf.

Only they didn't care. They didn't even know Billy was gone. Terry hadn't told a soul, and not one person had called to ask how he was. All right, the burning cross on John-Don and Peter's lawn was awful, but no damage had been done to their property. Terry was the one who'd suffered the real losses. But they couldn't understand that. They were all so caught up in that anti-ACA campaign that they had no time for him at all.

Terry hadn't told Leonora about the calamity, nor had he notified the police. There'd be questions he didn't want to answer. It could lead to a news story. And though he loved to see his prominent name in print, always paired with Leonora Halsey's, it belonged only in the society column. A vulgar story like this—a Terwilliger robbed by his houseboy—simply wouldn't do. He'd have to swallow his loss in silence and start all over again from the beginning.

At times like these, God, how he missed Delmont. A gay friend, one he shared a history with, a friend with taste, refinement, and a nonjudgmental understanding of the intermingled workings of heart and pocketbook.

He kept himself in a state of stupified daiquiried denial rather than admit to himself how unbearably lonely he was.

When the phone beside his chaise lounge rang he snatched it up. Maybe one of his neighbors. Maybe an invitation to a party.

It was Cornette, with an urgent twang in her voice. "Terry, I think you'd better come over here."

"Now? I'm busy."

"Make yourself unbusy then. There's something I've got to discuss with you. Now."

Something in the tone of her voice frightened him. Terry, still a hostage to her earlier threat to expose him, wasn't able to say no.

▼ ▼ ▼

It was the first time he'd set foot in Delmont's house since his cousin and her husband had moved in. The exterior, of course, was beyond redemption. That was her husband's doing. What Terry hadn't been prepared for was the interior.

The moment he entered, he could literally feel the foul atmosphere that had taken possession of the place. It was more than just Cornette's chronically bad taste and the revolting smells of her cooking. It was something else, that indefinable essence or personality that greets a visitor the moment he walks into a place not his own.

Confronted by it, and by the decorating horrors Cornette had inflicted on Delmont's elegant manse, Terry felt his knees go weak.

The heavy draperies—an ersatz, rubber-backed brocade—were drawn tight. Enormous lamps shaped like Spanish galleons and Conquistador helmets spread a slippery sheen of light over plastic slipcovers protecting massive lumps of furniture. Orange nylon carpeting covered the beautiful oak parquet floors. Delmont's built-in vitrines housed a grotesque collection of dolls, some in sequined dresses, others in Biblical garb. A tapestry rug with the scene of the Last Supper was suspended over the television set. Framed reproductions of Jesus at his dishiest hung in weirdly placed groupings. The house was as cold and airless as a walk-in freezer.

"Well, what do you think?" Cornette asked with a grand wave of the arm. "Haven't we done wonders with this old place?"

"Jesus," Terry muttered, trying to keep his teeth from chattering.

Cornette laughed. "Well, Terry, you're not the only Terwilliger who knows how to decorate. And you know, I was wondering—since you seem to know everybody, maybe you could put in a word with whoever's in charge of the Living section of the paper. They might be real interested in doing a story on the Labonnes at home."

A thin, sullen-looking girl with pale skin, long blonde hair and intense blue eyes entered the room.

"Dove, this is your uncle Terry that you've heard me talk so much about."

"Hi," Terry said. The girl said nothing.

"Dove was just saying how strange it was that her uncle lives right next door and he never comes over to visit," Cornette said. "I told her it wasn't that you didn't *care* about her, it was just that you were *different* from other people. When you don't have children of your own, you look for other ways to fill your time." She straightened the girl's slouching shoulders and lifted her chin. "Isn't she a doll?"

Terry, who found children excruciatingly boring and never knew what to say to them, nodded and asked her what grade she was in.

"Dove's going to be in the tenth grade this fall," Cornette said. "She's going to be entering high school. I can't hardly believe it."

"Don't you have a boy, too?" Terry asked.

"Oh, you mean Ron's son, Lester. He's not home right now." She fussed over the girl's clothing. "Dove, honey, your uncle and I haven't had a chance to talk in such a long time. Why don't you take Dumbo for a walk?"

It was obvious that the girl didn't want to go. She stared at Terry with a mixture of curiosity and disdain.

"But I want you back here when Ron comes home from his meeting. We're going to have a nice family dinner before we go off and do our show. Tuna fish casserole with potato chips on the top, just the way you like."

"Okay." The girl backed out of the room and disappeared.

The moment she'd gone Cornette said, "Sit down, Terry. I want to have a serious talk with you."

It was going to be more blackmail. He tried to work up his courage to refuse her the money she'd no doubt ask for. The plastic slipcover crackled as he sat down.

"You're a miserable homosexual, aren't you, Terry," she said.

"I beg your pardon?"

"It's all right, I'm not blaming you, I'm just concerned about your soul."

"My soul is none of your business," he said.

"Of course it's my business, Terry. You're kin. If you're sad and suffering, I want to lead you to a place where there's peace and happiness."

"I'd rather drive there in my own car, thank you."

"You can't get there in your own car, Terry, no matter how hard you try. Because the Lord's behind the wheel, not you. The Lord is in the driver's seat. He's got the road map. And he wants to take you on a spin down the highway of eternal life."

"I don't know what you're talking about," Terry said.

"I think you do. You're just afraid. You're trapped and you can't see the way out. But I'm telling you there is a way out."

"Yes," he said, "there is. By the front door." He got up to leave but she darted over so quickly that he fell back in the chair.

"We *know* you're a homosexual, Terry. And we know how ashamed you are of that. But that doesn't mean you can't be one of us. We're on your side, Cousin Terry."

"Yes," he snapped, "my bad side."

"That's just what I mean. Just because you're a homosexual doesn't mean we think you're bad. It's only the practicing homosexuals that we're trying to stop. And we know you're going to help us."

"What do you mean?" Terry tried to squash down the apprehension that was suddenly racing through his nerves. His cousin's eyes were as fixed and unreal as one of the gaudy dolls staring from the vitrine behind her.

"We know you're not part of this terrible group around here, Terry. We know you don't live the kind of filthy life they do. You're more of the eunuch type. But they're *deliberate* homosexuals. And you know they aren't your friends, Terry, they're your enemies."

"They're not my enemies," he croaked. "But even if they were, I'd rather have enemies like them than friends like you."

She sighed and shook her head, as if dealing with a recalcitrant child. "You're going to help us, Terry. We want you in our ministry."

"I've given you two thousand dollars. What more do you want?"

She calmly explained that not only did she want more money, she wanted him to appear on their cable-television show as a repentent homosexual. One who'd seen the error of his ways and had been lead, by her, into the evangelical bliss of normalcy. A sexless guilt-ridden pervert going public with the sordid details of his tormented life, that's what she wanted him to be.

The effrontery of it took his breath away. Faced with her pious stupidity—the way she idealized her own trashy life and pitied his own—Terry became livid. "You are absolutely crazy, Cornette. Even if I were gay, what makes you think I'd be so stupid or pathetic to go public on your behalf?"

"Why? Because you believe in what we stand for," she said.

"I don't believe in anything you stand for. This whole rotten organization of yours makes me sick. Burning crosses—"

"We did *not* burn that cross! The homosexuals burned that cross!"

"—persecuting people who just want to mind their own business—you're the sick ones, Cornette."

"If you feel that way, why did you donate money?"

"You know damn well why I donated money."

"Because you wanted to help us. You wanted to free yourself from the sins of perversity."

"You don't actually believe that?"

"Of course I do. And so is everyone in Portland going to believe that, Terry, when your name appears in the paper as a contributor to the ACA. All your homosexual neighbors are going to see that you're not on their side, you're on our side. So this is just the next step in your rehabilitation."

He gave a violent shudder as the last vestige of warmth left his body. "What do you mean, when my name appears in the paper?"

"Gracious, Terry, didn't you know that we're required by law to submit a list of all contributors to the Secretary of State's office?"

"But that's private information," he cried.

Cornette laughed. "Nothing's private in politics, Terry. It's public information that anyone can see. And the papers already have their hands on it. So you see—"

"But I told you to list me as Anonymous."

"That's against the law. We had to give them your name and the amount of your first contribution. The ACA does everything strictly by the letter of the law, Terry. We want people to know we've got nothing to hide."

His dental implants were chattering. "I don't believe this. People are actually going to see that I've contributed to the ACA?"

"You act like you're ashamed of your generosity. Terry, people are going to look up to you. They're going to say, 'Why, look, Terry Terwilliger gave two thousand dollars to the ACA—if he did that, and he's a homosexual, why we'd better send the ACA a check ourselves.'"

"I never said I was a homosexual, goddamnit!"

"But you're going to. Just think of the relief, Terry. You'll be able to stop hiding. You won't have to pretend that you're happy. You can break free of the lies these evil gay libbers all around us want you to believe. You're going to inspire homosexuals all around the country to renounce their sickness and let Jesus enter their hearts."

Cornette's eyes widened in astonished disapproval as Terry slammed his fists down on the slipcovered arms of the chair and glared at her. "Shut up with that Jesus crap!" he shouted.

"Jesus is not crap, Terry, except to practicing homosexuals."

"You don't know the first thing about Jesus or homosexuals. You twist everything around to make it fit into your own ignorance. You're a stupid whore, Cornette. A stupid blackmailing piece of social-climbing white trash."

"Don't say anything you're going to be sorry for, Terry," she warned.

"The only thing I'm sorry for is that I let you blackmail me for two grand. I'd sooner eat my own shit than do anything to help you."

"Well, as a homosexual you've been doing that your entire life, Terry, so I suppose you must like the taste by now."

"Just remember, Cornette, I have friends in very high places."

"Oh, do you?" she scoffed. "Well so do I, Terry. I've got a friend in the highest place of all."

"You mean the lowest place, don't you?" He pushed her out of the way and started for the door.

"If you don't help us, I'm gonna ruin you, Terry Terwilliger," she cried, "the same way you ruined me. I'm gonna make you pay for your sins!"

Terry turned to look at her. "Well, that's what a blackmailer does, isn't it? All in the name of Jesus, of course."

"You're going to regret this, Terry."

He couldn't resist one final jab before he left. "By the way, didn't you know that this house used to belong to a homosexual?"

"What?" she gasped.

"Yes, but it wasn't until you moved in, Cornette, that we had any problems with perverts around here."

She stuck her head out the front door and screamed, "You're sick, Terry. You're all sick and you're all going to burn in hell!"

He raced home, slammed the door, and locked it. Moaned. Looked around his beautiful house, seeking comfort, but could only see what was no longer there. What Billy had taken, or destroyed. For a moment he thought of praying—but it wasn't prayer he needed, it was a drink, a friend, a life.

He was sick, all right, but not in the way Cornette thought. Sick at heart, sick of treachery, sick of revenge masquerading as religion, sick of this whole pointless political campaign that had turned his private life into a public issue.

Now all he could do was wait for the ax to fall. A looming sense of catastrophe dogged his every step. Oddly enough, it had less to do with the possibility of being exposed by Cornette than it did with the fact that his gay neighbors were going to see that he'd contributed to the ACA. How could he explain it? It made him a traitor. He would become a friendless pariah in Queer Corners. But wasn't he that already?

All he had left was Leonora. Maybe it was time to marry. Convenient, comfortable companionship in his old age. She'd agree. She'd been waiting for twenty years for him to propose. After twenty kissless years, she wouldn't expect a physical relationship, and their respective fortunes could be kept separate.

But when it came right down to it, he knew that marrying Leonora and spending the rest of his days amongst the stuffy bores in their social set would be a living death. Permanent exile from his heart's true calling.

He thought of flying down to Palm Springs. But he'd have to come back sooner or later. Sell the house? Who'd want it with the Labonne monstrosity next door?

The house felt so bare now that Billy was gone. Without him, Terry was nothing more than an echo trapped in a hollow shell. The only thing worse than being mocked by his own Mock Tudor was being a ghost in the neighborhood where he'd lived so comfortably for so many years.

After downing two strawberry daiquiris he wobbled out to his patio and collapsed on his chaise lounge. Stared dumbly at nothing. Sitting by the sparkling waters of his pool, behind the lovely stucco wall, under the umbrella that sheltered him from the harmful rays of the sun, Terry felt like a caged animal. An old beast captured and robbed of its natural instincts so long ago that it could no longer smell the freedom that lay just outside its luxurious pen.

CHAPTER 27

JAY WAS IN A FIGHTING MOOD. EVERY MORNING HE WAS AT THE GYM by seven, pressing weights, crunching his stomach, and climbing the existential Stairmaster to nowhere. Three times a week he attended aerobic boxing classes led by Camille Parr, former champion of the Portland Boxing Association's Women's Division.

"Jab! Jab! Protect your face! Feint!" Camille shouted to the sweating students as they danced around the suspended punching bags to ear-pounding techno-rave. "Upper cut with the right! Go for the belly with the left! Come on! Slam that sucker in the gut! Go for it!"

Jay slammed, punched, cut, feinted. The black punching bag was Hitler, Himmler, Goebbels and Ron Labonne, all rolled into one. If any of those ACA meatheads ever tried to mess with Jay Zucker again he'd show them what a faggot's fist could do.

He had to be prepared. Gone was the safe, cozy conviviality of Queer Corners. The Labonnes were dangerous. The ACA was dangerous. Only no one but gays and lesbians seemed to realize or understand this. Every queer in Portland was on the alert. There'd been more gay bashings. It seemed to Jay that he was living in a new version of the Old West. Only this time the vigilantes and evildoers were fundamentalist Christians.

After just one "sympathetic" story—the cross-burning on John-Don and Peter's front lawn—the local paper had reverted back to its usual homophobia. When a group of ACAers marched in Springfield, their comments appeared on the front page with a color photograph. The quote of one Christian woman—"Homosexuals are lower than animals"—was set off in large type. But when gays rallied, the event didn't warrant so much as a blurb on the back page.

The one bright spot in Jay's life was Too-Too. His gay bistro was a smash, and had been ever since opening night. In an ironic twist of fate, the ugly fracas with the ACA van had turned out to be a source of fabulous free gay publicity. The confrontation made it crystal clear to anybody who didn't yet know that the ACA was determined to foment as much anti-gay hysteria as possible. Their ill-timed attempt to evangelize had blown up in their faces. More importantly, it helped to mend at least some of the fractures in the gay community. Suddenly everyone knew that they were all in this nightmare together. The fundraiser had gone on as planned, but with an added sense of urgency. Then the cross burning. When a shaken Jay returned to report to the crowd what had happened, money poured in. And overnight Too-Too became a rallying point for the No on Three campaign.

The crowds were phenomenal. By noon every table was filled and the noise level pleasantly deafening. It was even busier at night. In their spare moments Jay and

Cassandra chatted with their customers and passed out information on the No on Three campaign.

Jay, riding this crest, had to keep up his energy. The old temptations of wine and Valium gave way to an ion-charged Met-RX fruit smoothie cocktail at five. Cassandra, with her uncanny talent for spotting trends, persuaded him to add a line of "all-unnatural" protein-saturated body-builder drinks to the beverage menu. Another hit.

Knowing he was short of money, Jay persuaded Wellfleet to do an Old Standards gig at the piano from eight to ten. Wellfleet, embarrassed and uneasy until he discovered that on a good night he could rake in fifty tax-free bucks in tips, was turning into a regular—if somewhat eccentric—performer. A jazz combo took over at ten-thirty. On weekends, to standing-room-only crowds, performers from The Mousehole Theatre staged No on Three floor shows with musical numbers and comic sketches that mercilessly skewered The God Couple, Ron and Cornette Labonne.

The only thing Jay hadn't anticipated in the heady glow of Too-Too's success was the growing number of straight customers. They were good for business, of course, but the last thing he wanted was to alienate his gay clientele, some of whom felt they were on display.

These days, as Jay well knew, the mere presence of straight people in a gay environment roused a certain gaytriotic resentment. Were these hetero-diners here out of a sense of solidarity or merely to stare and titter? Heterophobia was on the rise.

Resentment was bad for business. Jay feared that if his gay customers left, the straights would stop coming, too. Yet he couldn't turn people away at the door just because he suspected they were straight. Nor would he put up a sign, as some angry separatists had suggested, saying "Breeders Not Welcome." That was merely childish.

Now, more than ever, Jay felt it was important for gays and straights to find common ground. It was the only way to defeat the ACA. But did the straight liberals who showed up at Too-Too even have a clue as to just how important this battle with the ACA was? Did they stop to consider the fears it touched off among gays and lesbians?

As that beautiful, hot, hate-filled August wore on, Oregon was often in the national news. For years the state had basked in a rosy glow of nationwide admiration. It was viewed as a bastion of advanced, clear-thinking, fair-minded social policy. A national magazine chose Portland as the "Most Livable City in America." For people outside the state, Oregon was a halcyonic American fantasy. It was thought to be safe, unspoiled, and humanely concerned about the "quality of life."

But now that admiration was turning to ridicule. What kind of state was so backwards in its thinking that it would listen to the rantings of a Ron Labonne? What kind of state was so paranoid about homosexuals that it would openly attempt to legislate discrimination against them? Oregon's calm, liberal facade was cracked wide open to reveal a state in the grip of extremist right-wing fundamentalists.

It wasn't until the economic impact of Ballot Measure Three on the state of Oregon became an issue, Jay noticed, that straight Oregon voters began to take it seriously. The economic impact on *gays*, who could lose their jobs if the measure passed, didn't seem to matter much. But the possibility that the state would lose millions in revenue from cancelled conventions and tourism hit a sore capitalistic nerve. Some human rights became truly important only when they touched the heterosexual pocketbook.

Ron Labonne, when asked about loss of state income from boycotts, said just the opposite would happen. "It's another homosexual smokescreen," he insisted. "The state will lose nothing. In fact, more money than ever will come in because groups dedicated to Christian morals will want to have their conventions here, in a state that upholds the sanctity of the family."

Jay's New York friends, addicted to catastrophe, were appropriately horrified by the stories that appeared in national (if not local) papers and magazines. Even Brenda, his ex-wife, called to find out if he was all right. "I've been reading so many horrible things about Oregon," she said. "Don't you live on the same street where they burned that cross?"

"Yeah, I do." He was ashamed to admit it, since for years his reports on life in Portland had been geared to eliciting jealousy, not sympathy.

"It's sounds like it's really ugly out there right now," Brenda said.

"It is." He couldn't bring himself to tell her about the gala opening of Too-Too, nearly ruined by ACA creeps, or the swastikas that had appeared on the No on Three lawn signs, or the gay bashings.

"Is it just gays they're picking on," Brenda asked, "or is it Jews, too?"

"Not yet," Jay said. "Not unless they're Jew queers."

"Well, that's you, isn't it? You'll be careful, won't you, Jay?"

"Yeah," he said, "I'll be careful."

But he didn't want to be careful. That part of his existence was over.

For the first time in his well-dressed life Jay bought a button that read "Gay, Proud, and Here to Stay." He wore it everywhere.

It was both amusing and annoying to see the reactions of straight women who'd always found him so attractive. Once they noticed his button, their flirtatious looks often turned to pity or resentment. "Such a *waste*," he overheard one woman say to her friend.

Straight men seeing his button nervously averted their eyes, denying him membership in their club. Some tried, with a contemptuous glance, to impress upon him their masculine disapproval. He noticed that they were always bolder in a crowd. Jay did his best to ignore their sniggers and the "Faggot" that inevitably followed.

But he was also surprised and moved by the number of positive responses his button elicited. People of all ages and from all walks of life—people he'd never suspect of caring one way or another—acknowledged his visible statement with a word or a nod or a smile. With hate getting all the attention, it was good to be reminded that there was an alternative universe of quiet, decent, ordinary American citizens who still believed in equality. But would they vote? That was the question.

It was a relief for Jay to finally be out of the closet, openly gay and still in full possession of his masculinity. But it was definitely a consciousness-raising experience. Now that he was out, he could more clearly see why so many gays weren't. As long as they remained formless ectoplasm they could pretend—like that traitor, Terry Terwilliger—that the straight world accepted them. The moment they materialized into visible human beings they became fair game, *fairy* game, open targets for persecution.

The situation was not so dissimilar to that of Jews who hated their Jewishness because the goyim hated Jews. It was part of that same terrible human need to fit in, to erase and declassify oneself in order to escape detection. Jews had their own special knowledge of the closet.

Jay had never been religious, but now his heritage as a Jew began to take on a new meaning and call to something deeply buried in his spirit.

When he overheard frightened gays talking about being sent to "the camps," he couldn't dismiss their fears, the way so many did, as paranoid fantasies. Members of his own family had perished in camps that people refused to acknowledge or see. And, of course, more than one American senator had already suggested that everyone with AIDS—meaning gays—should be sent to concentration camps.

As a gay Jew, Jay had two Holocaust histories to remember and learn from: the six million Jews who'd been exterminated because they were Jews, and the thousands of gays who'd been killed because they were gay. His Jewish forebears had been forced to wear the Star of David, his gay forebears the pink triangle. All the more reason to wear his "Gay, Proud, and Here to Stay" button.

▼ ▼ ▼

Terry's treachery was discovered in late August when *Willamette Wink*, the city's alternative paper, published a list of ACA contributors. There, for all to see, was the name Terrence Terwilliger III.

He made a futile attempt to exonerate himself. First he invited his neighbors in Queer Corners to a Sunday champagne brunch. No one accepted. Then he phoned the No on Three fundraising headquarters at Too-Too and said he wanted to "get involved." John-Don didn't return his call. Finally Terry showed up drunk at Too-Too and tried to talk to Jay. But Jay ignored him except to say there weren't any tables. It was a weekend, The Mousehole Theatre was performing *The God Couple*, and the place was packed. As he walked away, Jay said, "Traitor."

In desperation, Terry cornered Cassandra near the bar. "You can come back to the carriage house if you want," he shouted over the laughter.

She'd heard that Billy had left but Cassandra wasn't inclined to waste any sympathy on Terry the Turd. "Fuck off, you dirty collaborator. I wouldn't come back if you paid me."

Terry's face, lifted so often that it could no longer sustain a recognizable human expression, sank into a puddle of blank-eyed despair. "I should have listened to you," he said. "I'm sorry."

Terry Terwilliger saying he was sorry? She wanted to gloat, but couldn't. His pain was too obvious. "How could you do it, Terry? How could you betray us like that?"

He shook his head and let out a strange, whinnying laugh. "I thought it was just money. But then—" His voice quavered. He pursed his lips and blinked away tears. "The bitch wanted me to repent. Repent! Wanted me to go on her ridiculous television show and say I was . . . say I was gay . . . and ashamed of it."

"Well, aren't you?"

He bowed his head and didn't answer.

"You gave money to people who think you're a criminal. Racist homophobes who burned a cross on your neighbors' lawn."

"But I stood up to her," Terry insisted. "When she said they needed a gay person to help them, I refused."

"Sure, Terry."

"I did!" he whined.

She gave the bartender a drinks order and turned away from Terry, impatient and disgusted with his maudlin excuses. But he wouldn't leave. He wanted to chastise and exonerate himself at the same time. And also, it became clear, desperately wanted to get even with *them*. Cassandra pretended not to listen, but did. And pieced together a private strategy of her own.

▼ ▼ ▼

In September, a new log was thrown into the ACA's fire. It was a book called *Pink Nazis* and it made the outrageous claim that gays were responsible for Nazism in Germany. The media picked up on it at once. Most people laughed. Who would believe that? "The people who want to believe it," Jay said.

The very idea that such a distorted piece of fantasy could be used as a weapon by the ACA made him go ballistic. It was no different from the insane revisionist histories that claimed the Holocaust never happened. And here it was, given a bogus legitimacy in neo-Naziland by the sensation-starved media. Were these Oregonians crazy or what?

Pink Nazis was the last straw. Jay felt that he had to do something. Had to wake up all the people still slumbering in blissful ignorance. Had to fight, had to sound the alarm. It wasn't enough that Too-Too was a meeting place and rallying point for the No on Three campaign. It wasn't enough to wear a button identifying himself as a gay man, or to hang a Rainbow Diversity flag in front of his house. More was required of him— *but what?*

It was John-Don who suggested that Jay meet with Rabbi Mutterperl. "He's the most prominent liberal reformed Jewish rabbi in the state," John-Don said, "and we need his support. Maybe if you talked to him, he'd help us."

The idea of meeting with a rabbi, however reformed, made Jay *spilkes*. He dithered as long as his conscience would allow. In the midst of his agitation he realized that his fear of confronting religious authority stemmed from guilt. The guilt came from the fact that he was a gay Jew. He knew full well that when it came to homosexuality Jews could be as homophobic as Christians.

Finally he called and made an early-morning appointment to see Rabbi Mutterperl at his office in nearby Lake Oswego. At the last minute, giving in to cowardice, he removed the "Gay, Proud, and Here to Stay" button from his lapel.

Rabbi Mutterperl was a stocky, garrulous man with thick salt-and-pepper hair, a graying goatee, dark direct eyes, and a firm, friendly handshake. "So, Mr. Zucker," he said, motioning Jay to sit down, "were your parents fromer Yidden?"

"Were they what?"

"Were they observant? Did they keep the Sabbath holy?"

Jay shook his head. "Not really. They weren't very religious."

"German refugees?" asked Rabbi Mutterperl.

Jay nodded. "They escaped with my grandfather—my father's father—from Berlin."

"Did your family stop being Jewish after the Holocaust?"

"Sort of," Jay said.

"That happened to a lot of Jews," said Rabbi Mutterperl. "Very understandable, really. People asked, how could God allow this to happen? Personally, I think a better question would be, how could human beings allow it to happen?"

"We did celebrate Hannukah."

The most insignificant Jewish holiday. What about Yom Kippur?"

"No." His father refused to observe Yom Kippur because, as he said, "Jews got nothing to atone for."

"Were you ever bar mitzvahed?"

"No."

"Are you married?"

"I was." Until I realized I was gay, he was about to add, but Rabbi Mutterperl was already on to his next question.

"Was your wife a Jew?"

Yes, Brenda was a Jew. No, they didn't have any children. Where had Jay grown up? New York? How did he feel being a Jew in Portland?

"Well," Jay said, "the bagels aren't as good."

"It's the sesame kaiser rolls I miss," sighed Rabbi Mutterperl. They shared a New York laugh. Then, still smiling, the rabbi fixed his dark eyes more intently on Jay. "So. Mr. Jay Zucker. What can I do for you?"

The time had come. Jay crossed his legs and nervously cleared his throat.

"I'm here as a Jew who happens to be gay," he began. Then stopped, waiting for the expected sign of disapproval to flicker across the rabbi's face.

"A Jew is a Jew," shrugged Rabbi Mutterperl. "Are you troubled by your homosexuality?"

"No, it's not that."

"So tell me. I'm here to listen, not to judge."

An enormous sense of relief flooded through Jay as he began to talk, man to man, with Rabbi Mutterperl. Fifteen minutes later he had Rabbi Mutterperl's pledge to speak at the big No on Three rally planned for late October.

Driving back to Portland, Jay reveled in a state of hopeful exaltation. He felt physically lighter, as if a heavy burden had been lifted from his shoulders. It was a golden September morning. People looked happy and friendly. He honked and waved every time he saw a "No on Three!" bumper sticker. He had the top down and the Golden Oldies station was playing all his favorite songs. He smiled and sang along to "The Boy from New York City."

Would he be the man he was today if he'd stayed in liberal, sophisticated, gay-friendly Manhattan? No. Awful as it was, the homophobia in Oregon was the crucible in which he'd been forced to discover his personal strength as a gay man and a Jew.

In his ebullient mood it took him a moment to realize, as he pulled into his parking space behind Too-Too, that something was wrong. A squad car was parked out front. The door to the back office was hanging open at an angle, wrenched from its hinges.

Cassandra ran out to him, her face blotchy with tears and red with numbed rage. "Jay! Oh God, Jay!" She leaned down and squeezed him in a sobbing embrace.

He tried to numb the spurting panic, prepare himself for the worst. "What happened?"

"They broke in. Sometime last night." Cassandra took his hand in both of hers and slowly lead him around to the side of the building. Swastikas. He saw JEW FAGS MUST DIE. He saw DO GOD A FAVOR—KILL A KIKE QUEER.

His vision clouded over. He clenched his fists. He tried to find a deep solid breath in his rage-impacted lungs. "What did they do inside?"

What hadn't they done? It was as if a hurricane had raged through the restaurant. Cassandra's murals had been obscenely defaced. Chairs and tables were overturned, pots and pans hurled, china and glasses smashed, food thrown and smeared everywhere. JEW KIKE FAG QUEER everywhere. Too-Too's back office, where John-Don's No on Three fundraising committee met, had been completely trashed. The computer was shattered. File cabinets ransacked. Literature pulled from the shelves and pissed on.

"I want this investigated as a hate crime," he said to the police officer accompanying him around the premises.

"Do you have reason to believe this was a bias-related incident?" The officer's voice was a non-commital monotone.

"Are you blind? Look!" Jay pointed to the words painted on the walls. "You know who did this as well as I do."

"I'm afraid I don't, sir."

"The ACA!"

"I'm afraid I don't know what that is, sir."

Jay stared at him with disbelief. "The ACA!" he shouted. "The same group that tried to ruin my opening night. The same group that's beating up queers all over Oregon. The same group that burned a cross on my neighbors' lawn."

"What does ACA stand for, sir?"

Jay threw up his arms in frustration. "I don't believe this!"

Cassandra quietly gave the officer the information he needed.

"I want someone to take fingerprints. I want you to nail those bastards. I want you to go directly to Ron Labonne and accuse him of—"

"Sir, I have to follow procedure. If you'll—"

"Procedure, he says!"

"I can see that you're upset, but—"

"I'm not upset!" Jay shouted. "I'm fucking furious!"

When the officer finally left, Jay and Cassandra stood together in the destroyed restaurant. "I'm going to get him," Jay said under his breath. "I'm going to make that fucking pig squeal." He raced for the door.

"Jay! Wait! Where are you going?"

▼ ▼ ▼

She knew where he was going. And she was terrified of what might happen. Jay was in a reckless, mood. There was no telling what he might say or do. But Labonne had guns.

"Jay, wait!" She heard the spit of gravel as his roadster roared out of the parking lot. She ran for her car and set off in pursuit. She knew how fast Jay could drive in his powerful car. Her own car was like a golf cart in comparison. She got trapped behind a slow-moving bus and didn't have the horsepower to overtake it.

By the time she arrived on Skyview they were already in the midst of a heated altercation. Labonne stood on his porch, Jay below him. Their faces were alarmingly red and their mouths, in thrust-out jaws, were working furiously. Cassandra, who knew Jay's body language, could see that he was ready to pop.

She squealed to a stop and leapt out as Jay suddenly grabbed Labonne's shirt and pushed him. Labonne, screaming for his wife to come witness what was happening, threatened to charge Jay with assault.

"You fucking Nazi scumbag!" Jay screamed, raising his fists. "Come out into your pigpen and fight me—come on, fucker, just *fight* me—like a man—just you and me!"

He ignored Cassandra, standing frozen at the open gate and imploring him to come away. Labonne's steely eyes flicked over to her and then back to Jay.

He smiled as if he meant to take on Jay's challenge. He'd just taken a step forward when Cornette appeared in a quilted housecoat, her hair rolled up in fat pink curlers. With a cry of alarm she ran out and grabbed her husband's arm. He tried to shake her off but Cornette clung to him like a barnacle. "Don't hon, please don't!"

"Come on fatso—have to hide behind your wife?—come on, you fucking piece of SS chickenshit!"

"Jay, stop!" Cassandra darted in to pull him away. Jay brusquely pushed her aside. Labonne did the same with Cornette. The two women looked at one with dazed expressions. The men began circling one another.

"You have to be a man to fight like a man," Labonne said.

Jay coaxed him farther out into the yard with a steady stream of taunts. "You're a pig, Labonne, not a man, but I'll fight you anyway. Come on you pigfaced porker—oink, oink—here I am—queer, Jew—everything you hate."

"Come back inside, hon," Cornette pleaded. "Can't you see he's dangerous?"

"Dangerous?" Labonne spat. "He's just a screaming Jew fairy."

"You're the one who's going to be screaming, Labonne. Come on, you pigfaced goy. I'll show you how a fegalah can fight." His fist shot out and jabbed at Labonne's face but missed.

Labonne, his eyes narrowed and steady, let out a mocking grunt. "You call that a punch?" He ducked, rose, and rammed his meaty fist into Jay's stomach.

"Oof!" Jay doubled over and stumbled backwards.

"Jay!" Cassandra cried. She placed herself in front of him so Labonne couldn't hit him without hitting her first.

Cornette, with a babbling frenzy of Biblical quotations, entreated her husband to remember the moral values he stood for. Labonne whirled around as if he were going to strike her, then looked back at Jay and Cassandra. Laughed in contempt. "Next time I won't be so nice. Now get off my property." He let Cornette lead him into the house. The door slammed.

Cassandra took Jay home. He could barely stand. "I wanted to kill him," he kept mumbling.

Cassandra stroked his hair and thought, *Let me do it for you, darling.*

▼ ▼ ▼

Later that evening a stunned John-Don stood with Jay in the fund-raising office of Too-Too. The stench of stale, beery urine rose from the littered floor. In a final, doglike display of territorial aggression, the vandals had pissed everywhere.

Jay took a deep breath. Winced and held his stomach. "I wanted to kill him," he murmured. "I've never felt that way before."

John-Don put a hand on Jay's shoulder. He felt oddly disconnected from the chaos around him. Couldn't take it in. He remembered the stories his parents had told of their days as radical socialist agitators. The unbelievable lengths the government went to to stop them. Not unlike this.

The two men stood together in silence, surveying the wreckage. The hard drive of the computer lay smashed at their feet. The locked box of back-up copies on disk was gone. The names, addresses and phone numbers of nearly three thousand contributors and volunteers had vanished. All confidential.

"What do we call it?" John-Don said. "Gaygate? Hategate?"

"Too-Toogate sounds a little fey," Jay admitted. "How about Everyone-Knows-It's-The-ACA-But-No-One-Can-Pin-Anything-On-Them-gate?"

Because, as they both knew, there was no tangible evidence to connect Labonne and the ACA to the destruction of Too-Too and the theft of the fundraising records. Just as there was no evidence to connect Labonne and the ACA to the cross-burning on John-Don and Peter's lawn in July. Both were being investigated as hate crimes—"bias-related incidents" in sterilized police parlance—but Labonne vociferously disavowed any ACA involvement and, like a good Republican, redirected the blame back to the victims.

John-Don scratched his head. "Jay, I'm sorry. If we hadn't been using the place maybe this wouldn't have happened."

"A gay restaurant owned by a queer Jew? It would have happened. Sooner or later. Thank Somebody I had insurance. I'll get them to pay for a new computer. I'll say it was mine."

Together they hoisted up an overturned filing cabinet.

"Don't you love being gay?" John-Don said.

"Love it."

The odd thing was, they both meant it.

CHAPTER 28

SEEING HER CHILD, MAKING CONTACT WITH THE *REALITY* OF HIM, HAD detonated a psychic depth charge in Carolyn Corbett. She could almost hear the crackling snap as her corroded maternal synapses were reconnected. Carolyn had deliberately provoked the blast but was not prepared for the lacerating force of the emotions it produced. Dislodged from her hiding place. the old Carolyn who cowered in perennial darkness, fearful of discovery, was propelled, kicking and screaming, to the surface. There she was forced to stand naked, stretch marks and all, in the violent glare of her past.

The circumstances surrounding Lester's birth were horrible to remember. Carolyn still wanted to run, escape, hide, deny the truth of them. But she also felt a strange, fatalistic desire to throw her hands into the air and give herself up—not to any earthly authority but to those incomprehensible forces that seemed to be guiding her. Towards what? She didn't know. She couldn't know until she got there. She sensed that she'd pushed her karma way beyond the speed limit and was now being ticketed, warned, given one last chance to set things right. She saw with dizzying clarity that her life with Susan, in Bilitis Cottage, had no real meaning because it was based on a lie.

The lie was that she didn't know Ron Labonne. The lie was that she'd never had a child with him. The lie was that she'd never been part of a right-wing paramilitary cult called the Bruderschaft. She was the lie. Dear, sweet-natured Carolyn Corbett, whom everyone thought they knew so well, had for eighteen years lived the duplicitous life of a fugitive.

It would never end, that tormenting sense of disconnectedness, unless she acknowledged her actions and faced their consequences. Only then would she be free to move on.

Once, long ago, when she'd been talking to Ito, he'd said something she'd never forgotten. "Life is a spiritual journey, whether we recognize it or not." The old Carolyn balked at the steps she had to take, the trials she had yet to undergo, but over the summer she had finally embarked on her journey.

There were three paths she had to take to reach her goal. Each one required a daunting and dangerous trek back into the dark wilderness of her past. On the first path, the one she'd already taken, she found her son and lost him again. On the second path, the one she was on now, she would reveal herself to Susan. And on the third, the path Carolyn dreaded most, she would confront Ron Labonne. After that? Terra incognita.

▼ ▼ ▼

Life in Bilitis Cottage couldn't go on the way it was for much longer. Susan was quietly cracking under the strain. It wasn't just the situation with Carolyn that had sent her into a tailspin. Patient, self-effacing Carolyn was, in fact, the least of Susan's worries. Carolyn's transgression with the puppies now seemed almost laughable. But Susan wasn't laughing much these days. A series of vulgar human crises had sent Susan the Unbreakable crashing to the floor.

Among other things, she was on the brink of losing her entire inheritance. She didn't know how much, exactly, it amounted to, but hundreds of thousands pounds were involved.

The unexpected news that Mrs. Bark hadn't left Susan, her only child, so much as a dog biscuit in her will was the first slap in the face. The Bark money was really Cumberland money. It was Susan's mother, née Felicity Cumberland, who had the fortune. Susan's father, Reginald, was virtually penniless when Felicity married him. It was the strong-willed and financially independent Felicity who controlled everything: her money, her husband, and, until she fled to America, her daughter. Upon her death, Mrs. Bark's entire mouthwatering estate, including the Regency house in Brighton and a 16th-century cottage in Dorset, went to Susan's father. Upsetting as it was to be cut out at this stage, Susan had blithely assumed that when her father died the delectable properties would finally come to her.

But clever, malicious Felicity had other plans. Mrs. Bark decreed that when Reginald died the properties should go not to Susan but to Felicity's sister Posie. Both Susan and her father absolutely detested Posie, whom from time immemorial they had secretly called "Posie the Nosey."

Susan, completely bypassed, was stunned by her mother's posthumous contempt. But her father was a surprisingly sly old devil and he quickly figured out a way to keep Posie the Nosey from nabbing the real estate. It was quite simple, really. Reggie couldn't alter his wife's will, but there was absolutely nothing in it that legally prevented him from disposing of the Cumberland properties during his lifetime. So long as they belonged to him he could do with them as he wished. Mrs. Bark's one fatal mistake was to assume that once she died her husband would continue to obey her frequently stated command that the houses forever remain in the Cumberland family.

On her first trip back, to attend her mother's funeral, Reggie told Susan his plan. He would sell the properties and everything in them and turn the cash proceeds over to Susan. The implicit understanding, of course, was that in exchange he would go to live with Susan in Portland. The daunting prospect of caring for her 70-year-old father was mitigated by the thought of getting her hands on the fortune she was entitled to.

Reggie was prepared to act immediately—living in America was his lifelong dream—but Susan stalled for time. She couldn't just spring her father on an unprepared Carolyn. She hadn't even broached the subject with her lover, since the moment Susan returned home the two of them were embroiled in the ridiculous "dog fight." And during their resulting estrangement, Reggie, who'd never been sick a day in his life, collapsed, poor darling. The doctors didn't know what or how serious it was.

Susan flew back to be with him. She was mortified to find Posie the Nosey sniffing around like a dog at a smorgasbord. Susan noticed that some valuable 18th-century paintings were missing from the Brighton house. Posie the Nosey, with her ever-so-refained accent, told Susan that Reggie had "given" them to her. Susan grew alarmed. Her father was so weak he could barely speak and his thoughts were muddled. In his fragile state, without Susan at his side, he'd been unable to withstand Posey's forceful claims. If he were to die suddenly, before selling off the estate, Susan would be left with nothing. She stayed in Brighton as long as she could, and although she was rather clumsy in the nursing department, Reggie seemed to recover under her care. "I need you, Susie," he said before she left. "You're all I have."

"I can't leave Daddy alone any longer," she told Carolyn on her exhausted return. She and Carolyn had reached something of a truce by that time. "The poor darling's too confused and unhappy and I simply can't trust him to sell the estate if I'm not there." To do it for him, she meant.

Susan had a business to run, she couldn't keep flying back to England. She told Carolyn that she would be making a final trip to England in October to help Reggie dispose of the family houses. After that her father would come to come live at Bilitis Cottage.

"Just tell me when," Carolyn said, "so I can move my things out."

"Move out?" Susan sputtered. "But I want you here."

"Why? So I can nurse your father? No thanks."

Susan, so good at commands, so bad with emotions, went to pieces. Broke down and wept. Said she'd never realized how much Carolyn and the "stability" of their life together meant to her until now, when her last ties to England were disappearing. "I don't feel like I belong there anymore," she said between sobs, "but it's still wretched, losing one's homes. One's precious heirlooms. And you've always been such a brick, darling. A soft American brick for me to lay my head on."

"I'm not a brick," Carolyn said. "And you've always treated me like a dumb wife. I'm not a dumb wife. I think it's time to call it quits."

Susan's habitual sang-froid deserted her entirely. She pleaded, wept, cajoled. She began trailing after Carolyn, gazing at her with adoration, hoping for a crumb of reciprocal affection. She brought Carolyn flowers and gifts, cooked terrible meals, cleaned the cottage, walked Lady Caroline and took to calling her "our little girl."

But Carolyn kept her at arm's length. Her behavior was so completely bewildering that Susan wondered if Carolyn was going through menopause. Or was she sick with the emotional plague being spread by the pestilential Labonnes and their ACA ballot measure? It was infecting lesbians and gays throughout the city. Even Susan, so concerned with her money and her father, was feeling the demoralizing effects of the homophobia spreading like a virulent new strain of virus through Oregon. Perhaps Carolyn's constant, sharp-edged agitation and ferocious mood swings had something to do with that?

She knew that Carolyn was drinking more than usual and was smoking. These were sure signs of distress. Susan should know: she was drinking and smoking again, too.

Then fate, as if making up for lost time, lobbed another grenade at Susan. When the Senator Peckerwood scandal broke, she became so anxious that even Valium didn't help. A fierce anger took possession of her as she obsessively watched the unfolding story. It was on the news night and day. Susan pored over the newspaper stories, saw familiar names. Woman after woman, an entire disgusted brigade of former Peckerwood staffers, were coming forward to tell of the assaults and indignities they had suffered at his hands. Peckerwood, the Republican family-values man, was spewing venomous denials right and left.

The state's going insane, Susan thought, and it's taking all of us with it. For months gays and lesbians had been living with the outrageous lies and slanders of Ron Labonne and the ACA. Now the women bravely coming out of their straight, middle-class Republican closets to tell the truth about the revered senator were being reviled and their names and reputations smeared in the mud. There was no justice. It was a man's world.

"Can you believe it?" Susan cried in exasperation one morning when Carolyn entered the kitchen.

"Believe what?"

Susan threw down the paper. "Peckerwood! Those poor women. It's Anita Hill all over again. Revolting!" She pulled out a chair for Carolyn and fussed over getting her a cup of tea. "Straight men. Honestly. Every time they're caught with their bloody pants down they try to blame the woman. It's contemptible."

"Didn't you work for Peckerwood once?" Carolyn asked.

Susan nodded. "Ten years ago. When I was married and trying to live a Republican lifestyle." She glanced back at the paper. "I know most of these women. I *know* they're not lying." Her voice was hoarse, her hands were shaking with rage.

That night, after three brandies, she finally told Carolyn the hideous truth. She, too, had been sexually harassed by the senator. "He backed me up against a desk," Susan said. "His hands were all over me, clutching, clawing at my breasts. He was drunk. He grabbed my neck and forced his tongue into my mouth. Vile, disgusting." She covered her eyes and shuddered at the memory.

Carolyn was more sympathetic than she'd been in weeks. "What did you do?"

"Nothing!" Susan cried. "Well, I registered as a Democrat the next day, but other than that I did nothing."

"You didn't tell any one?"

"No. One didn't tell such things back then. It was too dangerous."

"Why?"

"Why? Because he's got all the power on his side! No one would have believed me. My God, when I think we were all going through the same thing, and all of us were too frightened to say a word! That's what happens, my dear, when you're stupid enough to become a little Republican wifey."

"You're not a Republican wifey now," Carolyn said.

"I know what you're getting at, pet. You think I should come out and add my sordid tale to the rubbish tip."

"I didn't say that."

"I'd love to!" Susan smacked a fist into her palm. "Oh, I would just bloody love to see that pious hypocrite get his comeuppance. But look what's happening to the women who've already given testimony. It would be even worse for me. Peckerwood's staff would ferret out every last detail of my life, especially my lesbian life, and use it to discredit me. They'd put my tits through the wringer."

Carolyn took a deep breath. "But at least you'd know that you told the truth. Weren't meek and frightened any more."

"Yes, yes, yes, I know, I know, I know." Susan wailed. She looked Carolyn squarely in the eyes. "Is that what you think I should I do?"

"It's up to you," Carolyn said.

"God, it could be such a hideously embarrassing mess. A total invasion of privacy. But I think I could do it, darling,"—a hopeful glance at Carolyn—"if I knew you were behind me."

Carolyn was very quiet. Bit her lower lip. Impulsively lit a candle and stared into its small, wavering flame. "Susan?"

"Yes, pet?"

"There are some things I have to tell you."

"Oh, darling, I wish you would. I wish you'd start talking to me again. I miss you so much. I was such an idiot about the dogs. It's just this endless strain—Mummy's death, the fact that she left me nothing, and now Daddy—the estate—the Peckerwood thing—I simply haven't been myself."

"Susan," Carolyn said abruptly, "do you love me?"

"Yes, darling." Susan actually went down on her knees in front of Carolyn. Her dramatic gesture was so sudden and heartfelt that she didn't see Lady Caroline hiding under Carolyn's chair. The dog let out a squealing yelp as Susan's knees crunched down on her paws and darted away with an aggrieved look in her bulging eyes. "Yes, I love you."

"Then don't interrupt me. Just listen. And then tell me if you still want me behind you."

▼ ▼ ▼

Carolyn had been seduced by the promise of love. He dangled it like a carrot in front of her. Or a caret, since for all her youthful rebelliousness she still secretly dreamed of a diamond ring, a church wedding, old shoes and streamers tied to the back of a car that proclaimed "Just Married." Despite evidence to the contrary, she believed what she wanted to believe—her romantic fantasies—and that made her a poor judge of character.

When she met him she was a fat, lonely, resentful 22-year-old living in affluent misery in Southern California. Her forceful, enigmatic seducer, who called himself "Eagle," was a good judge of poor character. It didn't take him long to figure out that insecure Carolyn Corbett had a desperate, hungry, insatiable need to be loved, to be wanted, to be a part of someone or something. There was a reckless streak in her. She was pointlessly rebelling against her well-to-do family. She espoused no angry feminist ideals. In short, under the right tutelage—his—she could be talked into anything.

He was a recruiter. He'd perfected his skills. He looked for gullible, love-starved girls with a vague anti-authoritarian streak in them. Carolyn was one of many he'd found. Like the others, she wanted to believe she was the only one. First he worked on her flesh until she panted at the very sight of him. Then he began working on her mind.

He would disappear. Long mysterious absences. Just when she feared she'd lost him he would reappear, reclaim her. When she said she wanted to be with him always, he alluded to the mysterious "commune" he lived in. Painted intoxicating scenes but left her out of the picture. Waited until she asked, then pleaded, to join him there.

Like a docile puppy she followed him into hell.

The "commune" was a bleak compound in the arid foothills of the Chocolate Mountains east of San Diego. The group called itself the Bruderschaft. Carolyn thought it sounded Germanic and brotherly. To foster a sense of group allegiance and identity, the men adopted aggressive, animalistic names suitable for brave hunters. That's why her lover was called Eagle. The women—who acted like dutiful squaws—were given soft, passive, elemental names. Carolyn, the eager new member, was christened "Feather." She never did understand why, but liked the airy sound of it.

She was thrilled to discover that the Bruderschaft was a secret society. She knew few details because she wasn't really allowed to talk to anyone. She was never alone, however: during her first weeks in the compound Eagle stayed comfortingly close by her side. She thought of it as a honeymoon.

As in any secret society there were initiation rites. Carolyn was finally allowed to attend a group meeting. The men talked. The women and children listened. In her excitement to belong, to be the Feather in Eagle's hat, Carolyn didn't pay much attention to the grandiose ideals being espoused. She heard and responded to the passionate anger; it chimed and boomed in the hollow recesses of her being. A revolution, and she could be part of it.

She still wasn't certain when she woke up and realized that the dream was a nightmare. She was drawn in so carefully that by the time she knew what has happening it was too late.

The group slowly forced her to sever her ties to the outside world. It sucked up her bit of savings. The money was her contribution, her investment in freedom, and she was promised a big return. Next, after virtually blackmailing her worried parents out of thousands of dollars, she was forced to renounce them. Now she had nowhere to go; the stifling Bruderschaft compound in the Chocolate Mountains became her universe.

Guided by the Bruderschaft, anxious to show Eagle how much she was willing to sacrifice for him, she kicked away the supports of her upper-middle-class life one by one. She did this even as she was collecting details. Such as: the group was living in a compound with armed guards. Such as: members were under constant surveillance. Such as: the other women were mindless drones relegated to cooking and cleaning. Such as: children were taken from their mothers and became communal property.

Then the obligatory "Mental Restructuring" sessions began. Induced paranoia. Bullying threats. Forced denunciations. Everyone outside was an enemy. The world was a conspiracy. The U.S. government, the United Nations, NATO, Communist Russia, all the universities, all the Jewish-run banks, the Black Panthers, multinational corporations—they were all in sinister, cancerous cahoots, preparing to take over and establish a dictatorial New World Order.

"Shed the blood and cleanse the world!" they had to shout a hundred times a day.

Then forced sex. A nightly open-door policy. The men could take whatever women they wanted. Drugs diminished the need for courtship preliminaries of any kind. It was rape. Carolyn, already pregnant by Eagle, was terrified. She pleaded with him to protect her from the others. And then she realized that he couldn't and wouldn't: he was one of them. There was no allegiance to one woman, there never had been. This had been planned all along.

She was on her own. She no longer belonged to Eagle. No longer belonged to herself. She belonged to the Bruderschaft.

Five a.m. target practice when she was six months pregnant. Kill or be killed they said now. They were preparing. Armageddon was at hand.

The brutal craziness of it slowly, sickeningly, dawned on her as her unborn child grew and her protective instincts ripened. Her sanity, once it returned, wouldn't go away. Lights blinked on in her feverishly working brain. She saw the Bruderschaft's grand revolutionary ideals for what they really were: a slop of crude supremacist ideology thrown over the most primitive biological urges. She was at the mercy of a group of violent, paranoid, dispossessed, emotionally retarded white men ranting about dictatorship and too stupid (or clever) to realize they were a dictatorship themselves. Racist, misogynistic neo-Nazis who captured stupid, will-less women like herself and clubbed them into believing that biological subservience was divinely ordained.

She was supposed to blindly surrender her life to the Cause. If she didn't, she was a traitor. Traitors were executed. No one who entered the Bruderschaft was allowed to leave. If she left, it meant she didn't believe. If she didn't believe, she would certainly reveal the Bruderschaft's secrets. In short, she would be exterminated.

Desperation wrings bold, cunning, ancient juices from the brain. As her belly swelled and her breasts grew heavy with milk, as the child that would become Lester Labonne shifted and kicked within her, Carolyn plotted her escape. Because she was pregnant they left her alone. She managed to steal the keys to Eagle's pickup. She knew there would be no doctor. One of the other women would act as a midwife. When labor came it was long and excruciating. The child, gray as cardboard, made his appearance. She saw him take his first wailing breath and turn pink with the miracle of life. Her piece of creation. She wasn't allowed to nurse him. The infant was immediately taken from her and put in a communal "nursery." She had to wait until she was strong enough to walk—or, rather, to run.

Her plan was to take the baby with her. But in this she had underestimated the Bruderschaft. Had other desperate mothers tried to collect their babies and escape? Was that why an armed guard was posted outside the room where her child was kept? Was that why the guard was Eagle?

She pleaded with him for a look at their child. He refused. He had his orders. "But he's mine!" she cried.

"He's not yours," Eagle said. "He's ours."

And she knew he meant the Bruderschaft.

"Go back to your room."

"I need some fresh air." It was three in the morning. She knew from the woman who'd helped her give birth that most of the men were away. Now in the final planning stage of their first major assault they were scattered throughout southern California, loading up on weapons. "Please. Can I go outside? Just for a minute." She touched his cheek.

He hesitated. "Okay, just for a minute."

Carolyn made her agonizing decision as she slowly walked down the quiet, desolate corridors of the compound. The desert night sky was weeping stars. She had the keys. She had nothing else but the clothes on her back. She didn't run. She didn't hurry. She saw that she was alone. She knew that she would always, now, be alone. Her freedom was the opposite of freedom. She drove off and left her baby behind. With him. With them.

She didn't live after that. She haunted a body. She was always fearful of being caught, of getting a bullet right between the eyes when she was least expecting it. And worst of all, she'd never be able to see her son, the sole fruit of her womb, that tiny spirit she'd seen come to life. She'd never be able to tell him her side of the story, never be able to stroke or comfort him in any way as he wandered motherless through life's confusing quagmire.

She hadn't told anyone. The Bruderschaft's paramilitary secrets were still safe. Two years later they were involved in a shoot-out with federal marshals in the Coyote Mountains near Plaster City, California. Four cult members had been killed, the rest escaped. She did not know if the cult was still in existence. But, of course, it was. It lived on in her head.

▾ ▾ ▾

The room was booming with silence.

Susan stared at her, dumb with amazement. Let out a baffled snort. Snatched up Lady Caroline and paced through the house, shaking her head, frowning, staring out windows. "Why didn't you tell me?" she finally asked.

"I was afraid to."

"Afraid? Of *me*?" Totally oblivious of her power to make dogs and humans heel on command.

"Afraid you wouldn't want me." But in that clear, calm, radiant moment Carolyn suddenly felt lighter than air. It no longer mattered if Susan wanted her or not because finally she'd broken through to herself, the Carolyn imprisoned behind eighteen years of anguished deceit.

Susan made no attempt to wipe away the tears streaming down her face. She knelt in front of Carolyn, took her hands, pressed them to her wet cheeks, kissed them. "You never told me any of this because you were afraid of me? Oh my poor brave darling. You've suffered all this alone, all these years? I'm so ashamed." She looked into Carolyn's soft blue eyes. "And it was him? That hideous cretin across the street?"

Carolyn nodded.

"That awful boy—he's really yours?"

Carolyn nodded. "I don't know if I'll ever see him again." She told Susan how she'd met Lester in the park and given him money to escape. "I had to. I had to give him his freedom. That's all I could offer him."

Susan squeezed her lover's hands. She rose and began pacing again. Her fear was breaking out like a rash. "But what happens now? What happens if Labonne recognizes you?"

Carolyn's voice was dull. "I don't know," she said.

"We have to get out of here, we have to leave. It's not safe. My God, what are we going to do?"

"I'm not running anymore, Susan. And I have to do it sooner or later."

"Do what?"

Carolyn looked at her. "Expose him."

CHAPTER 29

THERE'S NOTHING WORSE, DOVE THOUGHT, THAN NOT HAVING ANY friends. No one wanted her in their group. When word got out that she was the daughter of Ron and Cornette Labonne, they didn't treat her special, like her mom said they would. They laughed, sniggered, whispered behind her back, snubbed her. She'd been called a dweeb, a cracker, a Jesus freak, and a nerd. It was torture.

Slouching through the crowded hallways of Hamilton High she kept her head down and tried to remain invisible. A familiar voice in the back of her head reminded her that she was better than all of them. Jesus was her friend; she didn't need anyone else. But still she was ashamed of her clothes, her hair, her everything.

She always waited until the last minute to enter her classrooms, slipping in and taking a seat as far in the back as possible. And today she'd dawdled so long that she was going to be late for geometry. She raced up the stairway to the second floor. She wasn't looking, as usual, and collided head-on with a teacher hurrying in the opposite direction. Her book went flying.

She looked up. Her embarrassment turned to horror. It was the man who lived across the street. The one who'd chased her in the park. *Him.* Cassandra's friend. The one who'd demonstrated against her mom and Ron. A homosexual. A teacher, here at Hamilton High. Dove's knees felt rubbery, her face flamed hot.

John-Don Webster quickly scooped her book from the floor and thrust it back at her. "Sorry," he mumbled, dashing off down the hallway. He didn't even seem to know who Dove was. Or—the thought suddenly crossed her mind—maybe he did. Maybe he was afraid that she would tell someone what he'd tried to do to her in the park. So far she hadn't told anyone except Cassandra. It now occurred to her, like a neat geometry equation, that she didn't have to be frightened because she was the one who had power over him. All she had to do was tell her mom or Ron, and they'd do all the rest. The thought was strangely exciting. Maybe she would get her picture in the paper. The other kids would look up to her as a heroine.

When she got home from school her mom excitedly announced that she was flying off to an evangelical conference in Texas in two days time. "It just took me completely by surprise!" she exclaimed, breathless with excitement. "I've got to get ready. I've got to make a good showing."

Dove forgot about the teacher at Hamilton High. Now she was terrified at the thought of being left alone with her stepfather. "Don't go," she begged.

"Honey, I have to go. The Lord wants me too. It's His will, not mine."

"Can't you take me with you?"

"You've just started school, young lady."

"*Please.*"

"Dove, I've got an obligation to go. They called me. It's a huge conference, honey. Pat Robertson's going to be there. And Chuck Colson. It's a great honor that I was invited. It means they know who I am!" She beamed with self-absorbed pleasure.

"I don't want you to go. I'm afraid to be here alone."

"Oh, Dove." Cornette gave her an exasperated hug. "You're a big girl now. And you won't be alone. Ron's going to be here. He'll take care of you. And it's only for two days."

There was no stopping her mom. She bought new clothes and had her hair done. Ron was jealous and kept up a round of snide comments until Cornette silenced him with: "Sorry, hon, but when the Lord talks I listen." She acted lovey and concerned. "Don't you see? This is His way of telling us He's on our side. He's giving us this opportunity to tell the entire country about all the good work we're doing here in Oregon. Think of the support we'll get. This is the big time, Ron. There's no telling what they might do to help our cause."

"Financially, you mean?"

"Of course! It's just what we've been praying for."

"Then why aren't they paying for your ticket?" Ron asked.

"Oh, hon. I'm sure that was just an oversight. Helen won't mind if we write a check for the airfare. She'll see what this could lead to."

Dove pretended to be sick, which had always worked in the past, but not this time. On the day she left, her mom was more radiantly happy than she'd been for a long time. Well, why shouldn't she be? She was getting away from Ron.

▼ ▼ ▼

During the week that Too-Too was closed for clean-up and repairs, Cassandra laid her trap. The September weather was glorious, so she stayed outside as much as possible, clearing brush, hacking away more ivy, planting spring bulbs, and washing windows. Hard satisfying manual labor that kept her in Ron Labonne's line of vision. Jay was gone most of the time. Dove was back in school. The boy, Lester, was nowhere to be seen. Cassandra had no idea where Cornette was; Ron's wife never stepped foot outside the house except to get in her car and drive away.

When she finally saw Ron peeping at her from his window, half-hidden behind the draperies, Cassandra walked over to the property line, folded her arms, and stared back. His face remained impassive. A stand off. Finally she beckoned to him to come out.

He disappeared from the window. A few moments later he came outside and stood by his back door.

"Can I talk to you?" she called.

He kept his distance. "What about?"

"About us."

"Who's us?" he asked.

"You and me," she said.

He rocked on his heels, squinting in the sun, eyeing her with suspicion. "I don't have anything to say to you."

"Are you afraid of me or something?"

He laughed. "Afraid of you?" He slowly made his way down through the tiers of Delmont's ruined garden, a smug, complacent grin on his face, until he was by her side, the two of them hidden from view by the holly tree. "I think it's the other way around," he said. "I think you're afraid of me."

"You don't know me very well," Cassandra said. She wanted to leap on him, pummel him, bash his ugly face in, but kept her voice calm and ever-so-slightly mysterious. "What do I need to know?"

"How I . . . feel about you," she whispered with tortured intensity.

"How you feel about me? I know how you feel about me. I saw you out there with all your homosexual friends. Accusing me of burning that cross. And then that crazy pansy you live comes over and accuses me of destroying his homo restaurant. Accuse, accuse, accuse, that's all liars know how to do. I guess I showed him a thing or two."

"Look me in the eyes," she said, forcing herself to take his beefy hand. "Look me in the eyes and tell me that you had nothing to do with those awful things."

"I don't have to defend myself to you. I know whose side you're on."

She could feel him slipping away and tightened her grasp. "I want to believe you're a good man, Ron. I really do."

He drew his hand away. "Are you a lesbian?"

"I . . . thought I was. I don't know anymore. You've confused me."

"I have?" He sounded cautious but pleased.

"Yes." She snapped off a berry from the holly bush. "I keep thinking about you. Wondering."

"Wondering what?"

"How it would be," she whispered. "With you."

"Haven't you ever been with a man?"

She shook her head. "I'm afraid it'll hurt."

"Hurt? Making love?"

She nodded. "It does, doesn't it?"

"Not if the man knows what he's doing. Not if he's tender."

"Are you tender, Ron?" she asked. "When you make love?"

He brought his hand up with a sudden, impulsive jerk. She winced, thinking he was going to strike her, but he quickly, nervously, stroked the side of her face. "I can be."

"But that's what I don't understand about you. You seem so—powerful. You're so strong. How can you be that way and tender too?"

"Well, I know what gives a lady pleasure."

"It's just that—I don't know if I could ever *feel* pleasure with a man."

"Look," he said, furtively casting his eyes back towards the house, "do you want to be normal?"

"How can I know until I've tried it?"

His breath grew heavier. "Are you saying you want to try it with me?"

She closed her eyes and bravely raised her head. "Yes. But you're married. With a beautiful wife. So I'll just have to go on dreaming."

"Well, look," he said, clearing his throat, keeping his voice low, "if I could do that for you—if I could help you escape from being homosexual—I'd consider it an honor. It's my duty, in a way."

"Your duty? I don't want it to be just a duty, Ron."

"I mean, I'd be helping God bring you back to normal."

She nodded. "It wouldn't be a sin then, would it? Not if you were helping God."

"No, it wouldn't be a sin," he murmured, caressing her neck with a hand that smelled of hamburger and onion. "It would be releasing you from sin. Taking you out of a trap you've fallen into. You hate the way your are, don't you?"

She averted her face, as if ashamed to answer.

"They all do," he said knowingly. "They hate it, but they're brainwashed by the gay libbers not to say so."

"Oh, those gay libbers," she sighed, shaking her head. "I don't know what they'd do if they found out I was even talking to you."

"Look," he said with noble resolve, "if I do this for you, if I help you to escape from their clutches, would you do something for me?"

"Oh, Ron," she said earnestly, "I think I'd do anything for you."

"Would you come on my television show and talk about your conversion? How God led you away from perversity and made you normal?"

She gazed at him with wide, innocent eyes. "You mean tell everyone you lead me to God by fucking me?"

"No!" he spluttered in alarm. "No, you can't tell anyone that. That part has to be kept secret."

"Oh, I thought—"

"That's just God showing his mercy and understanding through me. I'm more like a—like a—"

"Like a shepherd," she suggested, "leading a stray lamb back to the family fold."

"Right."

"Well, I can't promise anything, Ron, until I really know if making love with a man is better than making love with a woman."

"Don't worry about that," he laughed. "There's no way you could ever experience real sexual gratification with another woman. It's unnatural. They don't have the right equipment."

"Well, they have tongues and fingers," she said.

He licked his lips. "Yeah, but you need a man to show you the true heights of ecstasy. Only a man can shine a light down that tunnel."

"Can you come over tonight?" she whispered.

"Uh—no, tonight's out. I gotta go to a dinner with Senator Peckerwood.

"You know Senator Peckerwood?" she said adoringly.

"Oh sure, he's one of my biggest fans."

"How about tomorrow night then?"

He considered. "Ten o'clock? Give or take?"

"I'll be waiting, Ron. I'll leave my door open."

"What about him—that crazy homo you live with?"

"He won't be home. It'll be just you and me."

She held her breath, stood on tiptoes, and brushed his cheek with her lips. A Judas kiss, but appropriate for a man who thought of himself as her Messiah.

▼ ▼ ▼

Another wearying round of meetings. That's all his life was now. When the committee finally adjourned around ten, an exhausted John-Don left the fund-raising office in the back of Too-Too and headed towards his Jeep. He was startled to see Peter standing in the parking lot next to his car. "Hey, what are you doing here?"

"Waiting for you."

"Why didn't you come into the office?"

"Didn't want to disturb you," Peter said. "I'd just be in your way."

John-Don felt a sudden pang of guilt. Instead of helping Peter deal with his depression, he was channeling all his extra time and energy into the campaign. They were now in the midst of planning the big No on Three rally to be held in late October, just before the elections. "You're never in my way, you know that," he said. "And there's so much you could do to help."

"Well, actually, I've been thinking about that." Peter cleared his throat and stared down at the asphalt. "My parents called today. I talked to my father." He looked nervously at John-Don, willing himself not to break down and cry like a twerpy sissy. "He called me. He saw us on the news, after the cross burning. He said he wanted to call then but he was too sick. He had another stroke, and he's been in the hospital. But no one told me because my mother's been sick, too."

John-Don could hear the anxiety in his voice. He put his arm around Peter's shoulder.

"It was hard to understand him," Peter said. "His voice is slurred. But he said he'd been through that himself. Cross burnings. He asked me if I was all right. He asked what I was doing about it. And I felt so weak, like a stupid coward, because I haven't done one damn thing."

"It's been harder on you because of the racist shit."

Peter nodded. "I freaked. I took it so personally. And he said—my father said—that was the worst thing to do. Because then you start believing that you're weak and powerless and that everyone's out of get you. And you've got to believe that it's not everyone, it's just some, it's just a few. If you stop believing that there are more good than bad, you're lost. That's what he said, anyway."

"He's right, you know."

"I know, I know, I know!" Peter said impatiently. "Honey, I just couldn't deal with it. All I could think of was myself. Like, how much shit do I have to endure just because I'm black and like to suck cock? My parents are embarrassed by me, all my old friends are dead, I'm trying to make a go of it in a new city, and then I come home and see the whole fucking history of my race and sexuality burning on the front lawn. And you're never around."

John-Don clumsily pulled Peter into his arms. "I know I haven't been there for you. I'm sorry. I don't know why, but I just freeze up when it comes to dealing with personal stuff." What he couldn't bear was feeling vulnerable or "weak" in any way. Especially now, when every last ounce of his energy had to be funneled into the campaign. He'd always hated marshmallow-soft emotions. Peter's neediness irritated him. But standing there in the parking lot, holding Peter, John-Don suddenly realized how important this simple human connection was. He could feel Peter's eager, almost hungry response to his embrace.

"I thought I was losing you," Peter said. "But I couldn't pull myself out of it. I just felt so fatalistic about everything. Like why bother because the other side is always going to win."

"You've got to fight anyway. You can't make it easy for them."

"That's what my father said."

They went home and shared a bottle of wine. It was like meeting again after a long absence. Amorous, but a little shy. John-Don kept his vow not to talk about the campaign. They deserved one night of their own, away from the conflict that had nearly split them apart.

Peter couldn't get over the fact that his father had actually called him. It was a call he'd been waiting for his entire adult life. The weird thing about it, he said, was that it came when he'd finally *stopped* waiting for it. And yet it came when he most needed it. A simple expression of love and support from the parents who'd always made him feel that he'd somehow disappointed them—it meant more to him than he'd ever realized.

In bed that night, John-Don held nothing back. He was fiercely passionate. He made Peter's wildest fantasies come true. Afterwards, as the panting subsided and they lay in one another's arms, Peter said, "I didn't tell you, but Ito came over today."

"Ito did? What for?"

"To have a talk."

"About what?"

"Oh, we just talked." Peter smiled secretively and fit his body into the contours of John-Don's. Spoons in the warm dessert of their bed. He didn't want to tell John-Don what Ito had said: that if Peter didn't do something, he'd lose John-Don; that John-Don was "most concerned" about Peter and felt Peter was cutting him off; that Peter would be a fool to let John-Don slip away.

And then, most surprisingly of all, Ito had said, "He is a rare individual—one in a million—and if you don't want him, there are others who do."

▼ ▼ ▼

Dove had worked out her brave plan for freeing the rabbits. She looked in Ron's appointment book and saw that he'd be away both evenings. By the time he discovered the rabbits were gone, her mom would be back.

She didn't want to make Ron suspicious, so she pretended that everything was fine. She obsessively cleaned the house, which seemed to please him. The second night of her mom's absence, she microwaved a teevee dinner for herself and two for Ron. Ron seemed distracted and was wearing too much cologne. He didn't pick on her, didn't nag her, hardly looked at her. After he left, her mom called and gave a breathless report about meeting all the wonderful people at the tel-evangical conference.

"They're treating me like a star!" she exclaimed. "When I got up there and stood in front of two thousand people, my image was projected on a huge screen."

"Weren't you nervous?" Dove asked.

"Yes, a little, but then I was filled with the Lord. You should have heard the applause when I told them about the ACA and our campaign in Oregon. Put Ron on, honey, so I can tell him all about it."

Dove said he wasn't there.

"Oh dang," her mom said. "Well, honey, you'll be sure to tell him everything, won't you? Tell him Momma Bear sends a gweat big kiss and says she wuvs him. And she wuvs you, too."

When she hung up, Dove felt alone and more cut off than ever. The rabbits. It was such a kind, simple thing to do, but she got jittery just thinking about it. She tried to concentrate on her geometry but couldn't. Instead, she wandered around the house making sure all the doors and windows were locked. She turned on all the lights and locked the basement door so the ghost wouldn't get her. She looked at Ron's guns and wondered if she'd ever need to use one. She thought of all the perverts in the neighborhood, including her Uncle Terry. They were everywhere! If she set foot outside, the man across the street—the teacher at her high school!—might be waiting. She could almost feel his hand grabbing her—pulling her into the bushes . . . getting even with her for what her mom and Ron were doing. She took comfort from the fact that all she had to do was tell them what he'd done. Once she did that he would vanish, like an evil ghost. Maybe they'd lock him up.

But it was now or never. Screwing up her resolve, she slipped out the back door and stood in the darkness. Dumbo, weighted down by his heavy chain, barked and dragged himself over to her. Crickets were rasping. She shivered in the cold. The stars were out. A sliver of moon hung in the sky like a crooked, terrible smile.

Dove instinctively looked over towards Cassandra's windows. Soft light glowed and flickered inside the studio. Candlelight. An enormous sadness—resentment, jealousy, longing—clutched her heart. She wanted to be there, with wonderful Cassandra.

She soothed Dumbo, then carefully picked her way down through the tiers of garden, past the satellite dish, until she was at the rabbit hutch. The rabbits were huddled up in a corner. Dove unlatched the door and reached in. Felt the tickle of their whiskers, the warm softness of their fur.

"I'm letting you go," she whispered to them. "You don't have to be afraid of him anymore." But the rabbits, even when she put them down on the ground, didn't move. She thought they'd be so thrilled with their freedom that they'd skitter off immediately. "Go on," she whispered, irritated, angrily nudging one with her toe.

Then she saw a flash of headlight skid past the garage and heard a car in the driveway. The sensor spread out its wide skirt of light, silhouetting the house. Ron! She froze. Her heart began to race. There wasn't enough time to get back in the house. Dumbo began to bark.

Gripped with terror, she darted behind the hutch and crouched down between two rhododendron bushes. A car door. He didn't slam it, the way he usually did. The sensor light quickly went off—which meant he'd flipped the switch in the garage. A figure appeared behind the house. Dove tried to catch her breath. In the darkness she could hear Dumbo dragging his chain and eagerly whimpering.

Why hadn't Ron gone in the front door? Why was he petting and quieting Dumbo? He never had before.

She could see Ron—it had to be Ron—slowly making his way down into the garden. He knew she was there! He was coming for her. Or maybe he was coming to kill one of the rabbits. Dove flattened herself and wiggled further back into the bushes. *Oh God*, she desperately prayed, *don't let him find me. I'll put the rabbits back, I'll be good, I won't ever question my parents again. I'll be good, I promise. I'll help them any way I can.*

Ron's bulky, menacing figure moved steadily closer, like a figure in her worst nightmares. He slowly descended into the garden, tier by tier, until he was so close that she could smell the sweet, sickly odor of his Brut cologne.

She didn't move a muscle. She hardly breathed. He loomed over her, passed the rabbit hutch, and felt his way towards the path that lead over to Cassandra's studio. Stopped and pulled something out of his pocket. Dove craned her head out, like a turtle from its shell. Ssst! Ssst! Ron sprayed breath freshener into his mouth and moved on, leaves and twigs crackling under his feet.

A new fear crashed over her like a wave. Why was he going to Cassandra's? What was he planning to do?

She heard a quiet tap on Cassandra's door. Heard the door open. Heard Cassandra's low voice. Heard Ron's low, answering voice. Heard the door close.

She didn't know what to think. She inched her way out and huddled near the rabbit hutch. One of the rabbits slowly hopped away. She quickly got up and angrily pulled the rest of them out, not knowing why she was angry except that it had something to do with the rabbits' cowering passivity. Their fate was in her hands and they didn't even know it. They didn't even want their freedom. One by one she threw them to the ground, then stood there, numb, her pulse throbbing in her ears, trying to decide what to do. Her first instinct was to run back into the house. But if Ron hurt Cassandra, it would be her fault. Why was he there? Why would Cassandra let him in if she hated him so much?

The lingering, suggestive smell of Ron's cologne hung in the air, teasing her nose. It troubled her, but she didn't know why. The darkness seemed to laugh at her bewilderment, her fear, her ignorance. The night was for ghosts and grown-ups and all their sneaky, terrible secrets.

She couldn't stop herself. She followed Ron's scent through the trees, past the holly, over to the brick patio in front of Cassandra's studio. Crouching behind Cassandra's redwood chaise lounge, she peered around towards the studio door. Soft, inviting light from within. Dreamy music. She'd heard that music before.

She crawled closer, on her hands and knees, until she reached the woodpile at the corner of the house. The second-floor balcony made an overhanging porch. Voices. Dove strained her ears, trying to hear what they were saying, listening intently for anger, shouts, screams.

A shadow passed by the curtained window above her. Dove quickly scrambled over to the other side of the woodpile. Waited for what seemed an eternity, until the voices moved further back into the studio, where Cassandra's bed was.

Her heart was beating so fast it hurt, but she had to know what was going on inside. Something tugged at her, a dark breathless desire to uncover a secret hidden in herself, an irritating mystery she almost knew the answer to but couldn't quite unravel. She crept over to the door, slowly lifted her head, peered through the slit at the bottom of the curtains.

She bit down hard on her lips. Her stomach contracted and she burned all over. She started to shake. Her head felt like it was going to explode.

They were both naked. Cassandra was lying on the bed. Ron was sitting on the side of it, pulling off his socks and scratching his hairy, sagging belly. At first Dove thought Cassandra was dead, that Ron had strangled her. But then she saw her move over to make room for Ron. When Ron stood, she saw his thing standing straight up in the air, like the stubby barrel of a gun. He looked down at it, smiled, waggled it back and forth in front of Cassandra. Then, on his knees, he crawled across the white comforter and covered Cassandra's body with his own.

Dove watched, but she couldn't see, couldn't take it in, couldn't admit to it. All she could think of was her mom, off in Texas, her image projected on a huge screen, praying with two thousand people. While Ron—her husband, the Poppa Bear she wuved so much—was here, naked, like a fat hairy pig on top of Cassandra.

Cassandra, who said Ron was stupid and evil. Cassandra, who said she couldn't be friends with Dove because of Ron.

How could she ever look at either of them again? Hate, fear, revulsion—Dove was consumed. She went up in flames. The world spun, obscene voices chattered in her ears. She knew she would never be the same, that the sight of them would be forever lodged in her heart, like an ax.

She tried to stand but her legs were wobbly. She reached out for support, grabbed for the woodpile. A log clattered down onto her foot. She gave a startled cry. Then couldn't move. Couldn't breathe. Couldn't do anything but stand there, rooted to the spot, staring in tear-blinded terror as the curtains suddenly parted, the door flew open, and Ron, his eyes wild and then coldly furious, stood before her as naked as Adam.

▼ ▼ ▼

Cassandra caught a brief glimpse of Dove's terrified face, just outside the door. Saw her standing out there, frozen in the tortured, cringing posture of a figure from Rodin's Gates of Hell.

She watched Ron's transformation. He was seized by a blind, terrifying rage, the same kind of monstrous, eye-popping fury Cassandra's father snapped into whenever his authority was subverted. It was like a visceral replay of her own childhood. She recognized the same cold nausea of terror in her body. "Daddy" was on a rampage and she had to hide before he got her.

She leapt out of bed and ran upstairs, naked, cowering in Jay's bedroom. She heard Dove's faint, high-pitched squeaks of terror—oh God, so pitiful, like an animal being slaughtered. What would he do to her?

Crouching beside Jay's bed, her heart pounded out a furious indictment. *Look what you've done! Look what you've done!* Hiding up here to save yourself when he's out there murdering Dove. Because of you.

She forced herself to move. Her limbs felt boneless, rubbery, weak. She had to help Dove.

▼ ▼ ▼

The world was a dark, malevolent place. She'd always known that. But now even Jesus seemed to be laughing at her terror. When Ron stepped back inside and began to pull on his clothes, Dove ran. He commanded her to stop. No way! She remembered all the things he did to Lester. Now it was her turn. She didn't know where to go. She ran until her foot got snagged in a tangle of ivy and she fell with a startled grunt. By that time Ron was outside. Now he was after her. Those big hands. The blind rage in his eyes. She scrabbled to her feet and bolted around the holly tree. His voice slashed through the darkness. He was hunting for her. Dumbo began to bark. She dove down to the ground and was trying to wriggle under the holly when he seized her foot. She let out a scream and clawed at the sharp-edged holly leaves as he pulled her out. "No, no!" she cried, flailing like a worm on a hook, trying to shake him off.

But he had her. She was caught. His grip was like iron. He reached around her waist, pulled her up, spun her around to face him. She couldn't look at him. He was panting, telling her to be quiet. She couldn't. She sobbed and screeched and gibbered and thrashed until he put a hand around her neck and grabbed her by the hair. "Shut up!" His voice was a furious hiss. He gave her a threatening shake. His eyes were bulging. "I won't tell, I won't tell," she sobbed. "I didn't see anything." Because she knew that was what it was all about. Secrets. His face loomed closer, his expression so weird that she thought she would faint. For a moment she thought he was going to plant his lips on hers, do to her what . . .

It came to her in a flash. Salvation. A way to save herself. The words spewed out in a breathless rush before she even knew what she was saying. "I won't tell, I didn't see anything, and I know something else, too, something about that homosexual man across the street."

▼ ▼ ▼

By the time Cassandra got back downstairs it was ominously quiet outside. She pulled on a robe and tiptoed out to the brick terrace. All she could hear was the steady, rhythmic thrum of the crickets. She cautiously made her way over to the rabbit hutch. She stood in the darkness, looking up at the windows of what had once been Delmont's beautiful Queen Anne house. The curtains were drawn.

I have to go in there, she thought. But she knew she couldn't. She didn't have the courage. She jumped as something soft tickled her ankle. Looking down she saw a fat white rabbit.

CHAPTER 30

"AND YOU NEVER TOUCHED THE GIRL?" BILL LONSDALE, WITH THE
tired, solicitious air of a department store Santa, peered at John-Don over the tops of
his half-moon reading glasses.

John-Don, sweating and too furious to speak, clamped his hands on his knees to
stop his legs from shaking. His stomach was in knots.

The principal sighed. "I have to ask, John-Don."

"They're out to get me," John-Don said. The frantic jiggling of his legs grew worse.
"This is the best way to do it."

"Yes, it will be if he gets her to press charges."

"It's insane! He wouldn't dare. Do you think he will?"

"I'm not sure." Lonsdale flipped his glasses onto the desk and wearily kneaded his
face. "He says he won't if, in his words, we get rid of you."

"*Get rid of me?*" John-Don let out an incredulous laugh. The phrase, with its
ominous double edge, roused every anti-authoritarian cell in his being. "You know
what I'd do if you tried to get rid of me, don't you? You know the fight I'd put up."

"No one's going to get rid of you," Lonsdale said patiently. "I told him that straight
out. But look, we need to discuss this, John-Don, calmly and like rational adults. Let's
get the facts—"

"There are no facts! It's a complete fabrication! I was out running and I saw this
girl. It was almost a year ago. I had no idea who she was. She'd fallen down and she was
crying. So I tried to help her. And she started screaming. That's it! I left her there,
screaming like a maniac." He tried to shake off the nightmarish suspicion that Bill
Lonsdale didn't believe him.

"And you didn't touch her?"

"No! Maybe I touched her hand, trying to help her get up. But I was trying to *help*
her." He couldn't control himself any longer and shot up from his chair. He felt as
though he'd been running for miles, not out of pleasure but because he was being chased,
hunted down by an obsessed lunatic. No endorphic high, just a winded breathless panic
as adrenalin pumped through his body, sharpening his senses, burning his skin. "I should
refuse to even discuss this without a lawyer from the teachers' union here in the room."

Lonsdale kept his voice calm. "If you want a lawyer present, just say so. Remember, nothing's happened yet. Nothing may come of it. All I'm trying to do at this stage,
John-Don, is talk to you. Off the record, as a friend. I can understand how this makes
you feel—"

"No, you can't." John-Don ran his hands through his hair and let out an incoherent yelp of frustration. "To be falsely accused to attacking a young girl—who just happens to be the daughter of Ron Labonne—who just happens to be a political opponent—who just happens to be out to get every gay person he can, using every dirty trick he can think of—no, I don't think you can understand how I feel."

"Why don't you give me a chance?"

Why? Because the situation had slammed John-Don into the same paranoiac and reactionary position he despised in others, snapping off his empathy, sucking the juice from his heart, polarizing his vision. Heterosexuals, especially white male heterosexuals in positions of power, were not to be trusted. Not even Bill Lonsdale, whose first concern was no doubt saving his own ass instead of helping John-Don save his.

"These maniacs have burned a cross on my lawn and destroyed a friend's restaurant," he blurted out. "They've stolen confidential records from the No on Three fundraising office. They've painted swastikas, accused us of recruiting and murdering children, and beaten us with baseball bats. Maybe you didn't know about any of that, Bill. Maybe you don't want to know. But it's part of *my* daily life as a gay person."

"I knew about the cross burning."

Well, who didn't? The cross burning, and the twenty-two charges of sexual harrassment recently filed against Senator Peckerwood, had put Oregon in the national news.

John-Don took a deep breath. "Tell me again what the bastard actually said."

It sounded even uglier in the retelling. That morning Ron Labonne had called Bill Lonsdale and told him that he was removing his stepdaughter, Dove, from school. The girl claimed that John-Don Webster, a teacher at the high school, had attacked her in Forest Park. She was supposedly in a state of emotional shock as a result. Labonne said he hadn't yet decided what he was going to do about it. If he allowed his stepdaughter to press charges and the case went to court, the girl would have to testify. The resulting publicity might do her irreparable harm. What he wanted above all else, Labonne said, was to protect his stepdaughter.

But then, in a move that shocked even cynical Bill Lonsdale, Labonne said that he would, in effect, keep the girl quiet if John-Don Webster were dismissed from his teaching position. "He's a known homosexual," Labonne said, "and I'll make that fact known to every parent in the school if I have to. He's not fit to be in contact with children."

That implicit threat was Labonne's undoing, as far as Bill Lonsdale was concerned. As a principal, of course, he had to be extremely cautious. This was an inflammatory situation, as Labonne well knew. And it was precisely because it was so deliberately inflammatory that Lonsdale refused to be pulled down into the hysterical flames Labonne was so desperately trying to fan.

"So it ended in a stalemate. I told him that a teacher in the public schools couldn't be fired on the basis of unfounded allegations. Or because he was a homosexual." Not yet anyway, he thought.

"I've *never* told my students that I was gay," John-Don said defensively. "I've *never* made sexuality an issue in the classroom. I never even mentioned the goddamned ACA because *you* wouldn't let me."

"I know that," Lonsdale said. "But you have to admit that you've become pretty high-profile over the summer. People know that you're—" He gestured vaguely.

John-Don slammed his fist on Lonsdale's desk. "That I'm gay. I'm queer! Say it, for Christ's sake!"

"I respect you, John-Don. I hope you know that. But coming out so publicly, at this time—"

"I've put my ass on the line, so don't think I'm going to disappear now just so *you'll* be more comfortable. I'm not going to sit back like a terrified wimp and accept the lies this madman is spewing out."

"No, of course not. It's just that your visibility makes it easier for him to—"

"To what? Smear me? Ruin me? Goddamnit, there are times when a person has to stand up for himself, stand up to evil, regardless of the personal consequences. You just don't get it, Bill. You're straight. You don't have to spend your life proving that you're not a criminal."

"No," Lonsdale said, "but I'm a battered old liberal and a tired secular humanist educator, so I'm at risk, too." Because if Labonne won, Lonsdale knew he'd be bound and censured for his beliefs as well. It was all there, in the vague, sloppy, insultingly unconstitutional wording of Ballot Measure Three. If the measure passed, the schools would ultimately be forced to teach creationism, institute daily prayers, have their libraries ransacked for "objectionable" literature, and be compelled to condemn abortion and homosexuality. Once installed in power, Labonne and fundamentalist zealots like him would attack the increasingly fragile edifice of education.

It was already happening. They were chip, chip, chipping away at the humanities, at the arts, at the sciences, at the multicultural notion of tolerance based on human diversity. Given half a chance, they'd keep at it until they'd extinguished every frail, feeble light of Western culture. Armed with bibles and fortified by religious bigotry, they wouldn't be satisfied until life was as harsh, bleak and bare as their impoverished imaginations could make it.

Here it was, nearly 2000 A.D., and the Dark Ages were looming before him. Life was steadily being reduced to the lowest common denominator. People were relinquishing their minds, their rationality, and cowering in blind, fearful obedience to supernatural deities.

What did it mean, Lonsdale suddenly wondered, this golden "Information Age" everyone jabbered about as if it were some sort of salvation through technology? What value did all this endless "information" have if it never added up to one jot of human truth, wisdom or compassion? It could just as easily be called the "Misinformation Age," since people who refused to think for themselves ended up believing just about anything put in front of them.

John-Don was quietly staring out at the parking lot through Lonsdale's office window. "What do you suggest I do?"

"I say sit tight. We have to wait and see if he actually takes her to the police. My feeling is that he won't. I think he's bluffing. He wanted to see first of all if I'd knuckle under to fear and threats. He knows that if he gets her to press charges he's in for a real battle. And his case is weak. If this incident occurred last January why has it taken the girl so long to make her accusations? Why is she supposedly so emotionally distraught now?"

"Because the elections are coming up," John-Don said, "and he's desperate. It wouldn't stand up in court. They'd have to see the connection."

"Ever hear of 'recovered memories'? If they're desperate, they can easily hire a psychologist to testify that the girl was so terrified she blocked it out. It's not uncommon."

John-Don chewed on a knuckle. "So what happens if he does get her to press charges?"

"I'll be behind you and the teachers' union will be behind you. We'll fight him all the way."

"And in the meantime, I'm just supposed to go about my regular duties. Act as if nothing's wrong?"

"Under the circumstances I'm willing to arrange for an emergency leave of absence—if you want it." Secretly, he hoped John-Don would accept his offer. Lonsdale hadn't had the heart to tell him that other bible-thumping ACA parents who'd seen John-Don on the news or in the papers had also called and demanded his dismissal. The school year had barely begun and already his ulcer was killing him.

John-Don hesitated. "No. I'll stay."

"Good," Lonsdale said. Shit, he thought.

"I have to. I won't give that lying piece of scum the satisfaction of frightening me."

"Remember, it all depends on the stepdaughter. If he knows she's lying, or if he's coerced her to make up this story, he's going to be very very careful. And John-Don?"

"What?"

"I want you to be careful, too. Please. Look out for yourself."

"I have to. I'm queer, remember?"

▼ ▼ ▼

A strange floating sensation enveloped John-Don as he left Lonsdale's office. He'd had this sensation before. Once, only a week earlier, when with Jay at his side he surveyed the wreckage of the No on Three fundraising office at Too-Too. And earlier in the summer, when he came home with Peter and saw the cross burning on their lawn.

It was a feeling that reality had fractured, sucking him out of one dimension and spitting him into a parallel universe. Jarring. Alienating. The most ordinary sights—everyday objects and people—were suddenly imbued with a lurking malevolence.

Right now he wanted comfort, wanted Peter, wondered if he should call him. Or Ito. No, not until he'd had time to calm down. Calm down? How could he, why should he, when his entire professional life as a teacher was at stake? All because of one lying girl. It was grotesque, ridiculous, but in this hysterical climate sexual witch hunts were becoming daily events. Lonsdale was right: all around the country people were being tried and sent to prison by children guided into "remembering" episodes of satanic rituals and sexual abuse. There was no telling what twisted fantasies the girl was making up, or what Ron and Cornette Labonne might get their daughter to say.

For a moment John-Don wished that he, too, could believe in some generous supernatural force offering help and guidance instead of an eternal vendetta. But when he tried to dredge up from the God-shaped hole in his consciousness an image of a beneficent deity working on his behalf, all he got was a picture of their God, ugly, jealous, fiendish, implacably angry, small-minded, and bigoted. No different from their version of Satan. They hated life, that's what it all came down to. Glued their eyes to heaven and the hereafter because the here and now was a chaotic hell they couldn't deal with. But if they hated life so much, why did they work with such remorseless fervor to make it hell for everyone around them?

He fought back a sudden desire to sink to his knees and howl in despair. *I'm innocent!* His eyes stung, he couldn't catch his breath, he was cracking, losing control. They're closing in, he thought. I've got to keep moving, keep the energy flowing. If I stop moving, I'm dead.

But an enormous weight seemed to be crushing him into the earth. Squatting on his shoulders was that terrible twin, the twisted shadow, the monstrous reflection of the pervert they were determined to make of him.

Nature. He was suddenly ravenous for the mysterious, impersonal comfort it had always given him. He staggered up the stairs towards the huge light-filled windows on the landing. Grasped the sill, looked outside. A beautiful, buttery autumn light frosted the giant elms lining the street below. In a corner of the football field a flock of white seagulls glowed against the emerald-green turf. The west hills cut a soft, serrated edge across a mellow blue sky. He knew it was beautiful because he'd looked out the same window before with a keen sense of pleasure, of community, of belonging. But now he felt cut off, like a tree stump in a forest, disconnected from the life he'd once taken for granted.

A leaf floated down to the sidewalk. The summer was already gone. He'd always remember it as the summer that changed his life. The summer when he'd finally recognized that he was pitted against a way of life and a set of values more powerfully entrenched, and more jealously guarded, than he'd ever believed possible.

And it wasn't just he who'd been changed. Everyone in Queer Corners had been affected. Even his straight friends, who'd pooh-poohed and laughed at the ballot measure as somehow beneath their consideration, were now being sucked down into the same disorienting vortex of disbelief. They'd finally awakened from their smug liberal slumbers to the shocking realization that yes, indeed, it was possible for someone as mean-spirited, self-serving and patently offensive as Ron Labonne to wield power in what they'd always liked to think of as their wonderfully progressive state. Surprise!

He remembered Jay's remark: "I wanted to kill him." John-Don felt that way about Labonne now. Pushed beyond reason. Ready to kill. And yet that would get him nowhere, and he knew it. That was, after all, their real power: to reduce everyone to their primitive, reactionary level of existence.

Politics. Dirty politics. Filthy politics. Unseen forces hiding in the dark. As John-Don slowly walked back to his classroom, an image of whispering ratlike men excitedly planning their next rampage kept flickering through his mind.

As he entered the classroom, the excited babble of teenaged voices quickly died away. Thirty youthful faces turned expectantly towards him. To them, he still represented adult authority. They knew nothing about what had just happened.

Or did they? John-Don's gay radar—gaydar, as Peter called it—was searching for homophobic signals. He could feel their attention turned on him. In the parallel universe they were all potential accusers, just like Dove Labonne, filled with secret, sullen, vindictive malice.

But then he began see their individual faces—Joyce, Shanara, Sean, Tiffany, Brad. Just kids, good kids for the most part, facing their own problems, trying to fit themselves into the anxious puzzle of life. Hopeful, most of them; already lost and desperate, others.

John-Don didn't envy them because the world they'd been brought into was, as far as he could tell, on the verge of extinction. He didn't know if they'd be different, if they'd be the generation that finally realized everyone was in this mess together. That they'd all sink into the mud unless they could overcome their differences and work together, side by side, to harness the incredible potential of all humanity. But for that to happen, they'd have to overstep the rigid boundaries set up by past generations. And that took courage and the ability to think for oneself. Most of them would ultimately be swallowed up in the system, become the cogs and pistons that kept the brutal, life-destroying machinery going. But maybe one or two . . .

He did envy them their youth, however, because youth gave them an elasticity he no longer felt in himself. And that's my job, he thought: to give them the tools of hope and resiliency that are being taken away from me.

"Let's talk about democracy," he said. "Can anyone give me a definition of it?"

Silence. He surveyed the room. There they sat, unformed pieces of the perennially unsolved human puzzle, shaped by forces beyond their control—genes, environment—and a slew of fantasies cobbled together from song lyrics, videos, movies and television. "Anybody?"

"Everyone living together equally, with the same rights, and able to vote for what they believe in." It was Sean Lewis, a thin, rigidly attentive boy who sat in the back row.

On the first day of school, John-Don had seen a yearning, almost adoring look in Sean Lewis's eyes. He saw it again now. It passed quickly, a shared flash of recognition between outsiders. John-Don suddenly knew that Sean Lewis was gay.

He couldn't acknowledge it, but it snapped him back into focus. I'm here to help you, he thought, but I can't help you. Not in that way.

That was his problem: he always, automatically, without thinking, wanted to help. To save others. That's how he'd been raised. As if he had some kind of superior strength and knowledge.

And look where it had gotten him. He'd extended his hand to help a crying girl in the forest, and it had been his undoing. Now he was the one who needed help.

▾ ▾ ▾

It wasn't the old kind of Queer Corners invitation, an embossed card requesting the pleasure of, or a cheery phone call mixing gossip with party details. All those lovely little civilized touches were gone. Peter called and said in a loud, frantic voice, "Get your ass over here right now!" And they went.

He called Ito, Jay, Cassandra, Wellfleet, and Carolyn Corbett. Instead of Carolyn he got Susan, who hadn't been seen in weeks.

None of the gay men in Queer Corners knew anything about the home life of Carolyn Corbett and Susan Bark. That summer, Cassandra had been the only person invited into Bilitis Cottage. But even she didn't know what was really going on between the dog-trainer and the librarian. And Wellfleet, Caroyn and Susan's closest neighbor, knew even less because he didn't know how to pry.

But there they were, Carolyn and Susan together, one sitting, one standing, in Peter and John-Don's post-modern Mediterranean living room. Susan, flitting about with a nervousness they'd never seen before, looked softer around the edges, almost vulnerable. Maybe it was a family crisis. Everyone knew that she'd gone back to England at least once since her mother died. Or maybe it was some deep-seated problem with Carolyn. Maybe they were on their last legs as a couple. Carolyn, who'd always been so nurturing, now sat like a poker-faced recluse who resented company. It was weird, jarring to see her so stiff and uncommunicative, a skeleton of her former chubby, sympathic self.

Their hosts didn't offer drinks to anyone. When people got together now it wasn't for parties but for emergencies. Cocktails were those delicious concoctions served back in the old days—a year ago—before Delmont died and the Labonnes moved in. Pre-ballot-measure days. Days when life in Queer Corners was quiet, decorous, and slightly soigné. Days when you knew what was happening in your neighbors' lives. All gone. Queer Corners was unraveling, disintegrating before their eyes, turning them all into desperate resistance fighters in their own neighborhood.

"Is Terry coming?" Susan asked.

"We're not talking to that traitor anymore," Jay said brusquely.

"Oh?" Susan raised an eyebrow and looked at Carolyn.

"I'll tell you later," Carolyn said.

"That wretched boy of his," Susan said. "Whatever happened to him?"

"Trashed Terry's house, stole a bunch of things, and disappeared," Cassandra told her.

"Poor dolt." Susan looked across the street at Terry's Mock Tudor. "Of course we all knew nothing good could ever come of that liaison."

Passing time, waiting for the meeting to start. Something awful had happened again, but what was it this time? Peter was pacing in front of the fireplace, exactly the way they'd all seen John-Don do. The top of Peter's nappy, close-cut hair, glinting with tiny silver threads, passed back and forth in the mirror behind the mantelpiece. John-Don sat off to one side, like a nervous contestant on a quiz show, or an anxious prisoner waiting to give his testimony.

"Okay," Peter said, waving his arms, "I called you over because I want you all to know that my lover, John-Don Webster—" he paused and took a deep breath—"has just been accused of raping—"

"—molesting," John-Don corrected him.

"—molesting the Labonne girl."

Shock. Disbelief. Outrage.

"Dove?" Cassandra cried, squirming in her chair.

Susan, obsessive when it came to lineage, wanted to make sure she knew exactly who they were talking about. "Dove Labonne," she repeated, like someone reading a passage from DeBrett's. "Biological daughter of the Labonne woman, a Terwilliger by birth, and the stepdaughter of the Labonne man. Is that correct?"

"The kid is fucking crazy!" Peter shouted. "John-Don tried to help her once—months ago—"

"I didn't even know who she was," John-Don cut in. "I was running in Forest Park, and she was sitting on a log, crying."

"Oh my God!" Cassandra covered her mouth, her eyes gaping. "You're the one she's been talking about!"

"Talking about? What do you mean, talking about?" John-Don demanded, his eyes zooming in on her.

Cassandra, her face burning, skipped a quick glance through the room. Only Carolyn was aware of her relationship with Dove; she hadn't told a soul about the catastrophe with Ron. "I got to know Dove over the summer," she said guardedly. "She was always talking about some man in the woods, but she'd never say who it was or what really happened."

"Well, it was me!" John-Don shouted angrily. "And nothing happened!"

"You're innocent, of course?" Susan sounded almost convinced.

Peter let out a disgusted huff. "Of course he's innocent. This is a frame-up, honey, and we've got to do something about it."

"No." Ito spoke with the assurance of one who'd had time to assess the situation. John-Don had tracked him down that afternoon, in the middle of a meditation session, and poured out the details. He'd broken down and wept as they sat looking into Ito's Zen garden. "We do nothing about it until the girl presses charges. She hasn't done that yet. She may not do it."

"If she does," Peter said, "it's because that fucking asshole tells her to. He's the one behind all this. She's just a pawn."

"We're all pawns," Wellfleet said. "I say it's time for a checkmate."

"We cannot react to what has not yet happened," Ito insisted. "We can only be prepared." And even then, that quiet voice within him said, one cannot be prepared because life never conforms to our mind-made conceptions of it.

"Shoot when the time is right." Wellfleet's head was tingling. Nothing more needed to be said. He'd crossed the line, here in this pleasant living room. Now it was just a matter of when. He began calculating, wondered if he had enough money for one last session at Crackshot, the firing range.

"I've had enough, I've just had fucking enough!" Peter bolted over to the front window to curse and shake his fist at the Labonne house. "I hate you, you fucking pieces of shit! I hope you rot in hell!"

"They are in hell already," Ito murmured sadly.

"Yeah, living with a bunch of faggots around them, I'm sure they are," Peter cried.

"I mean they are loaded with bad karma. It will come back to them. It always does. It will bring them down in the end."

"Is that supposed to comfort us? Ito, I don't give a shit about their fucking karma!" Peter screamed in a disgusted frenzy. "They can take their fucking karma and shove it up—"

"Darling, *please*," Susan said, nervously rubbing the upturned collar of her soft deerskin jacket. "We know it's serious. Sit down before you burst into flames."

Peter turned on her. "I want *them* to burst into flames. Get it? It's their turn to burn! I want to tie them up, douse them with lighter fluid, and flick a Bic right up their asses. But first I want to slice Ron Labonne's nuts off with a Swiss Army knife."

"I want to beat his brains out," Jay said, smacking his fist. "I want to beat him until he looks like boeuf bourgignon in wine sauce."

"Stop!" Susan might have been issuing a sharp command to a dog. "Yes," she said, "the man is beneath contempt, we all know that. They're coarse and demented homophobes, we know that. But really, why put ourselves on the same level? We are still nominally civilized human beings, I hope, even if they're not?"

Peter circled around her. "You haven't been here, Susan darling, you don't know. They're evil, my dear. They're out to get us any way they can. They fired Wellfleet. They gypped Ito out of a big garden commission. They burned a cross on our lawn. They trashed Too-Too. They stole the No on Three fundraising records. They're showing a sick anti-queer video with me in it—"

"You?" Susan said. "What are you doing in it?"

"Dancing," Peter said. "I'm at a Gay Pride Day parade in San Francisco back in the Seventies and I'm dancing on a float."

"I'm afraid I don't understand," Susan said. "It sounds garish, but what's the harm in dancing?"

"When a queer dances, honey, it can only mean one thing: he's having fun. Remember fun? It's what some of us used to have. And to a straight person, queers having fun are dangerous. We're mocking them. Because only straight people are allowed to dance."

Susan was puzzled. "I'm afraid this is all quite beyond me. What does dancing have to do with homosexuality?"

"Nothing! What I'm saying is, this trashy honky across the street won't rest until he chops each and every one of us off at the knees. You and Carolyn are the only ones he hasn't attacked yet, so you'd better be prepared."

"I have to smoke." Carolyn rose and banished herself to the deck, giving John-Don's shoulder a sympathetic squeeze as she passed. She stood outside puffing on a Marlboro and watching them through the open terrace doors.

The maternal, soft-edged, garrulous Earth Mother was gone, but no one knew what had happened to her, where she'd gone, or if she'd ever come back. The new Carolyn had the haunted, almost furtive look of someone battling a secret disease. She'd lost too much weight. With her drawn, sallow face, short black hair, and hollow, dark-ringed eyes, she looked like one of the ghoulish teenagers you saw hanging around, like harbingers of death, down at Pioneer Square.

As John-Don related the facts behind Dove Labonne's terrible allegation, Cassandra felt herself being dragged deeper and deeper into a nightmare. John-Don's nightmare, but hers, too. This accusation Dove was making against John-Don had to be tied up with what happened that night. But how? Was it Dove's malicious way of getting revenge on Cassandra? What was going on in that house? She had to talk to Dove—she had to find out.

"I say we go over there right now and torch the place," Peter was saying.

"Tell me, is that what Delmont would have wanted?" Ito asked.

"Yes!" Peter cried.

"I don't think so," Ito said.

"May I ask a question?" Susan, who'd been watching Carolyn out of a corner of her eye, turned her attention back to the others. "What is happening with the No on Three campaign? There's only six weeks left."

"A big media push starting next week," Ito said. "A huge mailing to all voters. Television ads. Campaigners will be going from house-to-house to talk directly to residents. And a phone bank—campaigners will be calling people throughout the state."

"That's what I told them they should do," John-Don said with irritated surprise.

That was just it, Ito thought: no one likes to be told what to do. A seed must be planted. It will grow in its own time, when the conditions are right. It doesn't grow because you tell it to. John-Don had yet to learn that lesson.

If he knew more about the campaign's direction than even John-Don, it was because Ito had recently, and quite unexpectedly, slipped into the inner ranks of the No on Three hierarchy. He hadn't told this to John-Don. But, as it turned out, Natalie Notale knew of Ito because he'd created a Gertrude Jeckyll knock-off garden for a former lover of hers. Natalie was accessible to Ito because she loved gardening. She listened to Ito's calm, unemotional *suggestions*—political strategems he'd garnered from listening to John-Don.

Soft, well-meaning, recalcitrant John-Don, tortured by his visions of an impossibly perfect world. The person who had stirred Ito's passions and awakened his heart, now sat like a terrified prince looking at the guillotine. There was a terrible, pleading look in John-Don's eyes every time he looked at Ito. *Help me!* Ito wished he could walk over and embrace him. But imposition was not in his nature. Spiritual trials had to be undergone alone. And he was also aware that Peter was keeping a sharp eye on him.

"And then there'll be a big rally, just before the election, down in Pioneer Square," Jay was telling Susan. "Rabbi Mutterperl's going to be one of the speakers."

"And so is my father," Peter said.

"He's really coming?" Jay asked.

"He's really coming." Yes, in the midst of all this, Peter's father was coming to Oregon. Coming to stay with Peter and John-Don. What timing! His parents finally meeting his lover, just when his lover was embroiled in a sordid sex-abuse scandal. Maybe it wouldn't come to that—*please God, don't let it come to that*—but if it did he, Peter, would stand by John-Don's side. He wouldn't hem or haw or apologize to his parents; they'd have to take him and John-Don as they were.

His only fear was that his parents would somehow see their son dancing in that inflammatory ACA video called *Homosexuals on the March*. The damned thing was everywhere, being shipped to churches, schools, and even television stations.

Peter had first seen it when he went out to talk to a Life Issues class at a high school in a small farming community outside of Portland. As part of the No on Three campaign's outreach program, Peter now gave these talks once or twice a week. He addressed civic groups, health classes, and private organizations. Wherever a queer was wanted, he went, answering their antediluvian questions ("Who's the man and who's the woman in a gay relationship?") and calming their irrational fears ("What if a teacher who's gay comes to school wearing a dress?"). The teacher, pro-gay, had been forced by the school's conservative administration to show *Homosexuals on the March* as the "other side" of the issue being discussed.

There, dressed in his Armani suit and tie, in an airless classroom stuck out in the middle of a soybean field, Peter had been horrified to see a clip of himself, younger and hunkier, dancing with wild, raunchy abandon. No one recognized him, but he knew he was there, trapped and condemned to dance forever in a bizarre time-warp created by the ACA. An example of sick behavior. And what infuriated him above and beyond everything else was that the people watching had no idea what that dancing queen had been through in the last twenty years, or how he'd changed.

"John-Don," Jay said abruptly, "do you think any of this is tied up with the Peckerwood thing?"

"How so?"

"It just occurred to me. Look, everyone knew that Labonne was hoping Peckerwood would give an endorsement to the ACA. He hinted at it in the papers. And then this sexual harassment thing blows up. Peckerwood, the family values man, is accused of sexually harassing twenty-two women."

"Twenty-three," Susan said. "Another woman came forward today." What she didn't say was that the twenty-third woman was herself.

Peter was suffused with a sudden, breathless hope. "Okay, what's the connection? Peckerwood pinched the asses of twenty-three women, so what?"

"He did more than that!" Susan was clearly irritated. It wasn't just an annoying tweak on the bum Peckerwood had given her ten years earlier, when she'd briefly lost her mind, turned Republican, and worked for the senator's re-election campaign.

"Okay, okay," Peter said, "but what's Peckerwood got to do with the Labonne girl accusing John-Don of molesting her?"

"Revenge," Jay said. "Damage control. They draw attention away from Peckerwood, because he's associated with the ACA, and then accuse someone who's gay—"

"Gay and highly visible," Wellfleet nodded excitedly.

"—of sexual misconduct. It's all politically motivated."

"I wouldn't put anything past them," John-Don said, "but it still doesn't get me off the hook."

"Such bad karma," Ito murmured. And all because of sex, because people were so out of touch with the natural processes of human desire. Even he, who fatuously thought he'd mastered the art of celibacy, had been attacked by the red-hot arrows of lust, of desire for an impossible sexual union. *Let it go, Ito,* the quiet inner voice whispered to him. Yes, but it wasn't easy.

I could still make a story out of it, Cassandra thought. I could still go public. That had been her plan all along. If she'd gotten Labonne to penetrate her, she'd be telling her story to the papers and selling it to the national tabloids right now: OREGON LESBIAN SEDUCES ANTI-GAY CRUSADER. The plan had blown up in her face, but it was still a story. She could forget about helping or protecting Dove, and tell the papers what actually happened that night. But she knew that Labonne would grind her into the dust if she did. She, after all, had been the seductress. She had said she wasn't sure that she wanted to be a lesbian. There were any number of ways he could get back at her. Cassandra, who'd always thought of herself as brave because she had nothing to lose, was suddenly afraid of losing the nothing she had.

Susan gave Carolyn her secret signal that it was time to go. "John-Don, I don't need to tell you how terribly sorry I am that this has happened." She waited for Carolyn, but Carolyn didn't move from the deck. "You know, of course, that we're there for you. Any way that we can be useful." Another tugging glance at Carolyn, who still didn't move. "If you need us as character witnesses—" She stopped, almost choking on her words. What about my character? she thought. If I'm asked to go public with my Peckerwood story, I open myself up to the same kind of character assassination John-Don is facing.

"Let's hope it doesn't go that far," John-Don said with an exhausted sigh.

"Yes," Ito said, "we can only hope."

There was an uncomfortable moment as Susan rose, tugged at her jacket, and waited for Carolyn to join her. "Coming, darling?" When Carolyn shook her head and said, "Not yet," Susan nodded curtly and left by herself.

Wellfleet, startled out of his dark revery, sat up and said he had to go as well. He peered at John-Don through glasses that magnified the wild look in his eyes. "Don't worry, John-Don. He's going to pay for this."

Jay and Cassandra were next. Cassandra, oddly quiet, gave John-Don a tight, trembling squeeze. Jay, so adept at embracing male bodies he didn't know, was clumsier when it came to showing physical affection for his neighbor. He stood there, his hands on John-Don's shoulders, and then impulsively kissed him. "I feel like we're prisoners of war waiting for liberation day."

Ito, who'd spent part of his childhood as a prisoner of war, sat quietly, his head bowed, as the others disappeared. He kept sneaking glances at John-Don. Would John-Don survive this? Would it lead him to a new place? Was Peter, so frantically protective, the best person for him now?

Let go of your attachment, the voice whispered. Now, when it is hardest, you must leave him to sort out his own fate.

He rose and solemnly shook their hands. "Goodbye, John-Don. Good night, Peter."

Carolyn remained out on the deck until everyone else had gone. Twilight had turned to dusk as she stood out there. Darkness flowed into the house. She was a shadow within it.

The three of them silently looked at one another.

"You'll be all right," Carolyn murmured.

Peter let out an anxious, barely audible moan.

"Carolyn," John-Don said, "are *you* all right?"

"The Goddess moves in mysterious ways," she said. She put on her dark glasses and slipped out the door.

CHAPTER 31

ON A WARM SATURDAY AFTERNOON IN MID-OCTOBER, CAROLYN picked up the telephone, called ACA headquarters, and asked to speak to Ron Labonne. She was told that Mr. Labonne was unavailable.

"Tell him it's Feather," she said. "He'll be available."

And he was. Carolyn kept her voice flat and unemotional. She said she wanted to see him. Labonne said no. She demanded to see him. Labonne dismissed her with a condescending laugh.

"Do you remember this?" She repeated the Bruderschaft's secret motto: "Spill the blood and cleanse the world."

In the silence that followed she could almost hear his brain ticking.

"Should I go to your house on Skyview Boulevard?" she asked. "I know right where it is."

"No!" A moment to consider. "Come here. It has to be here."

On his turf. Where he felt strongest. She agreed.

Next she dialed Susan's private extension at Windy Hills Kennel. When Susan picked up, Carolyn said, "I'm going out there to see him."

"What?" Susan gasped. "When?"

"Now."

"Darling, you can't! I absolutely won't let you! It's not safe!"

"I'm going, Susan. I just wanted to let you know, in case—"

"In case what?" Susan shrilled. "Wait until I come back. I'll go with you. I'll leave this instant."

"No. It has to be just me and him."

"Carolyn, you can't go alone," Susan cried. "There's no telling what he'll do."

"Don't worry. I'll see you later."

She hung up. A moment later the phone rang again. As Susan's voice came through the answering machine, imploring her to wait, to reconsider, not to go, Carolyn locked the door of Bilitis Cottage. She looked up at cirrus clouds in a dry blue sky. She got into her mustard-colored Volvo, backed down Santavista Terrace, and drove towards her showdown with the father of her child.

Terry Terwilliger, fragile and forlorn behind the wheel of his Mercedes, turned up Skyview just as Carolyn was turning onto Burnside. She noticed the new campaign sticker—"Equal Rights are Not Special Rights"—on his front bumper and double-honked a brief acknowledgement. Queer Corners called Terry a traitor. He had collaborated with the enemy. What would they call *her* when her secret connection to Ron Labonne came to light?

The penalties of silence.

As she sputtered down Burnside, dirty sparkplugs misfiring, Carolyn tried to calm her mounting anxiety. I am the Goddess, I am the Goddess, she chanted to herself. He might think he's almighty, omnipotent Zeus, but I am Hera, his equal, thundering through the heavens in my chariot pulled by six golden rams and full of a goddess-fury that will turn his blood to water.

She passed the spot where she'd stopped her car during the hailstorm and told Lester to get in. The place of that first unwitting encounter with her son was now enshrined in her memory, sacred, numinous with secret meaning. For seventeen years the ghost of a desperate mother had been trapped inside her, filling her head with its tormented moans: "My child is lost! I abandoned my piece of the creation, I left my son to a terrible fate! I'll never see my baby again!" But there, on Burnside Avenue in Portland, Oregon, they'd found one another. It was a sign. The Goddess was directing her towards the missing pieces of her soul. It was up to Carolyn to fit the pieces together and make herself whole.

Waiting for the light at 23rd, she lit a cigarette and looked down the street towards Too-Too. Jay was standing outside, arms crossed, face raised to the afternoon sun. Jay, who'd been through his own hell, had reached a place where he could relish a moment of warmth again. She wondered if she ever would. She'd incarcerated herself for so long that the idea of freely stepping outside, to plant bulbs or cut flowers or take Lady Caroline for a leisurely stroll, now seemed unimaginable.

And there was Sissy Parker, the realtor, waddling into Sarah Sue Seagull Realty with a Starbucks pastry bag in one hand and a heavy briefcase in the other. Carolyn squinted to see the decal on Sissy's briefcase: Hate is NOT a Family Value.

Yes, it is, Carolyn thought. Sorry, sweetie. That's where it all springs from. The love and the hate.

She headed down Alder and parked in a garage near the rental-car agency. The old renegade Carolyn, the woman who'd spent years covering her tracks, looking over her shoulder, erasing one personality and assuming another, didn't want Labonne to know what her real car looked like or to see her license plates.

Waiting for her cheap subcompact to be brought out, she glanced through the windows of Senator Peckerwood's re-election headquarters across the street. Saw the Republican campaign workers bravely pimping for their candidate.

The revered Senator Peckerwood was now confronting his hidden past and battling to maintain his political future. "He backed me up against a desk," Susan had told her. "His hands were all over me, clutching, clawing at my breasts. He was drunk. He grabbed my neck and forced his tongue into my mouth."

"Your car's ready, Miss Corbett."

Susan's frightened voice kept nagging at her as she hummed down Macadam Boulevard in a weird-smelling Mitsubishi: "You can't go alone. There's no telling what he'll do."

Very true. But there was no telling what she might do either. And here she was, on Military Road, turning up the driveway towards ACA headquarters.

▼ ▼ ▼

The grandmotherly woman guarding a makeshift reception desk in the foyer narrowed her puffy eyes, gobbling up the sight of the slender short-haired woman dressed entirely in black and wearing large dark glasses standing before her. "Y'ave'n appointment?"

Carolyn nodded.

"'Cause Mr. Labonne's a real busy man."

"He's expecting me," Carolyn said.

"Everyone's at church getting ready for the big rally tonight so I gotta do everything myself," the woman grumbled, hoisting herself up and painfully lumbering away. Her swollen feet, crammed into high heels, ballooned out like bread dough. She hobbled back to ask, "What's your name?"

"Tell him it's Feather."

"Heather?"

"Feather," Carolyn said sharply.

"Never heard that name before." A minute later, panting with curiosity, she told Carolyn she could go in. "Gonna be just the two of you, though," she wheezed. "He told me to go help set up the rally so I'm leaving."

Just the two of us, Carolyn thought. The tight ball in her stomach began to throb. "There's no one else around?"

"Unh-unh. Well, Mrs. Hill, upstairs. She's here, but she ain't all here, if you know what I mean." The woman tapped her head. "She's sort of been put away, if you know what I mean." She lowered her voice to a confidential whisper. "Makes trouble. Tries to run away. You know. *Crazy.*"

▼ ▼ ▼

Ron Labonne was sitting in a grandiose paneled library, behind a massive wooden desk. Composed, waiting, hands clasped, eyes riveted on her.

Carolyn, hidden behind her dark glasses, forced herself to look at the man she'd known as Corporal Eagle. Older, losing his hair, his body thick where once it had been lean. The youthful revolutionary had eased himself into the flabby comforts of the flesh. His mouth, following the lines of a drooping mustache, was turned down in a resentful grimace, like a baby nursing on sour milk. His bullish neck swelled from a too-tight collar. Hard to believe that she'd once found that coarse, pitted face attractive. For no reason other than that it was male and looked her way.

One thing struck her immediately: there was no love in him. There never had been. That vital instinct was missing. Flat self-absorbed eyes that took no pleasure in what they saw. Eyes that hunted, reducing their intake of vision to see only what they wanted to see. For a moment Carolyn almost pitied him. She saw a starving man who had never been asked to the table. He'd finally grabbed his piece of the pie, but there was no nourishment in it.

She stood, he sat, the chasm between them echoing with silence. Behind him, through the library windows, she could see the dusty grounds of the estate. A barren, rocky field, plowed up but left unplanted. Something stood in the middle of it. A scarecrow? She squinted. A cross.

"So," he finally said, slowly looking her up and down. "Eighteen years later."

Carolyn stiffened under his gaze. It was exactly how she'd felt when he first looked at her. The same fear, based on old insecurities. Back then she'd hoped that he'd see through her overweight, unattractive shell to the angry sexy daredevil hidden inside. He had, and as a reward she'd let him lead her into a world of lost souls. Not this time.

"Don't think I'm taking you back," he said abruptly.

The presumption took her breath away. "What?"

"Not after what you did."

Protecting himself by trying to shame me, Carolyn thought. Heaving the guilt onto my shoulders. Guilt had always been the best way to make her heel. That and fear of pain. "I don't want to come back to you," she said. "That's the last thing I want."

He spoke without listening, as if he'd carefully rehearsed in advance what he was going to say. "And don't think I'm ever gonna let you see him, either."

"Who? Lester?"

His face twitched.

Every move felt stiff, unnatural. Carolyn forced herself to sit down, to take her place at the bargaining table.

His eyes were like rifle sights trained on her across the desk. "You're hiding him. Where?"

A small flare of relief: Lester hadn't informed on her. "Lester's eighteen. He can go where he wants to. There's nothing you can do about it."

"There's plenty I can do about it," he said.

"Oh? There are things I can do, too."

He cocked his head. "How'd you find him?"

She didn't answer.

"He's my son, not yours. You gave up any rights to him when you ran off."

"I didn't run off. I escaped."

"You can call it whatever you want," he said, raising his voice, "but the truth is you ran off and left him. What kind of a woman abandons her own flesh and blood?"

The haranguing tones of her own conscience. "I was going to take him with me. I couldn't."

"Because you knew you'd be a bad mother."

"No. Because they'd posted you as a guard." To prevent desperate cult-mothers like herself from snatching their own babies. All part of the bizarre, nihilistic system the Bruderschaft developed to keep love, or any form of humanizing tenderness, from distracting cult members from their true task—to obey orders.

"You're a liar," he said.

"We'll see who the liar is."

"All those drugs you used to take " He shook his head. "Even when you were pregnant. I suppose you've seen the effect they've had on Lester."

"What I've seen," she said, "is the effect you had on him."

"I kept asking myself, What kind of woman cares so little for human life that she poisons her own son with drugs and then runs off and leaves him?"

"What kind of man beats his son, breaks his arm, makes him stand outside barefoot in the freezing cold?"

"Did he tell you that?" Another sad shake of the head.

"Were you punishing him or were you punishing me?"

"Of course you're so guilt-ridden you'd believe everything he told you."

"If I'd known how you were going to treat him," Carolyn said, "I would've killed you, just to get him away."

"You would have killed me, huh?" Labonne leaned back, nodding vigorously, tugging at his shirtcuffs, craning his neck up from the confines of his collar. Beads of perspiration glinted on his brow.

It was then that Carolyn noticed the gray aspirin-sized button affixed to a front corner of his desk. Almost inconspicuous. A microphone.

"You still want to kill me?" He opened a drawer, pulled out a small revolver, and slid it across the table.

She looked at it, her heart cramped and pounding. The fear behind all the other fears. The instrument of death, passively waiting for the hand that would give meaning to its existence. Ignore it, she thought. Don't give him the satisfaction of seeing you react.

He let out a hollow laugh. "Maybe it's just my money you want."

"You've never had any money. Except what you conned out of other people."

"I don't know what you're talking about."

She leaned closer to the microphone. "Oh yes you do. You were a corporal in the Bruderschaft. A paramilitary cult dedicated to overthrowing the American government. You needed guns and bombs. So you siphoned off money from me and everyone else who was stupid enough to believe you. And then you got us to get money from our parents."

He glanced down at the microphone. "Delusional. Always were. Thought people were out to get you."

"And you didn't?"

"No one's out to get me," he said. "Only a paranoid schizophrenic thinks that way."

"Then why did you build the compound? Why did you stockpile it with guns? Why do keep a gun here?"

His eyes narrowed. "Thieves."

"Do you remember the Great Plan, Corporal Eagle? Bomb federal buildings. Kidnap officials. Bring the government to its knees. Get rid of everyone who—"

He cut her off. "You show up after eighteen years and have the gall to sit there accusing me of imaginary crimes?"

"'Shed the blood and cleanse the world,' isn't that what we had to shout a hundred times a day?"

The facial twitch, a flicker of vulnerability before his features stiffened into an impenetrable mask. She saw one of his hands reach surreptitiously under the desk. Turning off what he didn't want to hear? Well, he'd hear it anyway. She wasn't going to stop now, not even with a gun on the table. He could pick it up and fire a bullet into her heart. It would be the end of her, but it would be the end of him, too, and that in itself would be a triumph.

"And you're still shouting that, aren't you?" she said. "Only now you've made yourself into the Chief Commando. So you can be the one who decides who lives and who dies."

"You're sick," he groaned.

"Oh, Great One," she mocked. "Oh, Voice of Truth. Finally found your platform. Finally found people gullible enough to believe your lies."

"Get out of here—now."

"Why? Are you afraid of me? Or what I might do to your new image?"

Again his face twitched. He stared at her. Then he let out a nervous grunt of contempt. "You should be locked up."

"I think it's the other way around."

"Coming here and threatening me—"

"I haven't threatened you." But her mere presence was a threat, and she knew it. She could topple the sick little empire he'd built for himself, and he knew that.

"Trying to make me pay for your sins," he said.

"My sins?"

"Oh, I get it. You've conveniently forgiven yourself. See yourself as a helpless victim."

"I was a victim. I'm not proud of it."

"I hear the voice of a sobbing feminist. 'Nothing's my fault. I'm not responsible for my actions.'"

His mocking, dismissive tone sparked into her. "I've paid every day of my life for what I did. For what I let you do to me."

"Boo hoo," he cried in a derisive falsetto whimper.

"Don't think you can sit there on your throne, like some fucking plaster saint, and intimidate me! I don't take that shit, from you or anyone. I'm not in your cult anymore."

"Cult? What cult?"

"Yes, what are your adoring followers going to think when they find out about that?"

"About what?"

"About the Bruderschaft," she cried. "I can tell them everything that went on inside that compound. The drugs, the brain-washing, the forced sex."

It all seemed to glance off him like rubber darts. "I don't know what you're talking about."

"You're a liar. You might be Ron Labonne now—Ron the Good, what a joke!—but I know who you really are. Corporal Eagle. A neo-Nazi hiding in a cheap new suit."

He leaned forward. "And I know who you are, Carolyn Corbett. Or are you still Wanda Bryce? No, she became Deborah Johnson. That was before Debby became Mary Higgins." He grinned, but his eyes were as hard as steel. "People don't believe prostitutes, you know. Especially one with as many aliases as you've had."

Goddess protect me, Carolyn prayed, the sweat trickling down her back and between her breasts. The air was stifling. All the windows were closed. The light was being sucked out of the sky. She couldn't focus on anything in the room. She looked outside, at the cross. A grotesque focal point, propped up like a dead tree on Gethsemane.

"Did you tell my son about your past history?" Labonne asked. "Maybe that's how you met him. He likes prostitutes."

Don't crack, baby, you're in the arms of the Goddess. She's telling you not to freak. This is information, that's all it is. It's what he'll use against you. At least you know.

"Did you really think you could get away?" he asked. "They had people watching you all the time. Tracking you. They still do."

"You're trying to frighten me," she said.

"Am I?" He sat back in his chair, studying her. "The moment you say one word about the Bruderschaft, Carolyn Corbett, you're dead."

She couldn't speak. She wanted to cry out. Eyed the gun. Bliss, bliss to blow his brains out. But that would be a victory for him. She felt something give way inside her. Choked as a brutal, suffocating pain grabbed her throat and seized her bowels. Lightheaded, ready to do anything.

"You owe your life to me!" Labonne suddenly shouted, banging his fist on the desk. "You will do what I say!"

She hadn't heard those words for eighteen years. Commands to obey had been hammered into her consciousness during the Bruderschaft's brutal "Mental Restructuring" sessions. Carolyn clutched the chair, steeling herself for takeoff. Moaned as the old dizzying terror revved through her body. Goddess, help me! *I want to kill him.* The same fearful desperation of the Carolyn who'd lived like an animal, running from hole to hole under cover of night. No, she wouldn't do that anymore. That Carolyn was so far away from the woman, the spirit, the Goddess inhabiting her body now. But she could still feel her, that old Carolyn, buried, fighting for breath, thrashing with tormented frenzy as she clawed her way up from the airless depths where she'd been hidden away like a madwoman. Carolyn let her come. She took into her heart the cowering, miserable creature she'd once been, embraced her, absorbed her pain, opened her mouth to let her speak at last.

The sound was like nothing she'd ever heard before. It gushed out of her in a harsh, scalding torrent, burning her throat, vibrating in her teeth. A terrifying wordless roar that literally pinned him to his chair.

And then it was gone. Expelled, aborted, released.

Ron Labonne turned pale. Gulped.

Carolyn couldn't help herself. Began to laugh, dizzy with relief. Another transcendence. As she laughed, the suffocating girdle of fear cinched around her for so long suddenly snapped open like a ripe coccoon. She emerged, as she was, as she'd waited so long to be.

"What's so funny?" he croaked, smoothing his hair.

"You are." She had slipped out of his grasp and he knew it. Now he was afraid of her. "Mr. God," she snorted. "Yahweh the Avenger. Tell me, how is Mrs. Yahweh? Is she the one who's going to save you now?"

"Leave my wife out of this."

"And how is Miss Yahweh, her lying daughter?"

"God help me, if you—"

"If I what?"

He didn't answer.

"God won't help you, Corporal Eagle, but maybe I will."

"I don't accept help from Satan."

"You are so unbelievably pathetic," she said, shaking her head. "You don't believe any of it, do you?"

He pressed himself back in his big chair.

"You don't give a damn about God or family. But it's the only way you can get anyone to listen to you."

"Plenty of people listen to me."

"Only fools listen to fools. Once they know how cynical you really are, how you've been lying to them—"

"Are you laughing at my faith in Christ?"

"Why not? It's a joke, isn't it?"

He leaned across the desk. "You think you know me, Carolyn Corbett, but you don't." His voice was thick with a mysterious fervor. "The person you knew is dead. He's been washed clean."

She saw movement outside. An elderly woman wearing a dirty blue housecoat was shuffling past the window, so close that Carolyn could see the thin, floating wisps of her yellow-white hair. She looked fiercely determined, as if it took every last ounce of her strength and willpower to totter forward. Pausing for a moment, the old woman stiffly turned to stare into the room. When she saw Labonne sitting in the leather chair her expression changed. Carolyn blinked in astonishment as she watched the transformation from kindly old woman to furious witch. Labonne was entirely unaware that just a few feet away an old, wrinkled woman was glaring at him with such wrathful intensity and silently screaming what appeared to be obscenities. Her watery eyes darted over to Carolyn, who sat transfixed by the spectacle. The toothless mouth rose in a terrible, mocking grin. And then she was gone. The Goddess, Carolyn thought, giving me the green light. She quickly shifted her attention back to Labonne.

"He's dead," Labonne was saying. "The man I was is dead. He's been reborn."

Carolyn shook her head. "He's not dead. He's just hiding." She slid forward in her chair. "And I'm going to tell everyone where he is and who he was."

"No, you won't," he snapped. "Because if you do, I'll make your life hell."

"You've already done that."

"Not the way I could now."

He knows his fate is in my hands, she thought. "Someone has to put a stop to you."

"Oh, they've tried. Everyone's tried. Because everyone's afraid of the truth."

"You're not the truth."

"God is the truth," he said. "I am His instrument."

"Your God is a pissed-off loser, just like you."

"Satan's plugged your ears," he cried. "You've always been possessed by him!"

His eyes told her to be careful. He was past redemption. And yet she wanted to fight, to pay him back for robbing her of her life and Lester of his. She wanted to grind his face in the filth of his own hatred. Wanted, like an avenging deity, to rip away his sanctimonious mask and force him to confront the rabid animal snarling behind it. "I'm going to ruin you," she said.

He looked like a bull when it realizes it's about to be slaughtered. His eyes bulged and rolled in their sockets. He twisted in his chair. "Satan told you to come here," he gabbled, plucking at his collar. "But I don't listen to Satan. I fight him."

"You're the Satan. And everyone's going to know it."

"God will punish those who stand in my way," he warned. "I'm fighting for the soul of my country!"

She laughed in his face. "Don't hand me any of your patriotic bullshit. I know your past, remember?" She made a tentative motion to leave.

"Listen," he said, dropping suddenly to his knees, his voice plaintive, "listen, we're so close. I'm so close. I've worked so hard. I've repented. I've prayed." He crawled around the side of the desk, his face red, dripping with sweat. "You've got to believe me. I'm not the man I was. I've changed, I've seen the light. I've put the past behind me. I'm looking to the future."

She rose and backed away, heart racing, as he slowly crawled towards her like a cumbersome amputee, his hands clasped, an anguished expression on his face. She heard a faint sound—a doorbell?—chiming in the distance. Who was it? The old woman?

"I won't let you destroy me," he panted. "If you destroy me you destroy God's plan."

"No," she said, "I destroy your plan."

"My plan is God's plan. Don't you see? No, Satan won't let you see. He guides you. He plants suggestions in your mind. Don't listen to him, Carolyn. Cast him out."

"That's exactly what I'm doing."

"Join me," he pleaded. "Join me. Now. Get down on your knees. Show your humility. Pray with me and I'll forgive you. Pray for Him to take the evil lodged in your heart and—"

Carolyn sucked in a startled breath. Susan was peering in through the library windows. Their eyes met. Susan looked down and saw Labonne on his knees. Her face blazed with alarm. She mouthed something to Carolyn.

"Say His name," Labonne implored, his arms raised. "Say it. Open your heart. Let Him in. He will forgive you as He's forgiven me."

Nails had been driven into her feet. She stood, unable to move, terrified that he'd see Susan. She shook her head: no, no, go away. But Susan rapped sharply on the window.

It all happened in one brief, terrifying moment. Labonne turned and saw Susan. Carolyn darted for the door. He lunged and pulled her back by the shoulders. She fell with a breathless grunt. He spun back towards the desk, grabbed the gun, aimed at the window.

"No!" All she could think of was Susan. She leapt on his back, pulling him down as he fired. A sharp crack. She gave a cry as they hit the floor. The weight of his body knocked the wind from her.

He scrambled clumsily to his feet. Stood over her, chest heaving, face twisted into an expression so naked in its desolate, disconnected cruelty that Carolyn couldn't bear to look. Man in all his glory. Fighting for breath, eyes squeezed tight, she drew herself into a fetal position and waited for the bullet that would end this round of her existence.

Another sound. The loud whining sputter of a motor. A grinding of gears. The floorboards shook as Labonne ran across the room. Carolyn opened her eyes, saw him staring out the window in disbelief.

"Goddamn her! How did that crazy bitch get out?" He slapped his forehead, moaned, turned in circles. "Shit, shit, shit!" He ran back to Carolyn, his face blazing, and pointed his finger at her. "You—you—" The sound of the motor grew louder. He darted back to the window. "Oh, fucking Christ."

He raced past Carolyn, flung open the door and slammed it behind him. She heard a key turn in the lock, then his lumbering footsteps pounding down the hallway.

Carolyn hoisted herself to her feet. Staggered towards the window. Where was Susan? Had he gone after her?

She couldn't register what she saw. It looked like an absurd dream. An old woman in a blue housecoat, bumping across the plowed-up grounds on a golf cart. Ron Labonne chasing after her.

Carolyn pulled herself together. Started for the door. Stopped. Went back to the desk and pulled open the drawer. The recorder was no longer running. Shit. But there had to be something on it. She yanked it free. Heard banging on the front door. She rattled and pulled on the library door. Locked. Don't freak. Escape. She ran for the tall library windows, cranked one open, hoisted herself up to the sill, and jumped down to the brick pavement. Ran around the house. Saw Susan banging frantically on the door.

"Darling! Darling!" Susan cried when she saw her. "What's he done to you?"

"Got to get out of here," Carolyn gasped, panting for breath. "Fast."

Carolyn raced towards the Mitsubishi. Susan raced for the Land Rover. Ron Labonne raced towards Mrs. Hill, who was jolting across her desecrated garden, headed straight towards the cross.

CHAPTER 32

"DOVE? HONEY? ARE YOU ALL RIGHT?" CORNETTE TAPPED A LONG PINK fingernail on the locked door of the ladies' room. The door was hollow, so flimsy she could have tapped right through it, like a woodpecker, if she'd wanted.

Cheap, she thought. Not like the luxurious Green Room in Dallas, scene of her recent triumph. The basement of the Foursquare Pentecostal Meeting Hall was as damp, dark and chilly as a tomb. With surfaces you couldn't quite see and certainly didn't want to touch. Glistening, snotlike streams of water oozed out from the concrete blocks, adding a musty odor of decay to the narrow hallway.

"Dove? You're not throwing up again, are you?" Cornette carefully lifted her sideflip and put her ear close to the door, listening for telltale signs of retching. "It's just stage fright, honey. I've been through it myself. Just be careful not to get any puke stains on that pretty white dress."

Still no response. The crowd upstairs was getting restless. Cornette could hear their bouncing, shifting impatience through the plywood floor. Mimi Strang, smart girl, was leading the choir through a reprise of "His Pain, Your Gain."

Everything was ready. The cameras were set up. The stage was decorated. She'd pleaded with Helen Hill to make it as pretty as possible, lots of flowers, extra lights, to show off Dove. Helen was getting cheaper by the day, pressuring Cornette and Ron for a "big return" on all the money she'd sunk into the campaign. She hadn't turned off the cash-faucet yet, but that suspicious, cheated look in her eyes was hardly reassuring.

Where on earth was Ron? Here it was, the biggest night of his life, and he was late! Well, she was an old show-biz veteran. She'd worked crowds long before Ron appeared on the scene. She knew what they wanted. She'd been a star at the conference in Texas.

"Dove? I'm starting to get worried, honey." She scratched on the door. "We should be up there." Cornette leaned closer. It was so dark that she misjudged the length of her eyelashes and with a tingle of alarm suddenly realized that they were stuck, like velcro, to the door's rough, unsanded surface. She couldn't close her eyes. "Oh Lord." With her fingernails she gently tweezed the lashes free, then groped through her purse for a mirror, to assess the damage.

▼ ▼ ▼

There was no mirror in the bathroom, so Dove had been staring at herself in the aluminum toilet-paper cover. A distorted fun-house image. She was supposed to be so pretty, so beautiful, but what she saw was a monster with a long chin, bulbous forehead and two frightened blue eyes. A freakish space alien wearing a big floppy white bow in its hair.

She heard her mother scratching on the door. An animal sound. Let me in. "Dove? I want you to open this door, right now."

She could still do it, the way they wanted. She had it all in her head. Her mom had coached her. "Now first you affirm your faith in Jesus. Use the Scripture, honey, and I mean use it. Say it like you mean it, like it's coming to you in a divine revelation. You'll feel self-conscious at first, with all those people staring at you, but use them, too. Take them with you on your journey to the Lord. The more you give to them, the more they'll give back to you. They want to believe you, remember that."

That was the worst part. They wanted to believe her. They would believe her. All she had to do was say what wasn't true.

"There'll be a moment when you'll feel them with you," her mom had said. "Sort of a melting feeling. That's when you know it's time to witness. That's when you begin to tell your story."

Her story. The terrible story she'd made up in a gibbering panic to pacify Ron, to divert his attention, to draw off the terrifying rage that was directed towards her because she'd caught him with Cassandra.

"Draw them in," her mom had said. "They're on your side. Let them feel your pain and confusion. An innocent young girl, looking for her lost dog in the forest. And then he approaches you. Someone you trust, a teacher from the high school, your neighbor from right across the street. You have no idea what he's after. No idea that he's a vicious homosexual looking for young children to prey on."

It was so awful, that bargain she'd struck with Ron out in the back yard. Promising she'd never breathe a word of what she'd seen. "I won't tell, I won't tell, I didn't see anything, and I know something else, too, something about that homosexual man across the street." She could still hear her squeaking, breathless voice, babbling out what she knew Ron wanted to hear. And she could still feel the strange and sudden sense of wrongness, that bleak awareness that she was lying about someone else in order to save her own skin. But she was so afraid of Ron she would have done or said anything to keep him away. He had her by the hair. His eyes were crazier than Lester's. He was panting with rage.

"What do you know?" he said, giving her a shake. "And don't lie to me."

She couldn't breathe right, couldn't think of what to say. "He—he—tried to—tried to—get me." Like Lester, like the ghost, like Ron himself. They were all trying to get her.

"Get you? What d'you mean? Tried to molest you?"

She nodded so fast it felt like her head had become unglued.

He'd clamped his hand around her neck and directed her into the house, moving her as if she were a doll. He'd kept his eyes on her the rest of the night, crushing her into submission. Once she'd made up the story, he refined it, putting words in her mouth.

"That's how you're going to tell it to your mother," he said. Yes yes yes, she nodded. "And that's how you're going to tell it in public." Yes yes yes. Not knowing that this was the public he had in mind. "And if you ever so much as breathe a word about what you saw tonight—" Yes yes yes, she knew what would happen if she told the truth.

▼ ▼ ▼

Wellfleet pulled up on a side street three blocks from the church. He never came to suburbia and now he knew why. There were no people on the streets because there were no sidewalks. Every house looked exactly the same. He could see the flicker of television sets. The orange light of the street lamps made everything look desolate and unreal.

It was dangerous to have an identity in a place so grotesquely anonymous. What if someone saw his anti-ACA bumper stickers? He drove on until he found a dark place under a willow tree away from the glare of the street lights.

He hid the spray paint under his jacket and obsessively felt in his pockets one last time. Fingers reassured by the familiar shapes of the knife and the gun, he set off down the street. He was accustomed to city blocks. Here the streets wound one into another with no discernable grid or pattern.

▼ ▼ ▼

"Dove!" Her mother rapped sharply on the door. "I'm going to count to ten, young lady. One . . . two . . . "

Her poor mom. It was so hard to even look at her. Because her mom didn't know what a sucker she was! Dove longed to tell her what she'd seen, but couldn't. Ron was always there, looking over her mom's shoulder. And Dove felt so sorry for her. Her mom was outraged by the story, believed it all. Wanted to go to the police immediately. Couldn't understand Ron's reluctance.

"Listen," he'd said, "this is what we've been waiting for. It has to be timed perfectly."

"Timed? Ron, my poor baby's been assaulted! I want the police to know about it right now."

They'd argued about it. Her mom had finally seen the value of waiting. Ron convinced her, although she sounded more exhausted than convinced when she finally told Dove. "Honey, we are going to tell your story. But we're going to use it to make a point. People have been calling us liars. Saying we don't tell the truth about homosexuals. So we're going to have you come to the rally. And you're going to stand up there, in front of the news cameras and reporters, and you're going to tell them exactly what that vicious pervert did to you."

While Dove sunk into catatonia, unable to eat, speak, or sleep, Cornette busied herself with the preparations for her daughter's "debut with Jesus." She bought yards of white taffeta and sewed up a long, stiff, weird-looking dress that made Dove look like a bride doll. "Oh honey," she said excitedly, "you're going to be so pretty up there, a picture of innocence. And we're going to be there right beside you, Daddy and Mommy, praying right along with you."

"Five . . . " Cornette said on the other side of the door.

▼ ▼ ▼

Wellfleet approached the church. It was a large rectangular hall with plywood siding and surrounded by cars. Inside they were singing. He recognized the tune: "His Pain, Your Gain."

He kept his head down as he skulked through the dark parking lot looking for the red Cadillac. Found it next to the ACA van. There was no one in sight. He ducked down, pulled out the knife, and plunged it into the tires of both vehicles. The air hissed out, the cars sank to their rims. Wellfleet peeked up, lightheaded and perspiring. Still no one. They'd launched into another hymn tune.

He ducked down again and began shaking the can of spray paint. Flipped off the lid. Started near the rear fin of the Cadillac and moved forward, forming large dripping letters. He sprayed ACA QUEER KILLERS on one side and WE ARE ACA LIARS on the other. On both sides of the van he sprayed ACA HATEMOBILE.

When he'd finished he wiped the paint canister and his sticky fingers with a handkerchief. His legs were stiff and aching as he loped across the street and and dropped the paint canister into an open trash bin beside a gas station. Then, his hand pressed to the gun in his pocket, he slowly walked back and entered the crowded suburban church hall.

▼ ▼ ▼

Dove banged her forehead against the wall, trying to make her mind shut up. If only Cassandra hadn't snuck into the house that day, just moments after her mom and Ron had left for an emergency meeting at ACA headquarters. Cassandra, suddenly there in *her* house, walking into *her* bedroom, saying, "Dove, I know you're lying."

Dove pulled the covers up over her head. Cassandra tore them away. "Dove, you can't do this. I won't let you." Shouting, making Dove listen to her, even though she had her hands clamped over her ears. "You can hate me, that's all right, you can say whatever you want about me, but you can't tell lies about John-Don Webster. You can't do that, Dove. You'd be destroying an innocent man. You'd be lying."

"Eight . . . " Her mom, on the other side of the bathroom door, had slowed down her counting and was starting to sound angry.

Cassandra's presence, her voice, had shaken Dove out of her numbed, guilt-ridden stupor. She was sucked, kicking and screaming, into a tornado so violent that she felt the Devil himself was behind it. She flew at Cassandra, flailing her arms, striking out, pummeling her, calling her every terrible name she could think of. Was caught. Held tight. Whispered to. Soothed. How long had it been since anyone had held her? Dove found herself clinging tight to the one friend she hated most in the world.

"Ten."

▼ ▼ ▼

The door opened. Cornette, through the scrim of her eyelashes, appraised her daughter. Wan, a little woozy looking. She straightened the white bow in Dove's hair. Plucked and brushed at the bodice of the white dress. "It's just stage fright, honey," she whispered, stroking Dove's face. "You've got to face it. Jesus will help you."

"Is he here?" Dove mumbled.

"Jesus? Why yes, He's here. Can't you feel Him?"

"No, *Ron*."

"Ron's been delayed. Don't ask me why, I don't know why. But we're here, the cameras are here, the reporters are here, and there's a huge roomful of people just waiting to hear you speak out. To tell the truth. So let's go." She took Dove by the elbow and steered her down the cold, dark, dank hallway.

▼ ▼ ▼

Wellfleet, cushioning the gun in his coat pocket, slipped like a nervous shadow through the crowd at the back of the hall. Mimi Strang, the malicious little bitch, was leading a choir through her favorite piece of drivel. The clear, juicy soprano of Tina Pedersen, floating through the hall, pierced Wellfleet to the quick. All that might have been!

Behind the earnest faces and excited smiles Wellfleet saw a group gathered to put an end to him. United in their determination to eradicate what they refused to recognize. Waiting for the leader who would guide them towards the victory they craved.

What he saw was the world he'd grown up in. Working-class America. Simple, direct, hardworking people eternally cheated out of the respect, decency, and rewards they felt were their due. White, God-fearing immigrant stock. Their parents and grandparents had come as strangers to the Promised Land and here they were, generations later, still strangers, still waiting for the promise to materialize.

The America they'd believed in didn't believe in them. It laughed at their values, robbed them of their hard-earned money, and rewarded the swindling irresponsible thievery of others. It revoked their employment benefits, made health care a luxury, taxed them to death, fired them before they could collect a pension. It wouldn't let their kids pray or salute the flag in school. After siphoning off all meaning and comfort from their lives it spat them out into a wilderness filled with other lost, disconnected souls.

Wellfleet understood all too well. They were angry. But oh, so was he. He was one of them. But he was queer, so he would never be one of them. They couldn't point their finger at the real culprits—they might end up pointing at themselves—so they found him, the one who had the least, the one who was and always had been the most vulnerable because no one would ever stick up for a queer.

Oh yes, he could see them massing for their triumphal march down the main streets and past the strip malls of America. An army of the disenfranchised, goosestepping past their beloved franchises—fast-food joints, giant supermarkets, home-handyman stores, video chains. A suburban jihad gathering strength as it passed tract homes, trailer parks, gas stations, and jerry-built churches on its way to the wicked city and the wicked people who must be conquered and punished. A groundswell of resentment that turned lunatics into visionary leaders and pissed-off losers into political heroes.

The assassination of this particular leader would be an historic event. The crowning achievement of Wellfleet's otherwise worthless life. If he could just hold on to his resolve. Not falter, not be blindsided by the doubts and fears that were crowding in to distract him from his mission.

In the front row he could see the elite corps of oppressors, seated and chatting affably with one another. Willard Lansgaard, the president of the college, Fletcher Davis, head of the music department, various teachers and board members. They were in for a nice unpleasant surprise. When their leader toppled forward in a gushing pool of blood and they looked around in panic, who would they see? None other than Wellfleet Stipple, the mousy musical little queer whose livelihood they'd taken away.

▼ ▼ ▼

The choir stopped singing. The restless crowd began clapping and whistling as Cornette Labonne, in pink, led her daughter, dressed all in white, onto the stage. From where Wellfleet stood they looked like two fairy-tale characters from Disneyland. All they needed were magic wands.

Where was Labonne? Wellfleet scanned the stage. Others wanted to know, too. "Where's Ron?" someone called.

Cornette said she didn't know but assured them he was on his way. She asked everyone to pray that he wasn't stuck in traffic somewhere. Told a couple of anecdotes about Jesus coming to their rescue in times past. "I know Jesus won't let him miss this rally," she cried, "because Jesus is the light guiding our campaign."

Right, thought Wellfleet. Jesus is up there sitting on his throne looking down at you in Beaverton, Oregon, and nodding his head in pleased admiration. Because you represent everything he stands for.

Cornette Labonne could obviously incite a crowd just as effectively as her husband. She began with the Christian pledge of allegiance: "I pledge allegiance to the Christian flag and to the Saviour for whose Kingdom it stands." That was followed by a gushing personal prayer, emphasizing that everyone was a worthless, miserable sinner until they saw the light of the Lord. Those who refused to hear His Word were cast out by their own deafness. Satan's personal assistants, as everyone knew, had infiltrated every level of government. They spread their filthy message through the airwaves, in movie theatres, in books, in the classroom.

Yes, particularly in the schools, where they stood every day in front of young, defenseless minds, battering away at their innocence, shattering their faith, seducing them into a world of perverted desire and unbridled sensuality. And they were protected under the law, these poisonous scorpions. They were allowed, no, they were *encouraged*, to tear down the foundations of democracy itself: home, family and church.

She's talking about me, Wellfleet thought, gorging on his familiar anger. He rubbed the palm of his hand against the comforting bulge in his coat pocket. Why just Labonne, he thought? Why not take her out, too? I could say Jesus told me to do it.

"And we are allowing it to happen," Cornette went on. "We, the Christian majority, who can still tell right from wrong, are commanded by God to cast out wickedness from our midst. Because if we don't, we are a part of that wickedness, and like them we will suffer the pain of hellfire and eternal damnation."

She paused. The crowd took a deep collective breath. Then she began talking about her recent "appearance" in Dallas. Dropped names. Pat Robertson. Chuck Colson. Said when she spoke about the ACA's sponsorship of Ballot Measure Three in Oregon, the entire convention hall stood up and cheered.

"They came up to me afterwards, hundreds of them, rich and poor, and they said, 'Cornette, how do we start a ballot measure like the one in Oregon in our state?' Because they, just like everyone here tonight, saw the way this beloved country of ours is headed. They were determined, as we are determined, to stand up and say 'Jesus says no to gay rights! Jesus says gay is the wrong word to describe miserable sodomites! Jesus says I agree with Three!'"

She worked them hard, like a skilled politician, using her evangelical fervor to ignite a flame of righteous, patriotic indignation. Wellfleet saw her transform a crowd of frustrated Americans into an angry mob determined to put their official stamp of disapproval on imaginary enemies. He stifled an overpowering urge to yell out, to scream, "You don't know me! You don't know any of us! Why can't you just leave us alone?"

And there were other things he could scream, too. What about Senator Peckerwood? What about burning crosses and painting swastikas and stealing files and trashing Too-Too? They'd even ruined his piano! What about their threat to ruin John-Don by saying he molested their daughter? Was all that part of God's plan for America?

Cornette moved onto a new tack. Grew somber. Began telling the congregation what the ACA had endured in the name of truth and moral decency. They were called liars. They were accused of crimes they hadn't committed. "And through it all we have held our heads up high, secure in our faith, knowing that God's truth can't be silenced."

She alluded to her startled discovery that there were homosexuals in her own neighborhood. Said she bore them no ill will. In fact, she prayed for them. Until she found out how truly evil they were.

Cornette beckoned to her daughter, who shrank back with a panicked look on her face. "Come here, honey. I want to introduce you to all these loverly people." The girl, after much coaxing, moved woodenly to center stage. She closed her eyes, as if she couldn't bear the sight of the crowd welcoming her with such warm applause.

Scared shitless, Wellfleet thought. He knew stage fright when he saw it. He'd felt the same way with Sid Charisse. He wondered what Dove Labonne would have to say.

"We have a story to tell you tonight," Cornette said. "A story that's going to shock you. I know it shocked me. It woke me up real fast. It made me realize what's really behind all the gay-rights rhetoric. Alot of that rhetoric has been used by one of our very own neighbors. Maybe you've seen him on teevee, or read about him in the papers. He talks a good line. So good that he's gotten lots of people to believe him. This man teaches in a public high school. He's with youngsters every day. He looks respectable. But now you're going to hear what he's really like."

Oh my God, thought Wellfleet, she's talking about John-Don. The girl's going to publicly accuse John-Don of assaulting her. He hadn't counted on that. He'd thought he was going to a big ACA rally. His heart was pounding out a deep, desperate coda. Shoot the girl, he thought. No, just take it out and start firing.

Like everyone else in the breathlessly silent room he kept his eyes riveted on Dove Labonne. She was being devoured by the crowd's lurid, hungry fascination. She stood utterly still in her long stiff white dress, her blonde hair tied up with a girlish bow. She pressed her lips together and opened her eyes.

"I've been raised to tell the truth," she said in a low, tremulous voice. "So I'm going to tell the truth. I'm going to tell you about a person who fools everybody." She paused, her eyes darting nervously towards a sudden commotion in the back of the hall. The doors flew open and Ron Labonne, panting, disheveled, covered in mud, burst into the room.

He put his hand up to stop the applause and when it didn't stop he simply stood there, nodding like a shy, reluctant hero. He'd stumbled in with a look of sweating, almost frantic alarm. That was changed by the applause and his sudden awareness that the cameras were on him. He didn't exactly smile, but his lips turned up in the pained grimace of a martyr accepting his fate.

Wellfleet slowly inched his hand down into his pocket. Made contact with the steel. Carefully moved his fingers towards the handle. Embraced the trigger.

"Okay, I finally made it!" Labonne shouted, lifting his arms in victory. "But I can see my wife had the good sense to begin without me." He started for the stage. Stopped as his stepdaughter pointed at him and cried,

"That's the man I want to tell you about!"

A murmur as the crowd's attention moved back to Dove Labonne. The cameras swiveled in her direction. Wellfleet slipped the gun from his pocket, holding it at his side. From where he stood he could fire directly into the back of Labonne's neck. He envisioned the bullet tearing through Labonne's throat, silencing it forever.

The girl's voice rang through the hall. "If you want to see a liar, look at him! If you want to see an adulterer, look at him! Because he's a liar and an adulterer, and I'm here to tell you the truth about him!"

Ron Labonne stood rooted to the spot. His wife shot across the stage and tried to lead Dove away. But the girl angrily shook off her mother's hand. And Wellfleet, once he realized what was happening, slipped the gun back into his pocket with a silent prayer of gratitude to a God he suddenly wanted to believe in.

Yes, he was one of them. As shocked as they were. Staring, transfixed, as Dove Labonne took possession of the stage, just as her mother had done, and used it as a pulpit to hurl an endless, unstoppable flood of denunciations against her stepfather.

▼ ▼ ▼

Wellfleet left the suburban church hall with a hallowed sense of wonder. No one noticed him. The place was in a pandemonium, but he was serenely calm. Reborn. Given new life.

Following some deep, mysterious instinct he drove to a lonely spot beside the Columbia River. It was his secret piece of sacred ground. In times past he'd come here for solace or to mull over his bewildering fate. And as the dry leaves of the cottonwood trees rustled and whispered in the October wind, he hurled the instrument of death into the dark waters of the river.

That night he slept as he hadn't slept in weeks. The moment his head hit the pillow he was pulled down into a deep, sweet, dreamless current.

The next day he received a call from the organizing committee of the No on Three rally. They needed music. The director of the Gay and Lesbian Choir had broken his arm and couldn't conduct. John-Don Webster had recommended him as a replacement. Wellfleet saw it as a sign and accepted immediately.

▼ ▼ ▼

Cheers, whistles, shouts, thunderous applause. The sounds of a community refusing to be silenced.

For over two hours they'd been packed, fifteen thousand of them, into Pioneer Square in the heart of downtown Portland. The old communal spirit, rediscovered only in times of crisis, bound them into one united, defiant family.

Wellfleet, sitting on a far side of the giant stage, looked out into the vast crowd. Picked out individual faces. Ordinary faces he'd pass every day without a second glance. The sight was so moving that he bowed his head in shame.

It's all there in front of me, he thought. Goodness, decency, compassion. It's still alive.

It was a miracle for him, being here, feeling this love for humanity welling up like music in his heart. He'd come perilously close to losing it entirely. Spiraling down to an underworld of darkness and shadows, he'd become a shadow himself. A mute shadow giving voice lessons to Death, which had no voice. He broke into a sweat just thinking about it.

Wellfleet pulled out a hanky, mopped his face, and turned his attention back to the sea of faces in Pioneer Square. Looked up at the sedate cupola of old Pioneer Courthouse across the street. There had been queers back then. Maybe some queers had helped to build it. Brave men who'd suffered a lifetime of defaced desires. Could they ever have imagined this scene, a mere 130 years later?

An earlier speaker had talked about the past generations of gay men and lesbians enduring in silence, "our brothers and sisters who couldn't speak because they had no voice." They were here today. Wellfleet could feel their spirit in the crowd.

Even if we lose, he thought, this is a victory. And the queerest part of this queer victory was that Ron Labonne had brought it about. Without him, none of this would have happened.

The rally had been going on for two hours. The heads of gay community organizations and coalitions Wellfleet had never heard of talked about the campaign from their perspectives. Teenagers, retirees, Native Americans, African-Americans, Hispanics, Asians. Politicians who'd kept quiet at the beginning of the campaign, trying to gauge the political winds, now stood up and addressed the crowd as if they'd never had any doubts.

Religious leaders spoke of love and compassion but had the good sense not to pray. The crowd warmed as Rabbi Mutterperl delivered an impassioned speech about the perils of silence. And now everyone was watching as Louis Love, a featured speaker, was helped up from his chair by his son, Peter, and lead to the podium.

The old civil-rights veteran stood there for a moment, blinking out into the cheering, sun-drenched crowd. He looked back at his wife and his son, seated on the stage.

His voice was slightly slurred from a stroke and it took a moment to understand what he was saying. But the slow, measured cadences of an old-fashioned, unhurried Southern orator were still there, unmistakable, overwhelming in their impact.

"I have come here by a very difficult path," he said. "I have worked for my people. Their suffering is my suffering. And now I am here because my son is suffering. I didn't know that. I'm sorry to say that I didn't want to know that. But I see now that it is all one and the same. It is all suffering. And it is based on injustice.

"I am his father. I liked to think that he looked up to me. That he found in me some hope for his own future. That's what parents are supposed to provide for their children. Hope for the future.

"But what is hope? Is it something we give to some of our children and deny to others? Isn't hope a gift that every one of us deserves? Isn't hope, in fact, our only hope? When we lose it, we become degraded. We lose our voices. And if our voices are not heard, then we lose ourselves. We lose our very souls as human beings.

"My son is gay." The words rang out through the enormous loud speaker system. Wellfleet looked over at Peter. There he was, fighting to control his emotions. Wellfleet couldn't control his own. Tears rolled down his cheeks. He felt a sudden keening pain for his own father, for a simple recognition that had been denied him. And that he had always denied to himself.

"I don't pretend to understand my son's life," Louis Love said. "I have my problems with it. But he is my son, and I love him. And I know that he is suffering. And I want to help him. That's why I am here today."

Time disappeared. Individuals disappeared. The crowd seemed to be breathing as one vast entity. When Mr. Love stopped and the roaring tumult began, Wellfleet leapt to his feet. Turned to his choir. They were ready. He was ready. He lifted his arms and delivered his gift to the world, a sweet, soaring stream of harmony.

CHAPTER 33

HALFWAY OUT OF THE GARAGE, TERRY'S MERCEDES GAVE A SUDDEN neck-snapping jolt and stopped dead. The old car, once so perfectly attuned and responsive to his touch, hadn't been the same since he let Billy drive it. Thousands of dollars in repair work, and still it bucked, rattled and whined like a fretful, unpredictable child. Sometimes Terry got the distinct impression that the car was as haunted by Billy's malice as he was.

He tried the ignition again. Nothing.

The fusty smell of mothballs wafted up from his winter mink as Terry got out of the car and stood rubbing his neck. How was he going to get down to the polling station? If he left the car and took a cab—ten dollars down the drain—he still couldn't close the garage door.

To hell with it, he thought. Let them steal whatever's in here.

He slipped on his peach-tinted glasses and wandered out to the driveway. It was the first Tuesday in November. A crisp, brilliantly clear day. So beautiful that he'd forgotten all about the *New York Times* crossword puzzle that morning and sat staring out at Mount Hood instead. Thinking about Delmont. Wondering what would happen in that day's momentous election. He might have sat there for hours if Aladdin, his new Persian cat, hadn't coughed up a monstrous hairball on the kitchen table.

The tiniest sounds were audible in the sharp, lucent air. Across the street he could hear Ito closing his front door. Terry watched as Ito, carrying an armload of flowers, made his way down those terrifying stairs. He has the step of a young man, Terry thought enviously. What's his secret?

Ito saw him and waved. A simple, neighborly gesture that Terry thought he'd never see again. He quickly waved back.

"How are you?" Ito called.

"My car died."

"Do you need a ride somewhere?" Ito asked.

"I was just going to vote."

Ito motioned him over.

Before they climbed into Ito's Landcruiser, both men stood for a moment looking over at the Labonnes' house. Garish and forlorn in the bright morning light, it stood like a hideous monument to a war no one wanted to remember and no one dared to forget. A war whose outcome would be decided today.

"I was thinking of Delmont this morning," Terry said.

"Yes? So was I."

"It's just over a year since he died and *they* moved in."

"I was going to the cemetery," Ito said. "I'll drop you off on the way."

"Would you mind if I went with you?"

As they drove west on Burnside, down the green corridor of Douglas firs and alders, Terry marveled at how ordinary everything looked. For straight people it was just another day. They'd go to work, send their kids off to school, vacuum the house, rake their yards, watch television, eat. They might vote, or they might not. If they did, they could release in the privacy of the voting booth every pent-up prejudice they'd ever felt about homosexuals.

But for gays, this ordinary, beautiful day was quite different. They'd be wondering about every person they knew, every person they passed: how did he or she vote? For me or against me? It was insane, almost too bizarre to comprehend, that total strangers had it in their power to deprive an entire group of human beings of their basic human rights.

Shameful, Terry thought. His forebears had come to Oregon as pioneers, in covered wagons, trekking along the Oregon Trail in the hopes of finding a better life out west. And they had succeeded. But what about him, a hundred and forty years later? As a gay man, he was part of Oregon's history, too. This whole ludicrous anti-gay campaign had turned him into an alien in the very state his family had settled.

His life wouldn't change if the ballot measure passed: he didn't have to worry about a job, housing, or public social policy. But for the first time in his life he found himself wondering, worrying even, about the others, the younger ones whose lives were still ahead of them. To be so unfairly branded, to feel that they were so unwelcome. It disgusted him.

Ito pulled off of Burnside and headed up into the hills of Sunset Memorial Cemetery.

Terry had yet to visit Delmont's grave. He hated cemeteries, hated that landscape of death, with decomposing bodies and dead lives buried under his feet and spread all around him. Somewhere beneath that smooth green lawn Delmont lay in a cobalt-blue casket, not the white one Terry had chosen. I failed him, he thought; I didn't even have the courage to demand that they rectify their mistake.

He couldn't have found the grave by himself and hurried alongside Ito, panting up a steep hill, through avenues of grave stones and monuments, past a small grove of conifers, fighting back a vague childhood terror that he'd be forgotten or left behind to fend for himself in a frightening, unknown place. The legacy of parents who'd take him to parties and then get so drunk that they'd leave without him.

Someone had been tending Delmont's grave, and he realized that it was Ito. Why not me? Terry asked himself. Delmont was my oldest friend in the world.

Ito pulled a small pair of clippers from his jacket pocket and snipped back the grass growing over the granite marker. "It is amazing how fast things grow," he said.

And how quickly things die, Terry thought, noting the year of Delmont's birth. "Do you come here often?" he asked.

"Every week," Ito said.

He treated the grave as if it were a tiny formal garden in need of the most exacting care. Terry watched, fascinated by Ito's precise, ritualistic movements. Each blade of grass was picked up from the headstone. The unruly turf around the base of the small cross was clipped. With a small stiff brush Ito swept away the dirt and pine needles that had settled in the letters of Delmont's name and in the eight numerals that encapsulated Delmont's time on earth.

"Ah, no," Ito groaned, digging in his jacket pocket.

"What?"

"I have forgotten my cleaning rag. This granite needs a good polish."

"Here." Terry opened his leather clutch bag and withdrew a monogrammed hand-kerchief. But instead of handing it to Ito, he crouched down and began gingerly rubbing the stone.

"Put some elbow grease into it, Terry. If you're going to clean it, clean it."

"I'm trying, but my hands are sore." Aching with the same arthritis that had turned his mother's hands into knobby claws.

Ito pulled a bedraggled heap of wilting, rotting flowers from a heavy bronze vase and substituted his fresh bouquet. When they'd both finished their tasks, Ito closed his eyes and bowed his head to the stone.

"Praying for him?" Terry asked.

"No. Just keeping his memory alive."

Memories. Terry remembered the parties, the laughter, the sublime food, the wonderful daiquiris, the conversation. Queer Corners as it had been, a special world unto itself. Back then, when they'd all been together, they didn't stop to consider what the world thought of them. They knew, but didn't let it interfere with having a good time. Secrecy provided its own private pleasures.

All that had changed.

Everything had changed.

And I've been left behind, Terry thought, crouching in the wet grass by Delmont's grave, his knees throbbing, his neck and hands aching. He got stiffly to his feet and buttoned up his mink, warding off the chill of melancholy.

On their way to the polling station, Ito asked if Terry was coming to the No on Three Victory Party that evening. Everyone from Queer Corners was planning to rendezvous there.

"I wasn't invited," Terry said.

"You don't need an invitation, but I am inviting you."

Terry fluffed his eyebrows and picked a stray pine needle from his coat. "What about the others? I don't think they'd want me." He waited for Ito to remonstrate, but Ito drove silently on. "And it may not be a victory party," Terry said, nervously smoothing the soft dark fur. "The last poll—"

"It is a victory party," Ito said. "Whether we win or lose."

Terry thought for a moment. "How much will it cost?"

"Whatever you care to give."

"Well . . . I'd have to take a taxi, I suppose. My car won't be—"

"You can ride with me."

"Who are the caterers? The food they serve at those—"

"I will be leaving at eight," Ito said. "Let me know."

He pulled up in front of the elementary school where Queer Cornerites had cast their ballots for presidents, senators, and state, city, and county representatives. Where they'd voted for or against tax levies and everything from light-rail funding to legitimizing assisted suicide. Where today, for the first time, they would be voting for or against themselves.

Terry was reluctant to end the brief camaraderie he'd had with Ito. "Aren't you coming in?"

"I've already voted."

Terry took his time getting out, then hovered by the open door of the Landcruiser, peering in at Ito's meticulously arranged tools and gardening implements. "Well—thank you. I suppose I can call a taxi from here. Such a nuisance."

Ito's dark brown eyes glimmered with amusement and annoyance. "Be grateful for nuisances, Terry. They let us know what's truly important."

What a curious thing to say, Terry thought, watching Ito drive away. The air was ringing with the sounds of excited, hyperactive children. He turned and caught sight of a small boy racing across the playground, a terrified look on his face. A larger boy was pursuing him, waving a stick. Terry watched as the smaller child stumbled and skidded across the asphalt. Saw the boy's pained grimace and heard his tearful howl as his heartless tormentor struck him on the head.

That's me, Terry thought, hurrying towards the playground. That's all of us.

"Hey, you!" He pulled the stick from the boy's hand. "What kind of a bully are you, anyway?" He helped the crying boy to his feet. The larger boy ran off. The other stood staring up at his strange mink-clad rescuer with timid admiration.

"Do you know how to fight?" Terry asked. The boy shook his head. "Neither do I. But maybe we should learn how." He handed the boy the stick. "Here, it's yours now. If he comes after you again, beat the living daylights out of him."

▼ ▼ ▼

Thanks to the schmoozing efforts of Peter Love, the No on Three campaign was using Montgomery Park, neé Montgomery Wards, as their election night headquarters. The old catalogue store, a victim of changing tastes and consumer demographics, had recently been revamped into a modern interior-design center with marble floors and tiers of showrooms around a central atrium. The evening was optimistically billed as a Victory Party, and the initial mood of the crowd was festive and upbeat. But as polls closed and returns came in, the atmosphere began to change.

The election results were relayed to the crowd from a stage and projected on a giant television monitor. Boos, hisses, cheers. It was an unbearably close race, closer than anyone believed possible. Several small towns and rural counties had voted in favor of the ballot measure. By nine o'clock it was neck-in-neck, hanging by a percentage point. The unthinkable was inching closer to reality.

Cassandra spotted the new vote tallies the moment they entered the noisy atrium. Filled with sudden, sinking alarm, she clutched Jay's arm. "Jay, what if he wins?"

"Then he wins," Jay said gruffly.

"But what will it really mean? For us."

"I don't know what it'll mean for anyone else," he said, absently patting her cold hand as they squeezed into the packed room, "I only know what it means for me."

Something was cooking with him, something big, but Jay wouldn't tell her what it was and Cassandra was afraid to ask. Ever since the trashing of Too-Too, he'd withdrawn from her. They continued to work side by side, they still lived in the same house, but emotionally Jay was simply not available. Over the last month, as the battle of the ballot measure grew uglier and uglier, his old *joie de vivre* evaporated entirely. It wasn't an uncommon reaction: gays all over the state felt they were literally being thrown to the dogs. There was mounting frustration, resentment, and anger over the way they continued to be portrayed, or ignored, in the media. And to see Jay, once so garrulous, generous, and open-hearted, hardening into a sour, disgusted cynic was unbearable.

In the final two weeks of the campaign Cassandra had done what she could, in her own way. They all had. Rallied. Manned the phone lines. Gone door to door. Entered heterosexual households, talking to sweet grandmothers, suspicious parents, old hippie radicals, disinterested Yuppies, single mothers, and more angry, overweight white men than Cassandra cared to remember. She'd even snuck into the enemy camp to confront Dove. She liked to think that it was because of her that Dove had made that scene at the ACA rally. And yet even his stepdaughter's denunciations couldn't stop Labonne and the ACA.

All Cassandra knew now was what she read between the lines in the local paper—hardly a reliable source of news. The ACA quickly closed ranks around Labonne, who said his stepdaughter was "disturbed" and in need of Christian counseling. But Cornette Labonne, who once would do anything to get in the news, was now perennially "unavailable for comment." And Dove, the only family member who dared to tell the truth, was called a liar.

Just as Carolyn had been called a liar: "a vicious drug-addicted Satan-worshipping lesbian-feminist who abandoned her child, became a prostitute, and now wants my blood," as Labonne described her in one rabid sound-bite. He'd been biting constantly in the last two weeks, ever since Carolyn's shocking revelations appeared in *Willamette Wink*.

Carolyn's story, with its lurid details of life with "Corporal Eagle" (Ron Labonne) in a right-wing paramilitary compound, and the astounding confession that she'd had a child by him, was evidently too incendiary for Portland's establishment newspaper. They said it was "politically motivated" and refused to run it, just as they had earlier delayed reports of the sexual-harassment suit against Senator Peckerwood.

When the next bombshell exploded, and Susan's name was added to the twenty-two others who'd already filed charges against the senator, the daily paper loaded its story with belittling remarks from Senator Peckerwood ("I don't kiss women who smell like dogs") and Susan's competitors in the dog world.

Carolyn and Susan had vanished. No one in Queer Corners had seen them for over three weeks. Cassandra's calls went unanswered. There was no sign of life in Bilitis Cottage. Windy Hills Kennel said that Susan was on "an extended leave" but wouldn't give out any other information. Rumors flew through the city's gay community. Carolyn Corbett had gone into hiding, afraid for her life. Carolyn Corbett had been murdered. Carolyn Corbett and Susan Bark had committed double suicide.

Nobody in Queer Corners knew what to believe. By then, anything was possible.

As they pressed on through the milling throng, Jay hardly looked at Cassandra. She followed his eyes, deciphering his little nods and winks. He was he being cruised by three different men in three different parts of the room. Aching with jealousy, she was about to slip away when Wellfleet caught sight of them in the crush and limped over.

"We're over there," he said, pointing.

His appearance was so startling that all Cassandra could think of to say was, "Wow, Wellfleet, look at you."

"Like it?" There was a wild glint in his eyes and a crooked grin on his face. His hair was disheveled. He'd covered himself with so many anti-ACA pro-gay buttons that he clicked and rattled every time he moved. Under his breath he was excitedly humming a refrain from one of the songs he'd directed at the big rally in Pioneer Square.

"Has anyone seen Carolyn?" Cassandra asked hopefully.

"No, but isn't that Phyllis Schafly in drag?"

Terry Terwilliger, in his mink coat and tinted, oversized glasses, had just strolled in with Ito. Wellfleet waved them over. "Ito, my friend, how are you?" Buttons rattling, he pumped Ito's hand and then turned to Terry. "I never would have guessed *you* were queer," he said.

Terry pursed his lips, trying to avoid the combined force of their contemptuous eyes.

"What's a Republican ACA contributor like you doing here?" Wellfleet taunted him. "Shouldn't you be with Ron Labonne or down at Senator Peckerwood's?"

"I've changed my party," Terry said primly.

"Oh, now you're a registered queer?" Wellfleet eyes sparkled with malice.

"Wellfleet," Ito said, "Terry came here to show his support."

"What support?" Jay snapped.

"Excuse me. I just gave the No on Three campaign a check for twenty-five dollars," Terry protested.

Wellfleet rolled his eyes. "Ohhh, twenty-five whole dollars? When you gave the ACA two grand? That's very generous of you, Terry."

Terry, his face blistering red, was on the verge of tears. With a sniff he pulled out his checkbook and Mont Blanc pen. "How much?" he asked. "How much do I have to give before you'll forgive me?"

"Three thousand dollars," Cassandra said.

"To help cover the campaign's shortfall," Jay added. "You'll make John-Don's night. He's worried that we'll be in the hole."

"Come on, Terry," Wellfleet coaxed, "show us what kind of a queer you really are."

Biting his lips, hands shaking, Terry made out a check for three thousand dollars. Jay, with no more than a flick of his finger, summoned a dazzled young man from the No on Three information table. "Our friend here wants to make a donation to the campaign," he said.

Terry tore out the check and handed it to the young man. "Here. In memory of Delmont Percy."

The young man ogled the figures. "Wow! Do you want a free No on Three coffee mug?"

"For three thousand dollars I think I should get a matched set," Terry grumbled. He heard their laughter.

"What's so funny?" Peter asked when the group came over to join him and John-Don. He saw Terry in their midst and frowned.

"Terry just gave three thousand bucks to the campaign." Wellfleet clapped Terry on the back. "For that, Terry, you can have your pick of any button I'm wearing. They're all collector's items. How about this one?" He plucked off a "Proud to be a Pervert" button and offered it to Terry.

"I don't like buttons," Terry said, backing away. "And this is mink, in case you didn't know."

Peter was wedged in between his parents on a long Italian leather sofa that allowed admirers easy access to his father. Mr. Love, a big hit at the rally, was holding court at one end, John-Don and his parents were at the other, so far away that Peter had to lean forward and shout, "John-Don, Terry just gave three k to the campaign."

John-Don, sitting glumly with his hands clasped between his knees, looked up in surprise. "Really?" He took a deep breath, rose, and dutifully went to shake Terry's hand. "Thank you. That's very generous."

"I did it for Delmont," Terry said. "I know that's what he would have wanted."

"I hope you did it for yourself, too," John-Don said.

Terry sighed. "I suppose so. Although it seems rather pointless to come out of the closet now. At my age."

John-Don tightened his grasp and looked into Terry's eyes, trying to make contact with the soul or spirit lodged behind the lifted flesh and dyed hair. He saw a man who thought he had everything but knew he had nothing. "It's never too late, Terry."

"What I want to know," Wellfleet said, "is what happens to Delmont's house when Ron the Con loses?"

"*If* he loses," John-Don said, glancing at the returns and gloomily returning to his seat.

"Oh, he'll lose," Wellfleet predicted. "And then what? I heard the ACA's bankupt. On-Air with Jesus is off the air. There's no way they can afford to stay in Delmont's house."

"Someone else will buy it," Terry said. "God knows it couldn't be any worse than it is now."

"Wanna bet?" Jay said.

"Yeah, what if another trashy straight couple moves in?" Peter saw instantly the effect his remark had on the elder Loves and Websters. They stiffened in self-conscious affront.

"So you want to live in a segregated neighborhood," Mr. Love said, grasping his walker. "Keep out everyone who's not like you."

"I don't want bigots taking over again," Peter said. "It's our neighborhood, whether they like or not."

"You can't expect everyone to like you, son. That's a hard lesson to learn, but you'd better learn it. Because if you don't, you're no different from the bigots behind this campaign." His slow, slurred voice boomed down the sofa. "Isn't that right, John-Don?"

"Yes, Louis, but you have to understand that we're all pretty angry right now."

"Everyone's angry," Mr. Love said. "Anger is the sorry legacy of this country. Everyone's divided. No one thinks about the future. And if no one thinks about the future, there is no future. It's as simple as that." He closed his eyes and raised his head, like an obedient child, as his wife leaned across Peter to dab away the bubble of froth that had collected in a corner of her husband's stroke-stiffened mouth.

A spokeslesbian for the campaign came out to announce that the final results were in from two counties in southern Oregon. "This shouldn't be a surprise," she said, "since it's Ron Labonne's old stomping grounds. But it's still a bummer." A groan of agitated dismay as she gave them the bad news. The margin was slim, but both counties had voted yes on Three. The scale had tipped in favor of the ballot measure.

"Bastards!" Wellfloat cried.

Cassandra clung to Jay. "They're going to win, oh God, I just know it."

"They are not going to win," Ito murmured, more to himself than anyone around him. He perched on a corner of the sofa beside John-Don. They looked at one another. John-Don was plainly exhausted, but his burning blue eyes ignited the passion Ito was still trying to extinguish. For a moment, Ito simply wanted to be absorbed, taken in, forget about the ever-present wall of hate surrounding human beings and lose himself, just once, in the heart of another. "Even if they win they lose," he said firmly. "I truly believe that."

John-Don moved his hand down, found Ito's, and gave it a brief, furtive caress. The clandestine physical intimacy took Ito's breath away.

Weeks of sleepless anxiety had robbed John-Don of his once-boundless energy. He looked older, like an endurance runner grimly willing himself on to the finish line. "You've really helped me, Ito," he said quietly. "I want you to know that. I admire you."

"Nothing to admire," Ito said uncomfortably.

"You don't let emotions get in the way."

"Some would see that as a failing, not a strength."

"I get very tired of emotions sometimes," John-Don confessed.

"They give you your passion."

"Sometimes they just give me a headache." John-Don lowered his voice so that Ito alone would hear him. "Through this whole thing—not just the campaign, but this cloud that's been hanging over me—you're the one who gave me strength."

Ito looked puzzled. "Me?"

"You seem to have a larger perspective. You don't panic, you don't scream, you don't blame the world for being the way it is."

Ito shrugged. "Blame leads to nothing but more blame."

"I know that," John-Don said. "But when you're falsely accused of crimes you didn't commit it changes your perspective. Mine, anyway." He stared sadly out into the room. "I never thought I'd feel so bitter. It scares me. I don't want to end up like that."

"Then you won't," Ito said.

"I want to have hope. The way you do." John-Don leaned still closer. "Help me to keep hoping, Ito."

He knows how much I love him, Ito thought, *and he is telling me that he loves me.* And suddenly, miraculously, he was freed. Released. The love he felt was just that— love, with no conditions, no if-onlys, no I-wants. It was just love, a warm flowing privilege of the human heart. He clenched John-Don's hand and nodded.

"Hello."

The Queer Corners corner looked over and saw a slender, elegant woman with short red hair and pearl earrings standing before them. She was dressed in a suit of creamy silk and her face glowed with the artful, professional wizardry of an expensive salon. The bulging eyes of a small dog peered out from the top of the canvas tote bag she was carrying.

Cassandra stared, as they all stared, in astonishment. "Carolyn?"

They crowded excitedly around her. Carolyn, crying, hugged and kissed them. So many questions. Where had she been? They were so worried. Where was Susan?

"She's coming," Carolyn said. "There she is."

Susan, clasping the arm of a short, dapper gentleman wearing a jaunty red beret, matching muffler and white gloves was moving slowly through the dense crowd.

"That's Reggie," Carolyn said. "Susan's father. He's come to live with us."

The three of them had just arrived from London. Endless delays and mix-ups. Lost luggage. On their way in from the airport they'd stopped to vote, arriving minutes before the polls closed, and then raced over to pick up Lady Caroline from the kennel before coming here.

There was too much to say. Yes, it was all true. Yes, Lester was her son. She couldn't go into it now. It had been so difficult. She was afraid they'd all hate her but knew she couldn't go on the way she had. She had to tell the truth, just as Susan had to tell the truth about Senator Peckerwood. "We knew if we never said anything we'd be helping the other side."

She and Susan decided to "elope" before the stories appeared. Why not? England was so beautiful. Absolutely gorgeous. They'd stayed in Brighton first. Right on the sea. No, it didn't rain once. The Regency terrace house was too adorable for words, and the Bark's thatch-covered cottage in Dorset—well, it had Anno Domini 1568 over the doorway and that wasn't the address, it was the year it was built. They helped Reggie to put the houses on the market, pack, and get ready for his first transatlantic journey. Then, at Reggie's urging, the two of them had holed up at the Savoy in London for four days. They treated themselves to the best salon in the city, went shopping, saw shows, bought clothes. "We're starting over," Carolyn said happily.

In her hyper, beyond-jet-lagged state, she could have rattled on for hours. She didn't allude to the fear that had prompted Susan's hasty decision to get them out of Oregon as quickly as possible. Susan was convinced that Labonne or someone from the ACA would put a bullet between Carolyn's eyes. Oddly enough, for the first time in her life, Carolyn hadn't been afraid. She was willing to stay. The fact that Susan had pleaded with her to go was the decisive factor. It meant that Susan really did love her.

"I can't tell you what's been like to get away from all this," she said. "To be in a place that's never heard of the ACA—" Scanning her neighbors' tired, anxious faces

Carolyn realized how callous she must sound. She'd gone, but they had stayed behind to fight. She'd been rejuvenated, but they clearly had not. She was back in the war zone.

"So tell me what's going on here," she said, struggling to hold on to her elated spirits. "Are we winning by a huge margin?"

Their eyes told her the sad truth.

"If Portland doesn't come through, we're dead," Jay said.

"When will we know?"

John-Don told her the final tallies were coming in now. By eleven they'd have the final outcome. Above them, the old giant clock, a fixture from the past, ticked on into the future, serenely indifferent to the changes it wrought. It leveled everything in the end, that old clock. Fifteen minutes to go.

Susan and her father finally reached the group from Queer Corners. "I'd like you all to meet my father, Reginald Bark." Mr. Bark, his eyes sparkling, smiled and gave them a cheerful white-gloved salute before Susan lead him over to the sofa, where he squeezed in beside Mr. Love. "Are you tired, daddy? If you're tired, we'll leave right now."

"Tired? Heavens no," he said. "I love a good party." He had an odd, high-pitched voice and once he started talking, as they were all soon to discover, it was almost impossible to shut him up. "This is my first time in America," he confided to Mr. Love.

"I hope you'll enjoy it," Mr. Love answered politely.

"I shall, I'm sure. Land of the brave and home of the free, isn't that what you sing here?"

"Well, some folks do," Mr. Love replied. "I don't think you'll hear anyone in this crowd singing it, though."

"I used to hear the lads singing that at the end of the war. Such lovely boys, those Yanks. So full of hope. That's what I like about you Americans. You're so bloody hopeful about everything."

"Daddy," Susan said sternly, "I don't want you to get too excited."

"My dear, I'm finally in America. I *want* to be excited." Mr. Bark took Susan's hand. "I want you to introduce me to all your friends, Susie dear. All the wonderful neighbors you and Carolyn have been telling me about. Oh, we had such *wretched* neighbors in Brighton," he said to Mrs. Love. "Too beastly for words. I'm so looking forward to living in a nice friendly neighborhood for a change."

The din grew more deafening by the moment. The atrium was packed solid. The clock ticked to eleven.

John-Don fidgeted and anxiously rubbed his knuckles. "It should be any minute now."

"Okay, everyone's invited to Too-Too afterwards," Jay said. "For a victory toast or a goodbye drink."

Goodbye? What did he mean? They crowded around him. Cassandra, pushed from Jay's side, went pale.

"If the ballot measures passes," Jay announced, "I'm moving to California."

They stared at him, mouths gaping. They didn't see the sudden wrench of anguish on Cassandra's face as she quickly turned away. But Jay did. He reached over and gently tried to tug her to his side. Cassandra didn't budge. Jay let her be.

"Yeah, well, I've been thinking a lot about this," Jay said. "I just won't stay and pay taxes in a state that brands me as a pervert. I won't do it. I've got too much respect for myself. I won't let myself be treated that way."

In the midst of all the clamor, Cassandra saw nothing, heard nothing, said nothing. If the ACA won, Jay would pack up and go. She'd be left behind to make a new life for herself in a state that didn't want her. Didn't want any of them. She could leave, too. But she was tired of wandering. She wanted to stay here, in Portland, at Jay's side. Too-Too was their joint creation, their baby, the closest she ever gotten to sharing another person's life. *Let go*, she said to herself. *Accept it. Things change whether you want them to or not.*

A breathless hush fell over the room as the head of the No on Three campaign made her long-awaited appearance. She was carrying a sheaf of papers.

"There's Natalie," John-Don said. "She's got the final tallies." He bolted up from the sofa. "This is it." He pushed his way out into the crowd. The others—except for Jay and Cassandra—followed him.

Jay gently stroked Cassandra's hair. "The big moment."

Cassandra nodded, unable to look at him.

"I know I should have told you," he said. "But I didn't make up my mind until today."

"Jay, kiss me. Please. I'm so frightened." She raised her lips and felt the soft warmth of his. A brother's kiss, gentle, protective, loving. It was all she'd ever get from him, she knew that, and it was futile to expect more. It was a kiss of farewell. But she held on tight, desperately pressing her lips to his, until Jay pulled away.

"Hey, you're going to ruin my reputation," he said, brushing the hair away from her face. "Come on, let's join the others."

Susan held Carolyn's hand. Peter stood behind John-Don, his hands kneading John-Don's tense shoulders. Wellfleet closed his eyes, hearing the glorious "Ode to Joy" from Beethoven's ninth symphony in his head. Terry took off his tinted glasses and rubbed his sagging lifted eyes. Ito visualized a tree, standing firm in the earth, its roots as deep as its canopy was high.

They made room for Jay and Cassandra, then huddled closer, all of them, waiting for the final results.

CHAPTER 34

THE CROWD SILENTLY WATCHED AS NATALIE NOTALE SLOWLY MADE HER way to the podium. Wan, tight-lipped and grim, she faced the sea of eager, expectant faces like a schoolmarm about to administer a severe punishment.

"Well, the polling booths are closed," Natalie said. The loudspeakers propelled her flat voice and nervous, heavy breathing to the far corners of Montgomery Park. "The returns are in."

In the pause that followed, everyone waited for a smile, a signal, some dramatic gesture to defuse the anxiety and spin it around to triumph. "And it looks—" she paused, then suddenly threw up her arms, "like Ballot Measure Three has failed!"

A huge, jubilant roar echoed through the glass-roofed atrium. The numbers on the "No" side of the giant monitor began to rise.

Natalie held up her hand. "We won't have exact counts until tomorrow—but right now it looks as if forty-nine percent voted for the measure, and fifty-two percent against."

The atmosphere, solemn and brewing all evening with a sense of impending catastrophe, suddenly crackled with life. A bolt of giddy joy shot through the packed room. Whistles, weeping, screams, howls of laughter and delight filled the air. Grateful eyes were raised, if not to heaven, at least to the glass roof of the atrium above. The crowd, united in victory, felt a collective need to move, to release the pent-up tension.

John-Don let out a strangled cry and shook his fists. "Three percentage points!" It was hard to tell if he was angry or exultant. "Three percentage points," he repeated. "That's hardly—"

Peter pulled him close and whispered in his ear: "It's only three percentage points, honey, but we won. That's all that matters." John-Don turned to him. His eyes were dripping. So were Peter's. "We did it, honey."

"We won, we won, we won!" Cassandra squealed and leapt up and down as if she were on a pogo stick. She bounced into Jay's arms. "Jay! You're not going now, right? You're not leaving."

Jay laughed and shook his head with relief. "No, I guess not."

Cassandra bounced over to Carolyn and Susan, hugging them both. "We won!" She bounced over to Wellfleet, to Ito, to John-Don, to Peter, and finally to Terry, throwing her arms around him. "Terry, isn't it wonderful? We beat them!"

Terry, unaccustomed to having a woman in his arms, started with alarm. He looked down at her radiant face and then slowly, clumsily, patted her on the back. "Wonderful," he said.

Susan turned to her sobbing lover. "Well, darling? The man is toast."

"Burnt toast," Carolyn sniffled, fumbling for a handkerchief.

"And you helped burn him. That took great courage, darling."

Carolyn dabbed her eyes and blew her nose. "He burned himself."

Lady Caroline barked and squirmed in the canvas tote bag.

Victories in the gay community were so rare that nobody knew quite what to do with their triumph. It needed music, celebration, a loud, memorable finale. Wellfleet, beside himself with excitement, conducted an imaginary choir in Beethoven's "Ode to Joy." "Freude!" he sang, hearing the orchestra and massed voices in his head. "Freude!" Which meant *joy*.

Ito closed his eyes and bowed his head.

One of Natalie's assistants came over and whispered something in the campaign director's ear. Natalie nodded, then tapped the microphone to get everyone's attention. "I have one final announcement to make," she said.

The clamor gradually ebbed away. Once again every face was turned towards the podium.

"I've just received word that Ron Labonne is about to make a statement from ACA headquarters. We're turning the big-screen monitor on so you can see and hear it for yourself."

Eyes rose towards the giant television screen. A huge image of Ron Labonne's face appeared. He looked thinner, drawn and haggard around the eyes, yet defiant and even triumphant.

"Tonight we lost at the polls," he said, speaking into a microphone, "but we can still claim a moral victory." He waited for the cheers in ACA headquarters to die down. "We lost by a couple of thousand votes. Think of what that means. We were outspent five to one. We were the victims of endless assaults on our integrity, our morals, our motives, our love of God and country. Three percentage points is *nothing*.'"

"But it's still three percentage points, you big bag of shit!" someone cried from the floor of Montgomery Park. It was Peter Love.

Ron Labonne jabbed a finger in the collective face of his television audience. "What this means is that we have been given a moral imperative to continue our battle. If we don't, the fabric that holds this great country of ours together—our families and our belief in the word of God—will unravel before our eyes."

He paused, unsmiling, gathering force like a dark storm cloud. "Despite their claims to the contrary, homosexuals pose the single greatest threat to the stability of the world today. If we don't stop them, you're gonna see homosexual marriages. You're gonna see homosexuals adopting innocent children and indoctrinating them into their deviant lifestyle. You're gonna stand by and watch helplessly as your children are taught in school that homosexuality is an acceptable lifestyle. You're gonna see your insurance premiums skyrocket because *they're* gonna demand insurance for their sex partners. You're gonna have to hire practicing homosexuals, even if you don't want to. You're gonna have to rent your apartments to them because if you don't, they'll slap you with a lawsuit. You're gonna see homosexuals *everywhere you turn*. You're gonna see them laughing at you and saying, 'We can do whatever we want and you can't stop us because we have special rights that *you* don't have.'"

"Turn it off!" Wellfleet shouted.

But everyone continued to gaze at the screen as if mesmerized by the unrepentant Labonne and his unending invective.

"Make no mistake," Ron Labonne said, "homosexuals are on the march. They're out to win."

"We did win!" John-Don cried to the televised image looming over them.

"But so are we!" Labonne shouted. "I'm not here tonight to announce the defeat of Ballot Measure Three. I'm here to say to all of you—everyone watching—that this fight is just beginning. And to that end, I'm making a public announcement that we will return. We will be there at the next election, and the one after that, and the one after that."

"Over my dead body," Carolyn said.

"We'll be there," Labonne warned, "as long as we have to be there, because we are soldiers of truth, democracy, and the American way."

His image blipped off.

Cassandra turned to her neighbors with a look of horror. "He's going to come back?"

"Oh my God!" A breathless Sissy Parker was pushing her way towards them. "I've been looking all over for you guys."

They moved into a self-protective knot, ignoring the realtor who'd sold Delmont's house to the Labonnes. "Come on," Jay said, turning to the others. "Let's go have our *temporary* celebration drink."

"I'll get daddy," Susan said. "We'll meet you there, Jay."

Peter nudged his lover. John-Don was still staring at the blank television screen. "Come on, John-Don, let's collect the folks and get out of here."

They were all just starting off when Sissy suddenly blurted out: "They're selling!"

They all stopped. They turned around and stared at Sissy.

"Yup," she said, nodding eagerly, desperate to reinstate herself in their good graces. She took a tentative step towards them. "It's all strictly hush-hush but I wanted you to be the first to know."

Still they stared. They appeared to be in shock but Sissy couldn't tell for certain. "Cornette called this morning. She wants to get out of town fast. Labonne's not going with her, but he agreed to sell the house before the mortgage company does a foreclosure."

Silence, in the midst of the roaring crowd swirling around them.

"I thought you'd be excited," Sissy quavered. But she saw no mercy in their eyes, only a horrible, damning denunciation. She flushed and took a step backwards, as if she'd gotten too close to a raging fire. "Why do you all hate me so much?" she cried. "I just sold them the house, I didn't collaborate with them." As proof she held up her briefcase with its "Hate is NOT a Family Value" decal. "They were my enemies too, you know."

"But they weren't in your front yard," John-Don said.

"They didn't burn crosses in front of your house," Peter said. "We're the ones who had to live with those—"

"Monsters," Terry said, shaking his head.

Sissy, suddenly on trial, launched into an agitated defense. "I'm just a real estate agent for God's sake. I didn't know what they were like. No one did."

Her comment was met with a tense, frozen silence.

"They made an offer," Sissy panted, beginning to sweat, "and it was accepted. I couldn't turn them down just because they were straight. That would have been discrimination."

"No," merciless Susan said, "but you could have been, how shall I put it, my dear, a bit more *discriminating*."

"How I feel personally about a potential buyer has nothing to do with selling a house."

"That's quite obvious," Susan replied.

"It can't," Sissy insisted. "There are federal guidelines against discrimination."

"Yeah," John-Don said, "for everyone but queers."

"I don't know what you want me to do," Sissy cried, turning in an agitated circle. "I don't know what I could have done. I'm sorry. I'm really sorry. What more I can say?"

"There's nothing more for you to say." Ito touched Sissy's arm. She stopped spinning. "You did not discriminate. They did. That's all we can say."

Sissy focused her grateful eyes on Ito, her only defender. "Anyway," she said in a meek voice, "they'll be cleared out by the end of next week."

"My God," Terry whispered, turning to his neighbors. "That means Delmont's house is on the market again."

Susan, narrowing her eyes, asked if Sissy was to be the agent.

"Yup." Sissy nodded. "I made certain I got an exclusive."

"How much?" Susan demanded, snapping her fingers.

"Four hundred," Sissy whispered, "but I know they'll take a lot less." She knew what they were thinking: she was responsible for a decline in their property values. "There's no way they'll get what they paid. They've absolutely ruined that beautiful house."

"It'll take at least a hundred grand to undo the damage," Peter said.

"And when is the house actually going to be listed?" Susan asked.

"Tomorrow."

"Tomorrow!" they all exclaimed.

"Unofficially," Sissy said. "That's when I can start telling potential buyers that it's available. It won't officially be listed until next week."

"And the real-estate market's going crazy," Jay said. "All those godawful Californians fleeing L.A. and moving up here." He'd already forgotten that he was going to become one of those godawful Californians if the ballot measure passed.

"They're snapping up everything in the hills," Peter said, oblivious to the fact that he, a former Californian, had snapped up his house almost the moment it came on the market. "The way things are going we could have new neighbors by tomorrow night."

"No one could move in that fast," Sissy assured him. "I can't even begin showing it until next week."

"Oh God," Susan wailed, wringing her hands. "Do you have anyone looking, Sissy?"

"Oh sure, I've got lots of potential buyers."

"Are they all straight?" Wellfleet wanted to know.

"No, not all of them." Sissy played her one and only trump card. "Actually, Freddi Jo Earle's looking."

"The tennis star?" John-Don's eyes widened. "The Freddi Jo Earle who took Wimbledon four years in a row?"

"Yup." Sissy nodded. "She used to be a Portland girl, you know. And now she's thinking of moving back here with her partner. Misses the rain."

Who, they excitedly asked, who was Freddi Jo Earle's partner?

"An architect." Oh, weren't they just eating out of her hand now! "Someone named Trudi Konig. She's darling."

"Cool!" Cassandra laughed. "Wouldn't it be fun to have a celebrity dyke in the neighborhood?"

"I just *love* Freddi Jo!" Carolyn cooed. "She's done *tons* for gay causes."

"So why didn't she do anything for her homo town while all this shit was going on?" Peter asked.

"Freddi Jo's been in Europe," Sissy explained, "starting her new line of unisex sportswear."

Carolyn turned to Susan. "Two lesbians in Delmont's house! It must be karma." Her face lit up. "We could play doubles!"

"They haven't moved in yet, darling," Susan reminded her. But mentally she was already practicing her backhand. "Sissy, just how well do you *know* Freddi Jo and this other woman?"

"Oh, we're old school pals. We talk all the time." This was stretching the point, since she had only talked to the celebrity tennis star twice in the past twenty years, but Sissy almost believed herself. "You'd just love her."

"Now it's really time for a celebration drink," Jay said. "Too-Too, everyone. Veuve Cliquot's waiting."

They collected parents, buttoned up coats and jackets, made hurried small talk with passing friends, then genially started off, as a group, leaving Sissy standing alone. Her hopeful smile faded when she realized she was not to be included. They've got one another, she thought forlornly, but who do I have? They'll never forgive me until I get someone like Freddie Jo in that house. And Freddi Jo was so goddamned slippery.

She looked up in grateful surprise when Susan turned back with what appeared to be a welcoming smile. "Aren't you coming with us, Sissy?"

▼ ▼ ▼

They were swept along in a surging sea of celebrants and had almost reached the doors when John-Don looked back over his shoulder towards the stage. Natalie Notale was surrounded by adoring well-wishers. She posed for photographs, answered reporters' questions, accepted congratulations.

She'd done her job. It wasn't how he would have done it, but doing it his way, at this point in his life, he might have botched the entire campaign. It was a humbling thought. Gay politics was still in its infancy. Gays and lesbians were still feeling their way around in the dark. The closet, even with the door open, still cast a long shadow over all of them. He felt a new respect for Natalie's courage, her willingness to fight.

But Labonne was right. The real fight was just beginning. John-Don could feel the impending battle in his gut. The more visible and demanding queers became, the more frightened and furious the straight population would become. They would dig in their heels, twist and tighten every law, enact new laws, do everything they could think of to keep their jealously guarded beliefs and privileges intact. Their enemies, already massing on the other side of the battlefield, were all the queers who were slowly beginning to realize just how many freedoms they didn't have, had never had, and who wouldn't rest until their equality and dignity as human beings was finally recognized.

For what, when all was said and done, had actually been accomplished in this horrific battle? Oregon voters had decided that queers should not be singled out for special ostracism. But the margin of victory was dishearteningly slim. Nearly half the state believed gays and lesbians *should* be labeled as perverts and discriminated against.

In the end, John-Don thought, this victory didn't give gays and lesbians one single thing. All it did, really, was prevent more from being taken away from them. But on the long, painful road to equality it was at least a first step. Queers, himself included, finally knew what they were up against. They knew there would be no fair debate on the issues that affected their lives, or if there were, it would be debated not by them but by those already in power. For John-Don, that was the most frustrating part. He had a powerful voice and he wanted to use it.

In time other leaders would emerge. And he, John-Don Webster, would be one of them. He suddenly knew that in every fiber of his being. He would never be silent again.

▼ ▼ ▼

Out in the parking lot huge, scowling effigies of Ron and Cornette Labonne were set alight as people jeered, cheered, danced and laid on their horns. Queers, so accustomed to suppressing their emotions in public, finally had a reason to let out the stops. Whooping, hollering, whistling, screaming, crying with relief, they sped off into the night like prisoners released from Death Row.

It turned into a night of impromptu queer ceremonies and celebrations of all kinds. Rockets illegally set off in Washington Park hissed up from the heart of the Rose Gardens and exploded over the sleeping city in a brilliant rainbow fizz of colors. Radical Faeries danced and sang in a grove of giant redwoods. The Lesbian Avengers ripped up and defaced "We Agree with Three!" lawn signs and posters.

Some, that evening, were almost sorry that the battle was over. Imminent catastrophe had united gays and lesbians as never before. Defeating the ballot measure had given them a common focus. It had forced them into areas they would never otherwise have explored. It had inspired courage in those who thought they had none.

On the east side of the city and the west, in bars, at parties, in suburban homes, in small towns, and by quiet rural firesides throughout the state, queers celebrated their temporary deliverance. For that's what it felt like, and especially to the neighbors from Queer Corners. At Too-Too they lifted their champagne flutes in exhausted triumph.

"To victory," Wellfleet said.

"To the light behind the darkness," said Ito.

"To No on Three," said John-Don.

"To John-Don Webster," said Peter

"To getting back our lives," said Jay.

"To Dove Labonne," said Cassandra.

"To our *new* neighbors," said Susan.

"To us," Carolyn said, "Who we were, who we are, and who we will be."

THE PURSUIT OF HAPPINESS

All citizens are entitled to life, liberty, and the pursuit of happiness—but if you're gay it's another story! As the rattled residents of Queer Corners soon discover, getting married, adopting children, and even falling in love can become everybody's business but their own. Join them as they battle a host of unnatural disasters and go for the gold ring in *The Pursuit of Happiness*, to be published in the fall, 2000.

AUTHOR'S NOTE

Queer Corners is a novel. Although it was inspired by two anti-gay rights campaigns that shook Oregon in 1992 and 1994, the events that actually occurred did not occur as I have presented them here. All of the characters and situations in this story are entirely fictitious.

In Oregon, the campaigns were public ballot measure initiatives meant to "define" gays and lesbians as inherently immoral and limit their basic civil rights. Both ballot measures were entirely legal under a state constitution that encourages the initiative process. Both were defeated at the polls by narrow margins. Heather Macdonald's 1995 documentary "Ballot Measure 9" is an excellent source of information on the first campaign. My beleaguered characters are nothing compared to the real individuals—brave, committed women and men from all walks of life—who worked to defeat the ballot measures.